CRITICAL ACCLAIM FOR ROBIN LEE HATCHER— WINNER OF THE *ROMANTIC TIMES* STORYTELLER OF THE YEAR AWARD!

Love Unspoken

She was so very beautiful! Never had Rory seen anything like her. She seemed to float down the staircase, her eyes behind the mask looking out over the heads of her audience. Young she might be, but at all the New York parties and teas and dances he had attended, the rooms filled with debutantes and older beauties, he had never seen such an entrance.

Rory moved through the crowd. His heart beat faster in his chest. He wanted to hold Brenetta, to love her, to cherish her always. Perhaps tonight....

Suddenly he stopped. Stuart had stepped out from the throng of onlookers. He held out his arm and Brenetta placed her palm on top of his hand. Like a king and queen among their subjects, Stuart and Brenetta moved toward the east drawing room, the assembly parting before them to let them pass. Both tall and slender and elegant, they made a breathtaking couple.

The spell was broken as they left the hall. People began to talk excitedly. "Have you ever seen anything so romantic?" someone said. "Oh, if only a man would look at me like that, I would do anything in the world for him!"

Rory knew then that it was too late. He had lost her....

Robin Lee Hatcher

Hearts Landing

LEISURE BOOKS   NEW YORK CITY

To Aunt Phoebe, Uncle Bill, and Aunt Dot,
a family you can count on.

A LEISURE BOOK®

June 1994

Published by

Dorchester Publishing Co., Inc.
276 Fifth Avenue
New York, NY 10001

Copyright © MCMLXXXIV by Robin Lee Hatcher

Printed in the United States of America.

PART ONE

How beautiful is youth! how bright it gleams
With its illusions, aspiration, dreams.
Longfellow, 1874

CHAPTER ONE

JUNE 1873—HEART'S LANDING

The sun was splashing its death colors across the Western sky in one final attempt to send its light and warmth across the already cooling earth. Brenetta Lattimer pushed back her ebony hair and curled her body into the arched branch of the giant oak tree and waited. He'd be coming for her soon.

A meadowlark's cry broke the stillness of dusk. She wondered if the nest was somewhere nearby and if she could find it. Just as she was about to leave her post and go looking, his voice reached her ears.

"Netta!"

She held her breath, knowing he would soon come this way. She peered through the dense foliage of her hiding place; her eyes strained to see in the gathering dusk. Yes, there he was. Her body tensed. She was as tightly coiled as an angry diamondback rattler.

"Netta . . ." he called again.

As he passed beneath her, she sprang free of her refuge, falling into his back with a shout. Swiftly he turned and rolled, catching her wrists with his strong hands. She tried to free herself before he could pin her to the ground but to no avail. As quickly as it had begun, it was over, and she was staring up into her father's laughing eyes, the green grass tickling her as it brushed her cheeks.

"This time I nearly got you, Papa," she declared.

Brent Lattimer laughed aloud and the lines deepened around his tawny-colored eyes, eyes identical to her own. "So you did, Netta. So you did. A few more years and I'll be helpless against these surprise attacks of yours."

He plucked her from the earth and swung her onto his back. Her arms grasped his neck, and she settled her chin on his shoulder as he started to walk toward the house. Her father's long strides covered the distance too quickly to suit her. She would have preferred more time alone with her favorite person in the world.

As they moved by the big, new barn, the house came into view. It was a two-story log structure with large windows in the living and dining rooms. From these windows, a panoramic view of Heart's Landing could be seen—the paddocks and stalls filled with fine horses, the lush grazing pastures, the green grass dotted with brown and white cattle, the tree-filled mountains erupting suddenly toward the sky, the outbuildings and barn, some whitewashed, others with weathered board siding.

Brenetta loved to stand at these same windows, especially in the early morning, and survey all that belonged to her parents and, therefore, to her. To her ten-year-old brain, it seemed the world. Other than a few brief trips into Boise, the territorial capital, Brenetta remembered no other place than Heart's Landing. Even their original crude cabin was only a wisp of a dream to her.

Looking over her father's shoulder now, Brenetta saw her mother standing on the porch near the front door. Taylor Lattimer's face lit up with a smile as they approached, her head shaking gently at the sight of them. Brenetta thought her mother the most beautiful woman in the world, and she knew her father thought so too.

"You two will never change, will you?" Taylor called to them, a lilt of laughter in her voice.

Brent set Brenetta on the porch steps. "I hope not. How 'bout you, Netta?"

"Never," she answered emphatically. "We'll be like this forever."

"Well, come on inside. It's past your bedtime, young lady."

"Oh, please. Can't I sit up with you and Papa just a little while?" Brenetta pleaded, knowing what the answer would be.

"Netta, you heard your mother. Off to bed." Brent's firm tone left no room for argument.

"Yes, Papa."

Brenetta reached up and kissed her mother's cheek softly, then turned to her father and repeated the kiss. His hand gently patted her bottom while at the same time it propelled her into the house and toward her room. As she climbed the stairs, she heard her father speaking softly to Taylor.

"And now, my love, is the best part of the day. The time when I have you all to myself."

Brenetta turned to see them locked in a tight embrace, so lost in each other they had totally forgotten her already. She felt an unpleasant pang of jealousy. Her rivalry with her mother was not something she clearly understood or was even consciously aware of, but it was there all the same.

With a sigh, she turned and resumed her ascent. Until tomorrow she was as good as invisible to them. The house seemed suddenly too big and too empty.

Brent finished kissing Taylor but kept his face close to hers. He gazed intently into her midnight blue eyes, the eyes that had held him spellbound from the first moment he saw her nearly fourteen years before. She had changed little in all that time. Her hair was still the same raven black, still long and unruly with its independent curls. Her skin was still milky white except for a splash of color on her high cheekbones, and as smooth and soft as down. She was as slim as a girl half her age. And he loved her completely.

His mind drifted back to a warm fall day. He remembered how he'd first seen her, laying on her back on a blanket in that secluded meadow, her eyes closed and a self-satisfied smile on her lovely mouth. He had thought her an angel.

"Where are you, darling," Taylor's whisper brought him back to the present.

He kissed her again. "I was remembering the Southern belle I fell in love with on a sunny day in Georgia."

Taylor sighed. "It was a lifetime ago, wasn't it?" she asked.

"We've built an even better life here, Taylor. I never dreamed my life could be this full, this happy. And you've given it all to me by loving me. And when I think how close I came to never having you . . ."

"Hush, Brent. You do have me. And you've given me ever so much more, my love." She kissed his lips, his nose, his eyes, and then his lips again. "Come, sit with me on the porch for a while," she said, tugging on his arm.

They sat quietly together, staring out at the friendly darkness. They had made this a practice early in their marriage, to spend a few quiet moments together each evening. They had learned in their first years of loving each other—before they were married—that nothing is ever for certain, that the unexpected always lurked nearby, waiting for its chance to wreak havoc in people's lives. The war had torn them apart and left its scars upon them. When fate had allowed them to reunite, they swore never to take the other for granted, never to assume the other would always be there.

"You know, I believe Netta is growing jealous of your love for me," Taylor mused, breaking the silence.

"What?"

"It's true, Brent. She idolizes you."

Brent leaned back from her. "Are you serious? She loves you."

"Of course she loves me," Taylor replied with a patient smile. "But she loves you more . . . or differently. I just think you should try to understand it. I don't want her . . . Well, I just want her to be happy."

Rory looked up at the main house as he closed the barn door. He saw the Lattimers, bathed in the light coming through the windows of the house, sitting close together, her head on his shoulder. He wished briefly that he was a part of that gentle scene; then with a shrug, he started off toward the bunk house. He passed through the darkness like a quiet ghost, his movements unconsciously fluid and graceful, the heritage of his Cheyenne Indian mother.

Only fifteen, Rory "Bear Claw" O'Hara worked as hard—or harder—than any other man on the place. Not only did he love Heart's Landing as if it were his own, he also had a deep-seated admiration and respect for Brent Lattimer and undying devotion for Taylor. He hadn't been too young to understand just what all the Lattimers had done for Garvey O'Hara and his family back in sixty-six and seven.

The O'Haras and the Lattimers had been members of the same wagon train headed for Oregon, and Rory's mother, White Dove, and Taylor had formed a quiet friendship. The two women were of the same age and both had young children to look

14

out and care for. White Dove was scorned, ignored and mistrusted by most other members of the train simply because she was an Indian and therefore different. Taylor was angered by their prejudice and had drawn even closer to her new friend.

As week followed week, the close proximity of so many varied people began to wear on nerves. Garvey O'Hara, never known for his even temper, was in the forefront of most disagreements, many of which led to fist fights. Because of their wives' friendship, Brent was usually the one to wade into the fights and drag Garvey back to his own wagon. Somehow out of all this, the two men built a friendship too. When the Lattimers decided to stay in Idaho, the O'Haras pulled out with them.

By the spring of 1867, Heart's Landing was already becoming a reality. Brent's younger strength and ready wealth, combined with the ranching and frontier knowledge of Garvey O'Hara, twenty-four years Brent's senior, brought swift changes to the mountain valley they had chosen to call home.

Garvey was happier than ever before in his life. He had his young Indian bride whom he loved passionately, though not always demonstratively; he had a fine, healthy son, and he had good friends nearby. At fifty-seven, he had finally found a place where he belonged, people to belong to, and an end to the vagabond existence he had always lived.

Then White Dove died in childbirth. His daughter was stillborn. The dream was over; the nightmare began. Only Brent's steadfast friendship kept him from finding a way into his own grave right then. Still, nothing was ever the same again. Though he continued for a time as the ranch foreman, his heart was not in his work, and he slowly retired to his cabin. Now, six years later, he rarely left his little house at all, spending his days rocking on his porch and his nights with his bottle.

Rory shook his head as if to shake away the memories. They weren't pleasant ones. He preferred thinking of those times with the Lattimer family. Taylor had spent many hours tutoring him, introducing him to what would be a lifelong love affair with books. Brent had taught him the workings of the ranch from the ground up. This last year he had even started Rory working on the ranch's account books. "Makin' a damned banker out of the boy, you are," Garvey had grumbled, but Brent was undaunted.

Rory even enjoyed Brenetta, though he tried not to let her know it. He allowed her to tag along sometimes as he did his chores, and occasionally he took her fishing with him in one of the mountain streams. He loved her gurgling laughter and her infectious grin as they walked through the forest. Her blue-black hair always hung in thick braids down her back and her gold-flecked brown eyes danced merrily as she watched for small forest creatures.

Rory stopped, looking at the cabin set slightly off from the bunkhouse, and thoughts of the Lattimers vanished. He knew he should look in on his father. He also knew he was probably already snoring in a drunken stupor. No, he'd wait until morning. It was already too late.

Taylor had seen Rory's silent exit from the barn. The boy works too hard, she thought to herself. He has so little time to just be happy. Somehow she would have to help him forget his responsibilities for just a little while.

She snuggled closer to Brent, thoughts of Rory slipping away as she did so. She could smell the faint scent of hay and horses and leather and sweat, a strangely comforting odor to Taylor. It was hard to imagine that she was once the pampered daughter of a wealthy planter, a girl whose most important decision each day was what gowns to wear for that day's activities. It was also hard to believe now that she was so happy, that she had ever actually gone through the war years. Her life before Brent seemed only a vague dream.

Taylor nibbled at the hairs at the base of Brent's throat. He responded by pulling her tighter against him and tilting her head back.

"You are a lovely nymph, you are," he whispered huskily. "Come to bed, wife."

Brenetta, too, had seen Rory leaving the barn. She had pushed aside the curtains at her bedroom window and was leaning on the window sill, her chin cradled in her arms. She saw him pause and gaze toward the house, then turn and disappear into the night shadows.

Dear Rory. Nobody could ever have a nicer brother than him. And that was how she thought of him, as the brother she'd never had. He was her best friend too. Actually he was her *only* friend, or at least the only friend anywhere close to her own age. There were no other children at Heart's Landing. Most of the ranch hands were single men; many of them only stayed a few months, through round-up and the cattle drive.

But Brenetta couldn't remember not having Rory around. It seemed he was always there, getting her out of one scrape after another. He'd saved her from more than one tanning by her father.

"Goodnight, Rory," she whispered after him.

A change in the air made her look up at the sky. Clouds were rolling across the heavens, blanking out the stars. She could smell the rain that weighed heavily within them, ready to break loose at any instant. The wind blew stronger, causing the curtains to flap madly on both sides of her. Suddenly the sky was rent by a jagged flash. The light was blinding in its brilliance. Following closely on its heels, the thunder boomed angrily, the fury of the storm shaking the house.

Brenetta's first scream was muffled by the thunder. By the time she caught her breath for the next one, her father was bursting through the door. He swooped her up from the floor where she had fallen in a fetal position and held her tight against his chest. She couldn't hear his crooning over the crashing thunder and her own screams and whimpers.

"It's okay, baby. Daddy won't let it hurt you. It's just lightning and thunder, Netta. It's all right. Hush. Hush now. Hush, love. It's all right."

Now her mother's words were added to his, her gentle accent pleasing, soothing. "It'll be over soon, sugar. Mama and Papa are here. We're all here. It's all right."

At last Brenetta was able to stifle her screams, but she continued to whimper and cringe with each booming assault. She closed her eyes against the bright flashes, but there was no shutting out the persistent pounding of the thunder or the fear in her heart.

Brent rocked her from side to side, silently cursing the weather . . . and General Sherman.

Brenetta had been just fifteen months old when the shelling of Atlanta began. She didn't remember it, but ever since that time, she had had an uncontrollable fear of loud crashing noises. Brent's guilt matched her fear for he had been fighting on the other side; he was a Yankee officer under Sherman and could have destroyed the woman he loved and the child he didn't know he had without realizing it. As Brenetta buried her face deeper into his chest at another angry roar from the storm, Brent thanked God for sparing them and prayed for the day when Brenetta's terror would be forgotten.

Taylor's hand on his arm told him she knew his thoughts, told him she loved him, had always loved him, Yankee or not. The guilt lessened. As if it was related to his emotions somehow, the storm receded with the guilt. The thunder became only a distant rumble from beyond the mountains.

Looking down at his daughter, he found her sleeping, the tension slowly disappearing from her face and body. He kissed her tear-streaked face as he placed her in her bed. Taylor tucked the blanket up under her chin, then brushed the dampness from Brenetta's cheeks with a loving touch. Silently, they slipped from the room.

Tobias sat on the porch of the bunkhouse, his chair tilted back, his feet braced on the porch railing. It had been quite a show, and now he waited for the promised rain. Heaven knows, we could use it, he thought as he pulled again on his cigarette. He closed his brown eyes and listened. He could still hear the thunder rolling through the air. It sounded like a herd of running buffalo. He smiled. He loved thunder and lightning storms, as long as they didn't start fires or stampede his critters.

His smile disappeared as he remembered the child's cry. Poor kid. She sure was afraid of the noise. And she was so happy and playful at other times, too. Downright mischievous, that's what she was! Little pest, he thought, and the smile returned.

Tobias Levi had been at Heart's Landing for over three years now. He had arrived in a spring snowstorm, a storm that dropped a foot of snow on them in one night. Brent had needed an extra pair of hands and Tobias had provided them. He'd never felt like leaving afterwards. Though only twenty-three, he proved himself indispensable and had followed Garvey in the position of ranch foreman. He did his job well and loved it.

Tobias was a loner, though not really by choice. He was a tall, slender man, his arms and shoulders well-muscled from his work. His face was sharp, dominated by his long, thin nose, his olive skin darkened by the sun and weather, and in summer, his sandy-brown hair became nearly blond. His brown eyes could sparkle with laughter or explode in anger. At the moment, they were smiling.

"Rory!" The angry shout was followed by shattering glass. Garvey O'Hara stumbled wildly out the door of his cabin. "Where the hell are you, boy?" He careened into one of the support posts on the porch and swore angrily.

Tobias tipped his chair forward, tossing away the butt of his cigarette. The rain began to drop in solid sheets, muffling Garvey's curses, but not before Rory appeared at the door of the bunkhouse, staring through the rain at his father.

"Want some help, Bear?" Tobias asked quietly.

Rory mutely shook his head, his square, handsome face expressionless. As if immune to the weather, he stepped into the storm and walked unhurriedly, deliberately towards his father's cabin.

Tobias shook his head. That boy had too much to carry. Old Garvey didn't deserve such a son.

"Where you been, lad?" Garvey yelled at him. "Have you got no shame but to leave your own da with no one to see to him? Don't you know that the rain sets the rheumatism to achin' in me bones?"

"I know, Da. I'm sorry," Rory answered. He took his father's left arm and placed it around his neck. Then he put his own right arm around Garvey's waist, and thus supported, the older man was guided back into the house.

The floor was littered with the glass from the

broken whiskey bottle. Rory stepped carefully over it to the bed. He helped his father lie down and began silently to undress him.

"I don't understand you, boy. Haven't I always done everything for you, that you should leave me here all alone? Haven't I given you the best home anywhere to be livin'?"

Garvey's words began to slur, and he slumped back on his cot. Rory pulled the blanket over his father's long-johns-clad, whiskey-filled body and left the cabin as he had come, silent and alone.

CHAPTER TWO

JULY 1873—HEART'S LANDING

"Rory, please let me go along. I won't be any trouble, I promise."

Rory looked into Brenetta's pleading face, then turned back to his horse, checking the cinch. She held her breath, knowing better than to ask again while he was deciding.

Finally he answered. "If your father says it's all right and you agree to do whatever I say, then you can come."

"Oh, thank you, Rory!" Her arms flew around his neck, and she planted a wet kiss on his cheek before flying off in search of her father.

Rory shook his head. He was sure to be sorry for letting her come with him, but somehow he just couldn't say no. Without waiting for Brent's approval, which he knew would come, he went to Chipper's stall and led out the small sorrel gelding. Before Brenetta was back, Brent in tow, he had brushed him down and saddled him with Brenetta's saddle.

Brent met Rory's wry smile after seeing the saddled horse and, with a chuckle, said, "Soft touches, aren't we?"

"Yes, sir. We are."

"Are you certain you want her to tag along?"

Rory shrugged. "She knows the conditions."

"Oh, yes, yes, I know, Papa. I'll do whatever Rory tells me." Her eyes, duplicates of her father's, glittered with anticipation.

"Then go get your things together. Rory's ready to leave," Brent told her.

She was gone in a flash, her braids flapping wildly behind her. The two men watched her leap up the stairs and disappear into the house.

"Where will you start?" Brent asked as he turned back to Rory.

"To the east. Best grazing this time of year, and he knows the area well. Don't worry, sir. I'll be sure to watch out for Netta."

"I know that, Rory. That's why I'm letting her go." Brent scanned the skies. "You shouldn't have any problem with the weather. How long do you plan to stay out?"

"With Netta along, four or five days. If I don't have them by then, I'll have to bring her back."

Brent nodded, hoping Taylor wouldn't be too angry at him for letting her go. "Well, I've got some fence work to see to. Good luck, and we'll see you in a few days."

Rory ran a knowledgeable hand over his horse's

flank as he waited for Brenetta. The animal was sturdy, built to handle the rigorous ranch work that was his daily life. He had both the speed and endurance which Rory would need if he got lucky in the next few days. Brenetta's horse, Chipper, was of the same type; in fact, the horses were half-brothers, sharing the same sire.

"I'm ready," Brenetta panted as she ran towards him, carrying her bedroll and canteen. Her pretty face was rosy with excitement.

"Then let's be off, little one, before the day gets any longer."

Rory tossed her easily into her saddle, then fastened her bedroll securely behind her.

Amen-Ra. An Arabian stud of the best blood. He was sired by Sheikh Hazad out of Tasha. Both were from the notable Spring Haven stock, stock that had been depleted for the Confederate cause. When the war was over, only the palomino mare, Tasha, and her copper-colored, three-year-old colt remained to come west with the Lattimers. Soon after they had settled in their valley, Amen-Ra had sought—and gained—his freedom. He had gathered a band of mares for himself and had been filling the mountains of Idaho with his sons and daughters ever since.

Last week, five of Heart's Landings's best brood mares, recently separated from their colts, had wandered out of their pasture through a hole in the fence that had gone undetected. Failing to find them within reasonable distance, Brent had surmised that Amen-Ra had acquisitioned five new wives for his harem. It was Rory's job to find them and bring them back.

Brenetta followed quietly behind Rory. She leaned forward in the saddle as they began to climb again. They had been riding like this for several hours. Every so often, Rory would stop and scan the area around him, his sharp eyes reading things Brenetta could never see.

As they reached the ridge, another valley opened up before him. Rory stopped again, dismounted and hunkered down, running his hands thoughtfully over the earth. His black eyes moved slowly across the terrain surrounding them. When they slid to Brenetta, his mouth turned up in a smile, his fine white teeth showing slightly.

"He's got them, little one, and unless I miss my guess, they're headed for Devil's Canyon."

"Will we see them today, Rory?" Brenetta asked, slipping down beside him, wishing she could understand how he knew about the horses and where they were going.

"No, not today. We'll make camp outside the canyon tonight and go in in the morning."

Brenetta looked hard around her. "Where's Devil's Canyon?" she asked.

"Can't see it from here," Rory replied as he stood up, pointing towards the east. "It's hidden in that mountain range. And if we plan to get there tonight, we'll have to get riding now."

Brenetta's stomach growled as she threw her leg over her horse, but she said nothing about her hunger. She knew that Rory had been generous to let her come, and she was determined to cause no problems or delays. She had learned early that Rory liked her and would share his time with her, but she had also learned not to push him past where he was willing to go. When his face closed up or his black eyes turned stormy or his silence became stony, it was time to leave him alone. She didn't really know why. She had never seen him lose his temper. It was just a feeling she had and she obeyed it.

"Netta, look," Rory whispered.

She followed his gesture. Below the ledge where they were riding was a small green meadow. Frozen in the midst of the long, wild grass were a doe and two spotted fawns. They stared back at Rory and Brenetta, only their white tails moving in quick staccato jerks.

"Rory, they're so pretty!" Brenetta exclaimed, forgetting herself.

At the sound of her voice, they sprang into action, leaping across the mountain turf toward the protection of the trees. Their tails stood straight up as they vaulted over ferns and brushes and disappeared from view.

"Oh, I'm sorry," Brenetta sighed. "I didn't mean to frighten them." It seemed very tragic to her that they were gone, that they had run away from her.

"We'll see others, Netta," Rory stated matter-of-factly.

Brenetta glanced behind her and down as they moved off, thinking how empty the little meadow looked without the pretty white-tailed deer.

Tobias removed his hat and wiped the sweat

from his forehead with his shirt sleeve. He squinted up at the relentless sun, then placed his hat back over his damp scalp and bent down again to his work. He was repairing the pasture fence where the mares had broken out the week before. As he set the new post in the hole he'd just finished digging, he thought how glad he was that Brent didn't fence off *all* the land. It was hard enough taking care of what there was for the horses. He'd much rather spend his days herding cattle than riding fence.

"Tobias!"

He looked up to see Taylor riding toward him, seated side-saddle atop her fine palomino stallion, another son of Tasha. She was wearing a pale blue linen riding habit. Her hair was tied back with a matching ribbon, and a saucy hat was perched on top of her head, shading her delicate complexion.

"Tobias, do you know where Brent is?" she asked, stopping her horse nearly on top of him.

He stepped back a pace, noticing her flushed cheeks and her angry eyes. "I believe he's checking the cattle on the south range, ma'am," he answered, and thought to himself, and from the looks of you, he's in big trouble.

"Do you know what he's done? He let Netta go with Rory to look for those mares! I only just found out."

"She'll be fine, Miz Taylor. Bear won't let any harm come to her."

Taylor appeared to calm down a little. "Oh, Tobias, I know Rory will look after her. But he's only a boy himself."

"No, ma'am," Tobias replied softly. "I don't believe Rory O'Hara ever got to be a boy. From what I've seen, he had to go from tyke to man in a hurry with that pa of his. Bear knows how to take care of himself and others. He'll take care of Netta."

"Well, I suppose you're right . . . Thank you, Tobias. I'm sure I worry too much. It's just . . ." Her words drifted off and she shrugged helplessly.

Tobias nodded and turned back to the fence post. He shook his head. Gads, what a woman she is, he thought. He never saw her that he didn't wish himself in Brent's shoes, even if she was seven years older than he was. The love she and Brent had for each other, and for Netta, too, was a wonder to behold. Tobias wished he had someone to love and to love him like that.

She should have a dozen children, Tobias thought. Then she wouldn't have so much time to worry over just one.

He turned around and watched her galloping back to the house. Again he shook his head. There probably wasn't a prettier spread anywhere than this one. It was in a large round valley nestled in the mountains with a small river running through its center. The grass was plentiful, the soil fertile. The house and barn and other outbuildings were attractive and well-built against the hard winters. Brent Lattimer was a wealthy man, and it showed in Heart's Landing. The place had a prosperous glow about it. "But he still has problems, just like everybody else," Tobias said aloud.

He swung onto his own horse and turned him

south. Taylor was right about one thing; Brent shouldn't have let the two of them go off alone in search of those horses. He'd meant what he said about Rory, but you never knew what might happen in these hills. Besides, he had a nagging suspicion about *where* Amen-Ra would be hiding with his mares, and if he was right, Taylor had even more cause for worry.

He nudged his horse into a gallop.

Devil's Canyon. The name fit. Impassible walls rose straight up on both sides of a narrow trail. Loose shale and large rocks fell without warning, making the mile long trek through the canyon to the lush valley hidden beyond extremely hazardous. This was Amen-Ra's favorite hideout.

A rabbit roasted over the campfire, and Brenetta eyed it hungrily. The horses grazed nearby, their legs hobbled. Rory turned the rabbit again, but his thoughts were on tomorrow, not his dinner.

He wondered now what to do with Brenetta. He couldn't leave her here with no one to watch her, but the passage through Devil's Canyon was dangerous. He remembered his promise to Brent to take care of her, and his frown deepened, drawing his thick black eyebrows together.

An owl hooted nearby, the sound a haunting one. Rory turned towards the cry. They had made camp in a small alcove of rocks with only a few pines guarding the entrance. He could make out the silhouette of the owl on one of the pine branches. Above the trees, the night sky was alive with glittering stars, like a black velvet cloth covered with gems. The air was crisp and refreshing after the heat of the day.

Rory inhaled deeply, feeling the tension and concern slipping away. He felt the rhythm of the earth pulsing around him, within him, and was content. At times like this, he could almost sense his mother close to him, her quiet strength and courage flowing from her spirit into his own.

"Rory, is it ready yet? I'm starving."

He turned to face Brenetta, momentarily surprised to find her there.

"Yes, little one. It's ready," he said. "And I'm hungry too. Let's eat."

The rabbit was quickly cut up and divided between them. Brenetta sank her teeth eagerly into the juicy meat, relishing each and every flavorful bite. They were both silent as they ate. The night was quiet save for the occasional hoot of the owl and the soft rustling of grass as the horses moved forward in their grazing.

Rory watched Brenetta eating and his worry returned. His only real choice was to take her with him, but he wasn't pleased with that option. He felt a strong protectiveness for her. She seemed to be his link to a better life, to being part of a real family. Somehow, she could *share* happiness with him, even *bring* happiness to him, when no one else could. Now he saw her eyelids grow heavy; her stomach was full, her hunger assuaged. He smiled, putting down his tin plate.

"Let't turn in, little one," he said.

She yawned. "I guess I am a little tired," she mumbled.

Brenetta crawled under her blanket, her head resting on her saddle, and was asleep almost instantly.

Rory straightened the blanket over her feet and returned to the fire. He added a few more logs, then checked the horses before turning in himself. They'd need their rest. Tomorrow promised to be a full day for them both.

Tobias broke camp at first dawn. He had ridden hard in the few remaining daylight hours of the previous day. As he hit the trail, he thought again of how hard it had been to convince Brent to let him go alone.

"Good Lord, Tobias! If you're right about where they've gone, I've got to go. What's the matter with him, anyway? If anything happens to Brenetta, I'll skin him alive."

"Brent, calm down, will you. First off, I don't think Rory was thinking about Devil's Canyon when he left here. He was just heading east, following a band of wild horses. But if they are in the Devil's, he's got a problem—leave Netta alone while he goes in, take her in with him, or come home without the mares. And you know darn well he won't do that. If he's that close to them, he's not going to come home without them. Second," he said sagely, "if you go running off half-scared after them, your missus is really going to be frightened. It's better you let her think it's no more than a few nights camping out, like they've done before."

Brent had mulled this over and finally agreed. Tobias had saddled a fresh horse and left quickly, the strange gnawing at his insides growing stronger with each passing mile. Now he was only a few hours away from the canyon himself, and he had seen several signs of their passing this way the day before.

If only I didn't keep feeling something's about to go wrong, he thought as he urged more speed into his mount's stride. He wasted no time enjoying the magnificent scenery around him. He was unaware of the rugged beauty of the purple-tinged mountains, the tall pines or stands of white birch, the granite rocks or the ebony and burnt ochre shale, or the persistent wild flowers, syringa and wild roses and forsythia among them, that covered the earth in small clusters and in sweeping seas of color. His only thoughts were of reaching the canyon.

Amen-Ra's nostrils flared. His head was turned into the wind, his mane dancing lightly above his neck. His copper coat gleamed like a well-polished brand new penny. His thick stallion's neck was arched, and his heavily muscled body appeared posed for flight.

He sensed danger but could find nothing to confirm it. He snorted and, with a toss of his fiery head, raced back down from his ledge. In a pique of authority, he bit and nipped at his mares, driving them closer together.

Finally he let them graze in peace, but Amen-Ra remained alert, his instincts honed to the ultimate after years in the wild.

Brenetta stared up at the canyon walls. From her viewpoint, they seemed at least a mile high and only a foot apart. She kept holding her breath and wishing she was back in the safety of their camp, or better yet, home.

She was leading Chipper along the narrow trail directly behind Rory's horse. Before entering, he had cautioned her to make no noise and to step carefully. Not only did they not want to bring loose rocks down on them, but they didn't want to alert the horses to their presence.

Brenetta hadn't been afraid at first. The thought of seeing the legendary Amen-Ra and his mares was too exciting. Now she wondered how Rory intended to get the horses out if he did catch them. Those wild horses certainly weren't going to walk quietly behind him like she was.

Brenetta's mouth became set in a grim, petulant line; a scowl furrowed her forehead. She wanted to scold Rory for bringing her here but didn't dare, which angered her even more. The trip was no longer a lark. It was just hard work. The sun beat mercilessly down into the canyon, the heat magnified by the rocks. No breeze reached the trail to bring relief. The very stillness was depressing.

She felt like crying. It was a bad day.

The remains of their campfire was cold; their tracks led away into the canyon. Tobias pushed himself up from the ground, wiping his sooty hands on his levis as he poked at the ashes with the toe of his boot. He gazed up at the sun. He figured he was about four hours behind them. Reaching over his saddle, he removed his canteen. After taking a long swallow, he poured some on his bandana and rubbed his face and neck, then tied it around his throat. Pulling on his hat brim to shade his eyes better, he swung into his saddle.

No point wasting anymore time, he thought. Darn those youngsters anyway. You'd think they'd have more sense than this, especially Bear.

But Tobias also knew that Rory was more than a bit stubborn and perhaps a little overconfident of his own abililty to handle all situations. As he entered the canyon, he hoped he wouldn't find himself facing a band of stampeding horses coming at him from the other direction. He pressed forward.

Devil's Canyon opened up into an incredibly serene valley, the grass kept green and lush by an underground spring and lots of trees to provide shade. The only other way out besides the way they had come in was over the steep, forbidding mountains themselves, a strenuous and difficult undertaking.

Rory let a small sigh of relief escape his lips as the trail they were following opened up into the pastoral glen. He motioned for silence as his eyes searched for their quarry. Finding them nowhere in sight, he beckoned for Brenetta to follow.

"First thing to do," he said softly, "is to close off this exit. Can you help me?"

Now that the canyon was behind them, Brenetta's sense of adventure had returned. "Of course I can," she hissed indignantly.

"Okay. Let's tie up our horses and get busy. They might show up any moment, and we need to be ready."

Rory led the way to a thick grouping of tall ponderosa pines. They tethered their animals securely but left them saddled in case they needed them in a hurry. Then they entered the canyon again. At its first narrow point, they rolled together as many large rocks across the entrance as they could manage. Next, they carried fallen lodge pole pines and constructed a crude fence about five and a half feet high. Rory knew it wouldn't withstand much force, but he hoped it would turn the horses if they came this way.

"Come, little one," he said as they stood back and looked over the fruit of their labor. "Let's see if we can find our missing mares."

And Amen-Ra, they both thought secretly.

They proceeded on foot, climbing steadily and keeping to the trees. It took them nearly twenty minutes to find them.

The herd consisted of about twenty-five horses, including the five from Heart's Landing, six or seven yearlings, and eleven or so sucklings. Amen-Ra stood off from the others. Every so often, he would lift his head from his grazing and survey his surroundings, sniffing the air carefully, and then continue eating.

Rory and Brenetta crawled foward on their stomachs for a better look. The five mares they had come for were huddled together in a group of their own. They had all lost weight and were covered with numerous bites and scrapes. They were all brood mares, pampered since birth. None had ever been used for anything but breeding purposes and were not in condition for the hard traveling required of them in the past week.

"Rory, look!" Brenetta whispered excitedly.

Following her finger, he spied a cream-colored mare grazing near a stand of trees. She had a refined, intelligent head and widely spaced eyes, a tall mare with strong hips and legs.

"One of his better thefts," he whispered back.

"No, no! Not her. The filly."

Rory looked again. Partially hidden behind its mother was a long-legged yearling. The mare stepped forward, placing the youngster in plain view. Brenetta's excitement was well deserved. Rory understood even better than she the promise that stood before him. The burnished copper of the filly's coat looked as though it would be hot to the touch. She had the finely sculptured head of her sire and had inherited the strong build of both her parents. She was full of promise, to be sure.

Rory motioned for them to slide back from the rim of their perch. It was time to make plans to capture the mares they had come for.

He was sure of it now. He could smell their approach. The scent of humans and leather and strange horses filled his nostrils. He tossed his head angrily as he sprang forward, trumpeting his warning. With bared teeth, he rounded up the day-dreamers and stragglers among his band. Once in motion, he led the charge toward the canyon.

The two riders appeared too late to turn them, and he whinneyed his triumph belligerently. The thunder of hooves, pounding in perfect rhythm, was amplified in the closed valley. One of the humans drove his own horse foward, trying hopelessly to reach the canyon before them.

His head stretched foward, his tail flying, Amen-Ra raced into the canyon. Suddenly the barricade loomed before him. For a brief moment he gathered himself for flight. Then, seemingly out of nowhere, there was another human beyond the fence, firing his gun over his head. Amen-Ra twisted his body, and with teeth bared, he plunged into his confused and frightened mares, driving them back the way they'd come. Before he could reach the front, the two humans in the valley had turned many of his band aside into a tiny recess in the mountain, a natural corral.

In a rage he stopped the rest from following those already trapped. Then a rope sang through the air, whistling by his ear, and he shrieked his fury. His front legs pawed the air, striking the unsuspecting horse of one of his attackers. Eyes flashing, he turned his remaining herd towards the opposite end of the valley, the mountains, and freedom.

Taylor was sitting in the shade of the porch, her sewing laying idle in her lap. Brent would be in soon, and she should be checking on their dinner, but she sat daydreaming instead. The last four days had been awfully quiet with Brenetta gone. Taylor had discovered it was *too* quiet. And with

Rory and Tobias gone too, the place seemed postively deserted. In the evening, it seemed as if she and Brent just rattled around the place.

With a sigh, she dropped her sewing into the basket beside her chair. She knew she'd best get busy before Brent returned to an empty table. As she stood up, her eyes caught a glimpse of the riders. They'd returned with the horses!

"Brent! Brent, they're back," she cried toward the barn.

She ran down the steps, stopping at the little white fence that bordered the lawn. When she realized she could only see two riders, she picked up her skirts and ran forward once again.

Brenetta was nestled in Tobias's arms, fast asleep. A bandana was wrapped around her head, covering the cuts and purple bruises she'd received when she hit the ground. Chipper limped along with the mares, his hip badly torn by Amen-Ra's assault.

"Tobias, what happened?" Taylor cried as they drew near.

Tobias stopped his horse and handed Brenetta to her father, who had arrived on Taylor's heels. "Just a few scrapes, ma'am. She's just fine; a mite tired, but just fine."

Brenetta opened her eyes. Seeing her parents, she whispered, "He was the most beautiful horse I've ever seen, and he's got a little flame that's going to be even prettier." She closed her eyes a moment, then opened them again, turning her head in Brent's arms. "Thanks, Rory, for letting me go. Thanks, Tobias."

Taylor kissed her daughter's forehead. With her eyes, she thanked Tobias for bringing Brenetta home safely. Then she followed Brent quickly into the house, her family whole again.

CHAPTER THREE

DECEMBER 1873—SPRING HAVEN

Marilee Bellman pulled her shawl tighter about her shoulders against the cold air blowing around the windows and under the door. Taylor's letter and the bank draft lay on the table before her. She rubbed her eyes, feeling the tension building across her forehead and pounding away at her temples; she felt incapable of facing another of Philip's rages right now.

She stood up and walked to the window, pushing aside the worn, heavy draperies. The plantation lawn was brown, barren. The gardens hadn't been properly tended for the last ten years or more. Philip worked hard at it, at everything, but at every turn the Yankees had put up another obstacle to keep them from success. Besides trying to raise cotton and scrape a profit from their land, her husband spent several days each week in town at his law office, though there was little work for him to do there. Most folks were too poor to hire an attorney; they could hardly feed themselves. So many of the old plantations were gone. Some were destroyed in the war; others had been sold for taxes and stood empty—or worse, they were occupied by dirty carpetbaggers or other white trash. If it hadn't been for Brent Lattimer's help, the same fate would have befallen Spring Haven long ago. If only he weren't a Yankee himself!

Marilee tried not to be bitter. She had never had wealth as a child, and when she married Philip, war was at hand. But just once—*just once*—she would like to have a day free from worrying over money.

She caressed the drapery fabric with her fingers, then looked around the room. The furniture showed wear, the wood floors were scuffed and dull, the carpets threadbare, but she saw it with the eyes of her youth when she had come to stay with her best friend, Taylor Bellman, and flirt with her handsome older brother, Philip, who didn't even know she was alive. She imagined the parties with tables piled high with food, the rooms filled with lovely, graceful people, their idle chatter the most urgent thing on their minds.

But war had changed all that.

"Miz Mar'lee, that boy done brung in another critter t' his room. I jus' ain't gonna clean up after another. I jus' ain't."

Marilee looked up and sighed. "I'll take care of it, Susan. Don't worry."

"Don' worry, she says. All I gots t'do is worry.

42

But no, she says . . ." Susan's voice trailed away as she went down the hall.

Marilee sighed again. Old Susan had been with the Bellmans since her birth. She didn't know exactly how long that was but guessed it to be around sixty years, maybe even more. Taylor had given Susan her freedom before the war was over, but she had stayed on to serve "Masta" Philip and his wife and child. She had refused the salary the law required they pay her, so Philip had been quietly depositing it in a savings account in her name all these years. She was a faithful old servant, and the children loved her, but Marilee had always found her a little domineering.

On her way out of the room, Marilee picked up the correspondence and check and stuffed them in her apron pocket. Later, she thought as she did so.

Sure enough, she found him in his room with a mongrel pup, both of them hiding under his bed. His sister, Megan Katrina, was with them.

"Out, the bunch of you," Marilee ordered. She waited as they slithered, grunted, and mumbled until they stood before her, sheepish heads bowed.

"What do you know about pets in this house?"

Nine-year-old Martin Philip looked at his younger (by barely ten months) sister, then answered, "We're not to have them 'cause they make Alastair cough and sneeze."

"And when you disobey, what?"

"Then everything's gotta be scrubbed down," Megan answered guiltily.

"And *who*," Marilee continued, "has to do the scrubbing?"

In unison they replied, "Susan."

Marilee looked at them sternly as she pushed a stray blond hair away from her face. "Well, not this time. This time the two of you are to clean this room *and* the nursery. Understood?"

They nodded.

"Good. Now get that dog outside where he belongs."

Philip traveled along the road at a fair clip. Georgia was caught in a cold snap, and the horse was as eager to get home as the driver of the buggy. Philip hardly noticed the passing landscape, he was so lost in thought. Christmas was only a week away, and there was no money for gifts for the children's stockings.

Philip Bellman looked ten years older than his forty-two years. His dark hair was streaked with grey. Worry lines were permanently etched around his blue eyes and across his forehead. He still had bouts with the fever that had seized him in sixty-four, and he had never recovered his robust health. Perhaps if he could have had some rest and lots of good food . . .

"Giddup there," he snapped, hurrying his horse towards home, a warm fire, and Marilee's loving ministrations.

Just thinking of her brought him a smile. They'd been married nearly thirteen years now, and he loved her more every day. They had four children, three boys and a daughter. It seemed Marilee and the children were the only rays of sunshine in his life anymore. If only . . . if only Spring Haven could be as it once was.

Turning up the drive, the manor house rose before him. She was still a beautiful, proud home, her columns straight and strong, even if the paint was peeling in places. A haven to those who loved her, her name promised. But Spring Haven was a weight that hung heavily around his neck. The taxes on her grew every year, and once again, he was faced with losing her or selling off some of her acres, land that had belonged to Bellmans for nearly one hundred years.

Megan carefully washed down the walls of the nursery. She was alone in the room, Martin having disappeared after a token swipe at the floor. She didn't really mind. She rather preferred the peace and quiet for a change. Having three brothers sometimes made her wish she was an only child.

Megan was a pretty little girl. She had inherited her mother's golden hair and her father's blue eyes. She always seemed ready to help when there was work to be done, but she often daydreamed about what her mama had told her it used to be like before the war, wishing they had dozens of servants and could have big parties with music and dancing and . . .

She heard the buggy coming up the drive and hurried to the window. Yes, it was Papa! She dropped the cloth in the bucket and raced down the stairs to welcome him home.

Martin Philip was a tall, skinny boy with dark brown hair and large brown eyes that dominated his oval face. At the moment his father was stopping his buggy at the front of the house, he was sitting in the hay above the stalls in the barn. The mongrel pup that had brought him his mother's disfavor was curled up at his feet, looking entirely innocent.

Martin tousled the dog's ears, wishing it was spring and not so cold. Then they could be out hunting frogs or something. He felt grumpy, as if he'd like to hit somebody. Why couldn't he bring General inside? If Alastair wasn't such a *baby*, he'd be able to have a dog in the house. Why did he have to have a dumb brother like that anyway? All he did was cause a fellow trouble.

With a kick at the loose hay, he crossed to the ladder. He put General under one arm and carried him down to the bottom.

"You stay here, General. I'm goin' in for supper. And if you see any Yankees while I'm gone, just kill 'em."

He stuffed his hands in his pants pockets, pants that were too short for him anymore, and hurried to the house. When he entered the front door, he could hear his father's raised voice.

"Couldn't he at least wait until I asked for it? Does he have to rub my nose in it? Maybe we could've had a good year. Maybe we wouldn't have needed his handouts. Doesn't he know how it makes me feel to have to take money from him? I don't care if he is my brother-in-law; he's still a Yankee. Always was, always will be!"

"Philip, remember," Marilee pleaded, "he saved Spring Haven for you, for us. If it hadn't been for his help, this would have all been ashes long ago. Please, darlin', please don't carry on so. You know we need that money. Please calm down."

Martin stood, frozen in his tracks near the doorway. The sound he heard now was worse than anything he'd heard before. His father was crying, his sobs torn from his throat in anguish. He pushed himself forward until he could see into the library. His mother was cradling Philip's head against her breast, tears running down her own cheeks.

"God knows I've tried, Marilee," his father sobbed. "We knew . . . we all knew it wouldn't be easy, but . . . but they won't let us *live*. They're grinding us into the ground with the heels of their filthy boots."

Philip stopped, raised his head, and gazed into his wife's eyes. "Look at me," he whispered hoarsely. "I'm a failure, Marilee. I'm an old man at forty-two. When we married, I was wealthy; I had a promising career and a thriving plantation, the best in North Georgia. Now I have four hungry children and a work-weary wife. I want to give you the world, but instead I'm forced to accept charity from one of *them*."

Martin turned on his heels and raced back to the barn. He leaned against the barn door, his face deathly pale, his knuckles turned white from his clenched fists.

"I'll get them. I'll get them all for what they've done to my father—to all of us. I *swear* it. I'll make those damned Yankees pay."

CHAPTER FOUR

MARCH 1874—HEART'S LANDING

Taylor sat at her dressing table, her brush stopped in mid-air. She leaned closer to her reflection, checking the tiny lines around her eyes. She looked for telltale grey, but there wasn't any. Not yet. She smiled. No, she really didn't look her thirty-one years.

Her deep blue eyes turned dreamy as she lowered the brush to the table. How very long it had been since she had felt like this. It was almost too good to be true.

"Ah, here you are, my lovely."

Brent leaned casually against the door-jamb, enjoying the view. The sight of him brought color to her cheeks and a smile to her lips. Brent crossed over to her and pulled her to her feet, taking her in his arms and kissing her soundly.

"Look at that," he said as he released her. "I can still make you blush."

"You flatter yourself, sir. It's thoughts of another that brings the roses to my cheeks this day." She batted her eyes coquettishly and curtsied.

"Tell me who it is," Brent cried in mock anger, "and I'll have him drawn and quartered."

The teasing left her voice. "Seriously, darling, there really is another on my mind." She lifted her gaze to meet his. "I'm going to have a baby."

Their bedroom was incredibly quiet. Brent's mouth worked but no sound came. Taylor read the shock in his face.

"Brent, is it all right? You don't mind, do you?"

"Mind?" he cried, his voice returning. "Mind? A baby! A baby here? I never thought . . . I'd given up . . . Shouldn't you sit down or . . . or something?"

She laughed, a joyous, tinkling sound. "Don't be silly. I won't break. But maybe *you* should sit down. You don't look very well."

He obeyed, pulling her down on the bed with him. He kissed her again, this time gently, filled from the depths of his heart.

"I love you, Mrs. Lattimer," he whispered.

"And I love you, Mr. Lattimer. And I love you."

Brenetta sat on top of the pole fence, the heels of her boots hooked behind the second rail. She was dressed in a long-sleeved shirt and levis. Her braids were twined around her head and hidden under her wide-brimmed felt hat. She stared gloomily at the horses.

A baby. Her mother was going to have a baby. She remembered her father's beaming face, her mother's tender smile, and felt very left out. They were replacing her.

"Hiya, Netta. How's our new crop today?" Tobias asked as he hopped onto the fence beside her.

She shrugged, wishing he would go away, but Tobias had seen her face and persevered.

"What's wrong, pet? You look like you've lost your last friend."

"Just about." She turned to look at him, then said grimly, "I guess it's no secret, so I can tell you. Mama's going to have a baby."

"But, Netta, that's wonderful news! Your folks've always wanted more children. Why, look at that big house they built and only the three of you to try to fill it."

Tears came quickly to her eyes. "But, Tobias, they won't love me as much with a baby around. Papa . . . Papa won't want to p . . . play with me anymore."

"Silly child," Tobias said gruffly as he put his arm around her shoulders. "Don't you know love's not something you use up? The more folks you got to love, the more love you got inside you to give away. You don't run short for anybody. Not ever."

"Really and truly, Tobias?"

"Would I lie to you, princess? Of course it's true."

Brenetta's tear-filled eyes turned back to the mares and new colts in the paddock. She had always loved the spring with all the babies arriving, colts and calves and piglets and puppies and kittens. If Tobias was right, maybe a baby sister or brother wouldn't be so bad either. She wiped her tears on her shirt sleeve and sniffed loudly.

"Thanks, Tobias. I *do* feel better."

He dropped his arm and jumped down from the fence. "No problem, Netta. Glad I could help."

"Whatayamean there's no more? Then *find* me some more. Would you let your own da die o' thirst?"

Rory caught his staggering father. "Da, I'm sorry, but I won't ask the Lattimers, and there's no place else for now."

"Won't? You *won't* do somethin' I'm tellin' you t'do? What kind of son be you then?"

Garvey stepped back and stared with his bleary green eyes. Suddenly his hand shot forward, landing hard against Rory's jaw. The sharp crack was followed by a heavy silence. Rory's face was totally expressionless as he returned his father's gaze.

"For the love of St. Christopher, boy! Don't you ever feel nothin'?" Garvey cried, then pitched forward in a dead faint.

Rory caught him and dragged him to his bed. He looked down at his father, red hair and beard matted, his besotted face swollen, and Rory felt the familiar ache in his chest.

"Yes, my father, I can feel," he whispered as he turned and left the stale-smelling cabin.

Rory walked swiftly to his tethered horse. He undid the cinch and pulled the saddle from his back, then kicked off his own boots. Holding a clump of mane, he swung up and turned towards the mountains. Should anyone have been around to see, his granite-like face would have stopped them from speaking to him as he rode off.

The ride to the top wasn't easy, especially bareback, but the strain and effort seemed to pull the tension from his shoulders. By the time he reached the top, Rory's head felt clearer even though his heart was still heavy.

He sat cross-legged on the rocky ledge, his eyes closed as he listened to his gelding grazing, to the wind whistling around the peak, to the sway of the trees. In the valley far below he could hear the gentle lowing of the cattle.

"Oh, Mother," he whispered, "how very alone I am. My heart is squeezed dry."

Brent relaxed in his saddle. The day was unusually warm for this early in the year, and he was enjoying the warm breeze and sunshine as he looked over the herd. The cattle had just returned from winter pasture. They looked good, Brent was pleased to see.

He sat a little straighter in the saddle as he saw Tobias riding his way with another man, a stranger. They rode through the midst of the cattle, separating them like a parting of the waters. Brent studied the stranger as they approached. He was a big man, both in size and weight. His dark brown hair was worn long and shaggy. He was clean shaven, except for the bushy mustache over his thin lips, revealing his deeply pock-marked face. The horse he was riding was equally large, his buckskin coat heavily lathered.

Tobias slowed to a walk, then stopped beside Brent. "Mr. Lattimer, this is Jake Hanson. Says he's just bought the Bowman spread. He's come this way to meet you and see the place."

"Pleasure t' meet you, Mr. Lattimer," said the big man, offering his hand.

Brent took it reluctantly. He had a strange feeling that he wasn't going to like or trust this man. He had no reason; there was just something about him . . .

"When did you buy the Bowmans out, Mr. Hanson?" he asked.

"Call me Jake. Just closed the deal last week. The old man and his wife'll be gone by the end of the month. Meantime, me and my gal, Ingrid, will be looking around for more stock to add to what the Bowmans have sold us." He stopped and looked over the herd. "And what kind of cattle do you call these? They're sure not Longhorns," he added with a chuckle.

"These are Herefords, Mr. Hanson. They came to this country from England earlier in this century. I'm attempting to prove that they can succeed here in the west. So far, I'm doing just that, as you can see for yourself."

" 'pears like it. How 'bout your horses? I hear they're special too."

Brent patted his horse's neck. "Yes, I like to think we have some good blood," was all he said.

"Any for sale?" Jake persisted, his close-set hazel eyes running greedily over Brent's mount.

"Not at the moment," Brent answered, thinking *and especially not to you.* "We're a few shy of what we like to have on hand."

"Well, Mr. Latti . . . it's Brent, ain't it? I guess I'll be movin' on, Brent. Now that we're close neighbors I'm sure we'll be seein' more of each other." He turned toward Tobias. "Thanks for bringin' me up here. Say, you never told me your name so I can thank you proper."

"Tobias Levi."

The eyebrows raised a fraction; the friendly smile vanished. "Sounds Jewish, don't it?"

"Perhaps because my parents were Jews."

Their eyes met and held. Brent could see Jake's undisguised scorn and Tobias's resentment in the face of prejudice. Finally, he kicked his horse forward, riding between the two antagonists.

"Tobias, check with Sam about the calves; see how he's coming."

Brent could almost feel the air charged with hatred, but at last Tobias broke eye contact and did as he was told.

"You sure hired a strange one for foreman, Lattimer," Jake said with a sneer.

"Mr. Hanson, I'm afraid I must go too. I wish you the best with your new place."

Jake understood his dismissal. His face darkened as he said a clipped goodbye and rode away.

Brent felt as if he'd just eaten something very spoiled, so strong was the bad taste in his mouth. He was certain Jake Hanson would mean trouble for someone. He was just that type of man.

"Mama, can I talk to you?"

Taylor turned away from the window where she'd been holding up new curtains. "Of course, sugar. Let me put these down."

She laid the curtains over the high-backed chair at the head of the dining room table, then beckoned for Brenetta to sit at the long walnut-colored table.

"I've just made some tea. Will you have some with me?" she asked Brenetta.

"Yes, please."

They were both silent as Taylor brought the cups and poured. Taylor settled into her chair with a soft rustle of skirts. She looked at Brenetta in her dusty shirt and canvas pants and bit back the urge to send her to her room to bathe and change.

Brenetta was chewing on her lower lip as she twisted her cup on its saucer, a tiny frown knitting her brows. Taylor waited patiently for her to begin, feeling sure she knew what the problem was.

"Mother," Brenetta began at last, "why do you want a baby?"

Taylor smiled; her blue eyes softened. "Netta, a baby is just part of the expression of love between a man and his wife. It's because your father and I love each other that we're so happy to be having another child. It's why we wanted you, too." She leaned forward and took Brenetta's hand. "Darlin', your father and I love you very, very much. You've been a treasure and a joy in our lives; that's why we're so thrilled to be having another baby. You'll see. Four of us will be just one more person to be happy."

Brenetta had been watching her carefully as she spoke, her uncertainty showing clearly in her thoughtful frown. "Will you still love me?" she asked.

"Love you! Of course we will!"

"And you won't send me away when it comes?"

Taylor's hands tenderly stroked Brenetta's hair. "No, my dearest daughter. You will always be just as loved and just as needed as you are right now."

Brenetta's dark eyebrows were nearly knitted together in consternation as she struggled with her conflicting emotions. At last she sighed and lifted her gaze to meet Taylor's.

"All right," she said, "I suppose it's okay with me if you have a baby, so long as Papa and you will still love me."

Taylor suppressed her mirth over Brenetta's serious permission and thanked her with a kiss on the forehead. Her heart sang with happiness. Her world was perfect.

CHAPTER FIVE

APRIL 1874—HEART'S LANDING

Brenetta was up at the crack of dawn. Today was her eleventh birthday. As usual, as a part of her birthday celebration, the family was going into Boise for a few days. Brenetta couldn't wait. She loved these semi-annual trips for supplies. The bustling capital of their young territory always thrilled her.

I don't even mind having to wear dresses for a week straight, she thought as she slipped one over her head. The pretty blue and white calico dress hit her at mid-calf, which suited her just fine. She wasn't in any hurry to get out of short skirts like some girls. Long dresses would be just that much more bother.

She hummed merrily as she splashed her face and began brushing her hair. Her mother would be in soon to braid it, and she didn't want anything to slow down their departure. She meant to have every tangle gone when Taylor arrived.

Finished with her hair, and still alone, she picked up her shoes and began to lace them. Her fingers felt clumsy and the lacing went slowly. She wished she could wear her loose fitting, black leather boots but knew they would never be approved by her mother. Taylor merely tolerated her canvas britches and slip-over shirts here at the ranch. In town it was an entirely different matter.

A light tap announced Taylor's arrival before the door swung open. "Good morning, Netta. Happy birthday." Her arms encircled Brenetta and hugged her tightly. As she stepped back, she said, "My, don't you look lovely in that dress. I do wish you'd wear skirts more often." She sighed. "Whatever happened to my little baby, all dressed in fluffy pink dresses, her hair in ringlets?"

Brenetta wrinkled her nose in distaste.

"All right. I know what you're thinking, young lady. Come here and let's get your hair braided."

Brenetta loved to have her mother work with her hair. Her fingers moved deftly, twining the strands into thick ropes. The gentle pulling on her scalp was somehow comforting. She watched Taylor's face in the mirror while she worked. Then she looked at her own reflection. Everyone said she was the image of her mother, and she tried now to see that for herself. Their noses were both small and their lips full. They both had high cheek-bones, deep-set eyes, and arched eyebrows. They had the same recklessly curly black hair. But where Taylor had dark pools of blue for her eyes,

Brenetta's were a tawny gold. They were a startling feature, looking as if they didn't quite belong with the rest of her. Also, Taylor's skin was still delicate and creamy white, while Brenetta's days spent in the sun had resulted in freckles across the bridge of her nose. No, she thought, I'll never be beautiful like Mama.

"There. All done," Taylor said, punctuating it with a kiss to the crown of Brenetta's head. "Let's have some breakfast and be on our way, shall we?"

Tobias backed the horses up and completed the task of harnessing them to the wagon. Rory was busy loading the back with food and bedding, enough for three days, although a trouble-free journey should take only two. With luck and fair weather, they would get to Boise by the following evening.

"Bear, you be sure to check on that brindle mare often," Tobias said as he walked to the rear of the wagon. "I've got a feeling she's fixin' to foal early, and I don't like it none either."

"I'll keep an eye on her, Tobias."

"I know you will. Oh, and Sam's gonna need some help with those yearlings."

"Mmm."

Rory's mumbled reply brought a careful look from Tobias. "You okay, Bear?" he asked, noting the stiffened jaw and masked eyes.

"Fine."

Tobias moved off, sensing Rory's reluctance to talk. The kid had been like that for days—no, come to think of it, he'd been that way for weeks—all tight and withdrawn. Tobias had always known Rory to be a very private, silent fellow, but this was different. Something was simmering just beneath the surface. He had a hunch it was Garvey's fault but knew of no help for it. A man had no business butting into another man's private life unless he was asked. One thing he did know; no matter what his personal worries, Bear would do his work around the ranch. You could always depend on Rory O'Hara.

"Things about ready, Tobias?"

Tobias looked up as Brent spoke. He'd been so lost in thought he hadn't heard the boss approaching.

"All set, Brent."

"Then I'll get the ladies."

Tobias waited by the wagon. Brenetta came running out of the house first. Her skirts flew wildly as she scampered down the steps, her petticoats and underdrawers carelessly revealed. Her face was all aglow with excitement.

"Happy birthday, princess."

"Oh, thank you, Tobias. It's a great day for a trip, isn't it?"

"Sure is," he agreed as he handed her up to the wagon seat.

"Good morning, Tobias."

"Mornin', Miz Taylor." Tobias tipped his hat, then held her hand as she climbed into the wagon.

With another quick glance over the rigging, he walked to his waiting horse and mounted up. Brent's saddle horse was tied to the back of the wagon while Brent took his turn at the reins beside Taylor.

"Let's go," Brent called to him as he flicked the leather reins in his hands across the broad rumps in front of him.

Rory brushed the stray black hair back from his eyes. His brown face was streaked with sweat. The barn seemed stifling, even with the door flung wide to the crisp April air.

The brindle mare had gone into labor around noon, ahead of schedule as Tobias had predicted. It had been a difficult labor as well. She, like Rory, was dripping with sweat. Every few minutes she would throw her head up and try to nip at her swollen side. At other times she would start to stand, then flop back, dropping her head to the floor, her eyes rolling back until only the whites glared out at him.

Rory had done everything he knew to do. A careful probing had shown the colt to be in the right position with no legs hung up or twisted back, but for some reason the mare couldn't budge it.

Rory knelt near her head, talking soothingly in a steady monotone as he stroked her neck. He wished Tobias was here. This was his mare, and a favorite mare besides. If something happened to her . . .

Suddenly she shuddered violently. Rory could see the contraction grip her belly. As she strained, two tiny hooves appeared, wrapped in the opaque, blue-veined sac. There was a long pause, then she pushed again. Her efforts produced the tip of the foal's nose. The brindle rested, and Rory stepped back from her. It looked as though she'd be all right after all. He breathed a sigh of relief.

Although she seemed to take her time, the remainder of her labor went smoothly. The colt was on the ground, his head poking through the membrane when Garvey entered the barn. Rory heard and recognized his step. He didn't turn to look, instead keeping his eyes on the wet colt before him.

"Say and it's a nice wee one for the Lattimers," Garvey said softly.

"He belongs to Tobias."

"Aye, is that so? Well, then, he's a richer man for this day's work."

Rory scrutinized him, disbelief written in his eyes. His father actually appeared to be sober. Garvey met his gaze with an even one of his own. As the colt struggled to stand, they both looked at it again.

"I've hurt you badly, my boy. I know what you've tried to do since the day I struck out at you. I know you've tried to do for your old da the way you think you should."

Silence.

"Don't know that I can be different than I am. I'm an old man, I am."

The foal wobbled crazily on spindly legs, his face a study in confusion.

"You're a fine son, like your ma was a good woman. Never was there a sweeter flower than White Dove, was there, an' I kilt her with me lovin'."

"Da . . ."

"No. Tis the truth I speak. I took her from her people, her so young t'was like a babe herself. And I an old man already. She died havin' the bairn because o' me wantin' her so."

Rory gazed at the new colt as he poked and jabbed at the dam's udder, seeking his first sustenance. He thought how close he'd come to seeing him die. Would it have been his fault? Tobias's? The stud's? No, it would only be part of the earth's cycle, the heart beat of nature, the natural order of life and death, day and night, beginnings and endings.

"I'm not a bad man, Rory," his father continued, "but I lost me reason for livin' with your ma's passin'. Has nought to do with you, mind you. I'm proud to be your da. It's just I'm too tired. Too tired, my boy."

Rory looked again at Garvey. For the first time he seemed to notice the streaks of grey in the red hair and beard. He saw the deep loss haunting those green eyes, sunken behind dark circles. Never had he seen so clearly how great a hurt his mother's death had been, how deep the wound ran.

"Da . . . I . . ."

Garvey shook his head and stepped away from the stall, from the fresh smell of hay and straw and new life. "No, Rory. Don't be tryin' t' say it. Just know I'm proud of what you've become despite your father. You're like your ma; your strength runs deep and strong—has for generations in her people . . . and your people. You're bound to be a name to reckon with some day. The O'Hara's won't go on disgraced after I'm gone." He turned and left the barn, his body bent, his shoulders sagging.

Rory watched him go, his feelings at war within his breast. He understood with a wisdom beyond his years how great a price his father's confession had cost him. Yet a hot anger rebelled at the compassion, the pity, that threatened to fill his heart. He wanted to strike out and hit something, hit it hard. He wanted to inflict pain, even to himself. What right did Garvey have to claim all the grief?

"It isn't fair!" he cried to the emptiness. "I lost her too!"

He looked back at the nursing foal. The muscles in his face jerked as he battled the feelings seeking to overwhelm him. He had worked too long and too hard at controlling his emotions to reveal them now, even to himself. He knew his duty, and he would do it. But he would not—*he would not*—open himself up again to the hurt, to the helplessness, he had felt from his father's rejection of him six years ago. He would not pity him, or love him, nor would he hate him. He would only do what he had to do.

The mask of control slipped back in place, his handsomely chiseled features revealing nothing, his black eyes blank. The barn was still except for the sucking sounds coming from the warm stall.

Brent's body swayed easily with the horse's gait, his broad shoulders relaxed. His hands rested on the saddle horn, and the reins were held lightly between his fingers.

They had left their mountains behind this afternoon, and now they were traveling across the sagebrush desert of Southwestern Idaho. The pungent aroma filled his nostrils. He looked ahead across the flatlands towards the purple mountains in the distance. The snow was disappearing from the highest peaks already. Below those same mountains, nestled in the river valley, was their destination.

Brent remembered the first time he had seen the town. Idaho was still in the midst of its gold rush, and the capital of the territory had been an exciting, bustling place. With a smile, he remembered Taylor's horror at the rowdy characters filling the streets and saloons. Even after months of hardship coming along the Oregon Trail, she had seemed to expect something more civilized and modern.

By 1870, most miners had left with the two hundred million dollars in gold they had picked and panned from Idaho's interior. The population had dropped drastically, seemingly overnight. But now they were coming again, slower this time, but still coming—men and women like themselves, seeking to carve a home out of this rugged territory, seeking a place to put down roots for generations to follow.

As they stopped to make camp, Brent felt a deep sense of contentment fill him. He looked over at Taylor. She was busy readying supper for the four of them. As she bent over the fire, her dress fell smoothly over her rounded hips and thighs, stirring his thoughts from one source of contentment to another. He moved silently up behind her;

his hands encircled her waist. He could almost touch the fingers of his two hands.

"Incredible," he whispered as he nibbled her neck.

She shuddered pleasantly, then relaxed against his shoulder, closing her eyes to the loving touch.

"You *are* incredible," he repeated.

She turned and kissed him, leaning against his taut, muscular body. "Incredible or not," she said huskily as their lips parted, "I have a meal to fix. Even if you're not hungry, Brenetta and Tobias are."

He laughed and swatted her behind lightly. "You win. I'm gone."

He climbed the steep bluff alone, his mighty legs pawing for sure footing, lunging even upwards. His copper coat glistened as it stretched over his straining muscles. At the top, Amen-Ra's sharp eyes surveyed the valley. His ears darted forward and back as his nostrils checked the gentle spring breeze. Satisfied, he shook his noble head. Amen-Ra had returned to his summer range.

The winter had been a mild one, and the snows had left the plains early. Forage had remained good throughout the season. He and his mares had lost little flesh. One early colt had died, a victim of coyotes. Otherwise, he had returned with all his band intact. Below him, the mares grazed peacefully, some large with foal, others with young ones already at their sides. Set apart from these were three young stallions. Soon they would try to assert some authority and Amen-Ra would drive them off. There was only room for one leader.

With a mighty shake of his head, he left the bluff. Once at the bottom he made a leisurely inspection around the perimeter of his band, then settled to grazing himself.

Like a magnet, the mountains pulled Rory O'Hara ever higher. They seemed to promise him something—peace, love, a sense of belonging. And so he followed their call, pushing deeper into the high forests, waiting for them to work their magic.

The cold water foamed and swirled over the smooth stones. Rory laid on his stomach, upstream from his horse, and drank deeply. Then, his thrist quenched, he sat back on his haunches and surveyed his surroundings. Nature had dipped her paintbrush in several shades of green and splashed the hues indiscriminately over the hills and valleys, grasses and trees. The chunk of blue sky overhead was flawlessly clear, and he was surrounded by silence.

It was amazing. He felt so often entirely alone when he was with others; yet here in the wilderness, when he really was alone, he felt a special closeness to everyone. Perhaps it was just that nature was his closest friend, his faithful companion.

With a sigh, he remembered last night. He had gone to see Garvey and found him drunk as usual. His brief trip into sobriety had proved too much for him. His only words to Rory were once again filled with scathing anger and rejection, rejection bordering on loathing. And so Rory had ridden out this morning to escape to a place of peace, and it was working. The cold hand that clenched his heart was easing its grip. He began to forget what had driven him away, and just enjoyed being here.

Rory led his horse along the stream and into the trees. He continued to climb on foot, his destination a rocky ledge from where he could see for miles in three directions. It was not far but it was steep. The last twenty feet of his route left the forest, jumping suddenly skywards. At its base, Rory tied his gelding to a tree and continued on alone.

He took his time ascending the cliff, checking every toehold. He placed his hands with care also, not desiring to surprise a sleeping rattler. The rocks were warmed by the April sun, and its southern exposure was a favorite spot for reptiles.

When he reached the top, Rory rested gladly. He was a strong young man, but the climb had been a difficult one. His eyes swept below him as his breathing began to steady itself. Suddenly he tensed and leaned forward. Entering the tiny meadow he had just left was Amen-Ra. Behind him were his mares and foals. Still further back were two—no, three—young stallions. From the looks of them, they'd be on their own soon.

The horses quickly lined the stream and drank. Amen-Ra sniffed the air suspiciously, then joined them. The breeze was blowing in Rory's face, and he knew the stallion was unaware of his close proximity. He gazed down at the proud animal, hardly breathing.

It was no wonder the Lattimer's horses were so desirable. This horse's blood was the foundation for them all. Before his escape, Amen-Ra had sired severeal sons and daughters by mares Brent had caught off the range or purchased from other ranchers. While they weren't the purebreds he would have mated in other times and other places, they were hardy, sturdily built animals, horses well-suited to their lives here in the West. It was a shame he had never been recaptured, but Brent had finally given up, settling for Amen-Ra's sons to carry on in his place.

Rory broke his study of the stallion and moved on over his followers. They were a fine looking band, strong and fit. They had wintered well. He recognized the mares they had captured with their five brood mares last summer. They had turned them loose, allowing them to race after Amen-Ra after securing their own mares. If Brenetta hadn't been hurt, he and Tobias might have tried to bring them along. As it was, they wanted to be able to get home quickly without fighting with four wild horses.

The mares and foals were branching out from the water, beginning to graze. Amen-Ra moved to the mouth of the valley, keeping a keen eye and cocked ear on any other possible entrances or exits. Even as he grazed he was wholly alert. Rory glanced at him with admiration, then resumed his perusal of the mares. When his eyes fell upon the two-year-old filly, they halted abruptly, desiring to go on further.

She had grown dramatically in the nine months since he had seen her last. Her refined, intelligent head was supported by a slender yet strong neck. Her body was short, built for quick turns. Her legs were straight and long, promising speed. Her copper coat shone even now at the end of winter; it still was the color of hot flame. The Flame, Brenetta had called her.

I want her, Rory thought as he sat there. I want her . . . and I mean to have her.

As stealthily as possible, Rory moved to the blind side of the cliff and began his descent.

Tobias stood outside the general store, smoking silently. Brent had left him to gather the supplies while Taylor dragged him off to another clothing store. Brenetta had reluctantly gone with them. Tobias smiled as he remembered her mutinous look. Five days in dresses and bonnets and laced shoes were beginning to get to her.

He dropped his cigarette at his feet and ground it carefully into the earth before turning to enter the store. His head was bent forward as he looked at his new boots, and he plowed directly into a young woman, knocking the packages from her arms.

"Oh, dear!" she cried as she knelt to retrieve her things.

"Sorry, miss," Tobias said, leaning down at the same time.

Their heads collided with a resounding *thwack*, and she fell over backwards, landing ignobly on her backside.

"Oh, dear!" she said again.

Tobias was totally flustered. "Miss, I do apologize," he said as he put out his hand to help her up. As he did so, he tripped over the bag of flour and flew forward, landing across her lap.

Embarrassment coloring his face, he looked up at her, expecting an indignant remark and possibly a slap for his ineptness, if not his impropriety of his choice of landings. Instead, he found her face crinkled up in barely suppressed laughter.

Tobias scrambled to his feet, and this time managed to help her up too. "Miss, I . . . I . . . Forgive me."

She actually giggled, covering her mouth with a hand. He didn't notice how red and calloused it was as he watched her sky-blue eyes dance out her merriment. Instead of making him feel better, he found he was even more flustered than before.

"I'll get your things," he mumbled and began gathering her packages. Fortunately, nothing was ruined or lost. As he stood up, his arms laden, he asked, "May I carry these to your wagon? It's the least I can do."

She controlled her amusement long enough to say, "Why, thank you, Mr . . .?"

"Levi, miss. Tobias Levi."

"Thank you, Mr. Levi. It would be most kind of you."

He fell into step beside her as she walked slowly along the board sidewalk. She was more than a head shorter than he was, even with her faded bonnet on. Light blonde hair fell down her neck in back, escaping the pins holding her bun in place. Her face was lightly tanned, exaggerating the paleness of her hair and eyes.

"Do you live here in town?" Tobias asked her.

"No, Mr. Levi. My pa and me . . . *I*," she corrected quickly, "just moved here from Texas.

73

We've bought us a little homestead south of here, about a day's ride or so." She turned a pretty smile his way. "And do you live here?"

"No, I'm a foreman for a cattle ranch. Heart's Landing. Maybe you've heard of it?"

She shook her head. "I don't think so, but my pa rarely repeats anything he hears to me. I'm sure it's a fine place if you're there."

Feeling shy but encouraged by her open, friendly face, Tobias said, "Maybe you'd like to see it sometime. Perhaps I could come callin' and ask your pa."

"Why, Mr. Levi, I think I'd like that very much. Oh, here's my wagon."

They stopped and Tobias put the packages in the back. Taking his hat from his head, he turned to her again.

"I suppose I'd best ask your name and find out where your place is."

Her eyes twinkled. "Yes, I believe that's a fine idea." She held out her hand for him to take, which he did. "My name is Ingrid. Ingrid Hanson. Pa bought the old Bow . . ."

"Get your stinkin' hand off my daughter, Jew."

"Pa!" Ingrid cried as she pulled away from Tobias.

Jake Hanson's face was mottled with anger as he grabbed Ingrid's shoulders and shoved her toward the wagon. "Get up there, gal, and don't you say nothin'."

"Mr. Hanson, I . . ." Tobias began.

"Keep your words to yourself, mister. I ain't interested in what no dirty Jew has t' say." Jake climbed into the wagon, shoving Ingrid to the edge of the seat.

Only the girl's frightened face kept Tobias from saying more, his own temper cooled by his concern for her. With his eyes he tried to tell her he would see her again. Somehow, he *would* see her again. Somehow . . .

Rory dogged their heels for four days. Amen-Ra felt his relentless pursuit and pushed his herd on at a breakneck pace. Rory was unconcerned; he knew the right moment would come and then the Flame would be his.

It was late in the afternoon when Rory saw the stallion's first mistake. He had turned unknowingly into a box canyon. Rory wasted no time. He knew that as soon as Amen-Ra reached the end he would be running back out. Rory pulled his lariat from the saddle horn, urged his horse through the mouth of the canyon, and waited.

He could feel the running horses before he could see them. The earth shook with the thunder of their hooves. Every nerve in Rory's body was alert and tingling, his muscles readied themselves for action. His mood communicated itself to his horse, who quivered in anticipation. Amen-Ra never faltered when he saw Rory at the entrance. He merely flattened his ears against his head and sped on. Rory had no intention of trying to stop the stallion. He had interest in only one member of the herd, and when his eyes caught sight of her near the rear of the panicked group, he pulled back even further, allowing Amen-Ra more room to pass by him.

Just before the Flame reached him, he spurred his mount foward, a startling cry coming from his lips. The surprised and frightened horses scattered, trying desperately to get around him and join the others. The red filly doubled over backwards and raced away from him. When she realized she was alone, she tried to turn again but her pursuer was right behind her. Rory let the rope swirl above his head several times before throwing it through the air. His aim was true; the loop came to rest around her throat. As it tightened, he slowed his horse, watching the filly carefully. Like a keg of dynamite, the Flame exploded into the air. Rory checked the dally around the saddle horn with one hand and gripped the rope with the other. His experienced mount kept the lariat taut while staying out of the crazed horse's way.

The battle continued for over half an hour. The filly threw herself away from her captor again and again. Each time her breath was cut off at her throat. She screamed out in anger and fear, her tortured cries filling the air.

Suddenly the fighting stopped. The Flame stood quivering with exhaustion, her head drooping, her nose nearly touching the ground. Tiny rivelets of mud striped her coat where dust had mixed with sweat. Her eyes were dulled with fatigue. Rory looked at her, the wild creature momentarily beaten down by man, and was tempted to turn her loose. It was a brief temptation.

"So now we can really meet each other," he said

softly as he moved his gelding forward a few steps. "I'm Rory, also called Bear Claw. And you are the Flame."

Her head came up slightly, and she cocked an ear in his direction.

"Yes, my lovely one. You have great spirit. You don't believe it now, but someday, we shall be friends."

CHAPTER SIX

JUNE 1874—HEART'S LANDING

Tobias sat on the moss-covered boulder, the smoke from his cigarette hanging in a blue-grey cloud over his head. He had been riding the boundaries of Heart's Landing all morning, keeping an eye out for strays. Things had been quiet and uneventful, and he was bored. He wished he'd gone on the cattle drive this year. He was so darned restless lately.

He pinched the end of his cigarette, making certain there wasn't a ghost of a spark left alive.

"Well, let's get with it, Spook," he said to the big white mare at his side.

They proceeded slowly west. The cattle grazing this section were primarily the Longhorns brought up from Texas the year before. Brent Lattimer was still experimenting with crossbreeding, and besides his Longhorns and Herefords, he had purchased some Scotch Shorthorns this spring. The boss of this spread would never be accused of living in the past. He was always trying new things.

Tobias was proud to be working for such a man. He looked on Brent as the father he'd barely had a chance to know. On his own at fifteen, both his parents gone, Tobias had drifted around the West until settling here. He'd seen a lot in the last ten years. Perhaps that's why he understood Rory so well.

Thoughts of Rory brought a smile to his wind-chapped lips. Rory had been working for two months with that filly of his, and darned if he wasn't going to win her over yet. Tobias turned a blind eye on how many hours Rory spent with her instead of at his chores. The Flame had captured a part of Rory's heart, giving him something he'd never had before, and Tobias wasn't about to interfere.

He dismounted at Crooked Creek and drank his fill. On the other side was the Hanson place. Their cabin was tucked back against the mountains some distance from here, hidden from his view. Tobias felt the hackles rise on his neck. The few run-ins he'd had with Jake Hanson were enough to bring a blistering hatred to his breast. Nothing could make Tobias Levi lose his temper faster than a slur on his racial heritage.

"Come on, Spook," he said gruffly. The horse followed quietly behind him as they followed the water downstream.

White birch trees lined the creek, their leaves

applauding softly as Tobias and Spook passed by. A kildeer called out, beckoning them to follow her away. The water gurgled and babbled as it hurried on its way to the valley, and later, to join the river. The laughter that rose to join nature's chorus was so much a part of the glad sounds that, at first, Tobias didn't recognize it as such. When he did, he halted abruptly, waiting to hear it again, but it was gone. He shook his head, wondering at his imagination, then moved on.

Tobias stopped again. He was not mistaken. He could hear laughter coming from up ahead. He tied Spook to a tree and proceeded quietly alone.

Crooked Creek fell suddenly into a small but deep pool. The clear freshwater pond was heavily shrouded in trees and ferns, the golden surface glittering in the sunlight. Tobias pushed aside the tree branch in time to see two small feet slip into the water, followed by a big Irish Setter paddling madly across the pond. The swimmer broke through the water at the other side, her blonde hair plastered against her scalp and then swirling freely around her white arms.

"Shauna, don't!" she cried as the dog reached her, placing its large paws on her shoulders, threatening to submerge her.

It was the first time Tobias had seen Ingrid Hanson since he'd met her in Boise. He had thought of her often, but always her father's face intruded on his daydreams, shattering their pleasure. He had forgotten she was so attractive. The soft swell of her breasts just beneath the water's surface, her pale blue eyes and nearly-white hair, and her charming laughter all blended together into a magnetic pull he couldn't resist. Unconsciously he stepped into view.

Ingrid turned startled eyes upon him. Tobias stared back, mesmerized. As the color rose in her face, he suddenly realized the position he had put her in and quickly turned his back to her. He felt like a schoolboy, the heat rising in his own cheeks.

"I . . . I'm sorry, Miss Ingrid," he stammered.

She swam to the bank and scrambled for her clothes. He could hear her and feared she would flee without forgiving him.

"Miss Ingrid," he said, again calling her by her first name, "please. I . . . I really am sorry. I . . ."

"It's all right, Mr. Levi," she said, behind him.

He twirled around at her voice, surprised by her nearness. A tender blush still colored her cheekbones, and her eyes were lowered, staring at his boots. Her fine, wet hair hung down her back, soaking her dress.

"I . . ." he tried again.

She looked up at him then, her pretty heart-shaped face open and guileless. "I thought I wasn't going to see you ever again after what my father said. I'm glad I was wrong."

Tobias's hand came up of its own volition and gently brushed away the drops of water trailing down from her hair. He couldn't understand what it was her closeness was doing to him. He had left boyhood behind long ago; he had known many women in his time. So what was this feeling striving to overwhelm him?

"My father . . . he really isn't always so . . . so unreasonable," she said softly, her eyes pleading

82

with him to understand. "You see, it was a Jewish family who took our home. I'm sure if he knew you, he would . . ."

Without thought, he gathered her in his arms, bending low to claim her lips with his own. Her brief protest was smothered in his kiss. Her temporary resistance changed quickly to acceptance and then to fire as she melted into his embrace.

Brenetta sat in the crook of the old tree. Her dress was bunched around her thighs, her feet rebelliously bare. Her pretty face was clouded as she rested her chin on her knees.

"Netta, it's time to go," her mother called from the porch, but she stubbornly stayed where she was.

"Netta!" Her father's tone changed her mind.

Brenetta scrambled quickly down the tree trunk, grabbed the discarded shoes and stockings, and raced towards the house. The buggy stood waiting at the door, and Brenetta arrived just as Brent was helping Taylor to her seat.

"Well, young lady, where have you been?" Taylor asked, looking at the toes peeking out from under Brenetta's skirts.

Sullenly, Brenetta replied, "No place special. Must I go?" she asked, turning a pleading look upon her father.

In answer, he picked her up and plunked her down behind her mother. He smiled at her as he climbed in himself, encouraging her to behave. She knew he wasn't eager to go either but was doing this for Taylor.

The cause of her rebellion, besides the dress and

shoes, was the family's destination. Taylor had insisted that too much time had escaped without a proper welcome to their new neighbors, and they were on their way now to visit Jake Hanson and his daughter, Ingrid. Brent's opinion of Jake's character had not swayed her in the least. "It's not Christian to ignore them," she had insisted, and Brent had relented.

To top it all off, Brenetta had been counting on watching Rory schooling the Flame. Never had she seen an animal with so much spirit and intelligence. She was totally captivated by the creature. And with Rory. She hadn't understood before what a way he had with horses. Slowly, but ever so surely, he had turned the wild hellion's fear into a solid trust. The pair was poetry in motion to watch —and today was the big day. Today Rory was taking the Flame for her first ride outside the corral. It was a big moment, and Brenetta was going to miss it.

The June sky overhead was dotted with cotton-ball clouds, and two hawks parried and swooped as they sought their prey. The long grass was starting to turn from green to yellow as the heat of summer began. Taylor took it all in, enjoying the magnitude of everything, the feeling of *forever* this country gave her.

The Hanson home was a mean little log cabin, set with its back against a rocky hill. The exterior had a sad, unkempt appearance, and the stoop looked dangerously shaky. A cracked flowerpot sat next to the door, the yellow flowers struggling valiantly to add color and cheer to their drab surroundings.

Brent stopped the buggy and helped Taylor out before he walked up to the door and knocked. He had told her he didn't expect either Hanson or his daughter to be at home this time of day. They were both surprised when the door was opened by Jake.

Taylor felt her smile freeze on her lips as she looked at him. He was nearly six and a half feet tall and seemed to tower over Brent, who was no small man himself. His brawny frame was covered by a soiled shirt and torn canvas pants. Several days growth of stubble covered his chin. He made her think of one of Brent's surly bulls and wondered if he would suddenly snort and paw the ground.

Bolstered by her early training of proper etiquette, Taylor walked up to the man, hoping her smile looked sincere. "Mr. Hanson, how nice to meet you at last. I have fairly badgered Mr. Lattimer to bring me here. I'm Taylor Lattimer, and this is our daughter, Brenetta."

He looked from her to Brenetta and then back again but said nothing.

"Is your daughter at home?" Taylor asked hopefully. "I thought perhaps she and Netta could get acquainted while we visit."

He spit a stream of tobacco juice on the ground. "Nope. She went out awhile ago and ain't come back yet." He paused in thought, then added, "Why don't you come in and sit a spell?"

Taylor was surprised at the clean and neat appearance of the interior. It was in sharp contrast to the outside. Though sparsely furnished, everything was in order, the floor swept and the two small beds made. Besides the two beds and the black stove, the only other pieces of furniture were a roughly hewn table and two stools. Taylor chose one of the stools and lowered her body into in.

"I'm sorry we haven't come calling sooner to welcome you but with calving and roundup and branding . . . Well, I'm sure you understand, being a rancher yourself."

"I'm surprised you *ever* come after the way your husband and I got on the first time." He turned an accusing eye on Brent.

Taylor stepped in hastily, not wanting to have their visit get any worse than it already seemed to be. "Where are you from, Mr. Hanson?" she asked.

"Come here from Texas. Wasn't much left for us there once the Yankees won the war and moved in on us. After my wife died, we pulled up stakes and come here. Seemed as good a place as any." He spit again, this time into a cuspidor beside the table leg. "Sounds like you're from the South yourself."

"How very perceptive of you, Mr. Hanson. I'm from Georgia, as a matter of fact. My family had a plantation about fifty miles from Atlanta. My brother still lives there with his family, although things are quite difficult for them now." She knew she was chattering and wished she had listened to Brent and never come.

Jake turned to Brent. "I got my doubts that you'd be a Southerner. Am I right?"

"You're right. I'm from New York."

"Figured."

Silence surrounded them. Brenetta shifted on the bed where she had chosen to sit. Taylor thought desperately for another topic, silently cursing Brent for not being more amiable and helpful. Her own mind seemed blank. She had no idea what to say to this man who looked at her with a mixture of admiration and disdain.

A shadow fell through the open doorway, and four pairs of eyes turned in that direction. Taylor knew this must be Ingrid and was surprised. She had expected more of a child; she didn't know why. The young lady before her appeared to be about seventeen or eighteen, but she was barely taller than Brenetta. She had apparently been swimming for her pale hair was still damp, falling freely over her shoulders and down her back. An excited color highlighted her cheeks, and her lips seemed slightly red and swollen. Her eyes sparkled from within, the sky blue color warm.

Why, she's in love, Taylor thought with sudden intuition, and she's just left him.

Ingrid quickly ducked her head, trying to hide all that was written on her face. Taylor glanced at Jake Hanson and knew with a certainty that, whoever Ingrid had just come from, her father would disapprove if he knew, and disapprove violently.

She doesn't want him to know, Taylor thought and stood up abruptly. She crossed the room, her hand extended.

"Ingrid, I'm so happy to meet you. I'm Taylor Lattimer, your neighbor." She placed herself between father and daughter in an act of feminine conspiracy.

Their eyes met; Ingrid's lit with understanding as she realized what Taylor was trying to do for her.

"Come here, Netta, and meet Ingrid," Taylor said as she motioned Brenetta to her side. "Why don't the two of you spend some time together while we adults get better acquainted? Go on."

Ingrid mouthed a silent thank you, then took Brenetta's hand and left. Taylor wondered a moment why she had so obviously stepped in where it was none of her business. When she turned back to her host, she ceased her wondering. This man was why. She didn't like him. But she did feel a kinship to Ingrid and wanted to help her any way she could.

"What a lovely mother you have," Ingrid said as the two girls sat in the shade of the mountain not far from the back of the cabin.

"Yes, mother *is* beautiful, isn't she. She's always been beautiful. Where's your mother, Ingrid?"

"My mother died a few years ago. She worked herself to death," Ingrid said thoughtfully. "But I think at one time she must have been very pretty. And she was a real lady, even if her folks were poor, and she always wanted me to be one too." Her eyes sparkled. "I'd like to learn to talk and walk like your mother. My ma spent hours trying to teach me right. Pa said it wasn't worth the time, but I've always tried to remember all she told me." She paused, then said, "My, I'm running on. Tell me about you, Netta. How old are you? Don't you just *love* Heart's Landing?" The color deepened in her cheeks.

Brenetta didn't notice the change. "Oh, yes. I love it, but I didn't know *you'd* seen it."

"Oh, no. I haven't."

"Well, you must come some time. I'm eleven. How old are you?"

"I'll be eighteen in September."

"Really?" Brenetta replied. She couldn't help noticing that Ingrid was no more than an inch taller than she was.

"Uh-huh."

"Do you ride?"

Ingrid shook her head. Her hair was beginning to dry and fine strands wafted around her face as she answered. "Not often. We only have the one saddle horse and no sidesaddle."

"You don't have to have a sidesaddle, silly."

Ingrid looked shocked.

"Well, you don't," Brenetta insisted huffily. "I ride astride all the time."

"My ma . . . she . . . What about your dress?"

"Oh, I wear pants and boots like the other wranglers."

"Pants?"

"Sure. Who wants to wear dresses, anyway?"

"I do," Ingrid sighed, her eyes taking on a far-away look. "I'd like to wear a pretty dress and look pretty for someone I love. I'd like to live in a nice house like the ones you see in town. Someday, when I'm married . . ."

"Married? Do you have a fella?"

"What? Oh . . . I . . . no. Do you?" Ingrid stammered.

Brenetta shook her head emphatically. "Not me! I'm not going to get married ever. I'm just going to stay and help my papa forever." She wrinkled her nose, then added, "Besides, I've got too many friends now. Rory and Tobias and Sam . . ."

"Tobias?" Ingrid whispered.

"Yes, Tobias Levi. He's our foreman. Next to Rory, he's my best friend, even if he is so much older than me."

"Old?"

"He was twenty-four his last birthday."

Ingrid smiled, her whole face lighting up. "Yes, I guess that does seem awfully old to you." She stood up. "Come on. I'll show you my garden. I've worked hard at it, and I'd like to show it off to someone."

Tobias stared down from the top of the ridge. Her cabin was only a dot in the distance—actually, he couldn't even be certain that was even it—but he felt as if she were near enough for him to see her. His lips still tasted hers. He thought he could still feel her petite, feminine body pressing tightly against him, her very soul responding to his embrace.

Only hours before he had wondered why he was so restless. Now he knew why. It was her, always thoughts of her. But now he knew she loved him and nothing else mattered. He meant to have her, Jake Hanson or no Jake Hanson.

CHAPTER SEVEN

JULY 1874—SPRING HAVEN

"Damn you! If I didn't have to worry about you, I could make it. I could make it without that Yankee's money. You brought it here. You brought the trouble."

"Philip. Don't!"

Their bedroom sweltered in the heavy summer heat. Philip stared wild-eyed at Marilee. To his mind, he had only spoken the truth. If he'd never married her, he would still be the handsome, wealthy master of a great plantation—an empire his father and his father's father before him had built out of the rich Georgia soil. She had tricked him somehow, she and Taylor. Yes, that was it. He'd been bewitched.

He'd forgotten how very much he had loved her. He'd forgotten that she had stood by him through his recurring sickness, a fever that was eating away at his mind. He'd forgotten that her love had never faltered through one failure after another. He'd forgotten the children she had given him, loving each one of them as she loved him. He was only aware of wanting to hurt her, to rid himself of the blackness that waited to overwhelm him, to destroy him.

"I'm getting out of here. I can't stand it here. Do you hear me? You've made me hate the only place I ever wanted to be. You've made me want to escape Spring Haven, my home. Why? Why did you have to do this to me?"

Philip stumbled from the bedroom, slamming the door behind him. He slipped more than walked down the curving staircase, hanging onto the bannister to keep from falling and rolling to the bottom.

He stopped, the cold gripping his heart. *It* was there again. He stifled the urge to scream as he turned to look into the east drawing room. It stood in the doorway, the emptiness, the black phantom that pursued him. It beckoned him to come, to slip into its eternal nothingness. Philip felt himself being pulled towards it and gripped the bannister with all his strength. His entire body shook.

"Philip, what is it?" Marilee stood at the top of the stairs, her tired eyes filled with concern.

The blackness vanished, and he whirled to face her. "You! You brought it here!" he yelled.

"Philip . . ."

He ran from the house, half-crazed and driven by fear.

"What you up to, Marty?"

Martin looked up to see Alan leaning over the side of the stall, his red-gold hair falling carelessly over his forehead. "Goin' fishin'," Martin answered, picking up his pole as he stood up.

"It's a might warm out there."

Martin shrugged. "Doesn't matter. It's a might warm everywhere, and General and I plan to go fishin'."

Martin wasn't sure if he liked Alan Montgomery or not. He was an odd-looking fellow, about twenty-six, with large green eyes and big ears sticking out from his head. He always seemed to be smiling or whistling or something, no matter what.

Alan had shown up at Spring Haven about five months before, looking for work. Philip had told him there was no money for hiring any help but said he was welcome to spend the night in the barn. For some reason, Alan had stayed on, working only for his room and board. He was a hard worker, doing the labor of three others, and everyone seemed to accept him as part of the family now.

Alan appeared ready to say something more when Philip burst into the barn, seemingly blind to their presence. He threw a saddle onto his horse and rode off without a word.

Martin tried to pretend his father's strange behavior didn't bother him. He flung his pole over his shoulder with feigned casualness and said hoarsely, "See you later, Alan. Come on, General."

Marilee sank down at the top of the stairs as Philip stormed out. She buried her face in her hands but her eyes were dry. She had cried them out long ago. She was filled only with fatigue. When was it she had last felt anything *except* fatigue?

"Oh, Philip. What is happening to you? To us?" she whispered.

For the thousandth time she tried to pinpoint exactly when she first noticed the change in Philip. When was it he first looked at her in fear, and then hate, instead of love? Perhaps it was after Brent's bank draft arrived just before Christmas and he had wept in her arms. Then again, maybe it began with his attack of fever last January.

"Well, there's too much to do to sit here all day long," she said aloud, her voice echoing her weariness.

Marilee grasped the oak railing and pulled herself to her feet. She moved down the stairs like an old woman, her dress hanging loosely from her thin shoulders. When she reached the bottom, she turned towards the back of the house, thinking she must see what Susan was preparing for their supper.

"Oh! Mr. Montgomery, I didn't see you," she cried as she bumped into him by the back door.

"I'm sorry, ma'am. Are you all right?"

His voice sounded genuinely concerned; his hands held her shoulders a moment longer than was necessary to steady her. She looked into his comical face and felt strangely comforted.

"I'm fine, thank you, Mr. Montgomery."

Alan smiled his crooked smile. "Don't you think it's time you called me Alan? I'd like to think I'm a friend by this time."

"Why, of course, you're a friend . . . Alan. And I *do* appreciate all you've done for us."

He nodded as he stepped aside to let her pass. Marilee had a funny feeling as she slipped by him that things were suddenly not the same as they had been moments before.

Philip raced his horse across the field, the animal's shod hooves pounding the fallow earth, throwing red chunks of clay high into the air. Philip spent hours like this every day now. It was the only place he felt safe. He could outrun the darkness on horseback. It couldn't call to him over the thunder of hooves.

July was nearly gone already. Since the day he stormed out of the house, Philip had been sleeping at the office in town. He went home for a short time each day to see the children, usually staying for supper. The rest of the day was spent preparing useless legal briefs—useless because he was a Rebel and the Yankees were in charge—or on horseback. These rides were his one link to sanity, and in his more lucid moments, he knew it.

The sun was setting now, the bright orange ball hanging brilliantly behind the silhouetted trees. He spurred his mount again, and they soared over the fence. He felt the power beneath him and revelled in it. *Why am I afraid to go home?* he wondered silently.

"I'm *not* afraid!" he said through gritted teeth and turned his gelding sharply in the direction of Spring Haven.

The sun disappearing quickly, Philip was forced to slow to a walk. The early night sky was illuminated by a million stars, and he felt a peculiar freedom. Nothing pursued him. He was free at last; he was able to think clearly once again.

Poor Marilee. It had been ages since he had been civil to her. Their only daily encounter was strained and unpleasant, Philip always watching for his phantom, Marilee always watching him. She had grown even thinner, almost gaunt, this last year. When was the last time he had seen her smile or heard her laugh, that laugh which had been so infectious when they were younger? Tonight he would make it up to her. He would tell her he was sorry. He would hold her, make love to her, and everything would be as it once had been for them.

He rode silently through the fields, feeling stronger with each step towards home. Now that the madness, the dark fog, had cleared from his mind he felt a surge of belonging to something wonderful. He knew this land so completely even darkness of night could not confuse him. Soon he would reach the slave quarters. Most of them stood empty now; the free negroes insisted on having their homes elsewhere so they would *know* they were free. Only Charley and Uncle Dan had kept their places, and Alan had moved into one.

The cabins rose up from the nightline before him. Philip dismounted and led his horse through them, remembering with nostalgia a time when this place bustled with activity, women bent over scrub buckets, pickaninnies running and laughing, old folks rocking on their porches while all the strong bucks labored in acres and acres of cotton. His memory was void of the poverty, the want, the absence of freedom of choice. He saw it all through the rosy remembrance of childhood.

A cabin door opened ahead of him, and Philip stopped short, not wanting to have to visit or answer any questions. He was in a hurry to see Marilee, to tell her now that his mind was clear, now that the darkness had fled, now that . . .

He heard her muffled laughter and lifted his eyes. A golden glow from the open door bathed the pair on the rickety porch. Alan held her possessively and ran a loving hand over her loosened hair.

"I love you, Marilee." The gently spoken words thundered through the night.

Philip felt the air turning cold nearby. Without looking, he knew the darkness had returned, deeper and blacker than before. He turned his head and watched as his phantom moved closer, piercing the July heat with icicles. It called to him, beckoning him to enter its emptiness, to join with its icy, ink-like nothingness.

"Oh, Alan," he heard Marilee sigh sweetly.

As her words faded, the phantom called him again, coaxing, promising him a place of peace, a place of feeling nothing. Stiffly, he stepped into the void.

Marilee had let herself stay too long. Alan's arm was lying across her stomach and she tried to slip out from under it, but his arm tightened.

"Don't go," he whispered huskily.

"I must, Alan. It's late and I . . ."

He kissed her throat, then nibbled her ear. "I know," he sighed by her earlobe, sending delicious tingles up and down her side.

They dressed without haste, comfortable in each others presence. It was as if they had been lovers for years instead of two short weeks. Marilee felt alive again. She loved and was loved. When she was with Alan she could forget everything else. She could pretend they were husband and wife, just the two of them alone—no problems, no worries, no decisions, no disappointments, no thoughts of watching as Philip lost his mind . . . no memories of a forgotten childhood . . .

"Marilee?"

She raised her eyes and looked at him across the rumpled bed. Funny how he no longer looked odd to her. There was strength in his flat nose and short stature. There was love and concern in his bright green eyes. He made her feel beautiful, like a young girl again. She seldom even remembered that she was seven years older than Alan. He seemed so much wiser, how could he be younger?

"Marilee, you must decide." He came around to her, his shirt still open, exposing the thick, curly hair on his chest. He pulled her to her feet. "Come away with me. We can't go on like this. We'll go someplace where no one knows us. We'll be man and wife."

"But the children, Alan."

"We'll take them with us," he insisted.

Marilee smiled sadly. "Alan, be reasonable. They'd never come. They're too old. They wouldn't leave their home, their . . . father . . ."

Alan embraced her, tipping back her chin so her eyes could meet with his. "Then come alone. We'll have children of our own."

His intensity frightened her; it frightened her because she felt it too. She knew she *could* leave it all, even the children, and go with him. She knew she could and was tempted.

"Alan, I must get up to the house."

His arms loosened their hold. "All right. I'll let it go—for now."

Marilee finished dressing but left her hair free. The children and Susan would all be in bed. No one would see her. Alan took her elbow as he opened the door and they stepped onto the porch.

"We could run away to an island in the South Seas," he whispered in her ear. "You could be the queen and sit on a throne eating berries until you burst."

She laughed, trying to hide the sound in his shoulder. He held her tightly, running his hand over her hair, his eyes burning into hers.

"I love you, Marilee." With those words he pleaded again for her to come away with him.

"Oh, Alan." It was what she wanted. She was going to say *yes;* they both knew she would.

A sudden movement in the shadows caught their attention. The man swung onto his horse and galloped past them, his face briefly identified in the light from the open door.

"Philip," Marilee breathed in horror.

They both had seen something terrible written in his features. It was more than just seeing them together. Something much worse.

"Get up to the house," Alan ordered. "I'm going after him."

Martin couldn't fall asleep again. He'd had another nightmare, bringing him sharply awake over an hour ago. He got up and lit a candle. Perhaps something to eat would help. He picked up the candle and walked to the door. Opening it, he peered around the hallway and then hurried to the stairs. As he reached them, the front door was flung open and Alan entered, carrying a man in his arms. Marilee appeared suddenly from one of the darkened rooms, as if she'd been waiting for him.

"Alan, what happened? What is it?" she cried as she rushed to his side.

"Where can I put him down?"

"In here. Quickly." She led the way to the library.

Martin crept down the stairs and followed after them. He blew out his candle, setting the holder on the bottom step.

"What happened?" he heard his mother ask again.

"He must have tried to force his horse over those downed oaks near the river. The horse refused. I found him lying between the trees. It doesn't look good, Marilee."

Martin looked at the crumpled body on the couch. His mother was cautiously removing the man's jacket. She took a cloth and sponged his face. When she moved away from him, Martin could see who it was.

He burst into the room. "Father! What happened? What's wrong with Father?"

Startled, Alan and Marilee were momentarily silent. Marilee recovered quickly, taking his arm and hugging him to her.

"He's had a fall, Martin. We don't know how badly he's hurt. You must be brave, darling."

Martin knelt beside the couch. "He was coming home, wasn't he? He was coming home to be with us again like it used to be."

He didn't see the pain in his mother's face.

Marilee stayed near him, sleeping on a cot beside his bed, never gone from his side for more than a moment, day or night. The doctor had been unable to give them much hope. Until he regained consciousness, there would be no way to tell what else was wrong with him.

Marilee rarely slept. She was filled with guilt and refused to see Alan, though her heart longed for his comfort. She kept seeing Philip's face as he rode by them, the pounding of his horse's hooves hammering out her guilt—fault, my fault, my fault, my fault . . . .

It was the fourth day since his fall when he began to groan, twisting his head from side to side.

"Philip. Philip, can you hear me?" Marilee called to him, coaxing him to awaken.

He opened his eyes slowly. Their total blankness sent terror down her spine. Then they began to clear. She saw recognition . . . and then confusion.

"Wh . . . what . . ." he croaked.

Marilee placed a glass of water to his lips, holding his head up with her other hand. "You had a bad spill from your horse, Philip. Do you remember?"

She could see him concentrating. "No," he finally replied.

"Well, you're going to be fine now." She put the glass on the table and then stood. Silently she was thanking God that he didn't seem to remember the events that preceeded his accident either. Turning away, she asked, "Would you like the drapes pulled open to let in some sunshine?"

When he didn't answer she looked back down at him. His face was contorted.

"Philip?"

"I . . . I can't move. Marilee! I . . . can't . . . move!"

CHAPTER EIGHT

SEPTEMBER 1874—HEART'S LANDING

Stunned, Taylor sat in her chair, the letter in her hand. This couldn't possibly be true. Philip paralyzed? And Marilee. Something was terribly wrong there too; she could tell by the things she didn't say as much as by what she did. When Brent came in for his midday meal, she was still sitting there, her eyes filled with tears.

"Darling, what's the matter? Is it . . ."

Mutely, she passed him the missive.

"I should go to them, Brent. Marilee needs me, and Philip . . . Oh, poor Philip!" She burst into fresh tears.

Brent rocked her gently, letting her cry it out before speaking. "You know you can't go, Taylor," he said when the sobs subsided. "The baby's due any time now."

"I know. I know, Brent, really I do. It's just . . . Oh, I feel so helpless, so awful."

It had been nine years since she had seen them. Philip had been so filled with determination to make Spring Haven great again. Marilee, so very much in love with him, had stood by his side as they said their last goodbyes to Taylor and Brent, the new baby, Megan, in her arms and young Martin Philip hanging onto her skirts. Funny how clear the picture remained in her mind. And she had two more nephews she'd never seen, Alastair and Kingsley.

Taylor was swept with homesickness. She wanted desperately to see her brother and Marilee and their family. It was knowing she probably never would that sharpened her grief.

She dried her eyes, sniffing quietly. "I'm all right now, Brent. Let's see to your lunch."

He helped her to her feet, holding her elbow securely in his hand. She smiled up at him, laughing at her own awkwardness. They walked slowly to the dining room where the table was all laid out, waiting for them.

"Where's Brenetta?" Taylor asked as her husband pulled out the chair for her.

"With Rory and his horse."

Where else? Taylor thought. Ever since Rory had brought that filly home, Brenetta had been awestruck. She spent as much time watching Rory work with that horse as Rory spent with the Flame himself.

"Taylor, I'd like to discuss something with you," Brent said seriously. "Do you feel up to it?"

"Of course, dear. Anything that concerns you, concerns me. What is it?"

"You know how I feel about Rory. He's been like a son to me."

"To us," Taylor interrupted.

Brent smiled. "To us. Well, with Garvey . . . The boy is grown-up, Taylor, but except for this horse, he's never had much, never seen much. He has a bright, quick mind."

"You needn't tell me that. I tutored him, remember."

"I think I'd like to send him back to New York next year. Have him work in the bank as an apprentice for a few years. Bob Michaels would see that he learned the business from the ground up. Rory would see some more of the world besides just these mountains."

Taylor was thoughtful. "Do you think that's so important? We've all been so happy here." She paused, then asked, "Do you think he'll want to go?"

"Maybe not at first, but he'll go if I ask him to. It would be good for him to get away from Garvey, too."

"Yes, I suppose it would. Netta will miss him terribly, though."

"So will I. But she'll have a brother or sister to occupy her time before then."

Taylor smiled that secret smile of an expectant mother, dropping a hand to her enlarged abdomen. "Soon, I hope. Very soon."

"Rory, do you really think she'll let me?"

"Sure she will, little one. Just tell her what to do and she'll do it for you."

Rory tightened the cinch, then walked to the Flame's head and stroked her nose. "Now you listen up, Flame. You behave yourself while Netta rides you. No showing off. D'you hear?" He scratched her behind the ears.

Satisfied that his message was understood, he looked at Brenetta. "Up you go. She's ready."

Brenetta swallowed hard. This was a dream come true, a chance to ride the Flame, and now she was quivering so hard she was afraid her legs wouldn't be strong enough to lift her into the saddle. She pressed her lips together in grim determination and reached for the saddle horn. With a sigh of relief, she settled into the seat, gazing down at Rory from what seemed a lofty height.

"Now what?" she asked.

Rory's eyes widened at her question. "I thought you knew how to ride a horse. If you don't, you'd better get down."

"Oh, Rory!" she cried, exasperated. "You know what I mean. I've never been on a horse like *her.*"

He chuckled. "Just ride her, little one." With two steps and a jump, he was sitting on the top rail of the corral.

Brenetta coaxed the Flame into motion, and within minutes, they were loping fluidly around the enclosure. When she stopped the copper-colored horse in front of Rory, Brenetta's face was alive with joy.

"Oh, Rory, she's incredible. I love her. Nothing

else in the world could be as wonderful as this."

"There's only one thing in the world that could be better than this," Tobias whispered against her silky hair. "Marry me, Ingrid."

They were lying on a blanket, Ingrid's head on his chest, surrounded by the remains of their picnic lunch. The afternoon warmth and full stomachs had lulled them into silence as each enjoyed the tender closeness of the other.

Ingrid raised her head, staring at him incredulously. "Marry you? You want me to marry you?"

"Don't you want to?"

"Tobias," she replied faintly, "or course I *want* to. But I thought . . . well . . . with my father . . ."

A calloused finger traced down her forehead, across the bridge of her nose, over her lips, and stopped under her chin, tipping her head back so the Indian summer sun could illuminate her beloved features. Huskily, he finished for her. "You thought I couldn't really love a girl whose father feels like yours does, a girl who would sneak out to meet me, spending hours alone in my company without a proper chaperone. Ingrid," he added, softly chiding her, "don't you know it makes you all the more precious to me?"

Ingrid dropped her eyes from him. He saw her fighting to control her emotions. When she looked at him again, her eyes were awash with unshed tears, but her mouth was curved upward in a smile. "You're right. I should have known. Yes, Tobias. I'll marry you."

There seemed nothing more to say. He pulled her back against his lanky body, holding her cheek against his chest, and stared up at the sky made of the very color of Ingrid's eyes. He felt an almost irrisistable urge to whoop for joy. Instead, his arms tightened around her possessively. In response, she nipped lightly at his neck.

Tobias growled low in his throat as he pulled her up so he could kiss her. He wondered crazily how someone so pale—her hair, her eyes, even her skin where the sun hadn't bronzed it—could be so vivid, so ablaze within. Her lips seemed to burn into his. He felt his desire for her begin to build, and he rolled her suddenly over onto her back, pinning her against the blanket. He rose above her, trying to slow his breathing.

"I think it's time you got home before something happens to make us regret this day."

Her eyes glittered at him in understanding as he pulled her up from the ground.

"I love you, Tobias," Ingrid whispered.

"And I love you, my little snow fox. When do we get married?"

A shadow crossed her face. "Pa's going to be furious. He . . . Well, you know how he is."

"Yes," Tobias said darkly. "I know."

Brent hadn't liked the feel of the air all morning. A storm was brewing. The grasslands, turned dry and yellow like straw, seemed to wait breathlessly for some rain. Rain that Brent suspected wouldn't come.

He stood outside on the porch, staring at the

eerie yellow-streaked grey clouds. He could smell trouble. Everything was unnaturally still, even the animals were silent. The glow of Tobias's cigarette as he sauntered towards the house seemed somehow an ominous sign.

"Not good," Tobias said without preliminaries.

"No," came Brent's simple reply.

Tobias stubbed out his smoke, his eyes thoughtfully studying the western skyline. "Sandman's got three men riding the South range with him, an' Sam took Virgil and Buck with him down by Crooked Creek. Thought I'd take Rory and bring in the horses to the corrals."

Brent nodded, his mouth grim. Tobias turned on his boot heel and walked away.

The prophesy became fact shortly after noon. The wind came first, sucked up through the valley like a funnel, battering everything in its path. The sky became black with broiling clouds, changing the day into night. As suddenly as it had come, the wind died down, and the valley was gripped in a tense stillness. The first bolt of lightning was almost a relief; it was as if the earth was able to breathe again.

Despite his vague impression that something worse was about to strike at Heart's Landing, Brent's first reaction to the lightning storm was to return from the stud barn to check on Brenetta. He found her cradled in Taylor's arms in the living room. There were no hysterics this time, but she was quivering violently.

"Everything okay here?" Brent asked.

Taylor nodded mutely, catching his eye over the

top of Brenetta's head, her glance telling him they would be fine. Brent placed a kiss on both the ebony heads and turned to leave. He stopped at the door, unable to shake the worrisome warning still nipping at his thoughts.

"You and Brenetta stay in the house. I don't like the looks of this storm."

Feeling caught in a web of unreality, Brent left the house. He threw his leg over his waiting horse, the big gelding moving restlessly beneath him.

"You feel it too," Brent said to his mount, sounding more natural than he felt.

He turned the horse south and urged him into a canter, feeling the need to get somewhere in a hurry. When another jagged flash of white spotlighted another rider racing towards him, he knew the time was here. Whatever bad news he'd been awaiting all day had arrived.

His felt hat pulled low on the old cowboy's weathered brow, Sandman brought his horse to a jerky halt, setting him back on his haunches and sliding his hooves into the dirt. "Boss! We've got a fire goin'!"

"Where?" Brent hollered above the thunder.

They were both riding at a gallop before Sandman had a chance to answer. "Indian Butte."

Brent spurred more speed into his mousey-colored buckskin. They swallowed up the ground, each mile drawing them closer to a rancher's nightmare. Fire. Range or forest, it made no difference to Brent. Heart's Landing had both kinds of land, and both kinds of fire brought the same horror. As if to torment him further, the wind picked up again. Brent swore angrily, his words disappearing into the violent air.

Before long, Brent and Sandman were joined by more riders. By the time they topped the rolling hillside leading down into the south range, every hand that wasn't already at Indian Butte was converging on it. Behind all the swift riders came Joe Simons, driving a wagon filled with shovels and axes.

The grey smoke looked almost white in contrast with the black clouds. It boiled furiously upwards and then rolled to the east. Before they could see the flames consuming the dry mountain pines at a fearful pace, they began choking on the thick smoke; hot ash blowing in the wind burned their nostrils. Silently, the men pulled out their bandanas and covered their faces.

At first she ignored the painful tightening in her back, refusing to believe the baby would choose this of all days to arrive. But she could pretend no longer.

Taylor stood on the porch, watching the clouds of smoke climb up to fill the empty sky. She had been so relieved when the lightning had finally abated and the wind carried away the storm clouds. Relieved until she saw what had taken every ranch hand from the place. Now she prayed silently that the fire would soon be defeated.

"Mother, is the fire going to come here?" Brenetta asked from behind her.

Taylor turned and held out a hand to her pretty daughter. "No, honey. It's a long way off. We'll be fi . . ." Another pain, this one a little stronger, a little closer to the last, cut off her sentence. Taylor sat down with a gasp, pulling Brenetta over beside her. "Netta, I want you to run down to Virgil Haskin's house and tell Mrs. Haskin I'm going to need her help. You hurry. Tell her it's the baby."

"Is the baby going to be born now?"

"Yes, dear. Now you run and tell her."

Taylor watched Brenetta scurry across the barnyard and past the bunkhouse, headed for the Haskin cabin. Erma Haskin was the only other woman living at Heart's Landing now that Joe Wilson and his young wife had moved on. Taylor's only servant, old Mima, whom she had brought with her from Spring Haven at the end of the war, had died several years before, and there was no one besides Mrs. Haskin to help her now.

She turned her eyes once again to the south. An orange-red glow was visible against the grey plumes billowing skyward, and she knew with a sinking heart that the fire wouldn't be out soon enough.

"Oh, Brent," she whispered.

"Mama!" Brenetta called as she ran back towards the house. "Mrs. Haskin's not there."

For a moment, Taylor was at a loss, her mind numb. What was she to do now? A baby on the way and only Brenetta here. Suddenly a thought came to her. "Netta, saddle your horse and ride over to the Hansons. Get Ingrid to come here."

"Will you be all right while I'm gone?"

Taylor smiled tensely. "I'll be fine, honey."

She waited until Brenetta galloped away from

112

the barn before entering the house. With an outward calm, Taylor gathered together several clean sheets, some twine, and a pair of scissors, then climbed the stairs to her room. She laid out the items on her night stand. Next she filled her wash basin with water, placing a wash cloth on the edge of the bowl. Satisfied, she removed her dress and slipped her nightgown over her head. Then she lay down on the bed and waited.

Brenetta kicked her little horse viciously, trying to force more speed from her. She was scared. She didn't really understand what was happening with her mother. She knew, from living on the ranch, that the horses and cows and other animals all got big and round with babies inside them, but her parents had always forbidden her presence during calving and foaling time, and she was never allowed around the studs or bulls during breeding season. The mystery only served to increase her fear. Would her mother *really* be all right?

Arriving at the Hanson home, Brenetta vaulted to the ground and raced to the door, pounding on it with open palms.

"Ingrid! Ingrid, are you here?" she cried breathlessly. There was no answer from within.

Her eyes wide and panic-filled, Brenetta turned her back to the door. She felt immobilized by indecision until she saw hay flying out from behind the barn into a corral. She bolted away from the house, crying aloud as she ran. "Ingrid! Ingrid!"

Brenetta rounded the corner and ran into Jake

Hanson. "Oh!" she exclaimed as he gripped her shoulders.

"Here now. What're you doing?"

Barely audible, Brenetta replied, "I'm looking for Ingrid, Mr. Hanson. Is she here?"

"Whatayou want her for?" he asked suspiciously.

"My mother needs her help."

Jake chortled. "So a Lattimer needs my gal's help, does she? Well, ain't that somethin'."

Panic was again threatening. *Please*, Mr. Hanson," she begged as tears filled her eyes.

"Pa, whose horse is . . ."

"Oh, Ingrid. Please, come," Brenetta cried, breaking away from Jake Hanson and taking Ingrid by the wrists as she reached her. "Mama's going to have her baby and Mrs. Haskin isn't there and Papa and all the others are at the fire and . . . and she needs you."

Ingrid hugged her, trying to calm her down. "Of course, I'll come," she answered softly. Raising her eyes to meet her father's, she asked, "Pa, what were you doing to her, frightening her like that?"

"Got troubles of our own, ain't we? I don't see 'em helpin' us," he grumbled.

"Pa!"

Ingrid pulled Brenetta along with her into the barn. She threw a saddle onto a jug-headed roan who looked as if he'd seen better days. As she put on the bridle, she said, "Go get your horse, Netta. I'll be right out."

Brenetta did as she was told, and Ingrid was true to her word. Before Brenetta had time to

114

more than gather the reins and mount up, the young woman was trotting out of the barn. Her drab brown skirt was hiked up around her legs as she sat astride; neither of them thought of the time Brenetta had suggested just that to her and Ingrid had been so surprised. The urgency of the moment was too great to try to ride sideways on her father's roping saddle or to worry about convention.

Together they galloped towards Heart's Landing.

His own tears streaked his sooty cheeks above his bandana as the smoke stung his eyes. Rory felt as if his arms were breaking as he swung the ax once more against the tree. Somewhere nearby, someone—he thought it must be the crusty old wrangler, Sandman, judging by the salty language —muttered as he smacked his shovel time and time again at the persistent flames.

Rory could barely hear Brent's cry for help as the flames jumped the fire line they had worked so hard to build. He forced his legs to carry him in the direction of Brent's voice, stumbling over the charred terrain.

Automatically, upon reaching the new line of battle, Rory started swinging his ax, trying to blank out of his mind the burning tiredness in his thighs, the rawness of his lungs, and the deep fatigue in his shoulders and arms.

Ingrid stood at the foot of the bed, unconsciously straining with Taylor.

"Push again, Mrs. Lattimer. We've almost made it."

Ingrid was both excited and frightened. She had been assisting her father deliver calves and colts since she was younger than Brenetta, but this was the first time she'd been called on to act as midwife for another woman. She was still afraid that something would go wrong, something that would be her fault. Yet the thrill of being present at the beginning of life could not be denied.

"It's coming, Mrs. Lattimer. It's coming!"

Only a few minutes later, Ingrid was laying the baby in Taylor's waiting arms, smiling brightly at mother and son.

"Thank you, Ingrid," Taylor said huskily as she gazed at the tiny babe at her side. Her black hair clung damply around her face, but she was still beautiful, a warm glow of happiness coming from within. "Why don't you tell Netta to come see her baby brother?"

Ingrid finished rolling up the soiled sheets and put away the scissors and other paraphernalia, then left the room in search of Brenetta. Instead of finding the girl, she found a hastily written note.

Ingrid, I thought Papa should know about Ma, so I've gone to tell him. Love, Netta.

She looked up the stairs, thinking of how upset this would make Taylor. But she could think of no way to keep from telling her. With heavy steps, she climbed the stairs to Taylor's room.

Garvey had watched the smoke for several hours, telling himself he should go help them fight it but knowing he wouldn't. What he really wanted was another drink. He hadn't had one since this morning, and there wasn't a bottle to be found in the cabin. He felt uncomfortably close to being sober. He looked towards the big house. Brent would have something. His old friend wouldn't care if he borrowed some whiskey until he could restock.

Garvey walked away from his cabin, stopping abruptly when he heard the baby's cry. It couldn't be . . . but it was. Mrs. Lattimer had had her baby. And her maybe all alone. He quickened his steps.

"Ma'am?" he called, pushing the door open before him.

Ingrid appeared suddenly at the top of the stairs, her face drawn.

"Who are you?" he demanded of her. "Where's Mrs. Lattimer?"

"What is it you want?" she challenged in return.

"I'm Garvey O'Hara. I live here." He could see her sizing him up and realized what he must look like, rumpled and unkept, and how unbelievable it must seem that he was a part of this place. "Is the missus all right?" he asked in a softer tone.

Ingrid relaxed a little. "Mr. O'Hara, the birth went well, but Mrs. Lattimer is terribly upset. Brenetta has gone for her father."

"Gone after—you mean to the fire?"

Ingrid nodded grimly.

"You tell the missus that Garvey O'Hara has gone after the wee lass, and she's not t' worry. You tell her that."

117

Brenetta was growing more and more nervous. The afternoon was waning; the smoke-darkened sky was becoming the darkness of evening, and still she couldn't find her father. Her throat burned from the dense smoke and her arms were tired from fighting with her skittish pony. The snapping and popping of the fire seemed to be everywhere, the land unfamiliar in the strange orange glow and smoky veil.

She was ready to turn back, to go home, when she thought she heard someone calling. It sounded like her father, and she pulled her mount's head around in the direction it seemed to come from. She was sure she would see him at any moment. Instead, she came suddenly upon a wall of fire. Her horse reared up, twisting his body sharply. His front lets struck at the air, his eyes wild and nostrils flared. Caught unprepared, Brenetta was thrown, somersaulting backwards and landing with a thump. Air rushed from her lungs, and she lay in a still lump as her terrified pony raced away.

With great effort, Brenetta pushed herself off the ground, still gasping for breath. Her stomach felt as though it was filled with lead as she stared at the fire consuming the land. She no longer knew which way was home; the fire seemed to be everywhere. She scrambled to her feet and began running, dodging the flames that licked at her from the trees and brush, seeking a way out of the inferno. She didn't see the drop into the narrow ravine in time.

Garvey had wasted no time covering the ground between the house and the Indian Butte area. He might never have found where Brenetta had gone if her pony hadn't snagged his reins in a fallen log. His terrified screams pierced the air, drawing Garvey into the edge of the forest. His own horse began to stamp and dance nervously as he stopped near the trapped animal.

"Netta!" he called. No answer.

He freed the pony and, hoping one of the men fighting the fire would see them and bring help, turned both the horses loose. As he plunged ahead on foot, calling her name between gasps for air, he noted the fire leaping from treetop to treetop and knew he was in trouble.

Brenetta regained consciousness, coughing and hacking from smoke-filled lungs. She ached all over from her fall down the rocky bank into the draw. It hurt to open her eyes and the heat was incredible. On hands and knees, she began to crawl along the bottom of the ravine, tiny sobs of fear squeaking by her lips.

When she first heard him calling her name, she thought she was imagining it. But, no! Someone was really there.

"Here. I'm here!" she half-cried, half-choked as she tried to pull herself up the bank.

"Netta, my lass, are you hurt?" Garvey asked as he appeared above her, reaching out for her.

"Not really, Mr. O'Hara."

"Then come along. We haven't much time."

He grabbed her hand and pulled her along

behind him. Time and time again, they were forced to change direction. Brenetta stumbled forward, totally lost and confused, her mind too tired to register her fear. Her eyes remained glued to the ground, both to watch where she was stepping to avoid another fall and so she didn't have to look at the consuming flames all around her.

Garvey stopped abruptly, his breath coming in jagged puffs. He twisted around and then back. The fire had doubled back, just as he'd feared it would, closing in on them. They were trapped in a circle of fire!

"Lass, we're going t'have t'go through it."

Her golden eyes opened wide to reveal her terror, the fire's reflection turning them to crimson. Her face was blackened by soot, her blouse torn in several places, her hair flying madly where it had escaped her braids. Garvey felt a heavy weight on his heart. Could he save this lass for Brent, the only real friend he had ever had? He *must* save her. He was nothing but a worthless, drunken bum, but Brent Lattimer had never deserted him. Now, Garvey had to repay him by saving his daughter. If he couldn't do this, he was better off dead.

He pulled off his canvas jacket and bundled it around her head and shoulders. "We're going to run," he told her as he picked her up, holding her firmly against his soft, out-of-shape stomach. "You just hold still, lass."

She thought they were going to die. Wrapped in the darkness of his coat, she thought she would suffocate from the heat. She was certain the fire would get her and waited to see it light up the darkness of her cocoon. But instead, she was suddenly thrust to the ground and rolled harshly about, his hands striking her legs. The jacket fell away from her face so that she could see again. Her pants were scorched, but she felt no pain. We've made it! she thought in amazement.

"Let's go, lass," Garvey shouted at her. He pushed her ahead of him as they ran, the fire still seeming to surround them. "Just keep goin', lass. I'm right . . . behind you. Just . . . keep running."

And she did. She ran as if the devil himself was at her heels, stumbling and tripping, but always getting up again. She had no other thought except to run. Just run. Run. Run. Run.

Rory, Buck Franklin, and Joe Simons trudged along behind Brent, shovels and axes resting on their shoulders. Their eyes were blank with fatigue, yet their bodies fought on. They couldn't quit, not until they'd won.

Rory was the first to see her. Despite the dense smoke and her wild and disheveled appearance, he knew her. He dropped his ax, calling to Brent as he ran away from the others. He caught her just as she tripped headlong towards the ground.

Looking at him in disbelief, she whispered, "Rory? Oh, Rory, we made it. We're safe."

Brent grabbed his daughter away from Rory. "Netta. Netta, what are you doing here? What happened to you?"

"Oh, Papa," she cried, "I came for you and was lost. Mr. O'Hara saved my life."

"Rory saved you?" Brent asked, puzzled.

"No, not Rory. *Mr.* O'Hara. He's right behind me."

Rory looked back through the charred trees, the fiery inferno rolling hungrily onward.

"Da. Oh God, not Da."

CHAPTER NINE

NOVEMBER 1874—SPRING HAVEN

Marilee sat in the buggy outside the small white house on the outskirts of Bellville. She gazed at it wistfully, remembering how happy she had been, growing up there. Her father, the Reverend Stone, had been a loving, gentle father, though sometimes stern. Friends and relatives had always been around; Taylor and Philip, Dr. and Mrs. Reed and their daughter, Lizabeth, her cousins Jeffrey and Robert Stone. Her father had passed away just after the war ended. After Lizabeth Reed was found insane, Dr. and Mrs. Reed had moved away, seeking help for her. Marilee had heard Lizabeth finally hung herself while in an asylum. Taylor had moved so far away that she seemed almost a dream. And her darling cousins—Jeffrey dying so gallantly in the midst of the War Between the States and Robert losing his arm.

She tried not to think of Philip's visits to her home when he had come courting her. Oh, how very excited she'd been. And her father . . . How proud he was that his daughter was going to marry a Bellman. To Marilee, it was a happy ending to her own private fairytale—the poor maiden marrying the handsome prince.

But it had soured, and the memories only made it worse.

With a flick of the reins, Marilee drove away from the house, heading back towards Spring Haven. She didn't hurry; she wasn't eager to return. All that awaited was a big house caught in a hushed atmosphere, children always tiptoeing everywhere and speaking in whispers.

"But it won't be so silent come spring," she said aloud.

Marilee had just left the doctor. He had confirmed it. She was pregnant again. But there was no joy in it for her. She was carrying Alan's child, and he was gone. She had sent him away following Philip's accident, her heart weighed down by her guilt.

"I'll go if that's what you want, Marilee," he had said that last evening. "But I'll return. Someday you're going to need me, and I'll be here for you."

"No, Alan. You mustn't come back. Our love is wrong. Look what it's done to Philip."

He had wrapped her tightly in his arms, his face grim, almost angry. "Our love didn't do that, Marilee, and don't you ever say it did. Philip was sick when I came and you know it. What's happened to him would have happened anyway, or something else like it."

He had kissed her then and walked away. He'd been gone by the next morning; she didn't know where.

Philip sat in his chair near the window, staring out at the balmy November day. He never left his room anymore. He found it took more energy than he had to face the world below, and so he stayed in his room, a sullen, self-pitying, and often frightened figure.

Philip had never been able to remember the events just preceding his fall. But he could remember how long he'd been pursued by the blackness, his phantom. He seemed to remember succumbing to it once, but it no longer called to him. Oh, it was always nearby. Right now, it hovered in the corner, its coldness pervading the room. It was waiting. Waiting, always waiting. Someday it would take him, someday when the moment was right.

And so they both waited.

Martin winced but made no sound as the schoolmaster brought the ruler down once more across his open hands.

"Now, Master Bellman. You shall sit over there until class is dismissed. I trust you'll remember not to repeat your offense again."

Martin made no reply. His big brown eyes were half-concealed behind lowered eyelids as he walked stiffly to the stool in the corner. He clenched his smarting hands into tight fists to repress the tears that threatened to fall. Several boys snickered, but a harsh glance from Mr. York brought instant silence.

His trouble had begun this morning when Peter Hale had made fun of Martin's worn breeches. Peter was the son of the Yankee carpetbagger who had bought Rosewood for taxes—*stolen* Rosewood was nearer the truth. When class had recessed for lunch, Martin had joined Megan, Alastair, and Kingsley on the grass outside. Peter and two other boys had sauntered over to resume their taunting. He was able to ignore them until Peter went one remark too far.

"No wonder you can't make your plantation produce enough so you can get any clothes. You got a crazy cripple for a pa."

Peter had had no time to escape. Martin had charged him so quickly everyone was caught unprepared. Head down, he had butted the bigger boy in the stomach and then began pummeling him with wild punches, all the time yelling over and over again. "You dirty bastard Yankee!" He might never have stopped if Mr. York's hand hadn't suddenly grasped his collar and yanked him away, choking off his air.

Now he sat on the stool, silently cursing the New England schoolmaster, the carpetbagger's white trash son, and all the fates that seemed to work against him.

CHAPTER TEN

MARCH 1875—HEART'S LANDING

She sensed something different about him. He stood on the other side of the fence, staring at her as he leaned on the railing. The Flame's ears swung forward, and she nickered to him softly.

The three-year-old filly, her burnished coat shining as it rippled over her firm, developing muscles, trotted across the corral to her master. She nudged his arm with her soft muzzle, encouraging him to stroke her neck. She had long forgotten the terrifying moment nearly a year before when his lariat had closed around her throat. Now she turned trusting eyes on him, listening to his soothing voice as he scratched her.

"Rory, is it true?"

He turned away from the copper horse and watched Brenetta run up to him.

"Is it true?" she asked again. "Are you really going to leave?"

"It's true."

"But why?"

Rory looked at her silently, wanting to capture her memory to take with him in the months and maybe years ahead. Almost twelve, she was as slender as a pole, almost shapeless under the baggy pants she still insisted on wearing. Her budding breasts were hidden beneath her loose shirt. A worn Stetson was pulled low over her forehead, vainly trying to keep the sun from her heavily freckled nose. He smiled, thinking how much he would miss her constant pestering to go with him wherever he went, to ride the Flame, to do this, to see that . . .

"I'm going because your father wants me to," he answered as he turned back to face the mare.

Brenetta touched his elbow. "But *you* don't want to go to New York, do you?"

He was silent a moment. No, he didn't *want* to go; he didn't *want* to leave his home, his friends, this land. But after all Brent Lattimer had done for him, how could he not? He was treated like a son around here, always had been. They had educated him, even supported him, made him an equal. They had never said a word against his father, not before or after his death. In fact, they thought of him as a good friend who had died saving their child. So if Brent wanted him to go to New York, to learn the banking business and to see another type of life, then he would go. And he would do his best in everything.

Stroking the Flame's nose, he answered, "I'll miss you, little one. And I'll miss the Flame, too."

Brenetta reached out and stroked the filly along with him, her forehead crinkled in thought. "You weren't meant to be caged up in a big city, Rory."

"Neither was the Flame, but look how content she is now. I want you to have her, Netta. Will you look after her, love her as I have?"

"Me? Oh, Rory, truly you want me to have her?"

"She's yours," he said. "Take good care of her."

He walked away, leaving an excited Brenetta slipping through the fence to get closer to her new horse. Hands in pockets, he walked quickly to the barn where he saddled a horse and then rode off in the direction of Indian Butte.

Small green sprouts pushed valiantly through the charred earth, promising someday to hide the devastation last fall's fire had left behind. Luckily, the rains had come in time to stop it destroying more than a few hundred acres. No grazing land had been lost, but some cattle had been trapped and perished in a box canyon.

Rory rode to the spot where they had found his father. Garvey had died a grizzly death, and Rory tried not to think of that part of it. He didn't even know why he'd come except it seemed something he had to do before leaving. He dismounted in the midst of the barren landscape, hunkering down to rest on his heels.

The past six months had been difficult ones for Rory. He had struggled with guilt over his father's death, feeling as though it was somehow his fault. If only he'd been more understanding, more patient, more helpful, more . . . more something. Tears silently streaked his brown cheeks. His father had died saving Brenetta's life. He had come selflessly just for her. But did he die not knowing how much Rory loved him?

How could he have known? Even Rory had refused to know it.

"Oh, Da. I'm sorry. I'm so sorry I didn't understand in time."

Rocking gently, Taylor nursed the baby. Young Carleton David Martin Lattimer was nearly six months old and such a good baby. He had been given his father's middle name, Carleton, and the first name of both his grandfathers. It seemed an awfully large name for such a small baby, but Taylor had been certain he would grow into it. But as she watched him sucking hungrily at her breasts, she was no longer so sure. She couldn't pretend any longer. Something was wrong with Carleton.

Lifting her eyes from him, she fought back the tears. How was she ever to tell Brent? He was so proud of his son. Having missed seeing Brenetta until she was nearly a year and a half old, Brent was fascinated with everything this miniature Lattimer did. How could she tell him she thought that little Carl was blind?

His appetite sated, the baby released the teat and gurgled contentedly. His eyes, the same deep blue as her own, stared upwards, and she tried to pretend that he was looking at her.

"Oh, please see me, Carleton," she whispered. "Please see me."

Ingrid placed the plate in front of her father, then dished up her own. She knew she wouldn't be able to eat a bite; her stomach was tied in a million knots.

She sat down across from him and watched as Jake polished off the biscuits and thick cream gravy while she shoved hers around on her plate with a fork.

"Pa."

"Ya?"

"I need to talk to you, Pa."

"So talk," he said thickly, his mouth full.

Ingrid swallowed hard, then said quickly. "Pa, I'm going to get married."

He stared at her, gravy caught in the corner of his mouth. "You're goin' to get *married?*"

Ingrid tried taking the offensive. "Did you think no one would ever ask me?"

Jake Hanson's eyes narrowed as he pushed his empty plate away from him.

"Do you want some more?" Ingrid asked nervously, her burst of courage dissipating.

"Who is he and when have you seen him so's he could ask?"

She jumped up and began clearing the table, afraid to look him in the face. She couldn't back down now; she had promised Tobias she would tell her father today.

"I . . . I met him last year in Boise. He's a ranch hand; no, he's a ranch foreman. That's a mighty responsible position, isn't it? He'll probably own his own spread someday. I know you'll like him if you just get to know him."

She peered around at him with guarded eyes. He was carefully putting a pinch of tobacco in his cheek as he tilted back his chair against the wall. "What's his name, gal?"

She couldn't avoid it any longer. Ingrid turned to him, her tiny shoulders thrown back, her chin lifted bravely, and her eyes flashing her independence. "Tobias Levi," she said clearly.

Without taking his eyes from her, Jake sent a stream of tobacco juice onto the floor. His face was as hard as granite, and she thought for sure his heart was made of ice, so cold was his gaze. Her father had always been a rough, coarse sort of man, but she had never feared him. Not until this moment.

Jake dropped his chair forward and stood up. He walked to the door, opened it, then turned to look at her again. "You may be a no good whore for all I know . . ."

"Pa! I never . . ."

" . . . but you won't never marry no Jew. Not even if I have to keep you chained up in this cabin like a mad dog. No, if I had a mad dog, I'd shoot it. Now you don't leave here 'til I come back. You hear me, gal?"

The cow had broken its neck in the fall, and the calf was squalling in hunger when Tobias found it. The calf's best chance of survival—in fact, its only chance—was for Tobias to take it back with him to the ranch house. They could try to pair it up with another nursing cow, try to get her to accept another baby, or they might have to hand nurse it themselves.

132

He caught the youngster with one arm around its chest, another around its rump, and packed it over to his horse where he laid it across the saddle before mounting up himself.

"Jew!"

He swing around to face Jake. He wasn't surprised. He'd been expecting this visit all day.

"I oughta shoot you, you dirty, thievin' sonofabitch. I told you to keep your stinkin' paws off my daughter."

"Mr. Hanson, I love your . . ."

"Shut your mouth, Levi, or I'll shut it for you."

Tobias stared at the big man, trying to think of something to say to bring some reason to him. But it was hopeless, he realized. He turned back to his horse, fully intending to mount up and ride off without another word.

The rifle stock splintered as it smashed into Tobias's skull. He crumpled forward, unaware of the second swing that ripped into his shoulder.

Brent was the one to find him the next day. At first he thought the young man was dead. The blood from his head wound had turned the ground around him to black. His face was a ghastly bluish-white with dark purple shadows below his eyes. It was obvious he'd regained consciousness a time or two for he had left a short trail of blood where he had dragged himself forward.

"Good Lord! What happened?" Brent muttered as he knelt beside his friend. He started to take him by the shoulders, but Tobias's painful groan as he felt the sickening give in the shoulder and upper arm stopped him.

With the help of two others, Brent made a

stretcher, and they pulled Tobias back to the ranch behind a horse. Taylor put him in the room nearest their own. They made him as comfortable as they could while Rory went for the doctor. Then all they could do was wait.

Ingrid threw the feed mechanically to the chickens, not even seeing them. She had managed to sneak away twice in the last week, but Tobias had never shown up at their meeting place nor had he left any sign that he'd been there. Perhaps she wouldn't have worried if her father hadn't seemed so unconcerned all of a sudden. Tobias's name and her plans to marry him hadn't been mentioned again. She was more certain with each passing moment that something terrible had happened to Tobias.

Suddenly Ingrid threw the bowl of scraps at the chickens, sending up a noisy squawk of complaints and flying feathers. Well, she wasn't going to wait *here* any longer. Her father had ridden out about half an hour before and shouldn't be back for another hour or more. That was plenty of time for her to head for Heart's Landing and see what happened to keep Tobias away.

Lacking another saddle, Ingrid gamely slid onto the big work horse's bare back from the fence. It was difficult to grasp his sides with her thighs through her bunched skirts, but she pressed him into a rough canter, grasping his mane tightly in her hands.

Brenetta sat on the floor with Carleton. He was

smiling at her as she helped him stand, his tiny legs pushing at the floor and then folding up on him. It was hard for her to believe that he was blind, even if the doctor had told her parents it was true. He had suggested that Carleton be seen by specialists when he was older. It was the only hope he could give them.

"Poor Carl," Brenetta said to him. "Not to be able to see how pretty the world is."

He laughed at her voice, and she laughed back. His cheeriness was infectious.

"Come on. Let's take a walk. I'll show you my new horse. Rory gave her to me. Her name's the Flame 'cause she's so red and shiny she looks hot."

The baby on her hip, Brenetta left the house and headed for the corral. The Flame saw her coming and came to the fence. She sniffed at Carleton, but the baby's surprised squeal startled her and she backed away.

"Carl, that's the Flame. She won't hurt you. Come here, Flame, and meet my brother. Come here, girl. It's all right. Come here."

The Flame cautiously stepped closer, her ears flicking forward and back. Brenetta took Carleton's little hand and stroked the Flame's muzzle.

"Someday you'll ride a horse like this, Carl, if you're lucky," Brenetta promised him. "Someday when you can see."

The Flame's head suddenly flew up, and she raced away to the other side of the corral, whinnying as she ran. Brenetta looked in that direction and saw Rory ambling towards them. The Flame actually seemed to tremble in anticipation as she called to him. Brenetta's heart sank.

The Flame will never really be mine, she thought.

Tobias stirred, sending pain stabbing into his head and arm, even down his back. The doctor had set his arm and wrapped his dislocated shoulder. It had taken twenty-five stitches to close up the wound in his head. Carefully, Tobias opened his eyes. The light pouring through the window hurt them, but he forced them to stay open.

"How are you feeling today, Tobias?" Taylor asked as she bent over him.

"Better," he answered through clenched teeth.

Every time he awoke, she was there. He wondered if she ever slept. Earlier—was it yesterday or the day before?—Brent had been there too. He had tried to get Tobias to tell him what had happened, but Tobias had feigned ignorance. He couldn't tell them that Ingrid's father tried to kill him. This was something he would take care of himself in his own way.

"Do you think you could eat something?" Taylor was asking.

"Yes, I'll try."

The doctor had told him it would take his arm and shoulder several months to be completely healed, but he was determined not to be bedridden for long. And he had to see Ingrid. He had to let her know he loved her and wasn't staying away from her on purpose.

Ingrid almost tumbled to the ground as she stopped the horse at the front of the house. Holding up her dress, she scampered up the stairs and knocked on the door. No one came at first and she knocked again.

"Hello, Ingrid."

She whirled around to face Brenetta and a dark-skinned young man, close to her own age, with broad shoulders and knowing eyes.

"Netta, where's Tobias?" she blurted out.

"Tobias?" Brenetta echoed. "Why, he's upstairs. I didn't know you knew . . . Oh!" she ended, understanding dawning as she noticed the expression on Ingrid's face. "Follow me. I'll take you to him."

Brenetta passed Carleton to Rory, asking him to put the baby in the nursery for her, then took Ingrid's arm and led her into the house and up the stairs. Brenetta paused at the door across the hall from where Ingrid had helped Taylor bring Carleton into the world and rapped softly.

"Who is it?"

"It's me, Mama. Someone's here to see Tobias."

"He's awake. Come in."

It wasn't until that moment that Ingrid knew for certain something had indeed happened to Tobias. Now she was afraid to step into the room for fear of what she would find.

Taylor saw that the guest was Ingrid Hanson, and her arched, black eyebrows rose a little in surprise. Tobias and Ingrid? Good heavens, no wonder the girl had been so frightened of her father finding out. Brent had told her about Jake's caustic comments about Tobias.

137

"Come in, Ingrid. Tobias, look who's here."

She saw Ingrid's worried eyes dart to the bed. She could see that the girl's worst fears seemed to be fulfilled when she saw him.

"Oh, Tobias," Ingrid cried, falling to her knees beside the bed. "What happened?"

"Just a little accident. I'm going to be just fine."

"How could he do this?" she cried softly, leaning her face against his good right shoulder.

Taylor saw Tobias glance quickly at her and she began to understand. Jake Hanson had done this to him. And he was silently telling her that she wasn't to repeat what she knew to anyone.

"Excuse me," Taylor said as she laid her embroidery aside. "Now that Ingrid's here to watch over you, I think I'll check on Carl."

Tobias was glad she'd understood his message. He was sure he could trust her to keep silent. He turned his gaze back to Ingrid.

"I'm glad you came," he told her.

"I had to. I knew something awful had happened to keep you away. Oh, Tobias, I'm so ashamed of him."

She was crying now and Tobias reached up and patted her back.

"But I'm all right, Ingrid, and we're going to get married. Don't cry, love."

Ingrid lifted her tear-streaked face from his shoulder. "I won't go back there," she swore fiercely. "I won't *ever* go back there. I'll stay right here with you. I'm old enough to decide what I want to do."

"Okay. Okay. We'll get married right away. No one's going to make you go."

Brent was waiting for him when he came. From the moment Tobias and Ingrid had told him they were going to get married, he'd known Jake would be coming. He'd also figured out just what had happened to Tobias, and Brent's blood ran hot with anger.

"Don't bother to get down, Hanson. You're not staying," he said from the porch.

"I come for my gal. Where is she?"

"Upstairs. With her husband-to-be."

Jake shifted his enormous body in the saddle. "You send her out t'me, Lattimer. You've got no right to keep a man from his kin."

"I've got every right to tell an attempted killer to get off my land."

Jake's hand went to his rifle.

"Don't do it, Hanson," Brent warned. "You'll be dead before you get it leveled."

Jake followed Brent's glance. From the side of the house stepped Rory, rifle ready. Two men walked towards him from the barn, the barrels of their guns pointed directly at him. From the corner of his eyes he could see others. He lifted his hand from his rifle stock.

"You win this time, Lattimer. But I won't forget what you've done here. You won't always be this ready. Sometime we'll meet up, just the two of us."

Brent nodded. He was sure that that was the truth.

"You've helped ruin my daughter, and someday you'll have t' answer for it."

Brent wondered if Jake really cared about

Ingrid as he replied, "If it helps any, they'll be married by a judge as soon as possible."

Jake jerked at his horse's mouth. "Don't help none," he growled, then galloped away.

Brent watched him disappear from sight. "Thanks men," he said, looking around at the others. "I think that's the last we'll see of him at Heart's Landing."

Tomorrow Rory was leaving. She wasn't going to see him again for a long, long time. Already Brenetta felt deserted and alone.

The two rode silently along, Brenetta leading the way. She kept the pace steady and swift. She knew Rory wondered where they were going, but he never asked. When they stopped at last, Brenetta seeming to have found the right spot, Rory looked at her with questioning eyes.

She dismounted and started to loosen the cinch. "Rory, I hope you'll understand what I'm doing, and I hope you won't be mad." She pulled the saddle from the Flame's back. "The Flame won't ever belong to anyone but you, and if I try to keep her, she'll die in that pen. She belongs with you or in the wild." She slipped the bridle off. "Just like you, Rory. You belong here at Heart's Landing. You don't belong all penned up in the city. I can't help that, but I *can* help her."

With a quick swing, Brenetta smacked the Flame across the rump with the bridle and yelled. Startled, the Flame jumped forward. She hesitated only an instant for a command from Rory to "whoa" before stretching into a full gallop and racing away.

Brenetta waited until she was out of sight before turning to face Rory. He was staring at her strangely, and she shifted uncomfortably, suddenly unsure if she'd done the right thing.

Rory's black eyes seemed to bore through her, then suddenly he smiled. "Thanks, little one. You understand more than I thought. Someday we shall capture her again, you and I, and she will belong to both of us."

He held out his hand and pulled her up behind him, and they started for home.

CHAPTER ELEVEN

APRIL 1875—SPRING HAVEN

"Please, Susan. Let me see the baby," Marilee whispered hoarsely.

It had been a long, difficult labor, and at times Marilee thought she and the baby were both about to die. But they hadn't. She could hear the little girl crying lustily, already protesting the cruelty of life.

Susan laid the swaddled infant in her mother's arms. Marilee gazed upon the angry red face. A light down of reddish blonde hair covered her head, and her tiny fists beat the air.

"Hush, little girl. Don't cry. Your father was always such a merry soul; he wouldn't want you to be unhappy. He always did his best to make me happy."

Philip heard the baby and cursed. Another

mouth to feed, and him as helpless and useless as a baby himself. Why did Marilee have to bring another brat into this miserable family? Why didn't she just smother it and stop the crying?

Martin couldn't believe how pretty Erin Alanna was. In just two short weeks, she had lost her red, wrinkled, old man looks. He wouldn't have wanted anyone to know just how captivated he was by his baby sister, but he found every opportunity he could to help his mother with her.

Never had Martin felt this kind of protectiveness towards Megan or his two younger brothers. Maybe it was because he was the man of the house now. After all, he was nearly eleven, and his father . . . Well, his father just wasn't able to take care of them all.

Martin tried not to think about his father. It frightened him to see the deterioration of the once vibrant man. It seemed he was forever in trouble at school for fighting because of someone's snide remark about his "crazy crippled father." But it was true. Philip didn't want to be with his children or his wife anymore. He had even refused to see the baby.

Well, he should see her, Martin thought. He'd love her if he did. Maybe it would even help him get well.

Quickly he picked her up from the bassinet and carried her from the nursery.

Philip's head swung around as the door opened. He had been watching the phantom moving slowly from the corner towards the window. For the first time since his fall, it seemed ready to beckon to him, to let him escape into nothing.

"Father, I . . . I've brought Erin Alanna to meet you," Martin announced in a shaky voice.

"Go away, Martin," Philip snapped. "I don't want to see her."

Martin stepped closer. "But Father, she's so pretty. I know she'll make you feel better."

He thrust the baby forward, and Philip's eyes fell on the sleeping infant. For a moment, everything was still. Then Philip began to moan, closing his eyes tightly.

He was there again, standing in the darkness outside the slave cabins. He saw them in each other's arms. They were lovers, and it was his fault, all his own fault. He had driven her there, rejecting her time and again. He had done it to all of them. And this . . . this was Alan's child.

Philip wasn't aware of Martin's hasty retreat. He opened his eyes and saw the darkness floating out the window. *Come*, it seemed to say. *Come with me and find peace. Come. Come, follow me."*

"Yes. Yes, I'm coming. "Wait! Wait for me."

He wheeled his chair towards the window. Grasping the ledge, he pulled his lifeless lower body out of the chair.

"Wait! Wait for me!"

Martin found his mother spinning yarn in the drawing room by the large windows where the light was good.

"Mother, something's wrong with Papa. Come quick!"

She jumped up, knocking over the spinning wheel. "What happened?" she asked.

"I don't know. I took Erin Alanna in for him to see . . ."

Marilee stopped and stared at Martin. "Good heavens!" she whispered in horror. She turned back to the stairs and, clutching her skirts, ran calling, "Philip! Philip, please . . ."

Marilee knew he had finally remembered. All her nightmares, all her terrible guilty dreams, were about to come true. She didn't know what he would do, but her heart was terrified. She burst through the door just as Philip pulled himself through the window. She saw him stretching out his arms and heard him cry, "Please wait!" as he fell from the window ledge to his death.

PART TWO

It is impossible to love and be wise.
Francis Bacon, 1625

CHAPTER TWELVE

MAY 1879-NEW YORK CITY/SPRING HAVEN

"Good morning, Mr. O'Hara."

"Nice day today, Mr. O'Hara."

"Top o' the mornin' t' you, sir."

Rory nodded to the various clerks as he walked toward his office. He only vaguely resembled the boy who had left Heart's Landing four years before. His black hair was cut shorter, and he was dressed in a suit instead of pants, open-necked shirt, and buckskin jacket. His long, relaxed stride had become the stroll of the cosmopolitan. His rugged good looks had matured, causing the ladies of his acquaintance to hope he would take notice of them. However, despite the confidence he had gained in his years in New York, he remained a quiet, private—although friendly—young man, a man who still longed for the mountains of Idaho.

"Mr. O'Hara, a telegram has come for you. It's on your desk."

"Thank you, Johnson. Is Mr. Michaels in yet?"

"No, sir."

"Well, when he gets in, would you please tell him I would like to talk to him?"

"Yes, sir."

Rory closed his office door. He still found it strange to have been promoted to an executive with an office and secretary of his own. Everyone, including Rory, knew he was being groomed as the heir apparent of this New York bank and trust company. He hated the "bowing and scraping," as he called it, that accompanied the new position. Before he had been just one accountant among many; now he was *Mr.* O'Hara, Brent Lattimer's protege.

Rory opened the telegram as he sat down behind the desk and began to read.

Chance for Carleton to see. Taylor and I taking him to London immediately. Netta going to Spring Haven. Proceed to Atlanta and escort her there. Meet her train on May 20. Brent

Rory turned his chair to face the window. He looked down at the bustling streets. It was like a pardon. He was escaping the confines of the city. Perhaps, if he'd ever told Brent how he felt . . . but Rory thought he owed it to Brent and Taylor and so he had tried to become what he thought they desired.

"Excuse me, Rory. May I come in?"

Bob Michaels closed the door behind him. Dressed in a well-cut grey suit, Bob was the picture of a professional man of wealth. In his late fifties, he had worked his way to the top, starting under David Lattimer's tutelege, then working with Brent, and finally becoming a general partner with on-site control since Brent was living thousands of miles away.

"I received a telegram from Bre . . . Oh, I see you've had one too. Seems I'm to expect you to be gone at least six months, maybe more. All depends on some operation, I guess."

"He didn't say much about that in mine, Mr. Michaels. Just that I'm to meet Brenetta at the train station in Atlanta on the twentieth."

"Well then," Bob said as he sat in a chair across the desk from Rory, "I think you'd best be getting your things in order. You've got just enough time to get there."

And so Rory found himself once again in a strange city. This time, however, he was not the young backwoodsman. Four years of living in New York had taught him to walk and talk and act so that people were willing to assist him, assured as they were that he was a young man of substance and importance.

He arrived in Atlanta with two days to spare and so had acquainted himself with the city. Evidence of the destruction Atlanta had endured just over ten years before was quickly disappearing. Atlantans seemed to be a hardy, industrious lot, and despite the ever-present Yankees and carpetbaggers, the city was rising above adversity. The burned out sections were rebuilt, and new businesses were beginning—and thriving—all around the city.

One thing his four years in New York had *not* taught him was what it was like to live in the conquered Confederacy, despised if you weren't a Southerner. He had to admit the hate was well-disguised. They hid their contempt beneath overwhelming politeness. Southern women had perfected it to an incredible degree, something they called "politing them to death."

The morning of the twentieth, Rory walked from his hotel to the depot. Dressed in a grey pin-striped suit coat and vest with charcoal slacks and a matching felt derby, he cut a dashing figure. His shoulders were broad, and although of only average height, about five foot eight or nine, he looked unusually strong. As he walked briskly along, he caught the eye of more than one early rising belle, and he returned their shy glances with a broad smile, his even white teeth seeming even whiter against his naturally olive skin.

Arriving only minutes before the train, he watched anxiously for the little girl in braids to disembark.

The train ride from Chattanooga had been most enjoyable for Brenetta. Her parents had found an elderly woman to act as her chaperone on the journey, but the old lady had slept almost the entire trip, leaving Brenetta free to do pretty much as she pleased. A young lady of Brenetta's looks and charm could not travel long without drawing the attentions of many a young man. So it was that she had met Stuart Adams.

It would have been hard for Stuart not to have noticed her. She was dressed in a pale yellow traveling dress, the skirt gathered and tiered at the back. A straw hat with yellow flowers sat jauntily over her meticulously coifed black hair. She smiled and laughed readily with the other passengers seated nearby, but it was her unusual eyes that captured their attention.

Brenetta caught him staring at her not long after he had boarded at Chattanooga. She lifted her almond-shaped tawny eyes, peeking out from under a veil of heavy black lashes, a small smile tweaking the corners of her lovely mouth. She knew *he* knew *she* knew he was watching her, but she still played it coy, waiting for him to approach her. As he got up and walked the few steps down the aisle to her side, she felt exhilerated by her own feminine power. Brenetta hadn't ever before realized how much fun it was to be pretty and sixteen. Long gone seemed her canvas britches, leather boots, and flapping braids.

"Excuse me, miss. I know I shouldn't really speak to you without a proper introduction, but I hope you'll forgive my boldness and allow me to join you."

Brenetta found him most attractive. Dressed immaculately in a suit of the finest cut and fabric, although somewhat threadbare and worn in spots, he had a roguish flair that she liked, and she admired his cornflower blue eyes and sandy hair. He was an inch or two over six feet tall. She liked that, since at five feet eight inches tall herself, she towered above most women and quite a few men as well. Although she couldn't have identified it as such, Brenetta found his lazy Carolina drawl enchanting.

"My name is Stuart Templeton Adams . . . from Charleston, miss, and I'm on my way to Athens, Georgia," he said as he sat across from her.

"How do you do, Mr. Adams," Brenetta said, her glance darting to her still sleeping chaperone and then dropping shyly to her folded hands in her lap. "I'm Brenetta Lattimer of Heart's Landing, Idaho, on my way to visit cousins near Atlanta."

"Idaho? My goodness, you've traveled far. You say you have family in Atlanta?"

"No, not *in* Atlanta. Actually, they have a plantation near Bellville. Spring Haven is its name."

Stuart looked thoughtful. "Hmmmmm. Seems I've heard of it. What is your cousin's last name?"

"Bellman."

"You're related to *the* Bellmans of Barrow County? My father used to talk about old Martin Bellman all the time, saying he had built the finest plantation Georgia would ever see."

Brenetta laughed merrily. "Goodness. Is it really so well-known?" she asked. "My mother was a Bellman; Martin Bellman was her father. Her brother, my Uncle Philip, and his wife stayed on after the war, but my parents moved west. It's Aunt Marilee I'm going to stay with while Mother and Father are in England."

Stuart's interest increased. "Your parents are

154

traveling abroad? Why didn't you go with them?"

"It's not a pleasure trip," Brenetta answered, a frown furrowing her forehead. "They've taken my little brother there to see if he can have an operation to make him able to see. Little Carl is blind."

"How awful," Stuart said softly, sympathizing with her.

Brenetta nodded, her attention miles away. Suddenly she smiled again, shrugging off her brief melancholy. "And why are you going to Athens, Mr. Adams, if I may ask?"

"I'm on my way to stay with friends of mine. Actually they're distant relatives. I'll probably stay a few months and then be on my way home to Windjammer. That's my rice plantation." He scowled a little. "Although I can't say there's much rice harvested anymore. You just can't get free darkies to work properly." His voice was filled with bitterness.

"Then why don't you hire white men?" Brenetta asked naively, thinking as she said it of Tobias Levi and Jim "Sandman" Sanders and Buck Franklin and all the other hands back at Heart's Landing.

Stuart laughed sharply. "I'm afraid it's not that simple, my dear Miss Lattimer." Changing the subject abruptly, he asked, "Is this your first visit to Georgia?"

"I was born at Spring Haven, but I don't remember anything about it. My father was an officer with the Union Army. My parents chose to start over in Idaho rather than live in New York where his home was or in the South on her plantation.

They don't talk much about it, at least not with me, but I suppose it was rather difficult for Mother, marrying a Yankee in the middle of the war and all."

"And what's it like in Idaho?"

"Oh, it's the very loveliest. Heart's Landing is our ranch. We have several thousand acres of grazing land and lots of mountains and forests too. My father raises cattle and horses. We have about twenty or thirty ranch hands most of the time, and they're all like a part of the family. Of course, there's quite a few more during round-up."

Stuart returned her smile. "It must be wonderful . . . and very exciting too."

When the young woman in yellow stepped down from the train on the arm of the tall, well-dressed fellow, Rory didn't give them more than a passing glance. The young couple, probably newlyweds, were not his concern. He was beginning to think Brenetta had missed the train, and he was worried.

"I haven't any idea where Rory could be. I know Father said he would meet me here."

Rory turned quickly in the direction of the voice, but the only people close enough that he could have heard so clearly were the young couple. As he watched, the man bowed over his lady's hand.

"I really should get back on board, but if you think I should stay until he arrives, I'll do so, Miss Lattimer."

Rory's eyes widened in disbelief. Could he have

heard what he thought he'd heard? Could *this* be Brenetta? He had left behind a freckled-faced, skinny little tomboy. Could this bright flower, so tall and shapely, with the dewy peach complexion be the same girl?

"Netta?"

Both she and her friend turned towards him.

"Rory?" she asked, equally surprised. He had forgotten how changed he was as well.

"Little one, it really *is* you!" Rory exclaimed.

Brenetta rushed forward and hugged him tightly. Her hat was knocked askew as she stepped back from him, smiling happily, her eyes twinkling. Their gazes met easily; they were almost exactly the same height.

"Rory, I didn't even know you!"

"You didn't know *me?* I was looking for a little girl and instead I find a beautiful young woman. What happened to the girl I called 'little one'?"

"Oh, Rory," she said, ignoring his question. "I want you to meet a new friend of mine. Stuart Adams. Mr. Adams, this is my very best friend in all the world, Rory O'Hara."

As they shook hands, Rory tried his best to be friendly, fighting the sudden, inexplicable urge to tell Stuart to stay away from Brenetta. Just like an over-protective big brother, he thought, and then smiled.

Stuart immediately saw in Rory a potential stumbling block to his newly formulated plan. Rory seemed a shrewd and intelligent fellow, and he had a slightly proprietory air about him towards Brenetta. Stuart would have to proceed with caution if he was to escape detection by this wary half-breed.

"I'm pleased to make your acquaintance, Mr. O'Hara. Miss Lattimer has been telling me all about her home and you and that horse you caught —the Blaze, was it?"

"The Flame," Brenetta interjected.

"Ah, yes. The Flame. Most interesting. Well, you'll have to excuse me. I must get back on the train before I'm left behind. Good-bye, Mr. O'Hara." Stuart took Brenetta's gloved hand again. Raising it to his lips, he said, "I shall look forward to seeing you again, Miss Lattimer. And I promise, I shall." He kissed her hand lightly and left quickly.

Once back in his seat, he looked carefully out the window, trying to see without being seen. Rory and Brenetta were still on the platform, Brenetta talking with great animation, her cheeks flushed with color. Rory was listening with a patient and adoring stance.

Stuart had never encountered such a charming, vivacious, and beautiful girl before—at least not all wrapped up in the same package. More important, she had what he needed most—a wealthy, doting father. Stuart had learned a lot from Brenetta's gay chatter in their hours together, including the fact that she was naive about men. Stuart was a bright as well as desperate young man; he knew when a good opportunity was knocking at his door. Brenetta Lattimer was his key to saving Windjammer, and he did not intend to let her slip away. This was his last chance.

Erin Alanna was the first to see the buggy coming up the drive.

"Mama. Mama. Comp'ny!"

Marilee heard her from behind the house where she was washing clothes. Wiping her hands on her apron, she hurried through the breezeway by the kitchen and around to the front of the house.

Erin Alanna was jumping up and down on the veranda, clapping her hands in excitement, her strawberry-blonde curls bobbing wildly. She loved to have visitors. Her emerald eyes glittered with joy as Marilee picked her up.

The buggy came to a halt in front of the house. The driver, a husky fellow in his early twenties, jumped out and helped the yellow-clad girl to the ground. It wasn't until she turned a brilliant smile towards Marilee that she realized who her guests were.

"Brenetta?" she cried, almost dropping Erin Alanna before hurrying down the stairs. "Can you really be Taylor's baby girl?" Brenetta laughed, a laugh so like her mother's that all doubt was wiped away. Marilee hugged her warmly, then stepped back to see her more clearly.

"I just cannot believe it. You were still only a baby when I saw you last. About two years old is all. My goodness, though, listen to me go on. In case you haven't guessed, I'm your Aunt Marilee and this is my youngest, Erin Alanna."

"I'm so happy to be here, Aunt Marilee. Mother's talked about you and Spring Haven all my life; I feel like I already know you. Aunt Marilee, this is Rory O'Hara."

"How do you do, Mrs. Bellman? It's a pleasure," Rory said politely.

"Well, come in, both of you. I'm sorry I wasn't better prepared for you. Taylor's note was scribbled off so quickly it's a wonder I knew you were coming at all. I'm afraid none of the other children are here at the moment. They're all in school today. Please, sit down; make yourselves comfortable while I get us something to drink."

Brenetta watched her aunt hurry away. It was hard to believe Aunt Marilee was only a year older than Taylor. Marilee looked closer to fifty with her wrinkled skin and greying yellow hair. She was thin to the point of emaciation. She must be very lonely with Uncle Philip gone, Brenetta thought.

She let her glance slip to the room she was in. It was quite a disappointment after everything her mother had told her. It was terribly run down. Still, she could see the quiet elegance of the place, and being here made her wonder what it had really been like, growing up here. She also wondered what it had been like for Taylor during the war years. There were many things her parents refused to talk about. Perhaps her time here would solve some mysteries.

"Here we are. Would either of you like anything in your tea?"

"Not for me, thank you, Mrs. Bellman," Rory replied as Marilee set the tray beside him.

Brought out of her reverie, Brenetta shook her head in answer.

"Mr. O'Hara, I understand you'll be staying to

do some business for Brent," Marilee said, making conversation.

"Yes, Brent wants me to look into the plantation inherited from his father, Dorcet Hall. I'm to look at several alternatives before deciding what should be done with it."

Marilee placed her cup in her saucer. "You mean he might sell it? Oh, dear? That would be terrible. It seems wrong that a Lattimer might not always own it, prosperous or not. But, heaven knows, Brent sinks enough money into this place without any profit to be bothered with one his father left to Tay . . . without worrying about Dorcet Hall."

Martin and Megan were the first to arrive home. Megan went running up the stairs and nearly collided with Brenetta on the landing.

"Oh!" Megan cried, jumping backwards.

"Hello," Brenetta said. "You must be Megan Katrina."

"And you're cousin Brenetta! How marvelous! Which room did mother give to you?"

Brenetta lifted a corner of her skirt and turned to walk with Megan. "She said it was my mother's old room."

"Really? I've always wanted that room myself. It's by far the loveliest bedroom in the house. But Mother would never let anyone use it. Saving it for Aunt Taylor if she ever came home, she'd say. But, of course, Aunt Taylor hasn't come, so she's given it to you. Are you going to stay with us long?"

"Until my parents and Carl get back from England."

Megan opened the door to her room. "I am sorry about your brother. I hope things work out for him."

"Thank you. I hope so, too, Megan."

Martin was suspicious of the dark-skinned man working on the old plow. He was wearing expensive trousers, but he had stripped to the waist, baring a massive back and muscled shoulders that glistened with sweat.

"What d'you think you're doin' with that plow?" he challenged.

Rory looked up a moment, then turned his attention back to his hands. "Fixing it, I hope."

Martin edged closer to see what he was doing. "Did my mother hire you to do some work around the place?"

"No," Rory grunted as he broke the rusted bolt loose. Turning to the boy, he held out his hand. "I'm Rory O'Hara. I work for Brent Lattimer and I brought your cousin Brenetta here for a visit."

Martin looked at the proffered hand but didn't take it. Yankees, he thought angrily. Yankees at Spring Haven!

His face clouded in anger, Martin burst in on his mother in the kitchen. "What are *they* doin' here?" he demanded of her.

Marilee looked up at her son. His lean face was mottled with anger; his voice broke as he spoke. At nearly fifteen, he was as gangly as a yearling colt, but he wanted to be regarded as the man of the family and Marilee tried to treat him as such.

"Martin, is that any way to talk about your own cousin? She is family, you know." She continued to work the bread dough as she spoke, hoping it would stretch enough to feed two more mouths.

Sullenly, Martin sat in the chair beside the stove, watching her busy hands.

"Martin, you must try to be friendly to Brenetta and Mr. O'Hara while they're here. It's likely to be for several months, and I can't bear it if you're hateful to them."

Marilee spent a lot of time worrying about her oldest child. Ever since he was a little boy, he had been filled with this excessive hate for anyone not born and raised in the south. It pervaded every aspect of his life. He blamed the Yankees for every difficulty, every problem, every failure. He even swore it was Yankees that had caused his father's death.

She sighed deeply, then pushed some stray hairs away from her face with a floury hand. "Please be friendly, Martin. Please," she begged softly.

"Mrs. Bellman, you've got to realize that I'm probably more familiar with the finances of this plantation than you are. Brent has given you only what aid you've asked for, which as I see now is barely enough to survive on, and no more. Your brother-in-law would be horrified to know the way it really is."

Marilee looked across the big oak desk at him, the circles under her eyes darkened by the dim light of the study. "I suppose that's true. But Rory,

Philip always resented the money Brent sent. I guess I just became accustomed to his refusals and learned to get by with what was here." She sighed. "I suppose I should have taken the children and moved back to town after Philip died. If it weren't for Martin I probably still would, but this place belongs to him. I can't take him away from it."

Rory stood up and walked to the window. "Mrs. Bellman, if something isn't done soon, there'll be nothing left for him. Brent and Taylor may keep it from being sold for taxes, but unless it begins to produce again, it may as well be sold. It's killing you by inches. Even a fool can see that."

"But what can I do?" she whispered, her head falling forward into her hands.

Rory's palms slapped the desk top in front of her, causing her head to snap back up in surprise. "You let me help you, that's what you can do. You can quit trying to do it all yourself. Martin and Megan are both old enough to do a lot of what you're doing. Netta would love to help. A lady she may be, but remember, she was raised on ranch-work; she'll do her share and then some. Stop living on pride, Mrs. Bellman. Let Brent *really* invest in this place. It can turn a profit again if we just try. Remember, Taylor still loves this place and thinks of it as her other home. You owe it to her as well as to Martin and yourself."

"All right, Rory," Marilee said, smiling wanly. "You win. I place it all in your hands. I'll do as you say."

They all sat around the ebony dining table, waiting for him to begin. The table's surface was marred by scratches here and there, but Marilee kept it polished to a high sheen. Rory could see each of their faces reflected in the finish. At the far end was Marilee, her tiny frame dwarfed in her high-backed chair. To her right was Martin, tall and lanky, his round brown eyes dominating his face as he watched Rory warily. On Marilee's left was Megan, a dreamy, sometimes moody girl, quickly approaching womanhood. Next to Martin and Megan, sitting opposite each other, were Alastair James and Kingsley Stonewall. Only a year separated them, and they looked so much alike with their dark hair and blue eyes, they could have been twins.

Beside Alastair sat Erin Alanna. Rory thought privately that she looked as if she belonged to this family by mistake, so different was she from the others. She had a pudgy nose covered with freckles. Her bright green eyes were touched with gold, and her hair was the color of Taylor's peach preserves, a pale golden-orange.

Last of all was Brenetta sitting on Rory's right. Tall and shapely in a blue linen day dress, she looked at him with only the hint of a smile on her full, pink lips. She was wearing her hair up, a blue ribbon woven through it, and her appearance was strangely disturbing to him.

Rory cleared his throat, feeling more nervous under their gazes than he had when he'd addressed his first board meeting at the bank. "Your mother has asked me to talk to you. I hope you'll listen carefully and be willing to follow my suggestions and instructions. You may think it's none of my concern, but I want you to know I really care what happens here.

"Spring Haven is in serious trouble. You're all old enough to know that. I'm arranging for a personal loan for your mother. If we succeed in making Spring Haven a productive plantation again, she'll pay it all back. If not, there are no penalties. But it's to your benefit to make it succeed."

Rory paused, looking from one of them to the next. Seeing Martin's face growing red, he decided to start with the hardest first.

"Martin, Spring Haven is destined to be yours someday and you're the man of the house. I'm going to expect to see you working harder than all the others put together. Tomorrow you and I'll ride over the place and discuss what crops it's not too late to plant yet this season and draw up plans for the coming year."

"What makes you think you know what should be grown on a plantation like ours?" Martin challenged. "You're no Southerner."

"No, I'm not. And I don't know," came Rory's truthful reply. "But I do know about the work that goes into a cattle ranch. I know it takes planning and ingenuity and gambles and sweat and lots of prayer. Are you man enough—or Southern enough—to take the chance?"

The gauntlet had been thrown at his feet and, as Rory was relieved to see, Martin was forced to pick it up. "I can do whatever it takes," he growled. "I'll work *more* than twice as hard as you or anybody else!"

Rory allowed himself a thin smile. "Good. It'll take everyone working just that hard to do what we have to do."

CHAPTER THIRTEEN

SEPTEMBER 1879—SPRING HAVEN

It hadn't been easy but they had done it. Spring Haven had produced a successful cotton crop. It was a pittance compared to the years before the Civil War, but when considering the past fifteen years, it seemed a windfall crop. In addition, Rory had overseen the planting and harvesting of corn and wheat for them to sell as well as a large garden for their own needs. They weren't going to make a fortune, but they might very well make a profit. At the very least, they would break even.

Leaning against the new wagon Rory had purchased with some of the loan money, Martin waited for the supplies he had ordered so he could load them and be on his way. The summer's labors had made a man of Martin. His extreme thinness had become a wiry strength. His skin was nearly as dark as Rory's, and his hair had been streaked golden by the sun. Although he complained often to his mother of having to "work like a nigga," he secretly enjoyed the feeling his labors gave him— the feeling of power as he tilled the land, the sense of being a part of nature and creation, the pure physical exhaustion that brought sleep to him quickly when his head hit the pillow each night.

Seeing Mr. Walker, the grocer, coming towards the door, Martin pushed himself away from the wagon and, taking the stairs three at a time, stepped inside the store before Mr. Walker could reach the porch.

"Everything's ready for you, Martin," the white-haired man said, speaking slowly. Mr. Walker had been running this store since Martin's grand-father's day, and he was familiar with everyone in the county. If Martin had indicated he had any time to spare, he would have begun telling him one story after another about early days in Bellville, about the first Martin Bellman and his lovely second bride, Taylor's mother.

"Thanks, Mr. Walker."

Martin threw a sack of sugar over his shoulder and carried it outside. His mouth watered just thinking of it. Martin couldn't remember the last time they had been able to afford the luxury of sugar. Tossing it into the back of the wagon, he turned back towards the store and found himself looking into the face of Peter Hale.

"Hey, Corey," Peter said to the boy at his side. "Look at this here red-necker. Isn't he the one that called me white trash?"

Martin glared at them but kept silent.

Peter snickered. "He looks just like that thievin' redskin his ma's got livin' with her."

With a lightning fast swing, Martin's fist connected with the other boy's jaw, snapping Peter's head back and causing him to stumble backwards against the wall of the store. He waited for Peter's retaliation. He was no longer the school boy who charged into a fight thoughtlessly. He had learned much from Rory O'Hara in the last four months, including the arts of self control and clear thinking.

As Peter charged him, Martin waited until the last moment, then sidestepped, sending the enraged antagonist barreling into the side of the wagon. Startled, the horse jerked forward, and Peter tumbled to the ground, landing face down in the dirt.

Martin kept a wary eye on Corey, but he turned his body towards Peter who was struggling to his feet. Martin's arms hung loosely at his sides, giving him an air of total relaxation and assurance. This seemed to infuriate Peter even more. He didn't charge Martin this time, however. Instead, he stalked closer, intending to score a punch to Martin's belly and then beat him to a pulp. Peter tried to circle around him, forcing Martin's back toward Corey in case he needed some help from that quarter. Martin recognized the tactics and carefully avoided the trap by sidling closer to the wagon.

"Come here, you dirty Reb. I'm going t'teach you some manners."

"How?" Martin asked. "You have to know some to teach 'em!"

Peter's swing went wide, and Martin brought another hook up to his jaw, followed by a left to the midsection. Peter was taken by surprise, both by the punches connecting and by the strength behind them. He doubled over at the waist, and Martin brought both hands, clenched together, down on Peter's neck, catapulting him to the ground.

When it seemed certain Peter was not going to get up right away, Martin turned to Corey. "Is there anything about me or my family *you* feel like sayin'?"

Corey shook his head quickly back and forth, his face white as he stared at his oversized friend, beaten and kneeling in the road at Martin's feet.

"Good," Martin said briskly, brushing the dust from his pants. "Then I'll get back to my business."

Marilee read the letter from Templeton Ashley with some surprise. Templeton was a distant cousin of hers on her mother's side. She hadn't seen or heard from him or his family since before the war began and so was curious as to why he was writing to her now. It seemed his son, Joseph, and a young relative of Templeton's wife were going to be traveling to Atlanta and were planning to drop in for a stay at Spring Haven. He ended by saying he hoped it would be convenient for her.

"Oh, my," Marilee said with a sigh. Harvest was just winding down and now she was to have house guests. Her thin, claw-like fingers tapped nervously on the table top.

In her childhood, when times were more prosperous and the county was inhabited with genteel Southerners instead of Yankee trash, people had thought nothing of dropping in for a visit and staying for a month or two or more. Everyone had lots of space and plenty of every necessity. There were slaves to tend to your every desire, and everyone seemed to belong to an extended family, related or not.

The soft rustle of Brenetta's skirts as she entered the dining room drew Marilee's eyes up from the pages. For an instant, as often happened, she thought the girl was Taylor, so much alike were they.

"Aunt Marilee, are you feeling well?"

Thoughts of Taylor vanished. "Oh . . . yes, I'm fine, dear. Please come join me."

Brenetta was dressed in a pale coral gown of the finest muslin, the fabric as light as the September breeze stirring the oak leaves outside the windows. She wished that Megan had a gown like this to wear, but they were lucky to have clothes at all. Another sigh escaped her.

"Something *is* wrong, Aunt," Brenetta said as she sat down across the table from her. "Won't you tell me what it is?"

"I've just heard from a cousin of mine. It seems we're to have some guests for an indefinite stay. I was just wondering how I would entertain them." She lifted her large brown eyes and tried to smile encouragingly. "I'm a bit out of practice. We have so little and all the servants are gone and the place looks so shabby and . . ." Her voice petered out.

Brenetta watched her silently for a moment, her lovely eyes filled with compassion and concern. Reaching across the table, she touched her aunt's hand. Softly, she said, "Tell me about it, Aunt Marilee. Tell me about life here at Spring Haven when you and Mother were girls. Tell me about the parties and your beaus."

The lines in the older woman's face seemed to smooth out as she began to reminisce, a bit wistfully. "Spring Haven was very grand when I was a girl. And your grandfather, Martin Bellman, was quite a man. Of course, I never knew his first wife, Philip's mother, but Taylor's mother . . . now, there was a beauty. She was from New Orleans, and she loved to entertain. The barbeques and the dances and the dinners . . . Of course, I was too young to attend a lot of the parties, but I watched from the top of the stairs along with Taylor whenever I was allowed to come. When your mother married David . . ." She stopped abruptly.

"I know about mother being married before, Aunt Marilee. Please go on."

"I . . . I wasn't sure you did." Again a thoughtful pause. "It was such a beautiful day. There wasn't a spot in the house that didn't shine like glass. The gardens were in bloom and the lawn was like a thick carpet. Philip hired an orchestra and both drawing rooms were filled with swirling dancers, the women dressed in hoopskirts of silk and satin and covered with jewels. And the food! I could feed my children for a year on what was thrown out!"

Marilee stopped, shook her head, and sighed again. "They were wonderful times."

"Aunt Marilee, why don't we have a ball when our company arrives? You'd know just what to do," Brenetta suggested, excitement lacing her words.

"A ball? Oh, Brenetta, you have no idea what it would cost—the food, the servants, the clothes. . ."

"You just leave that to me."

He was helping Martin unload supplies when she came swooping out of the house, her coral dress whirling around her dainty ankles. He never ceased to be amazed at the change wrought in her in just four years. He still expected to see her long braids flapping behind her, her little legs clad in worn britches. He remembered her looking up at him as she begged to go along with him somewhere.

Well, she was no longer a little girl. Brenetta had blossomed into a tall, lithe woman with a small waist, softly rounded hips, and high firm breasts—a disconcerting change for Rory, who found himself looking at her through a man's eyes instead of brotherly ones.

"Rory! Rory, I've *got* to talk to you."

Her face was flushed, her voice filled with urgency. A woman she might be, but Rory was glad to see still a hint of the excitable, impatient and even sometimes demanding child.

"Sure, little one," he said, putting the sack back in the wagon. "What is it you need?"

"Rory, you've *got* to give Aunt Marilee more money. If you don't, I swear I'll write to Papa and tell him what a miser you've been and how awful things are for everyone here."

His black eyes widened in surprise. "Excuse me, but have I missed something?"

Brenetta flounced over and sat down on an old tree stump. "Yes, you most certainly have. Everyone has been working very hard for months, and it's time they got to relax. Aunt Marilee's got more relatives coming for a visit, and she's worried sick about it."

"Surely she knows we've got food enough for more . . ."

"It's not *food*, you dolt-headed man. We *must* have parties. There hasn't been one here for years and years and my aunt and cousins deserve some fun. We'll hire some servants and everyone will get new clothes and we'll send out invitations and—"

Rory began to laugh, interrupting her flood of commands. "Okay, okay, I surrender," he said, choking back his mirth as her eyes sparked in amused indignation. "You make the plans. I'll see they're paid for."

Spring Haven bustled with activity the likes of which it hadn't seen in too long a time. House servants had been hired, and evidence of their labors under Marilee's relentless eye were beginning to be seen everywhere. Even the threadbare rugs and furniture looked renewed.

Megan stood in front of the mirror, a crown of afternoon sunlight settling on her hair as it streamed through the window of her bedroom.

Her blue eyes were wide with wonder as she looked at her reflection. She couldn't believe she was wearing a dress like this. And others were spread across the bed, the varied colors and fabrics adding a festive aura to the room.

"It looks marvelous on you, Megan. That shade is the same as your eyes." Brenetta smiled into the mirror as she spoke.

"Do you really think so?" Megan asked, pivoting around so she could see the tiers of fabric falling down the back of her skirt, each layer trimmed with a lighter blue ribbon, a matching sash circling her trim waist. "It's terribly grown-up, isn't it?"

Brenetta laughed merrily. "Of course it is, you silly goose. It looks that way because you've grown up yourself."

"Yes, you're right, I have. I've grown up and I'm pretty, aren't I?"

"Yes, Megan, I think so. Now, what can we do with your hair?"

As Brenetta fussed with Megan's fine locks, Megan allowed herself to daydream about the upcoming parties. Her mother had sent out invitations for a barbeque the first week in October. Megan had helped her address the white envelopes and had marveled at her mother's sudden animation, at how pretty and young she appeared. She was also amazed at how many people Marilee knew to invite, people with names as old as Georgia itself.

Even better than the barbeque were Brenetta's plans for a masked ball in early November.

Brenetta said everyone would be asked to dress as a famous person, past or present, real or from mythology, and all would wear masks. Identities would be guessed as part of the festivities. Megan found the idea thoroughly romantic, just like a fairy tale, and she was certain something wonderful would happen that night.

In between these two major festivities would be the entertainment of her cousin and his friend, or whatever he was. She wondered if they would be handsome and if they would take any notice of her. Catching Brenetta's image in the looking glass, she thought not. But perhaps, if she . . . Just then she heard a commotion in the hall, her door was thrust open, and Alastair and Kingsley came tumbling over each other into the room.

"They're here!" Alastair announced with gusto.

"They just arrived," Kingsley added. "Mother says come down."

"Don't you two know about knocking before coming into a lady's room?" Megan demanded as she angrily whirled away from the mirror. "Get out, the both of you!"

When the door had closed behind them, Brenetta said, "You go on down, Megan. I want to freshen up. I won't be long."

So Megan descended the curving staircase alone.

Stuart had planned carefully for several months for this visit. It had seemed too good to be true when he learned that his host's family was distantly related to Brenetta Lattimer's widowed aunt, but he was not one to waste an opportunity, and almost at once he had set the wheels in motion that had brought them here. Now, he was seated in a comfortable, if sadly worn, overstuffed chair, listening with only slight attention as Joseph lavished gallant attention on their hostess.

He had been watching the door with carefully hooded eyes, waiting for her to appear. The swish of skirts alerted him and he rose as she rounded the corner and stopped. But it wasn't Brenetta. The girl who stood framed in the arch of the doorway was as different from Brenetta as day was from night. Petite, almost fragile-appearing, her hair was the color of spun gold, her eyes the blue of a still mountain pond, her skin as pale and fresh as whipped cream. She was wearing her long hair pulled back from her face, held there with a shiny satin ribbon. She couldn't have been more than fifteen but her figure was as alluring as any he'd seen. Her smile was shy, yet he sensed an undercurrent of bravado, of ambition, and even a touch of the reckless adventuress.

"Megan, come in and meet our guests," Marilee called to her. As she crossed the room, her mother made the introductions. "This is my elder daughter, Megan Katrina. Megan, these are your cousins, Joseph Ashley and Stuart Adams."

Her eyes widened as she turned them on him. "We're related?"

"Very distantly and through a complicated maze of marriages, Miss Bellman," Stuart answered, bowing over her hand.

"And here's Brenetta," Marilee said warmly.

He pulled his hand away from Megan and turned to greet Brenetta.

"Mr. Adams!" she exclaimed before Marilee could make the introductions. "Are *you* one of the cousins?"

He smiled pleasantly. "So it would seem, Miss Lattimer."

"You two know each other?" Megan asked, obviously miffed by the loss of his attention.

"Yes, we met on the train last May," Brenetta replied. Then to Stuart she said, "How perfectly wonderful to have it be you. And this must be Joseph Ashley. We have such plans made for your stay, Mr. Ashley. I know you and Mr. Adams are going to have a marvelous time."

She was absolutely lovely, perfect in every way. She would grace a man's home, bringing a subtle elegance to it. Her voice was soothing, her manners excellent. She was young and strong and would bear healthy children to inherit the land after him. And because there was also her wealthy father, Stuart knew there must be no mistake in his pursuit of her. He callously discarded his initial attraction to Megan.

CHAPTER FOURTEEN

The doctor's office seemed incredibly dark and closed in, the walls paneled with walnut-stained wood, the desk a heavy black monstrosity, and the carpet a burnt shade of brown. Taylor sat across from the doctor while Carleton sat quietly on her lap, his blank eyes seeing nothing, but he was alert nonetheless. She could feel him listening to the doctor as carefully as she should have been. He probably understands even more than I do, she thought. Carleton was such a very bright boy.

"Mr. Lattimer," the doctor went on, speaking to Brent who was standing behind Taylor, his hand resting on her shoulder. "I cannot promise the procedure will restore his sight, but I can be fairly certain that it has a very good chance. You know, of course, as my respected colleagues have most assuredly told you before this, that this can be a very dangerous operation. Besides which we'll be operating on his eyes . . ."

The doctor's voice droned on, repeating what she had heard time and time again, by one doctor and then another. Taylor felt so tired and frigthtened. She wished they'd just do the surgery and be done with it. She had come to hate London, wishing only for the open spaces of Heart's Landing and her family and friends around her. She hated the fog and the rain and she detested the stark hospitals with their peculiar smells. They brought back too many painful memories of mutilated young men, soldiers missing arms and legs and eyes . . .

Brent interrupted the doctor. "Dr. Smythe, I'm sorry, but we've been through this so many times this summer. We've considered all the options, and I think we understand all the possibilities and complications that might occur. We feel it's time to get on with it. And Carleton thinks so too, don't you, son?"

"Yes, sir," Carleton answered clearly.

As Brent's hand squeezed her shoulder, Taylor looked at the doctor with pleading eyes. "Doctor, please tell us when you can perform the surgery."

He tilted his chair back from his desk, hooking his thumbs in the lapels of his coat. He looked at her over the rim of his glasses which were perched near the tip of his nose.

"This Friday."

CHAPTER FIFTEEN

OCTOBER 1879—SPRING HAVEN

Brenetta's laughter carried effortlessly through the autumn air from the veranda to the barn where Rory was shoeing a horse. Sweat beaded on his brow, and as he lifted his head to look towards the house, a large drop traced its way down his nose. He shook the offending moisture loose and looked away from the cheerful scene. Brenetta was sitting beside Stuart on the porch swing. In two chairs facing them were Megan and Joseph. Marilee sat apart from the younger folks, her hands working deftly with a ball of yarn and a pair of needles.

Brenetta had called to him earlier to take a break and join them, but he had declined, saying there was too much work to be done and he'd rather be doing it. Martin, too, had chosen not to be a part of the little group, choosing instead to stand holding the horse's halter while Rory put shoes on the big hooves. While Rory's face told nothing, Martin wore a sullen frown.

Having seen Rory's glance, he said, "Some people have it all. Look at those two. Nothing to do with their lives except sit around with a couple of dumb girls and practice their flattery. It makes me sick to see that Stuart Adams hanging on Netta's every word. They're so sweet on each other you could choke."

Rory dropped the draft horse's hoof, stood up, and stared at the veranda once more. Brenetta wore a cool linen dress of pale lavender, and she was waving a matching fan idly beneath her chin —an attractive gesture but it did little to cool the surprisingly hot fall day. Even from this distance he could see Stuart bending attentively towards her. When he spoke, she tilted her chin upwards, her smile full as her eyes—Rory couldn't see them but he *knew*—flirted with him.

"Put him up. I'll finish later," Rory said softly to Martin, then walked inside the barn.

Moments later, he rode out astride his favorite mount, a buckskin stallion. He had doffed his shirt and shoes and was riding bareback. His rock-like features seemed unreal as he trotted past Martin in the direction of the river. He looked neither right nor left, breaking into a canter as soon as he was out of the yard. For the moment, everything was blocked from his mind except the feel of the breeze against his skin and the horse between his legs. Suddenly he was free of everything—the plantation, the bank, even the Lattimer family. He was Bear Claw, Cheyenne brave, son of White Dove and grandson of Running Bear. He was part of the earth and the air and he was as free as the wind.

The smile was frozen on Megan's lips, and she hoped it didn't look as false as it felt. Inside her breast, her young heart seemed broken beyond repair as she watched Stuart and Brenetta. Caught in the throes of first love, she was certain nothing would ever be right again.

Her mind drifted back to the afternoon of their barbeque. The guests had come from near and far, arriving in all manner of conveyances. They were mostly from the generation that remembered the grand balls and barbeques, fox hunts and races, elegant clothes and great wealth. Now, for most of them, the wealth and all it had brought with it was gone, but their memories were clear, and they swore this was just like old times. Their children couldn't remember those days they spoke of, but they knew this was a grand day of its own. The tables were loaded with food, the conversations were gay, and the weather was perfect.

Megan stood with her mother and Martin, welcoming their guests. She watched and listened in amazement as her mother seemed to shed years right before her eyes.

"Marilee, you haven't changed a bit. As lovely as the day Philip swept you off to Charleston for your honeymoon."

"Marilee Bellman, you must have stolen these

children. You're much too young to really be their mother.''

"Why haven't we seen more of you, Marilee Stone? You simply must start acceptin' some of the invitations I know you receive. Times may be hard but we Southerners still know how to entertain.''

"I declare, those Bellman men always grabbed up the best and prettiest girls in all of Georgia.''

"Marilee Bellman, you have always been the county's most gracious hostess. Why, the Reverend Stone—God rest his soul—couldn't have managed at all without his pretty daughter nearby. Lord knows, it was the same with your dear departed husband.''

Megan looked at her mother through new eyes. Why, they were right. Her mother had once been young and attractive. She had been a girl, just like Megan, and had fallen in love with Megan's father and had felt all that Megan was feeling right now.

Much later, or so it seemed, she was able to wander away and join the other young folk. Suddenly she wasn't poor Megan Bellman in a thrice mended gown with turned collars and cuffs. She was the pretty daughter of a once renowned lawyer and planter. Her home was the magnificent Spring Haven plantation, and her days were all carefree, filled only with dresses and pretty baubles and senseless chatter with other girls just like herself. She could almost make herself believe it.

"You look very lovely, Miss Megan.''

She looked up into his handsome face, his smile

so warm it nearly melted her heart right there on the spot. "Why . . . why, thank you, Mr. Adams."

"The day is certainly lovely, and the barbeque is a great success. May I bring you something, some punch perhaps?"

"No. No, thank you."

He swept his arm before him, turning aside. "Will you sit with me a moment?"

Megan spread her dress about her on the bench which was tucked back into the trees. Her heart took wings, soaring with new hope. Maybe she'd been wrong about him preferring Brenetta. After all, they'd only barely arrived, he and his cousin, and Stuart *did* already know Brenetta. Perhaps there was nothing to it at all.

She smiled her prettiest, laughing gaily at his stories of life on a rice plantation and answering all his questions about Spring Haven and what they grew here and if the crops were successful and if she had always had such nice clothes and surroundings and many, many other things. Quite naturally, she began to assume the womanly art of flirtation. She needed no coaching or prompting from older, more experienced girls. It came to her as easily as slipping on her clothes in the morning or running a comb through her hair. She knew he liked her. She could see it in his eyes. He thought she was pretty too. It was all so very wonderful.

Then it happened. Brenetta came into view, walking with four or five young men, all set on impressing her with their masculinity and chivalry. Stuart rose, begging her to excuse him. Then he hurried after Brenetta, leaving Megan behind, feeling hurt and angry as she watched him take Brenetta's arm and lead her away from the others. The day was ruined.

"Megan, you haven't been listening to a thing Cousin Joseph has been saying," Brenetta scolded in mock firmness.

Stuart could see her pull herself back from her daydreams—not too pleasant a one judging by her down-turned mouth. He regretted her unhappiness, but there was no help for it. He was doing what he had to do. He couldn't let Megan ruin his plans.

He, too, remembered the day of the barbeque. He had sought her out, carefully gleaning what he had already suspected; Spring Haven had no money, at least not enough for his purposes. Brenetta Lattimer was his only hope. He had walked away from Megan knowing that he must never allow himself to turn in that direction again. He was in no position to look for a union with a kindred spirit such as he felt Megan to be. If he was to save Windjammer from his ever-looming creditors, he had to be cool and calculating about everything he did.

Stuart turned a practiced eye on Brenetta. His appearance was positively flawless, his manner perfect, his smile adoring. He was aware of everything he did as he did it all so very carefully. "Miss Brenetta, I feel the need to stretch my legs. Would you honor me with your company for a stroll about the lawn and gardens?"

"I'd love to, Mr. Adams," Brenetta answered,

placing her hand in the proffered crook of his arm.

Brenetta loved the feel of him pressing her hand against his ribs. It was a very protective gesture, and Stuart always made her feel protected and utterly feminine. The last few weeks had been so different from anything she had ever experienced; she felt like a different person herself. Though she had been in the South over four months, Brenetta was tasting true living and hospitality of the Southern aristocracy for the first time. Up until now, she'd been working as hard as everyone else, even harder than anything she had ever done at Heart's Landing. But suddenly, with the help of funds from her father under Rory's careful management, a magical change had occurred, sending servants and new clothes and parties and handsome young men into their lives.

She was aware now of the specialness her mother felt for Spring Haven. It truly was enchanted. Caught in the spell, Brenetta felt herself drawn helplessly into Stuart's web of attention and flattery. Her remote childhood had brought her no beaus, and Stuart was the first male who had ever treated her like anything besides a silly child or just another wrangler.

"Miss Brenetta, have I told you that your laugh is the lightest and most cheerful sound I've ever heard? No? Well, it is, and I love to hear you laugh."

"Really, Mr. Adams . . ."

He stopped. "Isn't it time I was called Stuart? After all, you call Joe by his given name."

Lifting her gold-flecked eyes rimmed by heavy

black lashes, Brenetta smiled coyly, a blush of color highlighting her cheekbones. "But Joseph is our cousin," she objected half-heartedly.

"But so am I!" he exclaimed, looking truly hurt although she knew it was only in jest.

"All right, then. From now on you are Cousin Stu. Is that better?"

Sweeping the ground in an exaggerated bow, he replied, "My lady, though I detest being called Stu, if the name falls from your royal lips, I shall love it forever."

"Oh stop!" she cried, giggling at his ridiculous charade.

He watched her a moment, joining her in her laughter. Then, in a flash, the smile vanished as he stepped so close she had to tilt her head back to meet his gaze.

"You must know I will never intentionally stop your laughter," he whispered huskily. "Brenetta, whatever I may do . . . whatever I might appear to be, I think you're a wonderful girl. I wish . . . I . . . I hope I'll . . . If I should hurt you ever, I will know my own heart is missing for I shall be a heartless fool."

Tiny shivers ran up and down her spine. For a moment she thought he would try to kiss her, and she wondered recklessly if she should let him. But the moment passed. He stepped away, offered his arm to her once more, and they walked on in silence.

He was as still as the rock upon which he sat. His black eyes smouldered as he mulled over his thoughts. Why hadn't he seen it before now? Was he so stupid? Brenetta's image flickered across Rory's mind—Brenetta on the Flame, riding across the fields; Brenetta stumbling away from the roaring forest fire, her face smudged and her clothing singed; Brenetta, a vision in yellow, at the train station in Atlanta; Brenetta with Stuart, her eyes twinkling at his wit.

He, Rory O'Hara, was in love. How had it happened? She'd been only a child. She was like his own sister might have been, his "little one." How could he have not seen the changes coming? If he'd seen it in time . . .

Rory jumped to his feet and glared at the river. So he was in love. What was he to do about it? Again he imagined Brenetta and Stuart together, imagined Stuart kissing her, holding her, loving her . . . It was intolerable.

"I should leave this place and go home where I belong," he said aloud.

Home. Home to Idaho. He was tired of playing the banker and the planter and the chaperone. He wanted to feel the crisp morning air and see the cattle dotting the land. He wanted to go trapping in the snow and swim naked in the creek. He longed for the smell of pine trees and sagebrush.

But he couldn't go. His sense of honor wouldn't let him. He had promised Brent he would look after Brenetta and everything at Spring Haven, and so he had to stay. Perhaps . . . just perhaps, he thought, I can make her see me as a man instead of as a brother or friend. Perhaps, if luck was with him, she might grow to love him too.

CHAPTER SIXTEEN

NOVEMBER 1879—LONDON

Brent dressed slowly. He was wearing his grey pin-striped suit, the one he had had made during their long stay in London, and it fit his tall, trim figure admirably. He looked ten years younger than his forty-five years and he was glad of it. Having a wife as beautiful and youthful as Taylor sometimes made him feel he needed that edge to ward off those who would try to usurp his position. It was a ridiculous notion. Taylor had eyes for no one but her husband. But his thoughts weren't on his suit or his wife's admirers this morning. They were in a tiny, grim room several blocks away.

He stepped out from his dressing room and gazed at the large four-poster in the middle of the bedroom of their suite. Taylor was still asleep, her ebony tresses spreading across the ivory sheets and pillow cases like an ink blot on a clean sheet of paper. She looked so very peaceful. He hated to disturb her, but it was getting late. His long strides carrying him quickly to her side, Brent bent over and kissed her brow. "Taylor love, it's morning. Wake up."

Her rosy lips drew into a pout as she opened one eye to peek at him. "So soon?"

He kissed her again, this time on the mouth. "Yes, so soon."

She caught his arm as he began to go, pulling him onto the bed beside her. His motion pulled the sheet away from her shoulders. Above the blue of her satin nightgown, the swell of her rounded, white breasts rose and fell with her gentle breathing. He felt his desire for her begin to stir as it always did when she was near. Quickly he pulled the sheet back over her.

"Get up," he ordered, his voice sounding harsh in his own ears. "We've got to get to the hospital."

Taylor's eyes snapped open. "This is the day."

"Yes, love," Brent answered as he walked back into his dressing room. "Today's the day."

Within hours the doctors would be removing the bandages from Carleton's eyes, and they would know whether or not he would be able to see. Brent's heart ached within him for his son. He was a game lad, bright and cheerful, and Brent desired the very best for him. He wanted his son whole. He wanted to see him riding high in the saddle at Heart's Landing, cutting cattle, wrestling steers, and seeing all that his mother and father had made for him.

Taylor stood on one side of the bed, holding Carleton's hand. She was unsure if the trembling was caused by her or her son. Probably both.

It hadn't taken her long to be up and dressed once she realized what day of the week it was. Still, she looked lovely, her dark hair covered by a wine-colored bonnet. Her blue eyes were darkened in concern, and her cheeks were flushed.

Dr. Smythe was unraveling the bandages from around Carleton's head. His hands seemed to move terribly slowly. Her anxiety grew with each revolution, and she looked up at Brent, seeking reassurance from the tower of strength she'd learned to lean upon so many years before. He smiled at her, nodding his head slightly. He slipped his arm around her waist as he stepped closer.

"How are you doing, son?" Brent asked softly.

"Fine, Father."

"Well," the doctor said, "that's the bandages." He dropped the tail of the long strip to the floor. "Pull the blinds," he ordered his assistant, who moved quickly to the windows.

The room darkened. Taylor tightened her hold on the boy's hand.

"Now, I'm going to remove the gauze from his eyes," Dr. Smythe told them. "Carleton, I want you to open them very slowly and then we'll find out what you can see."

Brent's grip on her waist nearly made her cry out in pain. Tension filled the room and Taylor wished desperately for some fresh air. Carleton's eyes fluttered open and shut. After so long wrapped up, they didn't want to obey him. Finally, he was able to hold them open.

"Can you see anything in this darkness?" the doctor asked him.

"N . . . no, sir. I don't think so."

"Let's open those blinds a little. Carleton, you tell me the moment you can see anything. Even just some light."

Carleton nodded. The curtains were silently pulled back. Taylor discovered she was holding her breath, and she leaned weakly against Brent's shoulder. He must see, she thought. He *must* see.

The room was flooded with morning light.

"Do you see anything yet, Carleton?"

"No, Dr. Smythe. Go ahead and pull the curtains. I'm ready."

Brent held her as she wept. His shirt was soaked with her tears, but now her crying was dry and jagged. Her body jerked spasmodically as she gasped out her grief. She gripped his suit coat with her hands, pulling at it in desperation.

She had been so brave. All these years since they discovered Carleton's handicap, she had seemed to serenely accept it, facing each day with optimism. She had treated him as normally as possible, loving and disciplining him as she had Brenetta. When they had come to London, she had been the one to appear outwardly calm even though he knew she was anxious for their boy to receive his sight. She had optimistically endured one test after another and then finally the surgery itself.

Even this morning, when they had realized the operation had failed, Taylor had maintained her poise. Brent had wondered at the strength she seemed to have in this hour of crisis. Her quivering anticipation as the bandages were removed had vanished. She had kissed Carleton, telling him what a wonderful boy he was and they'd be back soon. Then they had spent a long time in the doctor's office listening to his explanation of what had gone wrong and to him saying not to lose hope, there was still a chance Carleton's sight might be restored gradually. These things did happen sometimes.

Brent had hailed a cab outside the hospital, feeling as if someone had dealt him a telling blow to his stomach. He had urged the driver to hurry. Taylor had sat beside him, her expression calm and smooth, totally controlled. He should have known the facade would crumble quickly.

Once inside their suite, he had taken her in his arms and the dam burst. She came apart at the seams; her pain, stored up for five years, rushed out, ravaging her body, leaving her weak and helpless.

He rocked her now as the storm diminished. So much pain. She had endured so much. He wondered what kind of man he was that he couldn't protect her from life's cruelties. Wasn't it enough that she had been forced to marry—not once but twice—men not of her choosing? Wasn't it enough that he and she had been torn apart by circumstances, by differences, by war and by death? Wasn't it enough that she had borne his daughter alone, willing to face any scandal, any lies, to have his child, even though they weren't yet wed? Wasn't all that enough? Now must she suffer this too?

"Oh, my darling Taylor," he whispered into her hair. "Please cry no more. We've come so far together. We have each other. We'll make it through this together too. And Carl is a gutsy one. He'll conquer this if we show him how, and we'll be so proud of him. Don't cry, love. Don't cry. We're going home. It's time to go home, Taylor."

CHAPTER SEVENTEEN

NOVEMBER 1879—SPRING HAVEN

Martin was glad to leave the house and check on the livestock. He'd never seen so many blithering idiots in one place at the same time. The whole house was in an uproar over this dumb masked ball. He would be glad to have it all over with.

Mostly, Martin's objections to the ball stemmed from his own insecurities. Fifteen was an awkward age to be for a boy—unsure if he even liked the giggly females, yet drawn irresistably to them like a moth to a flame. And when he saw his reflection in the hall mirror, he was convinced no girl would ever care for him. He was too tall and thin; he looked to himself to be terriby gawky, all arms and legs, a veritable scarecrow.

He found Rory in the barn. An Irish Setter bitch had just had a litter of nine puppies, and he was adding some clean straw to the corner she had taken over for her nursery. Martin had gained a grudging admiration for Rory O'Hara in the months since he had come to Spring Haven, and unconsciously, Martin emulated many of his mannerisms. Though he still held a distant animosity towards Northerners, he rationalized his budding friendship with Rory by telling himself he wasn't *really* a Yankee. He was a half-breed, the son of an Irishman and an Indian squaw. Reluctantly, he included Brenetta in this reprieve. Although her father was, according to Martin's thinking, not only a Yankee and a Union officer but the wealthy swine who destroyed his father, Brenetta's mother was a Southern gentlewoman and his father's sister. Besides which she had been raised in the West, and Martin had discovered he just plain liked her, no matter how hard he tried not to.

"Hello, Martin. Things settling down inside yet?" Rory asked.

Martin sat on a bale of hay, placing his elbows on his knees and cupping his chin in his hands. "No. Megan's still wanting to be someone else than Red Riding Hood. She wants to be someone *'alluring and romantic!'.*" He quoted Megan with a deepened voice, a hand to his forehead, and fluttering eyes.

Rory chuckled. "Sounds like you're not too happy about it either."

"Not much. What's your costume going to be?"

Rory sat back on his haunches. "I finally decided on Robin Hood. How 'bout you?"

"I settled for something easy to wear. I'm going to be Francis Marion, the Swamp Fox."

Martin joined Rory beside the squeaking pups.

Carefully he picked one up and nestled it against his chest. "Looks like ol' General's become a papa again."

"Ya, I caught the resemblance too. Where is he, anyway?"

"My room. He snuck up there about an hour ago."

Rory pushed himself to his feet and walked over to the horse stalls, Martin not far behind him.

"Rory?" Martin said hestitantly, still unsure if he wanted to trust this man.

"Ya."

"You . . . you ever been in love?"

Rory gazed at him intently for a moment, then turned away. Martin breathed a quiet sigh of relief when he was no longer under Rory's scrutiny.

"Yes. I've been in love. Why?"

"I . . . I just . . . Well, I'm not too sure about this masked ball and . . . and everything."

A smile began to turn up the corners of Rory's mouth. "So you want to know about love and women. Is that it?"

Martin nodded, embarrassed.

"Sit down, Martin."

Brenetta's costume had arrived that morning from the dressmaker's along with Marilee's and Megan's. Megan and she had rushed to their rooms to try them on, and instantly upon seeing Brenetta in her Greek costume of Aphrodite, goddess of love, Megan had professed her hatred for her absurd fairy tale costume and began to cry. Marilee had been unsympathetic, telling her she was still too young, and if she kept acting like a child, she would miss the entire thing, spending the time in her room instead.

Although Brenetta felt a little sorry for Megan, she didn't dwell on it much. She was too pleased with the way her costume had turned out and was certain no one else would have anything like it. Once again she turned before her mirror, stretching her neck around to see the back, then turning to the front again.

The gown was made of sheer white linen. It draped her tall, slender figure, revealing the calf of her right leg. A cord of gold separated her breasts and circled her waist, then fell to the floor at her left hip. On her feet, she would wear gold sandals with long gold laces to weave up her legs. She had chosen more gold cord which would be woven intricately around her head and then down her back.

Brenetta knew it was a daring costume, sure to turn many a head. But the only head she wanted was Stuart's. She wondered if everyone felt this way when they fell in love for the first time.

Stuart rose early on the day of the ball. He had slept little, his nerves taut, his mind restless. Dressing quickly, he slipped down the back stairs and walked in the direction of the river. He clasped his hands behind his back and stared hard at the ground, chewing on his troubles thoughts.

He couldn't understand it. He'd always had a survivor's instinct; he'd always recognized the

202

surest road to reach his destination and taken it, no matter who he had to push aside or walk over to get there. He had come to recognize his own ruthlessness in matters of importance to him. He had accepted it as a necessary evil if he was to survive in this crazy world he'd been born into.

In addition, Stuart knew himself to be a consummate actor. So skilled was he at projecting any desired emotion, he had begun to wonder if he was able to truly feel anything honestly. Hardly a man yet—he would turn nineteen in just another week—he had nevertheless lived as a man for many years. He couldn't remember when he'd been just a boy, when he hadn't lived by his wits and cunning. So how was it that he was finding his head being turned by a mere child?

Stuart kicked at the ground as he thought of her again. Pretty Megan. She would never be the beauty Brenetta was and she would probably never achieve the natural grace and style of her older cousin either. She was spoiled and willful and impetuous, yet it was still Megan he was drawn to. It was still Megan he desired.

"Damn!" he swore under his breath.

He couldn't allow himself to think about her. It would ruin all his plans. He would lose his concentration, his air of assurance, and everything was so very crucial right now. For the past several weeks, he had courted Brenetta with all the flair and charm within him. He knew he had her right where he wanted her, and tonight he intended to propose. If he managed it right, he would be able to forestall his creditors. As soon as he could announce his engagement, they would be willing to pull in their teeth and wait for a chance to sink them into his father-in-law. They would know that that would be more profitable to them than foreclosing on a tired, little-worked plantation like Windjammer had become.

Megan was awake early. Her excitement over the ball, mixed with the certainty that the only man she could ever possibly love was lost to her, denied her another moment's rest. Thinking she would be the only one up in this predawn hour, she pulled a warm robe over her sleeping attire and left her room without even running a comb through her hair.

A light frost covered the lawn. She was glad for her warm slippers and robe, but it had been remarkably warm for November and Megan was certain it was going to be a perfectly lovely day for the party. She sat on a stone bench among the rose bushes and closed her eyes, hugging her shoulders against the chill. Oh, how she wished she had a beau for tonight. How she wished she had Stuart.

Looking up, it was as if her wish had been answered. Stuart was walking briskly away from the house, deep in concentration. With nary a thought to propriety or her appearance, Megan followed after him, no longer aware of the crisp air of dawn. When he stopped, leaning against a tree, she stopped too, trying to slow her racing heart, sure that he would hear it. She watched him for what seemed a long, long time, studying his face and form, wondering what it was really like to be kissed.

"Megan?" He had seen her.

She stepped closer.

"What are you doing out here so early?"

Suddenly she felt a little cold and unsure. She shivered. "I couldn't sleep. I . . . I saw you walking and followed. I'm sorry. I didn't mean to bother you. I . . . I'll go." She began to turn away.

"No! No, don't go."

She paused and waited.

"Megan."

He said her name softly, intimately, and she turned back around, finding herself staring into his eyes from less than a foot away.

"Megan, why did you come?"

The passions of her fourteen-year-old heart welled up and spilled forth, all other thoughts hopelessly lost to her. "Oh, Stuart, I love you. Please don't tell Brenetta. She has so much. I don't want anything, anyone but you. Can't you see that without you I'd rather be dead? Oh, love me, Stuart!"

She thrust herself against him and tilted her head back. His arms only hesitated a moment before they were wrapped around her back and his mouth was devouring hers. Megan was overwhelmed by the sensations his kisses ignited in her. Instinctively, she pressed herself tighter against his male hardness.

"Oh, love me, Stuart," she gasped as his lips released her. "Love me."

Yes. Yes, he would love her. Why couldn't he have them both, Brenetta for her money and Megan for . . . for everything else? She was willing. She had come to him and demanded it from him.

Stuart could feel her breasts through her robe; he could feel her arching, yearning body. Caution vanished. His only thought was wanting her, and he meant to take her now, right here in the cool morning with the trees as their bedchamber and the pine needles as their bed.

He released her just enough to cast a searching eye for the right spot. Instead, he met the cold gaze of Rory O'Hara. With a shove, he pushed Megan away, causing her to stumble and fall.

"Stuart!" she cried in surprise.

He didn't answer. Warily, he watched Rory's slow but steady approach.

"Adams."

"O'Hara."

Megan gasped and jumped to her feet, pulling her robe tighter about her. Neither of the men looked at her as she took a step closer to Stuart.

"Miss Bellman," Rory said gently, stopping her. "I believe you should be at the house. Come with me."

With that, the eye contact was broken. Stuart found himself staring at their receding backs. Upon the heels of their departure came panic. What if he told Brenetta?

"I've got to think," he said aloud. "I must think fast."

Brenetta had dressed with care this morning. Finding Megan's room already empty and the house still quiet, she had gone down to the library. She wanted to refresh her memory about Aphrodite so she could play the role with expertise. Pulling down a book of Greek mythology, she nestled into an oversized leather chair and began to read. She was only a little surprised when Stuart showed up at the door.

"I've been looking for you," he said.

He's so very handsome, she thought, laying her book aside and beckoning for him to join her. She smiled openly, her heart in her eyes. It wasn't until he sat down across from her that she realized he wore an extremely serious expression.

"Why, Stuart, whatever is the matter?"

"Miss Brenetta, I . . . I'm a little unsure how to tell you what I must."

"Can it really be so awful?" she asked, smiling at him.

His hand reached out and covered hers in her lap. She felt a tug at her heart as she looked upon the face she adored. He really was worried. Maybe he was going away. How awful that would be!

"Miss Brenetta, I think you know how fond I am of you. And I think . . . I *hope* you return the feelings."

"You know I do, Stuart."

"It's because I think you know me so well, and understand me, too, that I felt I could talk to you about this . . . unfortunate circumstance."

Brenetta was now thoroughly confused. What on earth could be causing him so much distress?

"I was out early this morning, getting a breath of fresh air, when I happened upon Miss Megan." He dropped his eyes, the color rising in his cheeks; then he cleared his throat. "She was obviously waiting for someone and she was dressed in her. . . er . . . rather inappropriately."

"Megan?"

He started to rise. "I'm sorry, Miss Brenetta. I don't think I can tell you after all. She is your cousin and your friend, and I don't think I feel right about . . ."

"You sit back down and tell me, Stuart. By the look on your face, someone in the family should know."

Looking grateful for her understanding, he continued as he lowered himself into his chair. "When she heard my step, she called out to . . . she called out a name as she turned around." He paused, then added, "A *man's* name."

"Oh, my! Whose?"

"Well . . . I . . ."

"Whose name did she call?"

"Ro . . . Mr. O'Hara's."

Her hand flew to her mouth. "No! You don't mean Megan and Rory . . ."

"I'm afraid so," he answered miserably, as if it were all his fault.

"Oh, what am I to do?" Brenetta groaned.

"I'm afraid that's not all, Miss Brenetta. When she saw it was me, she . . . ah . . . she threw herself at me. She swore if I told anyone, she would say it was me she was there to . . . ah . . . *meet*. Then she kissed me . . . rather shockingly well for her age, I'm ashamed to say . . ."

"Oh, Megan. Oh, dear!"

" . . . and when she let me go, *he* was there."

"Rory?"

Stuart nodded. "Yes. He gave her his arm and they walked off together." He looked so wretched. "I didn't know what was the right thing to do. I couldn't tell Miss Marilee that her daughter was making . . . assignations with . . . with Mr. O'Hara."

"Good heavens, no!" Brenetta cried, jumping up from her chair. She went to the window and stared out at the lawn.

"But," he continued, "I thought someone in the family should know before she . . . before she gets into any *real* trouble, before it's too late."

Brenetta turned to look at him. Her face revealed her inner disturbance. "You did the right thing in telling me, Stuart. I'll do what I can."

He crossed the room, stopping close, and took both her hands in his. He squeezed them firmly, then kissed them one at a time. He gazed into her eyes with love and concern. "You know I would do anything to keep from troubling your pretty head. If there'd been any other way . . ."

"I know, dear Stuart. Thank you."

He left then, and she turned back to the window, staring out without seeing a thing. Megan and Rory. It was more than she could believe; yet, if Stuart said it was so, how could she not believe him?

209

Marilee, as Marie Antoinette, greeted her guests as they arrived. She wore a powdered pompadour which was accented with topaz-colored stones of glass. An enormous farthingale supported her gown of bronze brocade. Her breasts were pushed high by the stiff corset beneath her low-cut bodice, and her neck was draped with chains of bronze and copper.

So busy had she been all day that she had failed to notice the strained air between Megan and Brenetta and Rory and Stuart. None of them had even come down yet. Alastair and Kingsley, dressed as court jesters, had been cheerfully running errands for her and the early arrivals. Martin was doing his best to play the host, mingling among their guests, complimenting costumes and making outrageous guesses as to who they were supposed to be and who they really were.

Most of them Marilee could recognize by their voices, but when a man entered dressed as an Arabian nomad—perhaps one of Ali Babba's forty thieves?—and refused to speak, she was stumped. His face was hidden in folds of material. Even his eyes seemed distant in the shadows of his flowing turban. He salaamed dramatically and moved on quickly, leaving her still puzzling over his identity.

Her mind was quickly drawn elsewhere, though, as three buggies and carriages, filled to overflowing, pulled up to the door at the same time. Laughter and gay chatter floated up the steps to her as the inhabitants untangled skirts and hoops, swords and spurs. Marilee felt her spirits rising in a joyous rush. Her worries over having everything be just perfect disappeared. She was young again, and she was going to enjoy herself as never before.

Megan met Stuart at the top of the stairs. Her face turned crimson, almost the same scarlet shade as her costume and mask. She hadn't seen him since this morning, and she seemed still able to feel his rough shove that had sent her tumbling to the ground. She wanted desperately to forget her disgraceful departure.

Rory hadn't said a word to her until they got inside the door. Stopping and looking at her grimly, he had said, "Remember, you're a young woman, Miss Bellman, and the daughter of a fine lady. Never forget who you are, no matter what." Then he had walked away, leaving her writhing with embarrassment.

But it was the scene with Brenetta that replayed in her head as Stuart bowed slightly to her, then hurried on down the stairs as if she had some terribly contageous disease. Brenetta had come to her room late this morning. She'd stood just inside the door, twisting a hankie with her hands as she chewed her lower lip.

"Megan, I must speak to you," she finally said.

"What about, Netta? Has something gone wrong for the party?"

Brenetta shook her head. "No, Megan. It's about you and . . . and what happened this morning."

Megan blanched. "How did you know?"

"That's not important, Megan," Brenetta said,

coming over and sitting beside her on the bed. "Really, dearest, I'm very worried. Have you been meeting him like this for long?"

"Oh, no!" she declared emphatically. "It just happened. I wasn't thinking, really I wasn't. And it wasn't his fault, either. I . . . I followed him out there," Oh, she was *so* ashamed. "I love him terribly Netta, and I just want him to love me."

Brenetta put her arm around Megan's shoulders and hugged her reassuringly. "I know, dear. He's a very wonderful and kind man. I've always thought so too. But I'm not sure he's right for you. You are only fourteen."

"I *do* love him, Netta. I really do."

"Then if it's supposed to be, it will work out. I only want you happy, and if you love him and he loves you, then you'll end up together. And I'll be happy for you both."

Megan was surprised by Brenetta's words. She was certain that Brenetta was after Stuart for herself.

"Well," Brenetta continued, "I won't say another word about it, and I won't tell Aunt Marilee, either. We'll just forget this morning ever happened if you promise to conduct yourself more properly around him."

"I promise."

She had been glad when Brenetta left. She'd been so certain Rory wouldn't tell anyone, but Brenetta had known so it must have been Rory who told. Now, as she watched Stuart hurrying down the stairs away from her, she felt like crying.

212

This was all Rory O'Hara's fault. Oh, how she hated him now!

Stuart, costumed in a smart Roman Centurion costume for his role as Marc Antony, could feel her watching him. He smiled at his hostess, all the time silently cursing her daughter. His slip this morning because of her wantonly chasing after him could have cost him everything. It was entirely her fault, and he wasn't going to let it happen again. In the hours since this morning's near catastrophe, Stuart had, with cold calculation and the skill of a surgeon, cut any romantic feelings he might have had for Megan completely from his heart.

One good thing—Brenetta had fallen for his story beautifully. Even in his agitation, he had performed as never before. He smiled now, remembering his words and actions. He had been truly superb.

He looked for her now. The rooms were beginning to fill with a myriad of costumed people—Henry the VIII, Napoleon, Jefferson Davis, Josephine, Queen Victoria, and those who were unrecognizable as anyone specific. He couldn't find Brenetta anywhere among them.

He did see Rory come in, dressed in Nottingham green, a quiver of arrows on his back and a long bow in his hand. Their eyes met and held briefly. Stuart was irritated to find he was the first to look away.

Carefully, he began to circulate. He knew it was

always important to be well liked by those in the proper circles. Even in times when so many were poverty-stricken, as was he, their influence carried much weight. He recognized Bellville's banker (no one else could be that fat) and moved steadily, yet unobtrusively, in that direction.

Brenetta was finally satisfied with her appearance. Her costume really was almost scandalously revealing, but she was unconcerned. She had caused sensations before in her shirts and britches. The only important thing to her now was that she knew she looked smashing. Stuart couldn't help but declare his love after seeing her in this.

The tunic fell softly over her body, emphasizing each and every curve of her figure. She had shaded her eyelids with a gold powder, then lined her eyes heavily with kohl. She had rouged her cheeks and lips and marveled at the difference this made.

Brenetta walked slowly along the upper landing, pausing at the top of the curved staircase. Looking down, she found the entry hall and both drawing rooms bustling with activity. She caught a glimpse of Rory and frowned. She hadn't found an opportunity to talk to him today. She was still surprised at Megan's profession of love for him. Though the girl had said she had followed him, Brenetta couldn't help but wonder if Rory just might return her feelings. She felt strangely piqued by the notion.

Then someone noticed her and the rooms began to fall silent. People moved closer to the doors of the drawing rooms to see what was causing such a breathless sensation. Forgetting all else, she looked about until she found Stuart. Then, eyes locked with his, she slowly descended the stairs.

She was so very beautiful. Never had Rory seen anyone like her. She seemed to float down the staircase, her eyes behind the mask looking out over the heads of her audience. Young she might be, but at all the New York parties and teas and dances he had attended, the rooms filled with debutantes and older beauties, he had never seen such an entrance.

Rory moved forward through the crowd. His heart beat faster in his chest. He wanted to hold her, to love her, to cherish her always. Perhaps tonight . . .

Suddenly he stopped. Stuart had stepped out from the throng of onlookers. He held out his arm to her and Brenetta placed her palm on top of his hand. Like a king and queen among their subjects, Stuart and Brenetta moved toward the east drawing room, the assembly parting before them to let them pass. Both tall and slender and elegant, they made a breathtaking couple.

The spell was broken as they left the hall. People began to talk excitedly.

"Have you ever seen anything so romantic?" someone said nearby. "Oh, if only a man would look at me like that, I would do anything in the world for him!"

Rory knew then that it was too late. He had lost her . . .

CHAPTER EIGHTEEN

NOVEMBER 1879—THE MERRY MAIDEN

The ship rolled and splashed as it had been doing for hours, yet Taylor hung tenaciously to the railing at the bow. Salt water sprayed her face, stinging her eyes. She welcomed the discomfort. It took her mind off their last days in London.

Brent had wasted no time making arrangements to leave. His concern for his wife and son had made him feel going home was urgent, and Taylor had agreed with him. She wanted to go home. She *had* to go home. She hoped she never saw any fog or heard a British accent again. Brent had managed to get them accommodations on the Merry Maiden, an American clipper ship heading for New York. They were the only passengers, the ship's purpose being that of transporting cargo, not people. The captain had graciously surrendered his cabin to Taylor and Carleton when they came on board.

"Glad t' have you aboard, ma'am. And might I say I'm hopin' things will go better for you and your family once your feet is set agin on the homeland," he had said in welcome.

"Thank you, Captain. I'm sure it will," she had replied.

As the sun began to sink into the sea, Brent joined her on deck. "Carl's asleep," he told her, gripping the rail to maintain his balance.

"Good. It's been a hard day for him. He was awfully seasick this morning again."

"He'll get used to it soon."

She agreed. "Maybe it will calm down tomorrow."

The skyline was on fire, the clouds near the horizon stained with red. Already the blue of the sky was turning a slate-grey color. A few stars were visible. Taylor gazed at the colorful scene and strained forward, urging the ship faster towards home as Brent's arm clung around her waist.

CHAPTER NINETEEN

NOVEMBER 1879—SPRING HAVEN

After the late supper was served, Stuart led Brenetta outside. They had said little all evening, spending the time mostly just looking at each other. It wasn't all acting on Stuart's behalf. He would have to be blind, and an idiot besides, not to want her. And he did want her. She was a very desirable woman. As Aphrodite, she seemed more available to him than she ever had before. As he led her into the gardens, he reminded himself to be careful not to move too quickly and frighten her away.

They sat on a stone bench, their only light coming from the midnight moon overhead, its rays filtering through the bare branches. Stuart sat a respectable distance away and again gazed at her. Her eyes were averted, her hands folded demurely in her lap.

"Miss Brenetta?"

She looked up at him.

"I know I should speak to your father first. I know I have no right to ask . . ." He paused for dramatic effect.

"Yes?" Brenetta prompted.

His confidence high, he proceeded. "Miss Brenetta, would you . . ." He stopped again and dropped to his knees. "Would you do me the honor of agreeing to give me your hand in marriage? I haven't much, mind you—just Windjammer, and it needs much work, but I'd promise to do everything in my power to make you happy."

There was a brief moment of silence before her smile lit the grove. "Oh, Stuart. I'd love to be your wife."

She fell into his arms. As he hugged her, instead of enjoying the feel of her through her scant costume, his mind began to drift to Windjammer. He could plant more fields, hire more hands. He could replace and restore. He could restock his stables. He saw himself dressed in fine new clothes astride a spirited horse as he surveyed his kingdom of Windjammer. Nowhere in this dream was Brenetta to be seen.

Many of the guests had departed; others who were staying overnight had retired. Marilee, exhausted yet exhilerated, bid goodnight to Charles Smith and his wife, Beth Ellen, then turned and found the mysterious nomad watching her. No one had ever guessed who he was, and he had remained mute all afternoon and into the night.

"Oh!" she gasped.

He motioned for her to be silent, then offered her his hand. I shouldn't take it, she thought. Perhaps he isn't even a friend. Perhaps he's a lunatic or something. She took it.

He led her down the hallway and out the back door. He never looked back at her, just kept walking at a steady pace until they reached the darkened, deserted slave quarters. Then he dropped her hand and without turning around, began to unwrap his turban.

Marilee waited, feeling a wonderful anticipation. Her heart seemed to pound to her ears as he turned to face her.

"Dear lord," she whispered, her knees crumpling beneath her.

He caught her before she fell, his lips brushing her forehead.

"Alan. Alan, it is truly you?"

"Truly, my love. It is I," he answered.

"I should have known your eyes. Even shrouded as you were, I should have known. Oh, Alan, it's been so very long!"

He helped her to her feet. Still holding her hand, he said, "You sent me away. I didn't choose to go."

Marilee nodded. "I had to."

"I know. And I promised to come back. Now here I am."

Suddenly, she pointed at his robes. "How did you know to come in costume?"

"This ball has been the talk of three counties for a month. I couldn't help but know about it." He smiled his crooked smile. "You make a ravishing Antoinette."

She curtsied low. "Thank you. And you make a noble khan, my lord."

He laughed with her as he salaamed once more. Then, sobering, he said, "I'm sorry about Philip."

She let him take her hand again and lead her into his old cabin where they sat on the thin tick mattress.

Alan pulled her head against his chest. "Tell me," he encouraged gently.

"Not now, Alan." She turned in his arms, brushing his lips with hers. "Not now. Just hold me close and let me be sure you're really here."

Rory closed his suitcase. Everything he needed to take with him was in it except the suit he would wear. He would leave as soon as it was light, riding to Atlanta and then catching the first train to New York.

He had tried to find Marilee but she had disappeared, and he hadn't wanted to disturb her if she had gone to bed. So he had settled for writing a note to leave for her, stating simply that urgent business had called him back to New York, and he was unsure when he would be able to return. He had added only a general farewell to Brenetta and all the others.

He poured himself a stiff whiskey and wondered if perhaps his father hadn't known more than Rory had given him credit for as he tossed the liquid back into his throat, feeling it burn its way down to his stomach.

Megan was the first one up, having been sent to

bed in the middle of the dancing. She'd had to miss the late supper and still felt insulted by being labeled a child by this action. Why, she could have had her choice of several men last night if she'd wanted. Brenetta wasn't the only pretty one.

Though it was early, the sideboard was already loaded with several breakfast choices. She was seated at the table, her plate filled with eggs, muffins and sausages, when Marilee and Brenetta entered together. No one spoke as they filled their plates, but Megan had the feeling both had something on their minds.

Brenetta took one small bite before laying down her fork. "Aunt Marilee, I just can't wait any longer to tell you. Megan, you too. Stuart asked me to marry him last night. I said yes."

Megan nearly choked on her muffin.

"Oh, I'm so happy! I'm going to write to Mother and Father today to tell them. I wish they were here right now. Of course, Papa will have to meet Stuart and give his permission before it's official but . . . oh, you *do* think he'll say yes, don't you? Papa *will* like Stuart, don't you think?"

Marilee smiled. "I'm sure he'll approve of Stuart, Brenetta, and I can see you're very much in love. That's the only way to be." She ended with a pleasant sigh, her face aglow.

Megan was barely managing to hold back her tears. She looked quickly down at her plate. Brenetta was going to marry Stuart! And after what she'd said yesterday about hoping Megan's love for him would work out. She was a liar. And a thief! She was stealing Stuart.

"I could hardly sleep last night," Brenetta continued. "I can hardly believe it's true! Wait until I tell Rory."

"Rory's gone," Marilee said abruptly.

"Gone?" Brenetta echoed.

"I'm sorry, dear. He left me a note. He said he was called to New York and left early this morning. I meant to tell you right away this morning but I forgot. Especially with your news."

"It's all right, Aunt Marilee, but I do wish I'd been able to share my happiness with him."

Megan couldn't take anymore. Bursting into tears, she ran from the room. She hated them. She hated them all.

Poor Megan, Brenetta thought as the girl fled the room. Rory left without even saying goodbye to her.

CHAPTER TWENTY

Rory sat behind the big desk, staring at the papers in front of him. The writing all seemed to run together, and at last he gave up and pushed them aside.

He'd been back in New York over a month now and all he could think about was Brenetta. He'd been seen almost nightly with one beautiful debutante after another on his arm, taking in the theatre and the opera, going to restaurants and private parties. A wealthy man now, having made many wise investments since coming to New York in seventy-five, Rory was an extremely desirable catch in the eyes of the young ladies as well as their mothers. Yet, no matter who he was with, it was Brenetta he saw in his heart, and he wandered from one brief romance to another.

He had been out late again last night and was now fighting off the sleep that was weighing down his eyelids. He didn't look up when he heard his door open, hoping whoever it was would go away.

"Rory, I've heard you were burning the candle at both ends. Now I can see it's true."

Rory jumped to his feet, wide awake. "Mr. Lattimer, when did you get back?"

They shook hands heartily. It had been almost five years since they'd seen each other, and they both stared, readjusting their memories to fit the present.

"Call me Brent, for Pete's sake. We arrived yesterday. Taylor and Carl are still at the hotel resting up. It was a difficult trip. Lots of bad weather."

"You must be tired, too," Rory said. "Let's sit down."

They moved across the room to a grouping of chairs near a large window overlooking the busy avenue.

"How's Carl? Was the operation a success?"

Brent shook his head sharply. "No."

"I'm sorry, Brent."

Rory could think of nothing else to say and they lapsed into silence.

"Rory, I . . ." Bob Michaels stopped short. "Gosh almighty! Brent!"

Once again hands were pumped and backs slapped. As they settled back into their chairs, Bob cleared his throat. "I sent you a wire. Now I see you didn't get it. Why didn't you let us know you were on your way back?"

Brent simply shook his head again.

"The operation failed," Rory answered for him.

"Brent, I'm sorry."

"Thank you. What was the news you wired me, Bob?" Brent asked, changing the subject.

"News from your daughter."

"Brenetta? Is everything all right?"

"Oh, yes. Everything's fine. She just asked me to try to get in touch with you. Thought I could get through to you quicker, I guess."

"What's the news?" Brent prompted.

"Seem's she's got herself engaged to some fellow from around Charleston somewhere. She's in a hurry for you to give your okay to this betrothel. Seems quite gone on him from her letters to me."

Rory listened mutely, his heart growing cold.

"What do you know about this, Rory?" Brent asked, shifting to look at him.

In a removed, impersonal tone, Rory answered, "Only what Bob's told you about the engagement. That happened after I left. I've met him, of course. He was a house guest while we were there."

"House guest?"

"Yes, sir. He's a cousin of a cousin of a cousin. That sort of thing."

Brent rubbed his eyes, looking bewildered. "What did you think of him?"

Rory's face revealed none of his true feelings. "She loves him, sir. That says a lot for him."

"No, Rory. That won't do. What do *you* think of him?"

"I'm not sure, Mr . . . Brent. To be honest, I'm a little over-protective of Netta." And I love her myself, his heart screamed. "He's a pleasant sort,

227

comes from a good family, has a plantation in South Carolina he's awfully proud of. I think you'd better meet him and decide for yourself."

"Yes, I'm going to do just that. And soon."

Taylor sat in the deep purple, chintz covered chair, her eyes staring at the picture on the wall, but her mind was a long way off. She was remembering the first time she had come to New York, nineteen years ago. She was eighteen at the time, wide-eyed and filled with the excitement of youth. Her first husband, David Lattimer, Brent's father, had brought her here as parrt of an extended, if somewhat delayed, honeymoon trip. She smiled now as she thought of the gaudy suite they had stayed in. She much preferred the warmth of this room. Perhaps it was having Brent and Carleton with her.

Rising from her chair, Taylor walked to the window. Below, she could see fashionable carriages carrying their passengers up and down the boulevard. The drivers were bundled against the icy air, their faces hidden in woolen scarves and their hands tucked back in the sleeves of their heavy coats. Occasionally one would stop in front of a shop, and the inhabitants would disembark and enter the store.

It hadn't been cold when she was here with David. It was late summer, and Taylor had enjoyed strolling along the avenues, carrying a frilled parasol, followed by her slave, Jenny, and shopping to her heart's content while David attended to his business at the bank. They had dined evenings in the best restaurants and been received into the homes of New York's elite society.

But it was their dinner with Brent she remembered best of all. Oh, how he had infuriated her with his "Yankee prejudices." Now she could admit that what had really troubled her was her attraction to him, but she hadn't recognized the truth then.

"Hello, love," Brent said as he opened the door.

Turning, she thought to herself, never could I have dreamed then that this man would fill my life with so much love and joy. She hurried into his arms, turning up her face to receive his kiss.

"Where's Carl?"

Taking his hand and leading him towards the couch, she replied, "In his room playing."

"I have some news from Brenetta."

"Really? How is she?"

"I'm not sure." He put his arm around her shoulders. "Rory and Bob tell me she's in love and has accepted a marriage proposal."

"Brenetta getting married?"

Brent laughed at her incredulous outburst. "Don't be so surprised, my dear. You weren't any older when you wed."

"And I wasn't in love, either," Taylor replied soberly, her earlier reminiscing still lingering in her mind. "Oh, Brent, I just want her to be happy."

"I know, Taylor. That's why we're going to get packed and head for Spring Haven now. I intend to meet this young man and see if he's right for my little girl. We'll leave tomorrow."

Taylor leaned her head against his chest; his

arm tightened around her. Brenetta engaged? Why, she was only a child! No. No, Taylor had to admit that Brenetta was no longer a child. And if she had found a man to love, a man who would love her too, then Taylor could only be happy for them both.

CHAPTER TWENTY-ONE

DECEMBER 1879—SPRING HAVEN

Brenetta couldn't believe the telegram. Her parents were back and would be at Spring Haven for Christmas. Quickly she pulled on her coat and went in search of Stuart. She found him with Alan Montgomery in the barn where they were applying salve to a colt's torn shoulder. She paused for a moment to watch them. She had never seen this side of Stuart. His coat off and shirtsleeves rolled up despite the chill, his hair falling carelessly across his forehead, his hands steadied the frightened colt while Alan worked in the medication. She liked the change from his usual perfection. It revealed his warmth, the love for animals she had known must be there.

When they turned the colt loose, he scrambled for his nickering mother with a cry, Brenetta hur-

231

ried on inside. "Stuart, they're coming! Mother and Father have left New York and will be here in time for Christmas."

He brushed the hair back from his face and slipped on his coat. "That's wonderful, Brenetta. I thought they were still in England."

"So did I. But they're not. They're almost here. Oh, Stuart, now Papa will meet you and we can plan the wedding!"

He kissed her forehead lightly. "Nothing could make me happier. The sooner you're my bride, the better." With a smile, he took her elbow and steered her towards the house.

His very touch seemed to burn her skin. She wished he would take her into his arms and *really* kiss her. He was always so proper, so reserved and polite. Just once she wished he would make love to her with his eyes and his kisses as she'd seen her father do with her mother.

Brenetta looked at him out of the corner of her eye and scolded herself. How could she want him to be any different than he was? He was absolutely perfect. And he was hers.

Stuart opened the door for her, and she stepped into the hallway. Things had changed radically since she had arrived here in May. With Rory's aid, Marilee had hired several negro house servants. Spring Haven, though still showing signs of the difficult years just past, was taking on the air of success, both in the house itself and in the land. And, remembering Alan's work with the injured colt just now, Brenetta had to admit that many of the most recent improvements could be attributed mostly to Mr. Montgomery.

In the excitement over her engagement and Rory's departure, Brenetta hadn't really noticed when he had become so entrenched as a member of the Bellman household, but there he was. And it wasn't until just last night that it had occurred to Brenetta that her aunt was in love with the peculiar-looking fellow.

Brenetta took off her cloak and Stuart hung it on one of the pegs by the back door. She shivered slightly from the cold air that had blown in with them.

"Let's get you by the fire," Stuart said. "I can't have you falling ill."

Fires were burning brightly in two of the three fireplaces in the east drawing room. Marilee was seated in a high-backed chair, her tambour frame set up before her. She was wearing a pair of wire-rimmed glasses and was concentrating hard on the embroidery pattern.

"Aunt Marilee, Mother and Father are coming here for Christmas," Brenetta announced, unable to hold back the news another moment.

"What?" Marilee cried. She had been so engrossed in her work, she had failed to hear them enter and so was startled as much by Brenetta's voice as by her announcement.

"It's true, Aunt. They're on the train right now."

As she was speaking, Stuart guided her to a chair facing her aunt, and she lowered herself into it. Stuart left her there and crossed to a long mahogany cabinet to pour himself a drink from the decanter of brandy sitting on its top. When he came back, he stood behind her chair, resting one hand on her shoulder.

"What do you think, Miss Marilee? Is Mr. Lattimer going to approve our betrothal?" he asked.

Brenetta thought be sounded nervous.

Marilee removed her glasses and laid them in her lap. Her expression was soft as she replied, "I'm sure he will, Stuart. He can't help but see the two of you are in love, and if I remember right, Brent could never deny Taylor or Brenetta anything."

Brenetta reached up and covered Stuart's hand with her own. "Aunt Marilee's right, Stuart. All my parents will care about is that you'll love and take care of me."

Stuart lay in his bed, tossing and turning sleeplessly. He didn't know if it was his conscience bothering him or if he was simply worried about whether or not the could pull it off. If he truly felt guilty, it would be the first time in a long, long time.

Throwing off the covers, he got out of bed and pulled on his pants. He lit a candle, then headed for the library, thinking that if he couldn't sleep, he might as well be doing something, even if it was only reading.

The house was caught in a quiet chill in the wee hours of the morning. Stuart made his way quickly towards his destination. Before he lit the lamp, he started a fire and waited beside it until he'd chased the chill from his bones. This accomplished, he picked up a nearby lamp and touched a flaming stick to its wick. He carried the light with him to a wall lined with books.

The library at Spring Haven was a treasury of the written word. There was a myraid of books, many dating back to before the American Revolution, a few even older. Ceiling to floor bookcases lined three walls, and a large, heavy oak table surrounded by matching chairs crowded the center of the room. Several more comfortable chairs were clustered near the hearth, and having chosen a book, Stuart nestled into one of these.

But instead of reading, he found himself staring into the fire. The flames disappeared from his vision, replaced by his memory of Windjammer. Gads, it would be good to go home. He had been away so long now, he was unsure what condition he would find it in. His mother was a pitifully helpless female who spent her days bemoaning all she had lost. His uncle, who had lived with them as long as Stuart could remember, was totally inept. Stuart's father, the older of the two brothers, had inherited Windjammer from his parents and had continued building and improving it. Stuart's Uncle James, however, had belonged to that special class of people whose only purpose in life was to be charming and gay and to spend money; it would never have occurred to him to actually *work* at anything.

Not so Stuart. By the time his father died when Stuart was thirteen, Stuart had absorbed all his love of the plantation along with all the knowledge he had to impart to his son. What he hadn't been able to leave was the money to make it all possible. Stuart had labored from sunup to sundown, trying to keep the place going, but he was working against desperate odds, two of the worst being his own mother and uncle. Finally, faced with disaster, he had learned to live by his wits, to take what he could, when he could, any way he could. The only thing that mattered to him was Windjammer, and he would do whatever was necessary to keep his home.

Stuart closed the book. It was no use; he couldn't read either. He was too conscious of the creditors closing in on him—like a pack of hungry wolves, their tongues hanging heavily from their powerful, teeth-filled jaws, the saliva drooling onto the ground. He hoped Uncle James would be able to use his charm to stall them just a bit longer until the official announcement of his engagement to Brenetta Lattimer could be made.

Once married, he could go home. He would be free to make Windjammer what it had been for his father and his father's father and *his* father before that. As for Brenetta, she could do what she pleased after the debts were paid. She could stay or go; it didn't matter to him. He was sometimes surprised at how cool his reactions to his bride-to-be were, and it was this that had kept him awake in his room. How it was possible for him not to care for someone as lovely and adoring as Brenetta, he didn't know. But the truth was he didn't care. He *really* didn't care.

And that was the crux of his entire problem. As Brenetta had said, all her parents would want was for him to love her. The strain of being constantly "on" was beginning to wear on his nerves; yet his work was only just beginning. He would have to play the lover for the entire engagement. He would have to press for an early wedding if he was to pull this off.

The carriage ride had been cold and miserable all the way from Atlanta despite the layers of warm blankets tucked around their laps and legs. Brent was sitting across from Taylor, Carleton in his lap. Both were sleeping fitfully. Taylor had pushed aside a corner of the window flap. A little more cold air would make no difference, and she wanted to be able to see. She couldn't believe it. It was as if she'd never left. Even with some homes gone and new ones having sprung up, everything looked surprisingly the same.

Once they had passed through Bellville, Taylor's anticipation increased. She was in truly familiar country now. She sat forward on her seat, leaning anxiously towards the home of her youth. If the carriage should break down now, she could still find her way, even blindfolded.

"Brent. Brent, wake up. Carleton, you too. Brent, we're almost there. Look!"

Pulling Carleton into her lap, she began to tell him about the passing countryside. "The road is lined with large oaks. Just the kind you like to climb at home. Do you remember? Right now, their limbs are all bare, but in the summer, they form a delightfully cool canopy. And if we stopped the carriage, we could walk to the river and then follow it almost right to Spring Haven's back door."

She fell silent, lost in one memory and then

another. The distance fell away under the pounding hooves and the spinning wheels.

"Oh, Carl, I can see the roof now. We're almost there."

Suddenly, they left the road. The driver slowed the horse to a jog.

"It's just as I remembered it," Taylor sighed as the house came into view. She hugged Carleton tightly, wishing he could see it. How could she describe it to a boy who had never seen anything?

Before she could begin to try, the front door opened and people began to pour out of the house. They stood on the portico, waiting for the carriage to reach them. As the driver pulled back on the reins, Taylor began pushing off the blankets. Brent opened the door and jumped to the ground, then held out his arms for their son. Taylor's feet had barely touched the driveway before Brenetta catapulted into her arms.

"Mama! Oh, Mama, you look wonderful. And you, too, Papa." She kissed each of them soundly, ending with Carleton. "Hello, little brother. I'm so glad you're back. I've missed all of you terribly."

Taylor looked at her daughter in disbelief. She hadn't realized—or had she just conveniently forgotten—how grown-up Brenetta was. When they bid her farewell seven months before, she had been dressed as a woman but Taylor had still seen the child within. Now it seemed that the child had disappeared for good.

"Come say hello to everyone," Brenetta was urging them.

Marilee was standing at the top of the stairs,

waiting her turn. They hugged each other, crying all the while. Then Taylor met the children.

"Little Phil?" she whispered as she shook Martin's hand.

He shrugged. "The name didn't stick. It's Martin."

Turning to the pretty blonde with the suspicious brown eyes and slight pout at the corners of her mouth, Taylor said, "Can this be Megan Katrina?"

Megan pecked her lightly on the cheek but said nothing, so Taylor moved on.

Alastair and Kingsley were entirely different matters. They jubilantly welcomed their aunt and uncle. Taylor laughed as she received their enthused hugs and kisses and tried to answer their many questions about the ranch and London and the ship and . . .

Erin Alanna was a charming little girl with a friendly smile. She was not really pretty compared to her sister or her cousin Brenetta, but she had charm and Taylor instantly loved her.

"And this is a friend of Aunt Marilee's, Mr. Montgomery," Brenetta said, finishing the introductions.

"How do you do, Mr. Montgomery?" Taylor asked, offering her hand.

He smiled a lop-sided grin as he took her hand firmly. "Very well, thank you, Mrs. Lattimer. I hope your journey here wasn't too uncomfortable."

Her eyes darted quickly back to Erin Alanna, then returned to him with the dawning of awareness. She quickly rejected her suspicion as impossible. "No, Mr. Montgomery. It wasn't too uncomfortable."

"Speaking of comfortable," Marilee interjected, "let's get inside where it's warm."

Taylor let Marilee link arms with her and guide them inside. Alastair and Kingsley quickly appointed themselves as Carleton's guides and caretakers, whisking him away up the stairs to their room. Eliza, one of the negro maids, took their coats.

Taylor and Brent were cozily settled on the settee in front of the fire before Brenetta approached them again, this time on the arm of an extraordinarily handsome young man. "Father. Mother. I'd like to introduce Stuart Adams. Stuart, these are my parents."

Stuart found himself looking into a pair of eyes identical to Brenetta's. Only these were decidedly more shrewd, belonging to a man who had lived through many different experiences and seen many different kinds of people. It would not be an easy job, fooling this man.

His lazy smile making him appear more self-assured than he felt, Stuart shook hands with his future father-in-law. "Mr. Lattimer, I've waited a long time for this opportunity. Perhaps we can have a private talk later." Turning to Taylor, he bowed, saying, "I can certainly see where Brenetta gets her beauty, Mrs. Lattimer."

"Thank you, Mr. Adams. Please, sit down so we can relax and have a friendly chat."

His hand on Brenetta's elbow, he took her to a divan nearby. They sat down, Stuart watching her with what he knew to be a loving expression.

"I understand you have a plantation near Charleston, Mr. Adams," Taylor said.

"Yes, ma'am."

"Has it been in your family long?"

Stuart didn't have to pretend now. He answered Taylor enthusiastically. "Since the early 1700s, Mrs. Lattimer. It's a fine old place, built to withstand the rain and hurricanes and whatever else Mother Nature can throw at her."

Brent was frowning thoughtfully. "I was with Sherman's Army of the West when it went through Charleston. You were lucky to keep your plantation."

Stuart's jaw stiffened. "I don't remember it, of course. I was barely four at the time. But I heard my father talk about it. They didn't leave us much, it's true. The paddies were ruined, the barns burned, the fences ripped up. Only one thing saved the house. My aunt had the pox. The soldiers wouldn't come near the place. After they'd gone, she said she was happy to know she'd saved Windjammer from those—excuse me, sir—dirty Yanks. Then she died."

"Mr. Adams," Brent said quietly, "I've spent nearly fifteen years trying to forget what we did to the South. I'm not proud of it. I'm only glad it ended so Taylor and Brenetta and I could leave, and go some place to start over." He paused, stood and walked to Stuart. "I'd like to think the South can forgive me my part in it. I'll start with you."

Stuart had also risen. The two men studied each other, the room totally silent around them. Then

Stuart held out his hand to take Brent's. "Sir, the South can rise above anything. I fell in love with Brenetta. I certainly can't hold being a Yank against her father."

They shook hands firmly and Stuart knew he had done it. Fate had offered him a sterling opportunity, and he hadn't failed to seize it.

CHAPTER TWENTY-TWO

FEBRUARY 1880—SPRING HAVEN

Her chin held high in resolve, Megan walked quickly along the side of the street. There was no sidewalks in this neighborhood on the outskirts of Atlanta, only the fronts of the delapidated buildings. Her heart was pounding madly as she paused before the squalid shanty that was her destination. A crude sign was hanging askew on the door, announcing that Mama Rue was in. Megan knocked. The door creaked open before her, but she couldn't see anyone. The inside was pitch dark; the stale air, thick with incense, rushed out to meet her.

"White gal, you got bizness wid big Mama Rue?"

Megan still couldn't see anyone, but she swallowed hard and answered the deep voice. "Yes . . . please."

"Come in, gal."

Quelling the urge to turn and run, Megan forced herself forward into the dark interior. The door closed slowly behind her. Then someone took her arm and steered her through another doorway, lifting aside a heavy blanket that served as the door.

Her eyes were becoming adjusted to the dark, and Megan could see a low table surrounded by ragged pillows. Her escort—she could see it was a man now—indicated she should sit on one of them and she obeyed quickly. A match struck against wood. The sudden flash threw a sinister contrast of light and dark on his face, giving the ancient negro a menacing, evil countenance. He touched the match to an urn in the middle of the table, then blew out the tiny flame. A heavy smoke began curling towards the ceiling from the urn. As the incense's sickly-sweet smell filled her head, the man shoved a battered tin cup into her hands and told her to drink. Too frightened now to refuse, she forced the bitter liquid down.

Then, from behind another curtain, stepped Mama Rue. A massive black woman, her head wrapped in a red turban and her body covered in a flowing, tent-like robe, she plopped down across from Megan, peering at her with cold eyes.

Megan wanted to get up and flee but her knees seemed to be made of slush. She wondered if she might even be dreaming all of this, so unreal did it seem to her now.

"You need magic from Mama Rue," the woman said.

Megan nodded in affirmation.

"You want Mama Rue get you man."

"Yes," Megan whispered. "Yes, that's right."

Mama Rue leaned forward. "You willing, girl, take chance?"

A drum began beating somewhere, the slow rhythm thumping against her temples. Megan was unconsciously swaying with it as she answered, "Yes. Yes, anything."

"Love spell dangerous work."

"I . . . I don't care," she replied.

"Cost plenty."

Megan, her eyes barely open as she rocked to the beat of the drums, took her coin purse from where it was hidden in her sleeve and pushed it across the table. Mama Rue dumped its contents onto the table. Her eyes glittered as the coins rolled and settled before her.

"Mama Rue get you man."

Marilee sat in the velvet-covered chair, eyeing the bolts of fabric Miss Harburough had laid out for her.

"What do you think, Marilee?" Taylor prompted her.

Marilee shook her head. "I don't know. They're all so lovely, I just can't decide. You choose, Taylor."

"But I won't be living with it, Marilee. No, you must decide for yourself."

Miss Harburough stepped closer. "Perhaps Mrs. Montgomery would like to see some other choices."

Marilee looked up at the woman, a lovely smile

lighting her eyes. How she loved to be called that. "No, thank you, Miss Harburough. These are quite enough. I'll just take a moment more to look them over."

"Yes, ma'am."

The proprietress moved away a respectful distance and waited as Marilee tried to resume her study of the fabrics.

"Marilee, are you daydreaming again?" Taylor whispered in her ear.

Looking sheepish, Marilee was forced to admit she had been and nodded guiltily.

Taylor stood up, her blue eyes twinkling in conspiracy. "Miss Harburough, I'm afraid we'll have to come back another time with our decision. Mrs. Montgomery isn't quite herself today." She took Marilee by the arm and propelled her outside.

"Taylor, really, I'm sorry."

"Don't be silly, Marilee. And perhaps you're right. Maybe I'd better make the choices. You're too much in love to think about new draperies and new fabric for chairs and couches. If it's left up to you, you'll probably end up with an orange and purple dining room or some other terrible combination to ruin a person's digestion."

The color rose in Marilee's cheeks. She had been Mrs. Montgomery for only four weeks, and she had found she was as bad as any young bride would be. Her thoughts were already drifting off to her husband, no matter what she was doing. The ceremony had been a quiet one in the parsonage in Bellville. With only her children, Brent and

246

Taylor, and Brenetta and Stuart looking on, Marilee and Alan had repeated their vows, becoming man and wife. Sometimes she was still unable to believe it was true.

Marilee was certain Taylor had guessed that Erin Alanna was Alan's child and was grateful she had never mentioned that she knew the truth. No one else had ever seemed to see the resemblance. Perhaps they were too used to Erin Alanna's looks, forgetting that Alan had been at Spring Haven before she was born. Whatever the reason, Marilee was glad she wasn't forced to acknowledge her guilt to anyone.

Of course, Alan knew. He had known the moment he'd heard her name, the moment he'd known Marilee had borne another child, even before he'd seen her. Bless his heart, she thought now, he never treats her differently than the others just because she's his own flesh and blood. He loves them all just the same.

Taylor led the way into the dining room of their hotel. They sat at a table near the window. Taylor ordered tea. "Perhaps we should go back to Spring Haven and return to Atlanta in a few weeks," she said to Marilee when the waiter had gone. "The wedding is still four months away. We have accomplished quite a bit actually."

"Yes, maybe you're right. It does seem we've been gone a long time."

"It's settled then. We'll all go home tomorrow." Taylor sipped the tea the waiter had served. "Do you suppose Megan would like to join us?"

Marilee shook her head. "I doubt if she's back

from shopping yet. She's probably going wild. Remember how it was for us when we were girls?"

Megan, her eyes glazed, stumbled along the uneven surface of the dusty road. Her hand clutched tightly the tiny vial Mama Rue had given her as she left. She was to drink it when she had Stuart alone. Mama Rue had promised he wouldn't be able to resist her then.

Eliza was waiting nervously where Megan had left her. "Miss Megan, I was gettin' powerful worried."

Megan didn't answer. She just kept walking. Eliza fell in behind her, carrying the few packages Megan had purchased before going to see Mama Rue. When they reached the hotel, Megan went directly to her room where she fell across her bed and was quickly asleep, her mind still filled with a ceaseless beating of drums.

Brenetta wandered aimlessly through the house, her hands trailing idly across the tops of nearby furniture. She felt restless and bored and wished she had gone to Atlanta with her mother and Aunt Marilee. She would have, but once she learned Megan was going, she changed her mind. Brenetta didn't know what had come over Megan in the past few months. What had begun as a warm friendship between the two cousins had soured suddenly. Megan was rude and surly whenever the two were alone together. When they were with others, she was coldly polite, but Brenetta was always aware of the hidden thread of animosity woven through her every word and action.

Pausing at the dining room window, she gazed out at the lawn. Already the grass was beginning to look a little greener. Soon the trees would be blossoming, birds nesting in their limbs. Soon the lawn would be covered with chairs and wedding guests, and she would walk down a grassy aisle in her grandmother Christina's wedding gown, just like her mother had done over twenty years before. She pressed her forehead against the cool glass. Oh, how she wished June was here already. And how she wished Stuart would get back. She felt lost without him.

Shortly after the new year began, Stuart had returned to Windjammer. He had told her that there was much to be done if he was to bring his bride home with him in June, but he had promised to return before March.

"Oh, I wish Papa had let us wed sooner," she whispered aloud. "Then I'd be there with him now."

"So, all this love and gush has made you lose your mind at last. Talking to empty rooms."

Brenetta swung around to look into Martin's teasing face. She smiled too. "I'm afraid so, cousin. Now you know the truth about me. Please don't tell a soul."

"Oh, I won't. How would I look if I had to admit to having a cousin who talks to empty rooms? It'll stay our secret."

Brenetta laughed at his mock seriousness. She had grown to like Martin ever so much more than she had at first. Even his bitterness towards her father seemed forgotten. She knew his friendship with Rory had made more of a difference in him than anything else; she also knew Martin corresponded regularly with him. She'd only written Rory a few times herself. His replies had seemed somehow restrained, but she had only noticed it in passing. The letters were quickly forgotten in the excitement and busyness at Spring Haven.

"Oh, I nearly forgot. There's a letter for you."

"From Stuart?" She stepped quickly forward, her face brightening.

Martin held out the letter, then pulled it abruptly back, hiding it behind him with a mischievous grin. "And what if it is?" he asked.

Her smile vanished. "You give me that letter, Martin Bellman. Right now!" She waved her arm in a threatening gesture.

"All right. All right. Don't lose your sense of humor over him. I don't think he's worth that."

Brenetta's face clouded at his thinly veiled insult. Whether he meant it that way or not, she resented it. Taking the letter from him, she swept by him into the drawing room where she seated herself by the large picture window and tore open the much awaited missive.

Brenetta, (no "darling," she thought with disappointment)

I apologize for not writing more frequently. There has been much to do here and little time to do it in. And I'm afraid money is in scarce supply. Mother again sends her best and looks forward to meeting you come June.

*I will be returning to Spring Haven in three or
four weeks. Say hello to all. I miss you and I
love you.*

> *Yours faithfully,*
> *Stuart*

She sighed as she let the paper slip to her lap.
His letters were somewhat less than exciting. She
wished he would be a bit more romantic or tell her
more about what he was doing.

"There I go again," she mumbled. "Thinking of
ways I'd like to change him. And I love him so just
as he is. Only . . ."

Only she wished he would sweep her passionately into his arms and beg her to run away with
him to New Orleans or to Rome or London or a
million other places. If only . . .

"Hello, Netta. How's my favorite daughter?"

Brenetta looked up as her father entered the
room. He had been working on the barn all day,
patching and mending and replacing. He looked
very tired.

"I'm fine, Papa. Sit down and let me get you
something to drink. Tea? Brandy?"

He stopped her from rising. "No thanks, pet.
Just sit beside me awhile. That's all I need. Just
your company."

She squeezed his strong hand, gazing at him
tenderly. "You miss Mother a lot, don't you? Even
when she's away just a few days." Suddenly she
understood better the special closeness between
her parents because of her own love for Stuart.

"You've pegged me," Brent said with a chuckle. "I'm worthless without her."

Brenetta laid her head against his shoulder, still holding his hand. She closed her eyes and relaxed. "When did you know you wanted to marry Mother? Was it long after Grandfather died?"

"I don't know, love. Seems I've always loved her."

"I know that, Papa. But when did you realize you were in love? How did you feel?"

Brent stroked her hair. "Well, I'd only met your mother a few times before the war started. She was quite the Southern belle, your mother was. She made my father very happy."

It was something Brenetta had always found incredible to think about, that her mother had been married to her Grandfather Lattimer when she was just Brenetta's age. Her parents had always talked about it with reticence. This time Brenetta persisted.

"Did you fall in love with her while Grandfather was still alive?"

His hand stopped its stroking for a moment. She could almost feel his struggle for the right words. When they came, she was not surprised.

"Yes, Netta, I did. And I suffered because of it. But your mother loved her husband, and I went away to keep from causing pain or worry to either of them."

"And then the war started," Brenetta continued for him, "and you came through enemy territory to see if she was all right and, since Grandfather had died, you proposed and were secretly married."

He took a deep breath. "Yes," he said finally. "That's pretty much how it was."

Brenetta sat up, turned and kissed his cheek. "Well, as wonderful as it's been for you and Mother, I'll be even happier because Stuart and I will have only had each other to love and no one to keep us apart."

"My dearest daughter," he answered gently. "No one could be happier for that than your mother and I."

Brent left the room a short while later. He was always uncomfortable when Brenetta asked him about those early years. He hated lying to her, but what else could they do? It would only hurt her to know the truth.

And it wasn't *all* lies, he thought as he left the house. He *had* gone away to keep from hurting his father. Taylor and Brent had both denied their love in order to protect David. But when Brent returned in the midst of war, only to find his father dead, murdered by Matt Jackson, their love flourished. Oh, he had wanted to marry her desperately, but how could they? He was a Union officer behind Rebel lines. Brent remembered so clearly the day Jeffrey Stone discovered him and warned him to leave or be captured. He thought Taylor would go with him and they would marry once they were out of the South, but she refused to go. Later they both learned she had misunderstood a remark she chanced to overhear and thought he didn't love her after all. So he had left her behind, not knowing she was pregnant with his child.

Lost in the past, Brent's feet had carried him beyond the barn, through the woods, and to the river. He sat down on a boulder and plucked a dry weed out of the ground. Sticking it in the corner of his mouth the chew on, he continued his train of thought.

Desperate and forsaken—or so she believed—Taylor had married Marilee's cousin, Jeffrey. He was a good man and he loved Taylor. Brent couldn't hold anything against him, even if it was Jeffrey who caused Brent to flee without Taylor, at least indirectly. Jeffrey had known whose child Taylor was carrying when he married her; he had known his wife was in love with the father of her child. Yet he had loved Taylor and loved Brenetta, too. Yes, Jeffrey Stone had been a good man. His death, like all the others during those gruesome four years, had been a tragic waste.

Perhaps they had been wrong to keep the truth from Brenetta, but what purpose could it have served? Someone so young couldn't understand all they had gone through, all they had risked and suffered because of their love.

No, Brent thought. It was best they'd never told her. Those who'd known Brenetta wasn't Jeffrey's child had thought she was David's, not knowing that his and Taylor's marriage had been a platonic one, a marriage in name and affection but never one in bed. Most were gone now, moved away or deceased, and none but Marilee were around who knew the whole story. Brenetta had grown up in Idaho where there was no one to dispute the years her parents had been married. She had been raised surrounded by security and love instead of shame and distrust.

"And, by damn, she'll never know anything except love if I can help it," Brent said to the river, tossing the weed into the water and watching it rush away on the current.

CHAPTER TWENTY-THREE

MARCH 1880—NEW YORK CITY

The sharp wind whistled around the corner of the building, blasting him in the face as he climbed out of his carriage. It was fitting weather for Rory's mood. His hand went quickly to his hat in order to keep it from flying away, and he walked swiftly through the door, held open by a smiling doorman.

"Good morning, Mr. O'Hara," he said in greeting.

"Mornin'," came Rory's curt reply.

His stony face warned the employees that this was a day to avoid Mr. O'Hara, and most of them quickly bent their heads and looked preoccupied with business. Rory stepped into his office and closed the door firmly behind him. After tossing his hat carelessly towards the hatrack, he removed his heavy coat and sat behind his desk, then twirled his chair to face the window.

New York. A bustling doorway of America. Home of commerce, industry, great wealth and opportunity, it was also the home of the homeless, the poor, the immigrants, and the hopeless. Rory was fed up; he was finished. He had awakened this morning knowing he couldn't stand it any longer. As soon as he could arrange it, he was going home to Idaho. If Brent didn't want him at Heart's Landing, then he would make a living on some other cattle ranch. There were other ranches, other herds to be tended, either in Idaho or Montana or Wyoming or . . . or someplace. It didn't matter as long as he was out of New York.

A timid knock on the door brought a growled, "Come in."

Mrs. Walters, a young widow who had replaced Mr. Johnson as his secretary, opened the door just enough to poke her head in. "I have your mail, sir."

"Thank you, Mrs. Walters. Just put it on my desk."

The plain little woman, dressed in a severe black dress, her hair pulled demurely to the back of her neck where it was caught in a bun, obeyed quickly. In her short time here, she had learned to recognize her employer's black moods and to leave him alone as much as possible until they blew over. Seeing her scurry away, Rory sighed. Gads! he thought. I've become a regular tyrant. Now I know I've got to get away from here.

Sifting through the envelopes, his eyes fell on

Martin's rambling scrawl. Unsure if he wanted to know what was going on at Spring Haven, yet unable to resist, he opened the letter and began to read.

Dear Rory,

You wouldn't hardly know this place since you left. In preparation for the big wedding, everything is being redone or recovered or replaced, compliments of Uncle Brent and Aunt Taylor. (My father must be turning in his grave!)

Alan is making his presence known in the fields. Already I can see we'll have double the crop from last year. He's got the boys and me working like darkies—but so did you!—and I really don't mind. I guess I kind of like him. I wasn't too sure about Mother and him marrying but I think it's all right now. He's kind of funny looking, as I've written you before, and he really isn't from a family of any prominence that I've heard of, but he's fair with everyone and he loves Mother. I don't think you'd recognize her anymore, she's so happy.

Stuart Adams is supposed to return any day now, and I'm sure glad. Netta's been moping around here like a sick calf. Her Prince Charming's not much for letter writing.

Megan is still acting weird. I don't even feel like I know her. Sometimes it seems like she looks right inside of you and her eyes are as cold and hard as ice. You'll see what I mean when you come for the wedding.

Hope all is well in New York.

Your friend,
Martin Bellman

"When I come for the wedding," Rory mumbled. As much as he had tried to forget, his heart still ached when he thought of Brenetta marrying someone else. He didn't think he could bear going to the wedding.

Again Mrs. Walter's knock brought his head up.

"I'm very sorry to disturb you again, Mr. O'Hara, but there's a gentleman out here who insists on talking to someone in charge. Mr. Michaels won't be in until much later. Can you see him?"

Rory tried to smile reassuringly, hoping to allay her fear of his temper. "Yes, I'll see him, Mrs. Walters. Send him in."

The gentleman who brushed past Mrs. Walters did not seem to be in a much better mood than Rory was. His agitation was clear on his round, leonine face. His greying mustache twitched as he pushed his glasses up the bridge of his short, broad nose.

Rory rose from his chair. "I'm Mr. O'Hara. How can I help you?" Indicating the chair opposite him, he added, "Please be seated."

"My name is Pinkham, Ross Pinkham," the man said as he settled into the chair, holding his briefcase on his lap.

Rory nodded and waited for Mr. Pinkham to continue.

"Mr. O'Hara, my family owns a small mercantile

and warehouse business in South Carolina. We are not wealthy but we have tried to help out our neighbors and friends whenever we could. Sometimes we would extend credit for staples from our store. Or at times we have advanced money on expected crops." Mr. Pinkham shifted in his chair, once again stabbing at his glasses with his middle finger of his left hand.

Rory waited patiently, wondering what on earth he was leading up to. New York seemed an unnecessarily long way for a small businessman from South Carolina to come for a loan.

Ross Pinkham cleared his throat. "Mr. O'Hara, one of the families we've tried to help since hard times befell them has . . . well, they seem to have taken a great deal of advantage of our generosity, as well as the generosity of many others. What I'm trying to say is they've borrowed heavily from everyone in the county."

"I'm afraid I don't follow the connection with our bank, Mr. Pinkham. Has this family borrowed from us too?"

"No. At least, not that I know of. No, Mr. O'Hara, my purpose is of a much more personal nature."

"Please continue."

"Well, it appeared as if the foreclosure on their plantation was inevitable. We all believed the widow and her son and brother-in-law would all soon be both homeless and penniless. And believe me, the plantation would not have brought the money that was owed, not in these difficult times. Only the more powerful of the creditors would have gained from foreclosure." Again he cleared his throat. "But, then the boy managed to arrange a brilliant marriage to a girl from a wealthy family, and so we have continued to wait."

A vague uneasiness began to nag at the back of Rory's mind.

"Recently we were all promised payment in full after the June wedding," Mr. Pinkham went on. "It's this that brought me to New York. While the others have agreed to hang on a little longer, I'm afraid if we don't receive at least part of that money now we will be in as serious a situation as . . ."

"As the Adams family," Rory finished in a dull tone.

Mr. Pinkham's grey eyes dropped to his hands, still clutching his case. He nodded.

"So Mr. Adams has promised all his creditors that his new father-in-law, Brent Lattimer, will clear his debts?" Rory asked.

Again the man nodded.

"Mr. Pinkham, I do not have the authority to release funds for Mr. Lattimer from his personal account and he is in Georgia awaiting the marriage. Just how much are we discussing?"

Rory's visitor opened his briefcase and slid the folder across his desk. Almost hesitantly, Rory opened it to peer at the figures. He sucked in his breath. "So much?" he asked Mr. Pinkham.

"I'm afraid James Adams has a very persuasive, golden-edged tongue. Somehow we always believed payment was on its way—just around the corner, so to speak."

"But five thousand dollars.?" To a *small* mercantile business? he wondered silently. "If he owes you this kind of money, what must his total debts be?"

Mr. Pinkham shrugged. "However much it is, it's a great deal, you can be sure."

Rory swiveled his chair around to the window. He was certain Brent was unaware of these debts and the claims for payment. He had no idea what kind of dowry or inheritance or allowance had been agreed upon between Brent and Stuart, but he was equally certain this had not been discussed. Although Stuart had never pretended Windjammer was a prosperous plantation, he had given everyone—Rory included—the impression that he was capable of supporting a wife. Suppose his only motive for marrying Brenetta was for money? Rory was convinced this was the case. Why else would Stuart hide the truth? If he'd told them the truth, he would have been recognized as a fortune hunter, that's why. But if he really loved Brenetta, wouldn't he have wanted to tell her everything? Wouldn't he have been honest with Brent and told him what dire circumstances he was in? Rory had to learn the truth, and he had to learn it in time. He would leave New York before week's end.

Turning abruptly, he said to a startled Mr. Pinkham, "I will personally clear this debt, sir, but only on the condition that you do not inform the other creditors I have done so. I will have the proper papers drawn up. Excuse me."

CHAPTER TWENTY-FOUR

MARCH 1880—SPRING HAVEN

Brenetta leaned against Stuart's shoulder as they stood together on the veranda. The quiet spring evening spread a blanket of contentment over the plantation, and Brenetta felt the peace of her own joy filling her heart. The house was drowned in silence; everyone else had retired long ago. As she stood beside her future husband, Brenetta wondered dreamily what it would be like for them as man and wife at Windjammer. A soft sigh slipped through her parted lips.

"It's time we turned in, Brenetta," Stuart said.

"Oh, not yet, Stuart. You've been away so long and we've hardly had a moment together."

"But I won't be leaving again. I've traveled a long way today and I'm tired."

She was ashamed of herself. "Of course. I'm sorry for being so selfish."

Stuart kissed her lightly on the cheek. "I'll walk you to your room. Come along."

At her door, he kissed her once again on the cheek and walked down the long hallway, disappearing around the corner. Again, she sighed. Her contentment vanished almost as quickly as it had come. She wanted so badly to spend more time with him. Why did he never seem to feel the same way? Were men so very much different or was he just in better control of his emotions? she wondered as she closed the door behind her.

Stuart paused at his own door, looking back down the hall. For the hundredth time, he wondered at himself, at his lack of feelings for Brenetta. For that matter, he seemed to have very little feeling about anyone, one way or another, anymore.

He opened the door to his room, expecting to find it dark. Instead, a candle flickered on his bedside stand, its light casting wavering shadows about the room. One of these shadows stepped forward.

"Megan? What are you doing here?"

He watched her drink quickly from a tiny glass vial before she answered. "I had to see you alone, Stuart," she said, tossing the vial into a corner of the room.

Stuart ran his hand through his hair, feeling too tired to deal with this. He was too worn out to pretend, to carefully think about each and every word as he was forced to do when with Brenetta. Dropping into a chair, he asked wearily, "What is it you want?"

"I want you. Don't you know that I love you? I would do anything for you. Anything at all."

Stuart stared at her. Her eyes seemed a bit glazed as she loosened her hair, shaking the golden tresses free to hang down her neck and over her shoulders.

"Megan, go away. I don't love you. I don't want you here. All I want in this world is to live at Windjammer and be left alone to enjoy the pleasant life my grandfather knew there."

"Do you think Brenetta can give you that pleasant life? Well, she can't. She can't!"

Her voice was rising to a dangerous pitch, and Stuart jumped up from his seat. He covered her mouth with his hand, but she shook free of it.

Whispering now, her eyes wide and dilated, she continued. "Mama Rue promised and you can't help it."

"What . . ." he began.

Megan's arms flew around his neck and she kissed him boldly, her breath coming in tiny gasps. She curved her body to meet his, demanding his closeness.

"Megan, stop that," he mumbled against her tightly pressed lips.

"No, I won't stop," she cried as he pushed her away. "I can't stop. Look at me, Stuart. You must love me. You have to love me. You *have* to!" She grasped the collar of his shirt and yanked him forward. The material gave under her frantic strength, tearing down the front.

"Are you crazy?" he hissed.

"Yes! Yes, I'm crazy over you."

With surprising quickness, she grabbed the

collar of her own dress and ripped open the bodice, the tiny buttons flying in all directions.

Stuart gaped, wondering what to do with her. Then suddenly he knew what he wanted to do. He grabbed her roughly, catching her hair in his hand, jerking her head back to receive his kiss. When their lips parted, his eyes felt as wild as hers as he pushed her onto his bed.

When Megan opened her eyes sometime in the wee hours of the morning, she was amazed to find herself in a strange bedroom. Turning her pounding head on the pillow towards the still flickering candle, she gasped. There beside her lay Stuart, his bare chest rising and falling in gentle slumber. It was then she realized she was also naked and her whole body ached. She felt as if she'd been beaten. But it was her head that caused her the most pain. She could remember nothing after she came to Stuart's room to wait for him.

Somehow she knew there was no going back; whatever had happened last night—and she had no idea what it was—would happen again. Naive she might be, but she knew only married people were supposed to share the same room and the same bed. Perhaps Mama Rue had kept her promise after all. Perhaps Stuart was really hers now.

Megan slipped out from under the covers. Gathering her tattered dress and chemise against her breasts, she crept out of his room and to her own.

Stuart lay still, feigning sleep until he was sure

she was gone. When the door clicked shut behind her, he opened his eyes, staring up at the ceiling. A self-satisfied smile began to stretch the corners of his mouth. At least he could say he felt something for someone at last. No, it wasn't love. He was a good liar but he never lied to himself. Though he had wondered briefly when he'd first met Megan if he couldn't love her, it was only desire he felt, a passion to possess her that she had awakened within him.

Megan had been a wild, desperate lover, and he knew now that her virgin body had been drugged by whatever was in that little vial. No matter the reason, he knew he would want her—and would take her—again. His confidence surging strong, he could think of no reason why it wouldn't go just as he wanted.

Stuart rolled over and went back to sleep.

Rory rode in unannounced. Finding the house empty and no one in the barn, he set out for the fields. As soon as the man looked up at the sound of his horse's hooves, Rory knew who he was. Only one man could fit Martin's detailed description. This had to be Alan Montgomery.

"Mr. Montgomery? I'm Rory O'Hara."

"Well, Mr. O'Hara, I'm happy to meet you. Were you expected? I'm sure Martin would have been waiting for you if he'd known."

"No. No one knew I was coming," Rory replied, receiving Alan's friendly hand clasp. "Where is everyone?"

"There's a big do in town for Brenetta and

Stuart. Sort of an engagement party given by Bellville's eminent citizens. Everyone's there."

"Why not you?" Rory asked.

Alan shrugged. "My blood's not blue enough; I don't fit in well. My own fault, no one else's."

Rory understood and felt a kinship with him.

"Well, if you've just arrived, you must by hungry and thirsty. Let's go back to the house."

"Thanks. I guess I could use a bite to eat," Rory said, his stomach growling at the suggestion.

They were just finishing a light repast when the doors burst open and people came pouring into the entry hall.

"Hello," Alan called. "Come see who's arrived."

Suddenly Rory was surrounded by welcoming faces—Alastair and Kingsley, as friendly and cheerful as ever; Marilee, looking brighter and younger, her once overly thin face now pleasantly filled out; Brent and Taylor, rested at last, Megan, something disturbing in her eyes that he would have to figure out later; and Martin, genuinely happy to see his friend, looking more grown up than Rory remembered.

Brenetta and Stuart were the last to come through the doorway. She rushed up to him and hugged him warmly. "Rory, what a charming surprise. Do you know how naughty I thought you were, leaving so suddenly? My very best friend from the time I was just a toddler and not here when I announced the happiest thing in my life."

Only by sheer willpower did he keep his arms from wrapping her up tightly and keeping her there. Instead, he gently held her at arm's length, noting how she had become even lovelier, how much more a woman she was.

"I'm sorry. It couldn't be helped. Stuart, it's good to see you again."

Stuart stepped forward and they shook hands.

"Thank you, Rory. Likewise you. I take it New York will manage without you awhile."

Rory tried to relax his stiff smile. "They'll have to manage longer than that. I plan on staying until after the wedding."

"Oh, Rory!" Brenetta exclaimed. "How absolutely perfect."

"Rory, if that's what you want, of course it's all right with me. I wish I'd known how you felt; you could've gone home years ago."

Rory and Brent were shut in the study. Both held glasses filled with bourbon, but Rory's went untouched. They stood beside the cold fireplace, arms resting on the mantle as they faced each other.

"I hardly knew myself. Besides, I'm not sorry I've had these years. I'm a different person because of them, a better person, I hope. I've seen new worlds, new people. Even the books I love to read couldn't be the same as living it." Rory paused, then added, "Please don't think I'm ungrateful, Mr. Lattimer."

Brent shook his head, noting Rory's lapse into formality. His arm reached out and he grasped Rory's shoulder. "I would never think it, Rory. You've been like a son to me. You've worked hard, harder than I could ever have asked, and you've always been the one I could depend on. And besides, I *do* undersatand your wanting to go back home. I'm more than ready myself. I've had a belly full of *civilization.*"

Brent's heart squeezed at his words, a reminder that when he did leave, he would be bidding farewell to his daughter, sending her off to face life under the protection of another man, to make her own decisions without her father's counsel.

From the depths of his heart, a father's heart, the memory of his first sight of her blocked out the present. Suddenly it was September again. He had just come from Atlanta, leaving behind him the victorious Union Army in the fallen city. He had come for Taylor, to make her his bride at last, and he had come to meet his child, the daughter he hadn't even known existed just a few short weeks before. And she was beautiful, a miracle. Curly black hair and a shining face, already wonderfully intelligent at seventeen months. That something so perfect could be a part of him, flesh of his flesh. It was so incredible, so miraculous. Together, father and daughter had run through the groves of trees—those very same trees that stood outside, unchanged by time—Brenetta's chubby legs and arms holding on tightly as he carried her piggyback, her squeals of joy ringing merrily in his ears.

Brent blinked away the memory and, with it, a sentimental tear. So fast. It had gone by so very fast. And I must be getting old, he thought.

"Well, Rory, at least you'll be here for the wedding. We're all glad of that. It wouldn't have been right if you'd gone before that."

"Yes, I'll stay 'til the wedding."

CHAPTER TWENTY-FIVE

MAY 1880—SPRING HAVEN

Megan tiptoed carefully into the house, her shoes in her hands. The quick brush through her hair had done little to correct its disheveled appearance, but she was unconcerned. The other inhabitants of Spring Haven had long since fallen asleep. And Stuart was not returning yet, maintaining his pretense of going into town overnight.

She was smiling as her foot touched the bottom step of the back staircase. It was really all so very easy, so simple, to make a man love you. She didn't understand why women were so secretive, so hush-hush about it. Soon Stuart would tell Brenetta he couldn't marry her, that he loved Megan and not her. Megan's smile broadened. That would show Miss Wonderful that she wasn't so perfect.

The changes which had been wrought in Megan

Bellman should have caused more concern, and would have if the house and everyone in it hadn't been so preoccupied with the wedding. As it was, they were all too busy to really notice the new wise look in her eyes or the sultry sway of her hips. They missed her sly glances and cool responses. They overlooked her curtness, which sometimes was really downright rudeness, blaming the excitement.

Low voices caused Megan to freeze, waiting motionless on the stairs. Ascertaining the direction from which the sound came, and unable to ignore her curiosity, she set her shoes on the steps and followed the sound to the study. The door was half open. Megan peeked carefully around it to see Taylor sitting in the large chair behind the desk. Brent stood behind her, gently massaging her neck.

Taylor was laughing softly, her eyes closed with pleasure. "Oh, but you have no idea how doubtful he must have really been, marrying that girl."

"That may be, but neither Brenetta nor Stuart seem the least bit unsure. Brenetta's terribly excited, of course, and Stuart is the calmest groom I've ever seen. But neither of them seem doubtful."

Taylor twisted her face toward Brent, took his hands, and pulled him around to the front of the chair where he leaned against the desk. "Oh, darling," she said. "Remember our own wedding? You didn't seem nervous at all. You were so handsome in your uniform. I was so proud and happy to become your wife."

"And you, my lovely bride," Brent said huskily, "you couldn't possibly know what was in my heart that day. To see our precious daughter, the result of so much love, standing beside us as you promised to be mine forever."

"If only they can find the happiness we've found without having to go through the heartaches," Taylor whispered, their eyes locked in understanding.

Megan slipped away, her mind rapidly processing what she had overheard. *Their* daughter at *their* wedding. Could it be true? The smile returned. Oh, Brenetta, I have such a surprise for you!

Stuart awoke, his body stiff from his night on the ground. The first rays of dawn were just beginning to peek over the trees, and he would have another hour or so to wait before he could begin his ride home. He washed up in the river, then changed into his spare clothes.

Chewing on a biscuit he had brought from the kitchen, Stuart contemplated his current circumstances. It would seem almost humorous if it weren't so tiring. He was only four weeks from taking a bride whom he cared little for except that she was wealthy. True, she was beautiful and he imagined he would enjoy the intimacies of marriage with her, but nonetheless, he would have married her if she was fat and ugly as long as she was Brent Lattimer's daughter.

And then there was the little cousin, Megan. What a flame was hidden behind that innocent, youthful face. He had spent many a splendid hour with her since that first wild night, hidden away in secret groves or dark rooms. Yet, she was as easy to fool as the others. She really thought he would throw Brenetta aside for her. So foolish . . . but she would learn. Stuart had seen her kind before. She was still young. She would learn.

"You're a cold man, Stuart Templeton Adams," he said aloud. "A cold, unfeeling man."

Then he chuckled. Actually, he did feel a bit amused. He had fooled them all. And it hadn't been nearly as difficult as he had feared it might be. His only worry had been Rory, who he knew suspected the worst of him. Yet even Rory was beginning to believe his sincerity. He could see it in his eyes.

Stuart stretched. Yes, it might be tiring, pretending all the time, but it was still humorous. And before long he would be home and he could quit pretending. Oh, he supposed he wouldn't want Brenetta to be unhappy there—no one should be unhappy at Windjammer—but he would have no time to waste pandering to her.

Windjammer. He would make it great again.

Brenetta leaned out the window, eyes closed, catching the morning warmth on her face, the light painting her heavy black lashes with prisms of blue. She breathed deeply of the fresh May air. One month. Only one more month and she would be Mrs. Adams.

It was wonderful to be in love. She wanted to shout it out loud to the world. She opened her eyes, a smile dancing on her lips. Stuart would be back in a few hours. Only gone one day and she missed him so. But her heart sang in anticipation of his return.

Brenetta dressed quickly and skipped more than walked down to the dining room. Her parents and Aunt Marilee were already sitting at the table. Megan was filling her plate at the sideboard, her back to Brenetta.

"Good morning, everyone," Brenetta said brightly, her words almost a song of joy.

"Good morning, honey," her father said.

"Good morning, dear," Taylor echoed, receiving Brenetta's kiss on her cheek.

"It's a beautiful day, isn't it?" Brenetta asked as she took a plate and began to fill it with generous portions.

Brent winked at Marilee. "Did you know? Stuart's back this morning?"

"No!" Marilee gasped in mock surprise.

Brenetta sat between her mother and aunt and began eating with gusto. She didn't mind their good natured teasing. Somehow today was extra special; she didn't know why. Maybe it was awakening to the song birds this morning. Maybe it was the pleasant dream she'd had. Whatever it was, today was a day to be in love and be loved.

Finished, she said to her mother, "I think I'll take a walk. Maybe I'll meet Stuart on the road."

"All right, dear," Taylor answered with a tolerant smile. "But he may not return this early."

"Netta?" Megan said suddenly, speaking for the first time. "May I walk with you awhile?"

Brenetta was more than a little surprised. The gap that had sprung open between them last fall had become a nearly unbreachable chasm. "If you'd like," she replied.

They walked silently down the long drive, Brenetta shortening her stride for the sake of her smaller cousin.

Out of sight of the house, Megan halted abruptly. "Netta, wait. I really don't want to take a walk. I know you're waiting for Stuart and won't want me along. Here, let's sit on this old log and talk, shall we?" They settled on the fallen oak tree. "Netta, I've been simply horrid to you, and I wanted to tell you how sorry I am. Will you accept my apology?"

Brenetta eyed her skeptically a moment, then smiled. How could she not forgive her? The world was too wonderful to not be friends.

"Of course, Megan. I'd like to be your friend again."

"Oh, I'm so glad!" Megan cried in a joyous shriek as she hugged Brenetta. "I've just been so jealous. You've been so very happy and I felt so left out, not having anyone to love me too."

"I'm glad too, Megan. I've missed sharing with you."

"Me, too. And I want you to know, I'm so glad you've got someone as special as Stuart to make you happy. After all, not every girl is so lucky. And, of course, many men wouldn't even marry a girl whose parents weren't married to each other when she was born. I suppose that's rather archaic, but my grandfather was a minister, you know, and I heard him say so often . . . Why, Brenetta, you're looking at me so strangely. Whatever is wrong? Oh! Oh, my . . . You don't know what I'm . . . Oh, dear. I had no idea." Megan jumped up. "I'd best go."

Brenetta's hand shot out, grasping Megan's wrist like a vise. "What are you saying, Megan?"

Megan's eyes were terrified as she shook her head vehemently, her lips tightly closed.

"Tell me!" Brenetta screamed at her.

Tears slipping down her cheeks, Megan sobbed, "I didn't know you didn't know, Netta. Honestly, I didn't."

"Know what?" she asked hoarsely.

"Why, that your father didn't marry your mother until you were old enough to walk."

"How do you know this?"

"Oh, Netta, please let me go," Megan pleaded.

Brenetta's grip tightened, causing the girl to cry out in pain.

"All right! All right, Netta. I . . . I don't remember who told me. I've just always known. Maybe I overheard Mother and Father talking when I was little. Oh, I'm so sorry, Netta."

Brenetta released her. "Please go away, Megan."

"Netta . . ."

"Just go. Please, Megan. Just go."

She sat quietly, her mind blank, her emotions numb. Around her the spring morning was as glorious as before, but she was unaware of it now. After a long while, the numbness began to drain away and in its place came understanding and shame. Not long ago her mother had carefully and lovingly explained the act of marriage to her, telling her the wonders of intimate love with one's own husband. But she and he . . . they hadn't been married!

Brenetta clenched and unclenched her hands in her lap. Her face flashed hot, then drained to a ghastly white as she imagined what might have happened, what must have happened. Then that terrible word entered her mind, a word she had heard from one of the cowpokes. She had badgered Rory until he told her what it meant. She was a bastard. Illegitimate. The child of unmarried parents. An unlawful offspring.

Oh, no! Not me. Stuart. What if Stuart finds out?

Her head snapped up. But he mustn't find out. She would die if she lost Stuart too!

Something was wrong, terribly wrong. It was written all over her face. Stuart stopped his horse and watched her. She was struggling with something, with some awesome decision or problem. A tiny alarm sounded in the back of his head. Maybe she knew about Megan and . . . If that little witch had told Brenetta, he'd kill her. With his own hands, he would kill her.

"Brenetta?" he called to her softly.

The pain and fear filling her rich tawny eyes as they turned on him tugged at even his calloused heart. He slid from the saddle. "Brenetta, love, what is it?"

She began to weep, and he held her face against his chest, letting her sob it out. Feeling her dependence on his strength, he was at least assured it was not what he had feared. Whatever the problem, she was still turning to him. As the tears began to dry up, Stuart passed her his handkerchief. She dried her eyes, then delicately blew her nose.

"Do you want to tell me about it?" he asked.

"No," she answered in a half-choked voice. "Just tell me you love me, Stuart. Please."

He stroked her lovely ebony hair. "Of course I'll tell you. I love you, Brenetta Lattimer."

He felt the sigh shake her shoulders, still wondering what had happened.

Megan's emotions swayed back and forth between triumph and panic. A week before, seeing Brenetta's face as she dropped her little bomb, Megan had thought certainly Brenetta's shame would bring on a broken engagement. Instead, Stuart had ridden up and tenderly comforted her.

But now . . . now it was different.

"But how does a woman know, Eliza?" she had asked the negro woman this morning.

"Miss Megan, you should be askin' your own mama these things?"

"Eliza, quit fiddling with those drapes and come here," Megan had ordered. "You know what mothers are like. Now you answer me."

So now she knew for certain. She was pregnant with Stuart's baby. He would have to marry her now. Megan laughed aloud at a new thought. Just like Brenetta's own parents, that's what would take Stuart away from her. And we'll be in love just like them too, she thought.

She began to brush her hair vigorously. She would tell him today.

For days, Brenetta had watched her parents, looking for a clue, an answer to her silent questions. No answers had come, but a hidden seed of bitterness began to push its roots into corners of her unconscious mind, blossoming into anger. Lies. Her life was just a lie and *they* had done this to her.

Brenetta was sitting on the shaded portico with her mother and aunt. Each of them was busy stitching on garments for the wedding. Brent and Alan were hammering away at more repairs of some storage sheds, and Rory and Martin had gone into Bellville for some supplies. The younger boys had taken Erin Alanna fishing with them. Megan had slipped away from the sewing group, claiming a headache and saying she was going to take a long nap. Stuart had locked himself away long ago in the study with some papers from his Uncle James.

"My goodness, Brenetta," her aunt was saying. "The time is slipping away so fast. I'm beginning to wonder if we'll get it all done in time."

It was an effort to drag her thoughts back to the present so she could answer. "It can't get here fast enough for me, Aunt Marilee."

"Ah, the eagerness of youth," Marilee sighed. "Remember how it was, Taylor?"

"Yes, I remember."

Were you so eager you couldn't marry him first?

Brenetta's mind screamed. She could feel her fingers tightening around the delicate cloth of the napkins she was embroidering. I hate you! I hate you both. Lies. My whole life, all lies.

"Excuse me, Mother. I'm afraid I seem to have caught Megan's headache. I'm going to go up and lie down."

"Brenetta, you're not getting sick, are you?" Taylor walked to where her daughter was now standing and put her hand on her forehead. "There's no fever but you do seem a bit flushed."

Brenetta barely controlled her flinch at Taylor's touch. "I'll be fine after I rest awhile."

Brenetta hurried into the house. She was just past the study door when she stopped and turned sharply. Her eyes stared hard at the heavy, finely carved door, the gold flecks amid the brown seeming to spark.

"Stuart? Stuart, can I talk to you a moment?" she whispered as she rapped softly.

At first there was no reply, no sound of any kind. Then she heard a slam of a cupboard door, the scrape of a chair, the thud of a book on the desk, followed by quick footsteps. The door was unlocked and opened, revealing Stuart looking slightly flustered.

Brenetta stepped back. "I . . . I'm sorry, Stuart. I've bothered you when you were working. I'm sorry," she repeated. "I'll go."

"No," he said, stopping here, smiling quickly. "No, please come in."

Taking her arm, he drew her into the room. His hands lay lightly on her upper arms as he looked gently into her face. She returned his gaze, willing him with her eyes to love her as much as she loved him.

Almost involuntarily, her arms wrapped around his neck. She pulled his lips down to meet hers, her kiss filled with all the passion, frustration, and anger she had been holding inside for what seemed like ages. At first his response was as reserved and proper as he had always been, but then something flared between them. Something she had never felt before burned deep in her stomach, making her legs weak as he pulled her hard against him. As Stuart's lips left hers, she opened her eyes to look up into his questioning gaze. Her body quivered as she met the look with an answer in her own.

"I love you, Stuart," she whispered. "Don't make me wait for you."

Disbelieving—or simply not understanding—he continued to stare at her.

"Take me some place, Stuart. Take me now."

"Netta, are you sure you . . ."

"Yes!" she cried desperately. "Yes, I'm sure."

Stuart took one of her hands in both of his. His voice when he answered was filled with an urgency to match her own.

"All right, Brenetta. There's an old cabin up the river a ways. We'll go there. Come on."

Megan could barely hear them over her own frightened breathing. The tiny cupboard where Stuart had shoved her was hot and stuffy, and she felt a creeping panic in so small a space.

But she did hear . . . and she understood. She

waited long enough to be certain they were gone before opening the door. She had to stop them. She had to. He couldn't do this to her. If she'd only had time to tell him about the baby . . .

"Rory! Rory, I've got to talk to you."
He tossed the saddle over the rim of the stall. "What is it, Megan?"
"You've got to stop them. She's making a terrible mistake."
He put up his hand, motioning her to stop. "Slow down. Who should I stop? And from what?"
Megan's lips trembled but she steadied herself and continued slowly. "It's all my fault. I didn't know, honestly, I didn't, that Brenetta hadn't been told the truth. So when I mentioned that I knew her parents weren't married when she was born, she was awfully upset. I think it's driven her mad because now she and Stuart are going to some place up river to . . . she told him she wants to . . . not wait for the wedding. Rory, you've got to stop them."
Rory had listened without any indication of his thoughts. When Megan stopped and waited, he couldn't deny the concern in her face, but as he had always suspected something in Stuart, so too did he sense a devious streak in this girl. It mattered not at all if she told the truth about Brenetta's parents. What mattered was what Brenetta would do if she believed it.
"When did they leave, Megan?" Rory asked as he swung the saddle back into place.
"After fifteen minutes ago, maybe twenty."

"I'll find her."

Rory vaulted into the saddle and rode quickly out of the barn. Behind his steely face, his thoughts raced on ahead. He couldn't bear the thought that she would turn to Stuart in her hurt and confusion, especially not in this way. If only she had come to him instead . . .

And Stuart. Rory was right about him after all. If he would take advantage of her inner turmoil, he was worse than Rory had thought.

He jabbed his horse in the ribs, pressing for more speed.

Now that they had arrived, Brenetta was unsure of what she was doing. From beneath lowered lashes she watched Stuart opening the small log house's door, wishing he would sense her change of heart and take her home. But she couldn't ask; her pride wouldn't let her. The die was cast.

The cabin had just two rooms and was sparsely furnished. There was a light layer of red dust over everything but it had a comfortable, lived-in look. She didn't wonder at this, however, as she was too busy staring into the tiny bedroom at the bed. Stuart, she thought. Oh, Stuart, take me home. Let's wait and make it right. Treat me as you always have. You should be able to tell what I'm feeling if you really love me.

But when he turned back towards her after sliding the lock, she saw a fire behind his blue eyes and knew instinctively that there was no turning back now. He pulled her into his arms and kissed her hungrily. Leaving her lips, his mouth traveled down her throat, then back up to her ear and back to her lips again. All the time, his hands were sliding up and down her rigid back, coaxing her one step at a time closer to the bedroom.

"Stuart . . ."

"Shh."

His hands seemed to stroke harder, more urgently. One swept up to her hair where it removed the pins, sending her thick curls cascading down her back. She was unaware that he had deftly unbuttoned the back of her dress until he began to slip it over her shoulders.

Alarmed, she cried, "Stuart!"

"You'll be fine. I won't hurt you. Just enjoy it. Trust me, Netta. You're so very beautiful."

She tried to relax, tried to succumb to his caresses as she knew she should—as she knew she *would* if the time was right, meaning if they were married. Well, they weren't married, but she was about to find out what loving could be like. She couldn't stop him now.

She couldn't . . . but the pounding at the door did. Stuart froze, listening.

"Open the door, Adams," Rory's voice thundered. "Netta, get out here."

Stuart stepped back from her as if her skin had burned him. "Gads, what do I do now?" he whispered.

She wasn't to know what he might have thought to do, for right then the door came crashing to the floor, the hinges knocked free under Rory's thrown weight. He stood framed in the doorway, his short but mighty body seeming to fill the empty space as had the door. Brenetta met his gaze and wanted to die.

"Come here, Brenetta."

"Now just a minute, Rory," Stuart began. "This isn't . . ."

Rory's quick look silenced him.

"Come here," he repeated, softly yet firmly. "And staighten your clothing," he added.

Perhaps it was her own shame, perhaps it was a combination of her confusion and tension, but perversely, she was filled with a white rage.

"No, I won't," she answered him defiantly.

She could read the surprise in his black eyes before his cool veil fell over them.

"Go away, Rory. This doesn't concern you."

His quickness was amazing. He was across the room and had her in tow before either she or Stuart could react. His words were as cold and hard as iron.

"All right, little one. It may be none of my business. Why I should spend my life loving you and caring about your happiness, I don't know. You don't want it anyway. So I'll forget the fact that I've loved you. That's over now. But, damn it, Brenetta! You have no right to do this to your parents."

"You don't know anything about it," she retorted. "You don't know what they did to me. The lies. I hate them both."

When she thought about it later, she would suppose Rory was as surprised as she was when he slapped her. Her head spun to the side, and as she slowly brought it back to look at him, he released his hold on her arm.

"Brenetta Lattimer," he said in a near whisper, "neither of us knows what really happened between your folks, and I can't say if it was right or wrong. But each of us in this room knows what you've come here to do is wrong. If it's what you want—if *he's* what you want—then to hell with the both of you. I wash my hands of it."

His departure was unhurried, but his back seemed somehow forebidding. Brenetta quelled the urge to run after him and beg his forgiveness. She had yet to realize what he had said about loving her, but she knew he had always been her most precious friend. Now she had lost him *and* her parents.

"Brenetta," Stuart said, placing his arm gently around her shoulders. "You're shaking. Come sit down."

He guided her to the bed and sat beside her quietly. She didn't cry as she laid her head on his shoulder. She simply quivered with a myriad of emotions. Brenetta failed to respond to his kisses in her hair or on her forehead. Then he was kissing her mouth and his hands were exploring once again, and she realized he still intended to make love to her.

"Stop it!" she cried, leaping to her feet.

"Don't make me stop," he pleaded, following her, grabbing her arms.

She pushed him away from her, disbelieving. "Don't you know what just happened here?" she cried. "Oh, Stuart, leave me alone!"

Running and stumbling, her tears coming at last, Brenetta raced away from the cabin.

She had been unable to listen to what had been said, but from her hiding place, Megan was pleased with the results. She had thought her plan had failed when Rory rode off, leaving Stuart and Brenetta alone together. But then a woebegone Brenetta came running out, disappearing into the woods.

Megan thought how marvelously well the truth, or at least a close proximity to it, had worked, much better than any story she could have made up. Confidently, she hurried towards the doorless entrance. Everything was working out just as she wanted it.

Stuart cursed himself for his own stupidity. What had he been thinking of to press himself on her like that? Was he such a fool?

At the sound of footsteps falling on the board floor of the log house, he looked up, hoping against hope that she had returned. Instead, his eyes fell upon Megan, a self-satisfied smile turning up the corners of her often petulant mouth.

"Not now, Megan," he said wearily.

"I've got something important to tell you, Stuart."

Uninterested, he sighed, "So tell me."

"You don't have to worry about how to tell Netta you won't marry her and don't love her. Stuart, I'm going to have your baby."

It felt like he had fallen into an icy river. The cold flowed through his veins, chilling him to the bones. Only through tremendous effort did he keep the shock from registering on his face.

292

"What makes you so certain it's mine?"

Dismayed, Megan's mouth fell open.

"I'm sorry, Miss Bellman, but I refuse to be blackmailed by a girl of your questionable character. If you are indeed with child, I suggest you look elsewhere for a father for it. You have certainly come to the wrong man by coming to me."

"Stuart, what are you talking about? You know . . ."

He brushed briskly past her, stopping just outside. Drawing on all his reserves, he donned his most confident air as he said lightly, "No one would ever believe what you suggest. I'm afraid they all know how devoted I am to my beloved fiancee. They would be much more likely to believe such disreputable behavior of a rogue like Rory O'Hara." He nodded. "Good day, Miss Bellman."

His brain was already fogged by the large quantity of whiskey he had consumed when she found him. Rory didn't object as Megan climbed the last rung to reach his sanctuary in the loft. She settled herself nearby without a word as he downed another glassful of the burning liquid.

He had no idea how long they sat like that, he on the floor, the crystal decantor between his crossed legs, and Megan on a pile of straw, her chin cupped in her hands as she watched him. He didn't know how late it had become; time had no meaning for him.

"I believe you understand, don't you?" he asked, breaking the silence. His words were slurred but he didn't know it.

"Yes."

"Did you know I loved her?"

"No."

She sounded so terribly kind; he must have mis-judged her.

Rory drank again. "How did you know where to find me?"

"I saw you take the whiskey and come to the barn. When you weren't at dinner, I thought I'd better check on you. I knew Brenetta wouldn't and no one else knows what happened."

"You're very sweet, Megan. Very sweet. Yes, you're very sweet."

He fell silent once more, concentrating only on drinking the whiskey, emptying his glass, then filling it once again from the decanter. By the time the final drop had traced its way down his throat, the barn was shrouded in the black of night.

"Rory. Rory, come on. We've got to get you to the house. We can't let anyone else see you like this. Come on. Here's my arm."

He felt as if his body was made of lead, and he leaned heavily on her shoulder as she wrapped his arm around her neck.

"Yes, Megan, you're so sweet."

He was never to remember how they made it down the ladder or up to his room, but arrive they did. Megan helped him over to his bed, then closed the door before lighting a lamp. The light threw dancing shadows against the walls; suddenly, the room began to spin and pitch wildly. Holding his head with his hands, he fell backwards on his bed with a groan. Megan got the washbasin to him just as he began to vomit, his stomach feeling like it was ripping away from his insides and trying to come up too.

The last thing he remembered before he passed out was her wiping his face with a damp cloth. He didn't know when she carefully undressed him and then removed her own clothes. He was too dead to the world to know that she had slipped beneath the covers beside him, staring at the ceiling, waiting for dawn and discovery.

CHAPTER TWENTY-SIX

MAY 1880—SPRING HAVEN

It was a somber wedding.

The groom wore the same grim expression he had worn since he awakened five days before. The bride's eyes were red, her cheeks blotched from crying. Quietly, Rory echoed the minister's words, promising to love, cherish, and care for her until death. Likewise, Megan promised to love and obey her new husband.

Brenetta observed it all with a hard lump in her throat as she stood between Stuart and her father. An aura of unreality surrounded them all, and she couldn't help thinking she would awaken soon and the hideous dream would be over. Looking at Rory, she felt again the stab of guilt. She couldn't help believing this was all her fault. If he hadn't had to come after her, if he hadn't been disappointed in what she had intended to do, he wouldn't have gotten drunk and then he wouldn't have . . . they wouldn't have . . .

"You may kiss your bride," the minister ended.

Brenetta could almost feel Stuart's body relax, as if, with those words, all the problems of the past week were solved. Oh, he had been so remorseful after what had happened between them, she couldn't help but forgive him. After all, she loved him so very much. But she had been subtly aware of some hidden tension ever since, particularly when Megan was around.

As Rory kissed his new wife lightly on the cheek, Brenetta wondered what kind of omen this might be for her own wedded bliss, now only two weeks away.

Megan thought she was going to begin crying again as her mother hugged her. She felt lost and totally friendless now that she knew Stuart had lied to her, had cheated her. She didn't want to be married to Rory. She didn't want to be pregnant. And most of all, she didn't want to leave Spring Haven.

It had seemed such a good idea at the time. If Stuart (see, even this was his fault!) hadn't said that people would believe someone like Rory would have fathered her child, it never would have occurred to her, but when she saw him with that decanter of whiskey, and knowing he rarely took even a sip of spirits, it had seemed an answer to everything. They would accuse him of taking advantage of the innocent, young girl who didn't know what she was doing, and then they would send him away in disgrace. Then, when the baby came, they would think what a remarkable girl she was, to come through such a terrible ordeal so surprisingly well. And no one would suspect any different.

Only it hadn't worked out quite that way. Doing the only honorable thing, Rory had offered to marry her. To Megan's horror, Alan and her mother had consented, agreeing it would be best for Megan to leave with Rory for Idaho right away, getting her away from the wagging tongues that would be after her. Something like this always had a way of getting out among the gossips.

Megan had barely seen Rory from the moment Alan, who had come seeking Rory for some work they had planned to do that day, discovered them. Rory had still been in a deep slumber, the effects of the alcohol holding tightly to him even in the morning light. She had been so certain she would get out of it somehow that she had avoided seeing Rory since she was pulled from his bed and wrapped in a sheet. She could still remember the shock and dismay written in his face as they led her away. But she hadn't gotten out of it. Now she was his wife.

As Brenetta came foward to hug her, Megan's eyes met with Stuart's. At that moment her despair vanished, leaving only the fire of hate and vengence burning in her heart. The fight had come back to Megan Bellman O'Hara.

I'll get even with you yet, Stuart Adams, her eyes promised him. Somehow, I'll get even!

"You tell Tobias we'll be on our way home in

another three weeks," Brent said as he shook Rory's hand.

"I will, sir." The formality was back.

"Rory," Brent said, trying to bridge the wall Rory had thrown up overnight between himself and all those who loved him. "Son. Just remember that we're all pretty much responsible for our own happiness. You've done the right thing in marrying the girl; now it's up to you to make it a good marriage." He clapped a hand on Rory's shoulder. "Many a marriage has started out on worse footing and been good."

He dropped his hand. "Well, I didn't mean to make a speech of it. You'll be fine. Have a safe trip home."

"Thank you. We will."

"Rory."

Brenetta's voice was soft, troubled. He turned away from her father to look at her, steeling himself against the flood of emotions that were sure to come.

"Rory, I do hope you'll be happy," Brenetta said. "I . . . I'm so sorry for all the trouble I caused you."

He tried to smile, unsuccessfully. "You were never any trouble, little one."

She kissed his smooth cheek, then whispered, "I . . . I didn't stay after you left." There were tears in her eyes.

"I know."

"I'm so sorry," she repeated.

"Don't be, Netta. Everything is fine. I'm sorry we'll have to miss your wedding, of course. Megan was looking forward to being your bridesmaid,

naturally, but we really must bet started home."
He tried to make it all sound so normal.

She nodded wordlessly.

"Excuse me," Rory added huskily, feeling ill at
ease so close to her. "I think it's time to collect my
. . . wife . . . and leave before we miss our train.
Goodbye, little one."

"Goodbye, Rory. Be happy."

Brenetta followed Megan up to her room to help
her change into her traveling dress. Megan had
already discarded the gown she had worn to be
married in, throwing the pretty blue eyelet dress
on the floor. As Brenetta entered, Megan was in
the midst of kicking it angrily across the room
with the toe of her matching blue slipper.

Brenetta kept her eyes averted as she said, "I've
come to help you change if I can, Megan."

The sheer hate in Megan's eyes was like a
vicious kick, seeming to knock the air from her
lungs.

"This is all your fault, Brenetta!" Megan yelled
at her.

"Oh, Megan. I'm so sorry. But you and Rory
have always cared for each other. He'll be a good
hus . . ."

"Cared for each other?" Megan cried. "That's a
laugh. And I'll bet I know where you got that idea.
Rory and I have hardly known the other was alive
since he came here with you last year. In fact, I
think we both decided we didn't even like each
other much when he came back again. Besides,
he's in love with you."

"With me?"

Megan yanked a dress from the closet, the only one not yet packed. "Don't play the idiot, Netta."

Brenetta sank down onto the bed, suddenly remembering what Rory had said to her in that cabin. Oh, dear God, she thought. What have I done to you, Rory? What have I done?

"You think I would have chosen a half-breed for a husband if I'd had any choice?" Megan continued as she buttoned the front of her gown.

"But then, why did you . . ."

Megan picked up her hair brush and threw it wildly towards the bed and Brenetta. It missed its mark, hitting the wall with a smart whack, breaking the tortoise shell handle in two. She was crying now, her face contorted into a grotesque mask of hate and despair and self-pity.

"Megan," Brenetta began softly, hoping to dispell the ugliness between them.

"Oh, you *are* a fool!" Megan cried again, wiping away the tears. Then she continued, the hysteria gone, replaced by a coldness unnatural for someone so young. "Brenetta Lattimer, I have been in love with Stuart since the day he arrived, but I had no chance with him. You threw yourself at him. Oh, I was pretty enough. I just wasn't wealthy enough. But he cared for me. While he was planning to marry you, he was loving me. Rory never touched me; he was too drunk. I tricked him. I tricked all of you," she ended triumphantly.

Feeling as if she couldn't manage even the one little word, Brenetta whispered, "Why?"

"Because I'm pregnant with Stuart's baby. But he won't marry me. He said . . . he . . . Oh, I hate

him! Well, now he's lost you too, so we're even."
Megan turned back to her mirror. "Go away,
Brenetta. Go find your betrayer and tell him you
know the truth."

It was almost impossible to get out of the room.
Her knees kept trying to buckle under her. Outside in the hallway, Brenetta leaned against the
wall. Dear Lord, she prayed, it can't be true. Don't
let it be true. Stuart would never betray me so. He
loves me. He loves me.

Brenetta forced herself to open her eyes, stand
straight, and begin to walk towards the staircase.
She could hear the subdued voices beneath her in
the entry hall. So different from the gala occasion
awaiting her—guests coming from miles around,
an orchestra for dancing, food and refreshments.

She lied, Brenetta thought as she started down
the stairs. She's upset and scared and ashamed. I
just happened to be the one she vented her feelings
on. Of course, she lied. He loves me.

Her eyes locked with Stuart's across the hall.
She wondered if it was fear she saw flicker across
his face before he smiled, sending a message of
love to meet her. But, of course, she knew that was
silly. He had nothing to fear.

CHAPTER TWENTY-SEVEN

JUNE 1880—SPRING HAVEN

Taylor threw off the sheet and hurried to the window. The sky was still the pewter shade of pre-dawn, but it promised to be clear and glorious. Elbows resting on the window sill, she found herself reminiscing about her own wedding day, twenty-one years ago last week.

Oh, it had been so different from her daughter's. She hadn't known the man she was about to marry. He was a stranger, come to save Spring Haven. But, of course, it had turned out well. She had learned to love him later, and because of him, Brent had entered her life. But, oh! Her wedding day had been torture.

Taylor smiled. How much better a life was promised to Brenetta, loving Stuart as she did and Stuart loving her. Perhaps they might even be as happy as Brent and she had been, as they still were.

Brent stirred and opened his eyes. "Awake already?" he asked in a sleepy voice.

"Mmmmm. Oh, darling, the day is going to be marvelous."

"Come here," he told her, "and tell me what's going through that lovely head of yours."

Taylor's bare feet padded softly across the floor to the bed where she knelt on the throw rug, laying her head on his chest. "I was comparing my wedding to what Brenetta's will be."

"I'm sorry I never saw you in that dress."

She looked up at him. "But you'll see Brenetta in it, and she'll be even lovelier. Besides, it's not the dress that makes the marriage. It's the love."

Brent drew her onto the bed beside him and kissed her tenderly. "Then we must have the best there is."

"We have."

Suddenly he swatted her behind and tossed her over him to the other side of the bed. "Well, my love, on a day like today, I would marry you again myself, but there's just too much to be done." He hopped up and poured water into the wash basin, then splashed his face. Looking back at her, water dripping off the end of his nose, he said, "So get up, lazybones. Look at me. I'm awake before you are."

Taylor shook a warning fist at him, laughing merrily. Yes, it was a glorious day.

Brenetta had been awake even before her mother. She too had gone to the window and stared out at the sky. But she wasn't checking the weather. She was looking for answers. She knew she didn't feel as a bride in love should feel on her wedding day. Night and day for the past two weeks, Brenetta had been assailed by doubts. She caught herself listening closely to and analyzing carefully everything Stuart said. She weighed everything he did for some hidden nuance that might tell her what he really thought, what he really felt.

And in the back of her mind was always the thought of Rory, who she knew loved her, with Megan, who hated both Rory and Brenetta herself. She had ruined both their lives. Was she about to ruin hers and Stuart's as well? If only she could talk to someone, but they all seemed so positive of her happiness, she didn't know what to do or say.

A long sigh escaped her as she turned away from the window. At least she was no longer angry at her parents. Knowing she couldn't approach either of them about it, yet also knowing she had to learn the truth—as Rory had said, whether it was right or wrong—Brenetta had gone to her Aunt Marilee. Marilee had told her the story of her parents' impossible desire to marry in the midst of war, of Taylor's heartbreaking attempts to find a minister to perform the ceremony in secret. She had also told her of the tragic misunderstanding which had separated them, leaving Taylor to marry her childhood friend, Jeffrey Stone. Brenetta had cried as Marilee related how Taylor had learned the truth of Brent's love for her just before Brenetta was born, and she cried again when she heard of Jeffrey's tender love for her, the child of another man, and again when Marilee told of his death. She had left with a better understanding of the closeness shared between her mother and father.

As she recalled the story, Brenetta realized that therein was her answer. A misunderstanding—a *silly* misunderstanding—had caused great pain for both Taylor and Brent because neither took the time to find out what the other thought or what had really been said.

"I'm not going to have the same happen to me," she said to the empty room. "I'm going to talk to him."

Stuart stood with his arm around his mother. Priscilla Adams was a tall, bird-like woman, thin with long appendages. She wrung her hands nervously, and Brent had the distinct feeling she had been doing it non-stop since the day she was born.

"Mrs. Adams, we're so glad you've arrived at last," Taylor was saying to her. "We were disappointed you couldn't come last week so we could have gotten to know you better. Please, come in and sit down."

Priscilla Adams looked at Stuart anxiously, then followed Taylor into the west drawing room. Already the room was filled with early arrivals, so Taylor guided them to a secluded corner where they sat in a close grouping of chairs and a sofa.

"I'm sorry Uncle James couldn't come too," Stuart said to Taylor and Brent, "but he just couldn't get away from Windjammer right now, even for my wedding." He looked at his mother.

"And it's been so long since Mother's done any traveling, I'm afraid it's been a terrible strain. Perhaps I should take her to her room to rest awhile."

"Oh, goodness! How thoughtless of me," Taylor exclaimed.

"Stuart?"

They all turned as Brenetta walked up. Brent thought she looked awfully drawn and wondered if she had slept at all these past few nights. Something wasn't right. It just wasn't right.

"Brenetta, love. Mother has arrived. Come meet her."

Following his introductions, Brenetta kissed Priscilla on each cheek before saying, "I've so wanted to meet you, Mother Adams. I may call you that, mayn't I?"

"Of course, child. How lovely you are. Stuart didn't tell me you were beautiful as well."

"Mother," Stuart interjected quickly, "didn't you want to rest before the ceremony?"

Priscilla nodded meekly, and the wringing hands quickened.

"Then let me take you," Stuart said.

Brenetta stopped them. "Stuart, I really must speak with you."

"Come with me, Priscilla," Taylor said, taking the woman's arm. "I'll take you up so these young folks can have a few moments together before everything gets too hectic."

"Let's walk outside, Stuart," Brenetta suggested.

Brent thought again that all was not right and wondered what he should—or could—do about it.

Stuart had feared that this moment might come ever since Megan's announcement that she was with child. He had seen the hate in her eyes for him and knew she might tell Brenetta. Yet Rory and Megan had gone and nothing had been said. With a sigh of relief, Stuart had hoped he could put the unpleasant matter behind him. Now he wondered.

They strolled silently down to the river, away from guests and family and servants. Stuart waited for her to begin, trying to appear calm and self-assured.

Stopping at the river's edge, Brenetta spoke at last. "Stuart, do you love me?"

"You know I do. Haven't I told you so?"

"Yes. You've told me. What's it like at Windjammer?"

Inwardly, Stuart sighed. She was only nervous, not suspicious. This he could handle. "You'll be very happy there," he answered her. "The rice paddies are very different from your cotton fields and the house isn't quite as big and richly furnished, but Windjammer has style, an elegance of age and a permenance, as if she says 'I am somebody and I will always be here,' You'll see what I mean when we get there."

Brenetta stared across the river, her eyes looking far beyond the horizon. "Tell me, Stuart, what kind of money will it take to get her back on her feet? I know Father has agreed to provide whatever you might need so that I might have the very best."

"He discussed it with you?" Stuart asked, but his dodge of her own question failed.

"Will it take a great deal of money?"

Stuart nodded, hoping he was doing the right thing in answering as he intended. "Yes, Brenetta, it will. I have accepted your father's generous offer to help reestablish Windjammer to her former condition, and there are a few outstanding debts to be paid. I wouldn't have accepted if it weren't that I want the best for you, you know. You needn't trouble yourself about these matters, however. You'll always be taken care of."

When she looked at him, it was with a searching gaze he thought must be able to see into the utmost secret corners of his soul. He found himself unable to maintain the eye contact, dropping his vision to the river bank at his feet.

"And you love me," Brenetta whispered, barely audible.

"Yes, I love you. Brenetta, what must I say to you to convince you, to allay your doubts?" He felt the panic rising along with his voice.

"What about Megan's child?"

Stuart had no idea how pale he had become as he turned a startled face towards her once again. "Megan's what? What are you talking about?"

"Megan was pregnant when she married Rory."

"No. I can't believe it. I had no idea Mr. O'Hara would stoop so low." Stuart, feeling his confidence returning, put his arm around her shoulders. "How very upsetting for you, my dear. I know he was a good friend of yours. For him to have acted so shamefully . . . and with your cousin.

But, I must say, I always suspected that he wasn't quite . . . shall we say, honest. And Megan. Well, she was a willful child. You must admit to that."

"Yes," Brenetta agreed softly. Then, "I'd best get back to the house."

So he had succeeded. Only a couple of hours and all would be well.

The dress had been her Grandmother Christina's. Taylor had worn it too. Now it was Brenetta's turn. The pearl-studded lace and glossy satin were as beautiful today as they had been forty years before. Tenderly, Taylor placed the mantilla on Brenetta's head, draping the delicate lace over her hair and shoulders.

Brenetta watched her mother in the mirror. She could see clearly the joy in Taylor's face.

"You're the loveliest ever to wear this dress," Taylor said to her, kissing Brenetta's brow. "I'm so very proud of you."

"Thank you, Mama."

"I wish you so much happiness, Netta. Just remember, as long as you love each other, everything else will be fine. Always be honest; never keep anything hidden or to yourself. Make him your world, your very life. You'll never be sorry." Taylor kissed her again. "I'd better go down. It's almost time."

Alone again, Brenetta turned back to the dressing mirror. She looked at herself critically. Even she had to admit the bride looking back at her was striking. Her skin was creamy smooth and white, the childhood freckles long since faded.

Her hair, clean and shiny, seemed blacker than ever under the white lace veil. It had been twisted in tight ringlets, reminiscent of Taylor's girlhood days, pulled high at the back of her head, then falling down her back. Her tawny eyes, framed by smoky lashes, seemed to catch the light, making them more golden than usual. Such a beautiful bride.

"But I don't want to marry him," she whispered.

Brenetta fought back the tears that followed her verbal admission. No, she didn't want to marry Stuart, for she knew without knowing how she knew that he really didn't love her, that he was really only concerned with the money which would accompany their union. And, with a sinking heart, she knew she believed what Megan had told her about the baby.

Perhaps it was knowing Rory as she did, knowing he would never have behaved as Stuart had tried to say he had. Perhaps it was the changes in Megan that hadn't begun until after Stuart came. Whatever it was, Brenetta knew at last that Stuart was not the man he had portrayed himself to be.

A tear slipped down each cheek. "But I have loved him so. I still love him," she said to her reflection.

Can you really love him after what he's done? she wondered. Yes. And no. I don't know. I don't know. What shall I do?

A knock at the door sent her scurrying for her handkerchief to dry away her tears.

"Yes?"

Brent, handsome in his black suit, grey silk

cravet, and diamond studs, poked his head around the door. "Are you ready? May I come in?"

"Yes. Come in, Papa."

Brenetta tried to smile her most dazzling smile. It would be what he expected.

Oh, Daddy, what am I to do? I can't disgrace you and Mother by backing out now. How would it look? I can't disappoint everyone that way. Look at everything you've done just for me and my wedding. And Aunt Marilee and the boys and Erin Alanna and our own Carleton. They're all so excited and happy. You've always done so much for us. I want you to be proud. Sometimes, to make others happy, you have to sacrifice a little happiness for yourself. Isn't that right?

"My little girl," Brent was saying with a shake of his head. "Where is my little girl?"

Brenetta threw her arms around him, beginning to cry again. "I'm here, Daddy. I'm still your little girl."

"Of course you are," Brent whispered. "Why the tears, Netta?"

She tried to sniff them away. "Every bride cries. Don't you know that, Father?"

Brent dabbed at her cheeks. "As long as that's all it is." He held out his elbow to her. "It's time to go."

Brenetta swallowed back the panic swelling in her throat, drew the veil over her face, and took his arm. Brent placed his right hand over hers in the crook of his left arm as they walked slowly out of her room, along the hallway, and down the stairs. Through the open doors, Brenetta could hear the buzz of the wedding guests out on the lawn. As she and her father walked across the portico, they fell silent one by one. The orchestra began playing the wedding march, and her father guided her to the end of the aisle between the rows of chairs.

Brenetta looked down the grassy carpet to where Stuart was waiting for her. Or was he really waiting for Brent? The tears were threatening again. She lifted her chin bravely, refusing to embarrass or hurt her family.

She could feel her heart palpitating madly in her chest when Brent suddenly leaned down and whispered in her ear, "Brenetta, for whatever reason, if you don't want to marry Stuart, then don't do it. Your mother and I only want your happiness."

Brenetta was surprised at how well he had read her feelings but shook her head stoically. She had come this far; she would see it through.

Locking her eyes on the small raised platform, she began the long walk on the arm of her father. Stuart looked so wonderfully handsome; her heart was squeezed between fists of doubt but her feet carried her forward.

Next to Stuart was Martin as best man and Carleton waited next to him, holding a satin pillow with the rings resting on top of it. With Megan gone, Brenetta had asked her Aunt Marilee to be her attendant, so she was waiting opposite Stuart. Little Erin Alanna, already having spread the path with Cherokee rose petals, waited beside her mother. A seeming multitude of strangers, their faces lost in a blur, looked up from the sidelines, but Brenetta was only vaguely aware of them as she drew closer to Stuart. Brent passed her hand to him, and Stuart drew her up beside him. She felt chilled, her heart turned to stone.

Looking up into his face behind the safety of her veil, she felt she could almost see the edges of the mask he so carefully wore. I don't even know you, she thought. I love someone who doesn't even exist. (The minister was saying something now.) Why, if I loved you, I wouldn't be so afraid. But it hurts. I *must* love you. Only you're not the same man. Stuart, who are you? Why did you take Megan to your bed? And why did you lie to me?

I can't! I can't! Her heart thudded painfully.

Quickly, she pulled her hand from his, and turned for flight. "I can't, Stuart. I can't!" she cried aloud, then began running back up the aisle.

A deathly hush was all she heard as she raced into the house and up to her room where she fell onto her bed, weeping inconsolably.

Taylor placed a protective arm around Brenetta's shoulders as they stood beside the carriage. Brent was lifting Carleton up beside the driver where they had promised him he could ride.

"I'm going to miss all of you so much, Taylor," Marilee said as a tear trickled down a damp path on her cheek where others had gone before it. "I hope it won't be so many years before we see each other again."

They knew it might be never again but that fact remained unspoken.

Brent shook Alan's hand, then clapped Martin on the shoulder. "You've done remarkable things here, Alan. You, too, Martin. Spring Haven has triumphed, just as all Bellmans eventually do." He stepped backwards to put his arm around Brenetta from her other side. "We've got to go. Have a boat to catch on Saturday. Goodbye everyone."

"We'll write," Taylor promised as Brent helped Brenetta and then her into the carriage.

"And we'll write back. Take care, all of you. We love you," Marilee called after them.

The carriage in motion, Taylor exchanged a speaking glance with Brent before turning to stare out the window. She was leaving Georgia once again, but this time it was without the expectation of adventure which they had shared when they departed for Idaho in 1866.

The past week had been a nightmare. Brenetta refused to tell anyone why she had changed her mind but it was obvious to Taylor that Brenetta's heart was broken. She had become apathetic about everything. She wouldn't see Stuart, sending him away from her door every time he tried to talk to her. Finally, there had been an ugly scene between Stuart and Brent—or at least that was what Taylor had surmised. The interview had been held in the library, the raised voices muffled through tightly closed doors. Stuart had left the same day, more subdued and not nearly so upset as he had been. When pressed, Brent had only told her that he and Stuart Adams had "come to a settlement." Stuart had been paid off.

Only at one time had Brenetta stirred from her lethargy. She had begged that they not go home, not yet. She didn't care where they went, only she didn't want to return to Idaho. Neither she nor Brent asked their daughter why. If she was that determined not to go home, then they wouldn't make her. Today they were on their way to Charleston where they would catch a ship to France. Taylor was not eager to travel abroad once again, but for her daughter . . .

Casting a sidelong glance towards Brenetta, Taylor prayed that whatever the cause, whatever the pain, her daughter would find peace in her heart once more.

PART THREE

Many waters cannot quench love,
Neither can floods drown it.
Song of Solomon 8:7

CHAPTER TWENTY-EIGHT

MARCH 1881—HEART'S LANDING

The heavy black clouds could have taken lessons from his face as he slammed out of the house. Rory jerked the collar of his coat up around his neck as he bent into the icy March winds. Having learned his lesson after one bad mistake, Rory had sworn never to touch alcohol again, but at the moment, he wished he had never made the vow. Total oblivian was what he longed for.

The barn was warmed by the animals inside. The air was sweet with the scent of hay and straw, horses and cows. Closing the door quickly behind him, Rory took a deep breath, trying to still his boiling anger.

That woman! Sometimes he'd like to . . .

Rory sat on a bale of hay and watched the newest arrival, a pretty black filly, pull hungrily at her mother's udder. Instead of soothing him, however, it increased his irritability, reminding him of Megan and the baby.

Pretty little Bellamie Starr. So fair-haired. Such big blue eyes. So sweet and happy. But not his child—and unwanted by her own mother.

From the very beginning, life with Megan had been pure hell. She had whined and complained her way to Idaho, making his homecoming a miserable one. Tobias had been so pleased to have him back, and Ingrid had done her best to make Megan feel at home. Poor Ingrid! She had been tried to the very limits of her good nature, but Megan would have none of it.

When she announced that she was expecting a baby, Rory was surprised and very, very pleased. He loved children and wanted many. However, Megan had been none too willing to accept his lovemaking, and when she did, it was with such resentment and scorn, he had little desire to attempt it often. He only hoped that with time she would forgive him for taking her virginity in a drunken stupor and learn to care for him.

Ever the proud father-to-be, Rory had set about waiting for his child. He never lost his temper with Megan. He catered to her every whim, pampering her as if she was made of porcelain, his eye always on the calendar, settling on the month of February and the baby's coming. But nearly two and a half months ahead of schedule, on a wintery December morning, Megan delivered a healthy, full-term baby girl, and Rory knew he had been deceived. Despite the knowledge, Rory lost his heart to the infant.

Not Megan. She wanted as little to do with the baby as possible. One morning she even refused to get up and nurse her, so Rory had found an Indian woman, the widow of a French fur trapper, to wet-nurse the baby. Gentle Deer's own child had died in the same fire that claimed her husband, leaving her with both empty arms and a lonely heart. She had gladly come to care for Starr.

Bellamie Starr O'Hara. The first name was, in part, for her Bellman heritage, but Rory had also chosen it for its old French meaning which Gentle Deer had shared with him: *beautiful friend.* Starr was for the light of love he hoped would surround her in all her life. O'Hara was because he loved her and would never have her hang her head in shame because of her birth. He never admitted to Megan that he knew the truth and she naively believed he was fooled.

Rory tried to be patient with his wife; he still wanted them to learn to live together amiably even if they couldn't learn to love each other. But to-night had been too much for him.

They were sitting at the table, eating their supper. Megan was wearing a pretty rust-colored woolen skirt and a white blouse. A bright yellow shawl was draped over her shoulders, a Christmas gift from Ingrid. She looked very fetching, a soft glow of firelight catching the gold shafts of her hair. She seemed very vulnerable and innocent as they ate in silence, only disturbed by the crackling of the fire and the clink of forks against their plates. Starr was sleeping in her basket across the room, Gentle Deer in a chair nearby.

Then the baby stirred, whimpering as she realized she was hungry. Rory watched Gentle Deer bend over the side of the basket and begin to change Starr's diaper, cooing softly all the while. She was such a pretty woman, quiet and unobtrusive, yet loving and caring. He smiled, thinking what a peaceful family they made tonight.

"If you want her so much, why don't you get on with it. She's just a squaw," Megan snapped.

Rory looked at her.

"Oh, don't look so shocked. I know you want to. You men have it on your minds all the time. It's disgusting. And all it gets a woman is a house full of babies—demanding, wet babies."

"Megan."

"Look at Ingrid. Already has four boys and here she is getting ready to have another one. As bad as a brood mare. She doesn't behave with any decency, else this would have stopped after the first one or two."

Across the room, Starr's whimpers turned to earnest wails. Gentle Deer was moving too slowly to suit her stomach.

"For heaven's sake, shut that brat up!" Megan cried. "Are you too stupid to do even that right?"

"Megan, that's enough," Rory warned her.

Her eyes were the blue of an arctic sky and held just about as much warmth as she fastened them on him. "Of course, if she didn't have to care for that baby, you could take her right now for your bed wench. Well, go on. I don't care. Just don't come to my bed anymore looking for favors."

The desire to strike her was almost overwhelming. Before he lost hold of the thin thread of control, he left the table, donned his coat, and stormed out of the house.

As so often happened in moments like this, Rory's thoughts went to Brenetta. He wondered where she was at this very instant and what she was wearing. Was she smiling? Had she gotten over Stuart, or was she still in love as he was with her? Maybe she had fallen in love with someone else. Was she dancing in the arms of some French duke or maybe relaxing at some country estate outside Paris? Perhaps she was . . .

The filly, her belly full, stopped her noisy sucking and nickered contentedly to her mother. The dam curled her neck around to nuzzle the youngster, and Rory's attention returned to his side of the globe.

Gentle Deer was with Starr like this mare was with her foal, her dark brown doe's eyes filled with warmth and love as she tended to the baby's needs. She had a shy smile and a quick mind, and Megan's abuse seemed to slide unnoticed off her back. Two or three years older than Rory, she was as slender as a reed, her trim figure always clothed in fringed deerhide dresses which were decorated with colorful beeds, sewn in intricate designs. She wore her black hair in two waist-long braids with a beaded headband around her forehead.

Rory stopped to consider Megan's suggestion in earnest. He knew he could take Gentle Deer as his second woman; she wouldn't protest. Although there would be no fire between them, they would share contentment. She would tend to his wants and warm his bed, and even, perhaps, sooth the soreness in his heart. In return, he would help ease her loneliness and give her other children to replace the one she had lost.

Yet, een as he thought of it, Gentle Deer's face was replaced in his mind by another raven-haired woman, this one with skin as white and aglow as pearls, and he knew he could never do it . . .

Tobias studied Rory from the other side of the barn. His presence had gone undetected, and after having seen his father's face, he thought it best to leave him alone for a while.

Tobias shook his head. Of course, he had never known Megan before Rory brought her here but he couldn't help but wonder what had compelled him to marry her in the first place. Her mouth was set in a perpetual pout; she was selfish and conceited, as spoiled a wench as he had ever known. He had seen her rebuff Ingrid's attempts at friendship too many times to think kindly about the girl. And the tongue lashings he had heard her unleash on Rory were enough to send a man running for a monastery.

He was a lucky man to have found a woman like Ingrid, and he knew it. Six years with her and every day was better than the last. She sparkled with laughter, joy flowing from her to everyone around. She had given him four healthy sons, and in August, there would be another Levi. Surely the God of Abraham had blessed him with a full quiver. The only shadow on their happiness was Ingrid's father. He refused to see her on her children, announcing that his daughter had died the day she married a Jew.

Tobias cleared his throat noisily as he stepped from the stall. When Rory looked towards him, he said, "Mighty fine filly, ain't she, Bear? That mare always comes through with a gem."

"I was just thinking the same thing, Tobias."

"I'm afraid it's gonna snow again tonight."

"You're probably right."

"Everything all right at your place, Bear?"

"Fine. Just fine."

"Good."

They fell silent, both gazing at the filly. Rory was the first to move.

"Guess I'd best get back to the house."

Tobias nodded. "Hey, Bear, I nearly forgot to tell you. Had a line from Brent. The family's comin' home in a couple of months. Said they've got a surprise for us too. You don't suppose Netta's found herself another fella?"

"Could be, Tobias," Rory answered in a strained voice. "Could be."

Rory pushed the door open and left Tobias alone with the animals.

CHAPTER TWENTY-NINE

MARCH 1881—MARCHLAND HOUSE

The Marquis of Marchland, a member of the landed gentry, leaned against the massive marble mantlepiece, detailing minutely the events of that morning's hunt. He was a man in his early thirties, of medium height, with a strong, straight nose and surpised eyebrows. He was also, in Brenetta's mind, a fop. He bored her to tears and she regretted daily her father's acceptance of the Marquis' invitation to stay at Marchland House during their visit to England. She knew a proposal was brewing behind his hazel eyes, and she wanted to avoid it at all costs. It wouldn't be the first one she had received since leaving Charleston. She had even been proposed to on board ship. Still, when those men had asked her to be their wife, she had still been mourning over Stuart and hadn't worried about what to say to them. The men themselves had had nothing to do with her refusal.

The Marquis was an entirely different matter. She simply—and very emphatically—couldn't stand him. "A brilliant match," people would say if she accepted, but Brenetta could only shudder at the thought of being his wife.

Time, at least, had healed her broken heart. She hadn't believed them when they said it would. She had seen Paris and Vienna through a veil of tears, but by the time they visited Rome, the pain was receding, and she had arrived in England with much of her former vigor for life restored. When she thought of Stuart now it was with a feeling of unreality . . . and sometimes a wistfulness for what might have been.

"Excuse me, March," she said, interrupting him, using the nickname he had insisted they all use. "I seem to have developed a headache. I think I'll go upstairs and lie down for a while. I'll see you again at supper."

The Marquis bowed towards her. "May I walk you to your room, my dear?"

"Oh, *please* don't bother. I'm sure Mother wants to hear the rest of your story about the hunt. I'll go alone."

She left quickly but not before she had seen the daggers flung in her direction from her mother's stormy blue eyes. Brenetta laughed silently, knowing Taylor felt the same way she did about the fastidious, dandified fellow who was their host.

Climbing the staircase, Brenetta let her fingers glide over the dark paneling of the wall. Marchland House was well over three hundred years old, rich with a history of the people who had lived here for centuries. She couldn't help but compare it with Heart's Landing, a home built less than twenty years ago on the frontiers of a country younger than this estate. While this house, with its dozens of bedrooms and ballrooms and parlors, its gold and silver, its grand pianos and opulent carpets, might be as beautiful as it was large, Brenetta found it depressing. It was time to go home. She longed for Heart's Landing, for its simpleness of life and struggles for survival, and for the people there—Tobias and Ingrid and Sandman and Rory . . .

Rory. A letter announcing Bellamie Starr's birth had reached them in Rome. Marilee had written how lucky it was that Starr had lived, as prematurely as she had been born. Brenetta had gone to her room after Taylor finished reading the letter and lay on her bed, staring at the ceiling and feeling sorry for Rory. While she had escaped, though painfully, from making a tragic mistake, Rory had not been so fortunate. She hoped for his sake that they had learned to care for each other and that he had forgiven Megan her deceitful tricks. As for her own feelings towards Megan, the bitterness was gone. Only a kind of pity remained, a pity for Megan's foolishness and ruthless pursuit of her own selfish desires.

Yes, she thought as she opened the door to her room, it's time to go home.

Every day they sat like this, father and son,

beneath the gnarled old tree, a book in Carleton's hands and a frown of concentration on his bespectacled face. The thick glasses gave the boy a strong resemblance to an oversized housefly, but Brent was unconcerned about Carleton's appearance. It was not even worth noting compared with the thrill of hearing his son reading to him from the old primer.

He couldn't be certain when Carleton first complained of the pain behind his eyes. First, they had thought it merely a result of the tension following their departure from Spring Haven, but he did remember that first moment of realization when he knew Carleton was gaining some sight. They were in their suite in Vienna. Brent had come into his son's room one morning and found him already up, sitting on the edge of his bed.

"Good morning, Carl."

"Morning, Father."

Brent lifted the blinds, flooding the room with light. It happened he was looking at Carelton in a nearby wall mirror as he did so, and he saw the boy's quick gesture to protect his eyes from the sun with the crook of his arm.

Brent whirled around. "Carl, why did you do that," he demanded.

Slowly the arm came down, but Carleton's eyes remained tightly closed. "My eyes hurt. I was just covering them."

"Come here," Brent ordered, sounding almost angry in his excitement. "Open your eyes."

"It hurts when I do."

"Open them," Brent demanded, taking

Carleton's hand and dragging him closer to the window.

With effort, the lids fluttering in objection, Carleton obeyed his father. As the light hit them, he winced, once again bringing up an arm to shade them.

"Good lord," Brent whispered. Then he shouted, "Taylor. Taylor, get in here!"

He caught Carleton up in his arms and began swinging him around the room. "Don't you understand, my boy? That's the light that hurts! Carl, you can *see* something!"

"What is it? What's wrong?" Taylor cried as she came running to his summons, her hastily donned robe flying out behind her.

"He can see. He can see." It was all Brent could say as emotion began choking his throat and clouding his eyes with tears. "He can see."

Little by little, Carleton's eyes had improved, moving from the pain of light to seeing shadows to observing colorful, though fuzzy, objects until finally, with the help of glasses, he was even learning to read.

As Carleton's voice droned on, Brent put his arm around his son's shoulder. "I love you, boy."

Carleton looked up from the pages. "I love you, too."

"Read me some more. I like to hear it."

"Sure," Carleton said with a smile. "I like to read."

CHAPTER THIRTY

JUNE 1881—HEART'S LANDING

It was one of those rare June days when the temperature climbed over ninety degrees in their high valley. There wasn't even a hint of a breeze to stir the air and bring some semblance of comfort.

The blacksmith had gone with the herd on the spring drive so Rory was shoeing his own horse when the buggy pulled up to the house. Sweat pouring down his face, he cast only a casual look in that direction before returning his attention to the large hoof resting between his legs. It was Ingrid's excited squeal that caused him to drop it and run towards the house. Instead of finding trouble, he found Taylor and Ingrid locked in an embrace.

"Rory?" Brent boomed in greeting, clapping the surprised Rory on the shoulder.

"Brent, we weren't expecting you yet."

"I know. We decided to surprise you. Worked too." Brent turned towards Taylor. "And we have an even bigger surprise, don't we, dear?"

Taylor was beaming brightly. "We certainly do. Carl, come here."

It only took Rory a glance at those thick glasses perched on the boy's nose to grasp what had happened.

"Carl, my young friend, you've become quite a distinguished looking young fellow since I saw you last," Rory said seriously, shaking Carleton's hand.

Carl looked him over carefully before saying, "You're Rory? You don't look anything like I expected. You're much darker than everyone else, too." Then referring back to Rory's greeting, he said, "It's the glasses that make me look different. I can even read with them."

"Read? Already? That's amazing."

"It is wonderful, isn't it, Rory," Brenetta said as she stepped from the buggy.

Heart in his throat, Rory turned to face her. She was dressed in a mauve linen dress and looked cool and composed despite the heat and dusty travel. Her hair was swept to one side, tied in place with a pretty lilac ribbon. The smile on her pink lips was warm and reached all the way into her eyes.

"Brenetta, it's good to see you."

"And you, Rory. It's so good to be home again."

Cosmopolitan. That was the word her appearance brought to mind. Not simply a woman of fashion, which she had been even at sixteen, but one who knew and understood about life. He thought how he must look to her—barechested with rivulets of sweat glistening on his brown skin, his hair damp and clinging to his scalp, his levis covered with dust—and then he thought of the men she must have known in Europe—suave, sophisticated dukes and earls. He felt more of a country bumpkin now than he had when he first went to New York.

"Rory O'Hara, you could have told me everyone was here."

Megan's sharp words made him cringe. What a pair they were. Him a disheveled, uncouth half-breed, and his wife, the screaming shrew.

"Megan, how good to see you," Taylor said sweetly, greeting her niece with an affectionate kiss. "Let's all go inside where it's cooler. Megan, we're all looking forward to seeing that baby of yours."

"Really? Well, I'll have Gentle Deer bring her up to the house later," Megan replied.

Brenetta's eyebrows rose in question. "Gentle Deer?"

"She's Starr's nurse," Rory replied.

"Is she ill?" Taylor asked.

Megan shook her head. "Of course not. But someone's got to look after her and I certainly can't be expected to do that day and night."

"Oh," Brenetta and Taylor said in unison, exchanging glances.

The Indian woman sat beside Rory on the sofa,

her eyes lowered, her hands folded in her lap. Rory was holding the blonde-haired, blue-eyed child, talking to her softly, paying no heed to the other conversation in the room. Megan was still going on to Taylor and Brent about the hardships she had been forced to live with in this primitive land and complaining of married life and motherhood in particular. Taylor was doing her best to reply politely and with tact.

Brenetta, meanwhile, continued her private study of the threesome on the sofa. Gentle Deer was really an exquisite woman, almost exotic looking with her wide-set limpid brown eyes, the high, thin eyebrows, her square chin and the broad, slightly flared nose. Her demeanor was demure and obedient, yet there was no mistaking the pride that kept her backbone straight and strong.

Brenetta's eyes shifted to Rory, and she couldn't help wondering if these two were lovers. They seemed so well-suited to each other. She wouldn't have blamed him, especially after listening for so long to Megan, but she couldn't help hoping it wasn't so. For some reason, she knew that Rory wouldn't be the same man she'd always known— the same man she cared for—if he had been driven to a liaison with another woman.

Rory's face fairly beamed from within as he looked at the child in his arms. It was almost heartbreaking to know Starr wasn't really his. Knowing that he must know it too, as everyone must guess, and seeing his love for her despite that knowledge made Brenetta feel closer to him than ever before. Any person who could love so unselfishly was a very special person indeed.

Starr laughed aloud, the merry sound ringing over her mother's continuing speech. Leaning towards Gentle Deer, Starr grabbed the bodice of the woman's dress and began tugging at it.

Gentle Deer took her from Rory, standing as she did so. "I'll go now," she said softly to Rory. She nodded to the others, then left.

"You're very lucky to have someone like Gentle Deer," Taylor said to Rory.

It was Megan who answered her. "Oh, we put up with her as best we can, but I'm never too sure about her. You can never *really* trust an Indian, you know."

Brenetta could see the anger rising in Rory's face. "Excuse me," he mumbled, "I need some air."

Brenetta waited a few moments, then got up herself. "I think I'll walk down to Ingrid's to meet the children."

"You can't get enough of the little rascals, can you?" Megan called after her sarcastically as Brenetta slipped out of the house.

She found him leaning on the corral fence. Wordlessly, she laid her hand on his shoulder. He didn't look up or acknowledge her presence in any way.

"At least you're home in Idaho," Brenetta said finally as the twilight deepened around them. "And you have a beautiful daughter."

His voice sounded far away. "I love that baby more than my own life."

She could feel his pain, his frustration as he spoke. Seeking to comfort him, she laid her cheek against his back. "I wish it was better for you."

"You know, don't you?" The question was barely audible.

"Yes."

"That's why you didn't marry him."

"Partly, yes."

Rory turned to face her then, the unreadable mask having fallen back into place. "Then it was worth it if it saved you a lifetime of hurt."

"No, it wasn't worth this."

He chucked her gently under the chin, forcing a smile. "Well, you're home now where you belong. We all are." For the first time in months, Brenetta felt like crying. He saw it and was immediately contrite. "Has it been terribly hard for you? Do you still love him?"

"No," she said, blinking away the tears as she shook her head. "It was bad at first but I don't love him anymore. When I think of him, I just feel nothing . . . except maybe sorry for everyone who was hurt because of it all." She leaned forward. "I only wish you were happier," she whispered as she brushed a kiss across his smooth cheek.

Ingrid, looking nearly as wide in her pregnancy as she was tall, brushed back the wisps of hair clinging to her flushed face. She had risen early to bake the bread, hoping to beat the rising thermometer, but the morning sun had brought with it another unusually warm day, making her little kitchen into an oven itself.

Five year old Reuben was already hard at work on his Hebrew. Since their marriage, Tobias had drawn more and more strength from the faith of his ancestors, a faith he had slipped away from in his early adulthood. He had begun instructing his sons when they were barely out of diapers, reading to them of a heritage that went back more than four thousand years. And Ingrid, out of love for Tobias, had embraced his faith as well, feeling as Jewish as if her name was Naomi or Ruth or Hannah or Simone. Now, as she watched her small son, his forehead wrinkled in concentration, she felt a great pride welling up in her heart. God had truly blessed them.

With a shake, she hurried to finish her morning chores. Soon Isaac and Elijah and David would be awake and clamoring for their breakfast. With their father away on the cattle drive, Ingrid was kept busy with her burgeoning household from dawn to dusk.

"Knock, knock."

Ingrid looked up to find Brenetta looking in at her from the open door. "Come in, Netta. You're out and about early. Sit down."

"You're the one who should sit down," Brenetta said as she stepped inside. "Don't you think you should take it a little easier?"

Ingrid laughed. "And just who would bake the bread and wash the clothes or make breakfast if I did?"

Brenetta sat down at the table across from Reuben. Looking at the boy, she said thoughtfully, "It's amazing how he's grown since I went away.

341

All of them have. And now you have David too and another one coming. How do you manage, Ingrid?"

"With plenty of love and lots of laughter," Ingrid answered as she planted a kiss on her son's head.

"Megan can't even manage one."

Ingrid's mouth grew tight. "Megan, I'm afraid, thinks only of Megan."

"Believe it or not, Ingrid," Brenetta told her, "she wasn't always like this."

Ingrid sniffed. "Well, she's always been *like this*, as you put it, since she came here. Poor Rory. Sometimes I . . ." Ingrid sat down at the table. "Netta, you should have seen him while he was awaitin' that baby. As if he was the first father ever. As mean and sharp-tongued as that girl could be, he treated her like glass. Course, her delivery surprised us all, coming when it did. All except her." She stopped suddenly, realizing what she had said.

"Don't worry, Ingrid. I already knew. Go on."

"Netta, you'd think that the sun rose and set on Starr's whim. My Tobias has always been right pleased, but Rory . . . Well, Starr is just everything to him. He's got a big empty place in his heart, and he's trying to fill it with Starr, if you ask me."

"He's that unhappy?"

Struggling to push her bulky body from the chair, Ingrid could only manage a nod.

"But, Ingrid, he seems all right."

"Netta, you grew up with him. You should know how he can hide everything behind a blank face.

Maybe I can see it 'cause of being so much in love with Tobias, but it's as clear as can be to me. Rory came back from the East with a pregnant bride, but he was in love with someone else—and still is."

"After so long?" Brenetta said softly. "Oh, Ingrid, I hope you're wrong."

Rory held onto the tail of his horse, letting the big buckskin pull him up to the steep, rocky incline. With a mighty lunge and scrambling hooves, the gelding pulled them both onto the ridge. Rory gave the animal and himself a breather as he let his eyes run over the terrain spread before him. Somewhere up here he would find her.

When he had come home a year ago, Rory had thought a few times of looking for the Flame, but somehow, he knew he couldn't try to capture her, not with the way he felt trapped himself. It was different now. He sought the mare as a homecoming present for Brenetta.

The trail he was following was less than a day old. He didn't want it to get any older. Rory swung into the saddle and turned his horse to the east.

It was mid-afternoon when he found them. He had to slide along the bluff on his belly to get a closer look. The first shock was finding another stallion in Amen-Ra's place. So the old guy finally died, Rory thought as he measured up the usurper. He couldn't help but wonder what had happened to Amen-Ra. He would have been nineteen this year. This stallion was definitely his father's son. Though his coat was not the same shiny copper, he had his sire's well-shaped head, short back, and strong legs as well as a deep chest. He was a sorrel color with a flaxen mane and tail and two matching stockings on his forelegs.

Spotting the Flame was his next surprise. Of course, he had known she would be six years older, but for some reason he hadn't expected her to have a colt at her side. But she did. He was a cute little guy, about three months old, not as red as his mother but still red enough to give a feeling of warmth. An Ember from the Flame, Rory thought, giving the colt his name.

He scooted back out of sight before standing and hurrying to his horse. He had found her. Now the real work began.

Brenetta was seated beneath the weeping willow when Megan joined her. The afternoon heat was oppressive, and Brenetta wished that Megan hadn't come. She only wanted to be alone.

"It was hotter back home," Megan said, "but that doesn't seem to help, does it?"

"No, it doesn't."

Megan spread her billowing skirts around her on the grass. "You've been home over a week now. How does it feel after Europe?"

"I'd rather be here."

"You must be joking! I would have loved to be in your place."

You've taken my place before . . . with Stuart, Brenetta couldn't help thinking.

"You've hardly talked about your tour. Tell me about it, Netta."

"Megan, it wasn't a tour. I went there to hide."

Her face the picture of innocence—after all, thought Brenetta, hadn't she apprenticed her deceit with the very best?—Megan asked, "Why did you break your engagement? I never heard."

"I just discovered I didn't love him enough," she answered. *Enough to live with his lying and cheating.*

"You must have broken his heart," Megan continued.

Why do we pretend? Why do we act as if we never had that conversation and that you didn't tell me you were pregnant with Stuart's child? Megan, who will you hurt next?

"Perhaps his heart twinged a bit, but I doubt that it was broken. I'm sure he's over it all by now," she said aloud.

Brenetta looked out between the branches of the tree and saw Gentle Deer walking towards the mountain. She was carrying Starr on her back like a papoose and had a bucket in her hand. "Where's Gentle Deer going?" she asked.

Megan shrugged. "Berry picking. Hunting for roots and herbs. Who knows? As long as she keeps Starr with her, I really don't care."

"She seems terribly nice," Brenetta said thoughtfully.

"Of course she does, but it's all an act. She thinks she's fooled me but I know what's going on."

"What's that, Megan?"

"She's after my husband. Well, what she doesn't know is, I don't care. She can have him, at least at night, as long as he leaves me alone."

345

Brenetta tried to hide her shock, knowing that was exactly the reaction Megan was after.

"Of course, you can't expect savages to behave like civilized people. They just don't know any better. They're like the darkies back home," Megan finished.

"Savages!" Brenetta cried. "Megan Bellman, Rory has more class, more integrity and intelligence than most of the men I've met on either side of the Atlantic. I refuse to believe he would behave less than fairly with you."

Megan was about to make her retort when a commotion drew their attention. Rory was riding towards the corral with a horse in tow. Reuben was shouting excitedly as he ran ahead of him.

"Flame!" Brenetta exclaimed as she leaped to her feet and started running. She reached the corral just as Rory had turned her loose. "Oh, Rory, you've brought in the Flame! How wonderful! She's even more beautiful than before!"

"Yes, she is, isn't she? Just like her mistress."

"Her mistress?"

"She's yours, Brenetta."

"Mine?" she echoed.

"Don't you remember, little one? I gave her to you years ago."

Brenetta stood beside him, leaning over the corral fence. "But I set her free."

"And I brought her back to you," he said, a bit gruffly. "But," he added, "the colt is for Starr."

Overwhelmed, Brenetta threw her arms around his neck and hugged him with gusto. "Thank you! Oh, Rory, thank you!"

"Isn't that cozy." Megan's waspish words were like a splash of cold water on her joy.

Brenetta drew back from Rory. "Megan, look. Rory has brought in the Flame," she said, trying to cover her suddenly blushing face by looking towards the horses.

"I'm sure that's wonderful."

"Megan, please," Rory said as he pulled her closer to the fence. "Look at the colt. He's for Starr. By the time Ember's ready to be ridden, she'll be ready to ride him. He's a beautiful colt."

"So's the mare. Why are you giving her to Netta? Why not to me?"

Rory's sigh was felt more than heard. "Because she already belongs to her."

"She couldn't have wanted her much if she set her free." Megan turned her cold blue eyes on Brenetta. "Perhaps you just always get what should be mine." With a flourish of skirts she left the corral.

Brenetta had a sick feeling in the pit of her stomach. "Excuse me, Rory. I must go," she said softly. "Thank you again."

CHAPTER THIRTY-ONE

AUGUST 1881—HEART'S LANDING

Megan threw the fashion magazine across the room. It hit the wall and fell to the floor, torn pages strewn around its battered cover.

Everything, simply everything wonderful was going on out in the rest of the world, and here she was, trapped in this God-forsaken place.

"I hate it! I hate everything here. So help me, we're leaving here. Somehow, I've got to make Rory take me someplace away from here. Somehow."

Strange how she had no desire to go home to Spring Haven, but it wasn't much different than here. Nothing happened there either. If only she could get him to take her to New York or New Orleans or Savannah. Even Denver would be better than this.

Megan jumped up to look in the small mirror hanging over the washbasin. Closely she examined her face. It was still flawless; after all, she was only sixteen. She had learned how to apply rouge to her cheeks and lips so as to add subtle color without appearing painted. Her figure had bloomed following Starr's birth, giving a womanly swell to her breasts and hips. With the right clothes . . .

"So help me, I'm getting out of here, come hell or high water."

The door opened just then, letting Gentle Deer and Starr pass through. Once again the Indian woman had been berry picking; her bucket was filled to overflowing. She set Starr free, and the toddler was off and crawling at once. She avoided Megan, whose only contact with her seemed to be a raised voice and an occasional smack. Starr's curiosity led her towards the fireplace. Gentle Deer was quietly sorting out the berries and looked up just in time to see her picking up the cold charcoal, ready to shove it in her mouth.

"Starr, no!"

The startled baby stopped and Gentle Deer quickly had it away from her but not before she had blackened her face and clothes.

"Starr knows better," Gentle Deer said softly.

Megan tossed her hair. "For goodness sake, that won't convince her." She grabbed Starr roughly from Gentle Deer. Kneeling by the hearth, she pointed to the cold ashes, saying, "No, Starr. No. No. No." With each word she whacked Starr's bottom or one of her hands until the child's wails filled the house.

A rage boiled inside Megan, a blood-red anger like nothing she had ever known. She had to stop that brat's racket. Clapping a hand over the baby's mouth, she cried, "Shut up, Starr. Do you hear me? *Shut up!*"

Starr squirmed and twisted, trying to get away. Megan shook her in response. Gentle Deer darted forward and snatched her away from her mother, cuddling the terrified child against her bosom.

"Starr's mother has punished enough," she said in a hushed tone.

Megan's face was white, her eyes sunken and wide. "I'll say when it's enough, you stupid squaw! And if she ever makes noise like that again, I'll put a pillow over her head and smother the noise out of her. Do you understand me? Then you'd have to leave. You'd have no job here and I wouldn't let you stay just to bed my husband."

Gentle Deer turned away in the midst of the tirade and went into Starr's little room, closing the door behind her.

The soft morning light sifted through the sheer curtains of the one window in their bedroom. It settled on his wife's golden hair which spread like angel wings over the pillow and sheet.

Rory propped himself up and stared at her. In repose, her face was soft, her mouth relaxed. He could almost believe she could smile an honest smile with those lips. She looked truly innocent, hardly capable of hurling such angry—and often vile—darts at him as she had last night.

Coming home from a long, hot afternoon of bronc busting, Rory had been met at the door by a simmering Megan. He could read the signs now and was tempted to turn and run before she came to a full boil. She had begged him to take her someplace else. He had all that money, hundreds, even thousands of dollars just wasting away in the bank. If he wouldn't move from here, couldn't he at least take her on a trip, someplace where she could buy some decent clothes and see some refined, elegant people?

"There's no place else you can get what you need better than around here," he had replied.

She threw a book at him.

"Rory O'Hara, you're a tight-fisted, low-bellied half-breed! You took me away from my home. You tricked me. You've cheated me out of what should be mine. And then you spend your time breeding with filthy squaws and dreaming about that harlot up at the main house. Well, don't you think you can share my bed any more. Go sleep with the other beasts where you belong!"

With silent fury he had forced open the door she had slammed and locked in his face. He hadn't wanted her; he had had no desire for her. Yet her words had stung him, driven him to take her forcefully in his arms and crush her mouth with his own. She raked the side of his face with her nails as they tumbled onto the bed. He was tearing the clothes from her body, intent on punishing her as she had been punishing him, when reason returned. He had rolled away from her, sickened at the thought that he had nearly raped his wife, sickened by what she had nearly driven him to do.

"All right, Megan. You win," he croaked. "We'll take a trip."

"Where?"

"Any where you want to go."

She had actually hugged and kissed him then, before turning onto her side and falling instantly asleep, leaving Rory to stare at the night-blackened ceiling, filled with shame and loathing.

Now he was trapped by his own guilt, and he knew it. Whatever she wanted would be gained by reminding him of his behavior last night. If only he hadn't lost his head.

He slipped out of bed and dressed silently. Megan wouldn't awaken for hours yet. He left the bedroom, noting the broken latch and sagging hinges that he would have to repair later. The door to Starr's bedroom was open. Gentle Deer's pallet was empty as was Starr's crib. Thinking they were out and about awfully early, Rory turned and left the cabin, headed for another day of backbreaking work, hoping it would be hard enough to drive the devils from his mind.

Tobias knew the moment he had crossed the border onto Lattimer land, even without fences. He was as familiar with it as he was with his own face, maybe more so. Even the horse seemed to sense that their destination had nearly been reached.

When he had left on the cattle drive, Tobias had certainly not known he would be gone so long. First a stampede had scattered the cattle, delaying them while they were all rounded back up again. Then they had been forced to detour around newly fenced farmland. Other cattlemen would have cut the barbed wire down and moved on through, but

Brent had never allowed such an act and neither would Tobias. Arriving in Dodge, he had had a hard time selling the herd for what he thought to be a fair price. Finally, the money in his pocket, he'd nearly been robbed. He managed to fend off the thief but not before he was stabbed several times and received four broken ribs.

With so much time to just lay around and think while he recovered, Tobias had decided it was time he had a place of his own. He had four sons, and by this time his last child had probably already arrived. Brent had always been generous with him. He knew he had enough money put back to get himself started, even if it was only in a small way.

Well, he had done it. On the way back to Heart's Landing, he had found the land he wanted, not far from Heart's Landing itself. Inside his shirt pocket was a slip of paper that said it was his. Tobias Levi was a landowner. He would buy all his stock from Brent, starting out with the very best. He knew Brent would let him include his herd with Brent's own every spring for the drive so that would save him on ranch hands and the worry of getting them to sale. Besides, with Brent and Rory both back, he could leave without feeling guilty.

Tobias was still a couple hours ride from home. Relaxed in the saddle, allowing his horse to set his own pace, he began planning for the hundredth time the home he would build for Ingrid and his children. It would be large. Nothing like Brent built for Taylor but bigger than what they had now. It would be shaded by tall pine trees and protected from the wind by them too. It would have two stories with lots of room for their children. With any luck, they could get it up before the first snow fell.

Ingrid sat in the shade behind her house, nursing the baby. Little Caleb had arrived two weeks before, their fifth son. Now if only Tobias would return so she could stop worrying about him. The other wranglers had brought her his letter, telling her he would be fine, he just couldn't sit a horse for a while, and for her not to worry. She thought it was terribly easy for him to say she wasn't to worry. After all, he was there and knew how he felt. She, on the other hand, had only her imagination, and it could conjure up all kinds of possibilities, most of them dire.

She and the baby were both nearly asleep when he found them. Catching a glimpse of his shadow through half-closed eyes, she sat up with a start. For a moment she couldn't believe it was really him. She was afraid she was still daydreaming. She said nothing as he walked over and knelt down beside her. As his gaze fell to the baby in her arms, she noticed the scar running across his right cheek and another one on his chest, visible through his unbuttoned shirt.

"A girl?" he asked.

"No. This is your son, Caleb."

"And the others?"

"Brenetta's reading to them to give me a rest. I'll call them."

He stopped her by putting his hands on her

arms. "Wait. Let me have a moment with just you . . . Well, almost just you," he added as he looked again at Caleb, who was now lying in his basket beside them.

Hesitantly, Ingrid reached out and traced the red line on his cheek. Tobias lifted his gaze, a rueful smile on his lips.

"It's really nothing. I wasn't much to look at anyway."

"Oh, Tobias. I was so frightened," Ingrid said, falling into his arms.

"Pa!"

Tobias and Ingrid broke apart in time to see Reuben running madly towards them. As close on his heels as their short legs could manage came his brothers, little David bringing up the rear. They piled onto their father, arms and legs seeming to come from every direction. Ingrid watched it all with a sense of total contentment. This was her family, her life, and it was whole again now that Tobias was back.

Tobias wrestled himself free. Calling a halt to the wild melee, he told the boys to line up so he could look at them.

Like four stair steps, they stood according to ages. Reuben, at five and a half, was the image of his father. He had the same sandy brown hair and brown eyes, and same long, thin nose and lanky build. He promised to be as tall as his father some day too. Isaac, on the other hand, had his mother's fair coloring and blue eyes and was much shorter than his older brother even though only nineteen months separated them. Next came two and a half year old Elijah. Tow-headed and brown-eyed, he seemed to resemble only himself, and his personality was likewise independent. Last of all was David, one year Elijah's junior. With his heart-shaped face, blond hair and blue eyes, he was a miniature of his brother Isaac.

"Men," Tobias said, smiling. "I have a surprise for you and your mother." He turned towards Ingrid. "We're going to be moving."

"Moving?"

"I've found some land north of here. It's ours."

Ingrid was speechless. Leave Heart's Landing? It was impossible.

"We'll raise our own cattle, have a house of our own. When the boys are grown, they'll have a place to inherit and a home for their families." He stopped. "Ingrid, aren't you glad?"

She could read the pride of accomplishment in his eyes and turned on a smile. "Of course I am, Tobias. It's just so unexpected, that's all."

"It will be a great place someday," Tobias said as he sat down beside her once again.

"Of course it will, Tobias. How can it help but be if it's yours?"

"It's ours," he corrected her.

As she nodded, her eyes turned towards their small cabin. When everyone was indoors, they were so cramped it seemed there was no room to breath, let alone move. It would be good to have a bigger place. Still, this was their first home. It was here they had come after their wedding. It was here all of their children were conceived and here they had all been born. It was a place of love.

Then she looked at Tobias and knew it was really *he* that was the place of love. So where he went, the love would be.

Whither thou goest, I will go, Ingrid said silently as she kissed his scarred cheek, *and whither thou lodgest, I will lodge.*

Gentle Deer and Starr hadn't come home and he knew beyond a doubt that she had no intention of bringing the little girl back.

"Rory, for heaven's sake, relax," Megan said irritably. "She'll take good care of her. If she wants her so bad, maybe the child's better off with her. Perhaps we should just forget that she was ever born."

In a chilling tone, Rory answered, "I don't want to believe that even you could say that, Megan. Gentle Deer is a good woman and she loves Starr, but the fact is that she took my daughter and I'm going after them." He gave her a piercing look. "I don't believe she would have taken her unless she thought Starr was in danger."

"Going after her!" Megan exclaimed, not acknowledging his last sentence. "But you promised me we'd take a trip. Why not at least let the woman take care of her until we get back? Then you can go looking for them."

Rory opened the door, turned and looked at her. "Megan, you are my legal wife. If I chose to, I could divorce you or I could even just walk out this door and never return. I know that you tricked me into marrying you because you were pregnant with Starr, and I know who her real father is. But I've stayed with you anyway. Do you wonder why? It's because of Starr. I love her that much. She *is* my daughter, regardless of the facts. So if you get a trip or even if you get food for the table, it's because of Starr. I want you to remember that while I'm gone." He turned, took another step, then faced her again. "And one more thing you should remember. You will never be half the woman of Gentle Deer. I don't love her nor have I ever desired her, but I do recognize her as a woman of quality which you will never be. You sicken me. Don't be afraid that I will ever again darken your bedroom door."

Rory was amazed at how quickly Gentle Deer could travel with a child. He also realized she was an expert at covering her tracks, forcing him to retrace his steps time and again. He held no anger in his heart for the woman. He knew she had done it out of love, but as one day became two and then two became three, fear began to gnaw at his heart. What if he should never find them? What if Starr should be lost to him forever? He would have nothing then. No one to give his love to. Nothing and no one but a wife who hated him and whom he loathed in return.

Brenetta paced the length of the porch. Surely Rory should have been back days ago. Any number of things could have happened to him. He could have been thrown or attacked by a mountain lion or a bear or he could have been killed by renegade Indians or outlaws or . . .

"Brenetta, sit down," Taylor told her. "You're

wearing a path in the boards.''

Dropping into the nearest chair, Brenetta asked, ''Do you suppose he's all right?''

Megan had been forced to explain Rory's sudden absence but had limited her explanation to saying Gentle Deer had run off with Starr and Rory had gone after them. Brenetta was certain there was more to the story.

Rory. And Starr. Both of them out there somewhere. Though she had been camping with him many times when they were growing up, and she knew how capable he was, in her mind he was suddenly as helpless as Starr would have been on her own. Oh, nothing must happen to him. It just couldn't!

''Netta,'' Taylor said softly.

Brenetta blinked away her troubled thoughts. ''Yes, Mother?''

''Netta, you must be careful.''

''Careful?''

There was a long pause before Taylor replied, ''About loving another woman's husband.''

''Mother, what are you . . .'' She stopped in midsentence, understanding dawning. ''I *do* love him, don't I?''

''Yes, Brenetta. I'm afraid you do.''

Brenetta covered her face with her hands. ''Oh, Mother, what am I to do?''

''Perhaps you should go away for a while,'' Taylor suggested.

''No. No, I ran away once before. I won't do it again.''

''Then I suggest, my child, that you learn to hide it better so that no one else will know.''

They fell silent, Brenetta thinking on what her mother had said. Yes, she would have to learn to control her emotions and expressions so that no one would guess the truth. *But I think he still loves me and he's hiding it too. Whatever am I to do?*

Rory found Gentle Deer with her people. It was a small tribe of Sioux, only about fifteen in all. They had left the reservation in search of better hunting and had wandered far to avoid being sent back to a place they hated. Gentle Deer came out to meet him, a frowning buck watching from about ten feet away, his arms crossed against his bare chest, his feet planted firmly beneath him.

"I've come for Starr."

"Starr would stay with me."

"No, Gentle Deer. I will take my daughter home. There is no danger for her there."

"The woman is gone?"

"No, she is still there, but Starr will not be with her. Bring me my daughter, Gentle Deer. I will not leave without her."

Gentle Deer seemed to measure him up, then left him to enter a wickiup. When she returned it was with Starr in her arms. Seeing her father, the little girl squealed happily in greeting.

Before Gentle Deer passed her to him, she said, "Bear Claw has great strength and much endurance to live with the white fire-tongue. I will ask the gods for peace for Bear Claw, mighty brave."

"Gentle Deer is a woman of wisdom," Rory replied, taking Starr and holding her tightly. "She has loved Starr and my heart is grateful. I will ask the gods to send a mighty brave and many papoose to Gentle Deer."

Megan had vacillated between anger and fear from the moment he left. She had been so certain she held the upper hand but she had pushed him too far. By not caring about Starr, she had lost all that she had gained. What would he do now? She had never considered he might divorce her. Where would she go if he did? She couldn't go back to Spring Haven, a scorned woman. Besides, though it wasn't much in evidence now, Rory was a wealthy man, and Megan intended to have a chance to enjoy that money.

By the time Rory returned, Megan had pledged to herself that she would be more careful, that she would play the role of adoring wife. She would be so convincing not even she herself would know she was pretending.

When she saw Rory riding in, she rushed to brush her hair and change her dress. But he didn't come to their cabin. Instead he had ridden up to the main house. Miffed but forcing herself to control it, Megan hurried after him.

The door was open, and as she climbed the steps, she could see Rory just inside the parlor. Before him stood Brenetta with Starr in her arms.

"Will you do it for me, little one? For Starr?" Rory was asking her.

"Oh, Rory, you know I will. I love her just as you do. But Megan . . ."

"No, Brenetta. She will not have the child."

Megan hurried inside. "Rory, you've found

362

her!" she cried, taking Starr away from Brenetta. "Oh, my baby. My little girl. Are you all right? Your mama's been so afraid for you."

Starr set up an immediate fuss at being jerked away from someone she liked into the arms of the woman she feared most. Megan managed to hide her irritation with Starr, but only barely.

"Oh, dear, she's awfully tired, isn't she?" she mumbled.

Rory removed the little girl from her arms and Starr's cries subsided.

"Brenetta, please take Starr to the nursery. I must speak to Megan alone."

Brenetta left silently with Starr in her arms. The room was ominously still until she was out of sight. Feeling the need to make the first move, Megan reached out and touched Rory's arm.

"I really have been frantic, Rory."

She couldn't help but notice that the soft expression which had filled his eyes while Starr was there had been replaced by a stone-cold one.

"Megan, I've arranged for Starr to stay here from now on. Netta will care for her as Gentle Deer has done. And I'll be moving my things to the bunkhouse today. Don't worry, I'll see that you're amply provided for, and should you want to go home to Georgie, I'll take care of all expenses."

The blood seemed to have all drained from her head. "Rory, you mustn't do this to me. I . . . I've made some mistakes. Bad mistakes. I'll change. I'll be a good wife . . . and a good mother. I promise. I promise I will. Please don't move out. Please don't put me through the embarrassment."

"Don't embarrass you? My dear wife, you don't need my help for that?"

Losing control, Megan stamped her foot and retorted, "You can't leave me. You promised to take care of me. You promised to cherish me. Aren't you a man of your word?"

"I said you'd be taken care of."

"You promised me a trip. Remember? That was right after you broke down my door and attacked me." Her voice had risen to a fevered pitch, easily reaching the farthest corners of the house.

Rory's face darkened. "I'll keep my promise, Megan, but when I decide the time is right." His hand clamped around her upper arm and he propelled her outside and towards their cabin.

She'd done it again. She'd gone too far. Why was she so careless?

"Rory, I'm sorry. I truly am, Rory. I'm just so upset, I didn't know what I was saying. You're taking away my baby, and I'm losing you too." She managed to squeeze out some tears. "Don't you know I've grown to love you?"

He stopped abruptly and glared at her. She continued with her tears and woebegone expression, letting her shoulders droop in a stance of hopelessness. She could see his jaw twitch as he fought within himself.

Finally he said tonelessly, "All right, Megan. I won't move out of the house. I'll stay in Starr's room. But Starr will not return."

"Thank you, darling," Megan said submissively, her eyes lowered. "I promise I'll show you what a good wife I can be."

As he lay on the pallet in Starr's room that night, Rory wondered what else he could have done. He didn't trust Megan. He didn't believe she had learned to love him as she said. But he *was* a man of his word. He had taken her for his wife. Could he do anything different by her? Wasn't he bound to give their marriage every chance?

Uninvited came the picture of Brenetta with Starr in her arms. The woman he loved and the child he loved—and neither of them really his.

CHAPTER THIRTY-TWO

OCTOBER 1881—HEART'S LANDING

The bright golds and oranges of fall were quickly disappearing. The morning air was crisp, its sharpness nipping at her lungs, but in a few hours the sun would bring a pleasant Autumn warmth. This was Brenetta's favorite time to go riding.

The Flame seemed exhilerated as well. Brenetta could feel the mare bursting with restrained energy and, reaching a level stretch of ground, let her have her head. Above the thundering hooves, Brenetta bent low, her hands holding the reins on either side of the mare's neck. The wind whistled in her ears and stung her eyes. Still she regretted pulling the Flame down to a walk again about a mile down the trail.

She patted the shiny red neck. "Good girl. Now we'd better get down to business."

Brenetta, as well as nearly every other hand at

Heart's Landing, was on the lookout for signs of the rustlers. In the past few months, they'd been hit hard. At last count, they were down about two hundred head. It didn't help much to know they weren't the only ranch suffering this fate. Tobias was hurt even worse. Half his starting herd had been taken.

As the trail melted away behind them, Brenetta's mind began to wander from thoughts of cattle and rustlers. Actually, the first to come to mind was because of the cattle and rustlers. Tobias and Ingrid. They had moved into their new place last month after a house raising attended by everyone from miles around. Brenetta tried to get over to see them at least once each week. Ingrid seemed very happy in her new home as did the boys.

She thought now of her last visit. The house was warm and friendly with its one main room downstairs. Tobias and Ingrid's bedroom was right off it. Upstairs were four bedrooms, but the three oldest boys shared one room; the others stood empty. David still slept in his parent's room along with baby Caleb.

"What are you going to do with all these extra rooms?" Brenetta had asked.

With a soft blush of her cheeks, Ingrid answered, "Fill them up, I hope."

They were such a happy family, full of laughter and mischief. The only cloud on their horizon was Ingrid's father. Brenetta knew she had tried to visit him once again after Caleb was born, only to be turned away by Jake Hanson, her own father, at the end of a shotgun. Brenetta had been horrified when she heard the story.

"How awful for you, Ingrid!" she had exclaimed.

"I'm afraid after all this time I've come to expect it, but I've got to keep trying. It's so sad, Netta. He's so very bitter and so alone. He's grown old and the place is so run down. It was never much but . . ." She sighed. "He could be enjoying his grandsons if only he weren't so stubborn. Maybe someday . . ."

Thinking back on how Ingrid had even forgiven Jake for almost killing Tobias, Brenetta decided that the woman came close to sainthood in her book. Certainly she was a happy woman, loved as she was by her husband and children.

Thoughts of the Levi children brought Starr to mind. The past few weeks, since the moment Rory had put her in her arms and asked Brenetta to care for her, Starr had become the center of Brenetta's life. She had agreed to do it out of love for Rory, but now it was because she truly loved the child as if she were her very own.

There had been a moment or two when she had looked at Starr and had seen the resemblance to Stuart so clearly it had been a shock. It had brought her a brief feeling of pain and sorrow for a lost love. But the feeling vanished quickly enough, replaced by an even greater ache—her love for Rory.

Rory, her beloved. Yet she couldn't touch him or hold him or kiss him because he belonged to Megan. Brenetta knew he still loved her. The message was in his eyes and in his voice whenever he came to see Starr, but he would never tell her because of Megan.

Damn that girl! She had ruined all their lives, especially Rory's. It hurt Brenetta to see him trapped by his own sense of honor. Yet, if he was different, would she still love him.

Memories of Rory flitted through her mind. Rory the boy—at nine, watching as they buried his mother and baby sister; at thirteen, helping his drunken father into their cabin or bent over his studies in Brent's library as Taylor tutored him; at sixteen, taming the Flame and at Garvey's funeral, tears streaking his face, and as he left for New York. Rory the man—at the train station in Atlanta, so handsome, so changed; working at Spring Haven, his bare skin glistening with sweat over his broad, well-muscled back and chest; at his wedding, his chiseled face once again withdrawn, closed; and home again, loving Stuart's daughter, a proud man, a determined man . . . a man married to Megan.

Her thoughts always came back to that. It was a fact she couldn't change. She knew he was doing his best to make their marriage strong. She also knew Megan was pretending to be doing the same, and the pretense galled her.

Brenetta was unprepared for the sudden rattle that sent the Flame flying up on her hind legs. She was thrown clear of the threatening snake but plunged down the side of a rocky ravine, sliding and rolling, until she landed in a crumbled heap at the bottom.

The Flame's reins were snagged between two rocks when Rory came upon her. At first he thought she was tied there while Brenetta had walked off to see something. Then he noticed one of the stirrups was missing. Closer inspection revealed that it had been torn away. The Flame's legs were cut and bleeding, as if she had struggled desperately to free herself, probably from the snagged stirrup.

"Brenetta," he called. No answer.

Rory removed the ruined saddle, leaving it alongside the trail to be picked up later. Next he removed the mare's bridle and replaced it with a halter. Mounting his own horse, he began retracing the Flame's trail, the tired mare bringing up the rear.

Jake Hanson had never thought he would be glad to hear a rattler give warning, but he certainly had been lucky. If it hadn't happened and her horse hadn't thrown her, Brenetta Lattimer would have discovered him for certain, him and the ten head of Lattimer cattle he was herding off Heart's Landing. If she had seen him, he would have had to kill her himself. He wouldn't have liked to have done that to such a lovely young woman.

When the flaming red horse raced away in panic, Jake had cautiously approached the edge of the ravine. He was certain she was dead. Nobody could lie as twisted and as motionless as she was and still be alive. Quickly he had returned to his horse and ridden away, leaving behind the cattle he had worked so hard to gather this morning.

Jake spit a stream of tobacco juice at the ground as he watched Tom Parker altering brands in the box canyon below him. Tom's brother, Pete, was helping him, the two young men working in an efficient and well-practiced rhythm. Over the past several months, Jake and the Parker brothers had managed to add nearly four hundred head of cattle to Hanson's own herd. Having put out the word that he was missing cattle too had removed him from suspicion, and having someone as expert as Tom Parker working for him had almost guaranteed that no one would discover the cattle weren't his.

It had begun as a way to sting Brent Lattimer, a man for whom he harbored deep resentment. After Ingrid's last attempt to see him, he had sworn to get even with all of them. Once he'd begun and he'd found how easy it would be, Jake had broadened his range of activity until he was striking nearly every ranch within fifty miles or more.

After today's near mishap, however, Jake had decided it was time to pull back and relax. There would be no more rustling until late winter or early spring. Maybe not even then. Maybe he could think of something even better by then to stick in Brent Lattimer's craw.

Brenetta regained consciousness. She wondered how long she had been out this last time. She was certain she hadn't pulled herself any further than ten feet before yielding to the pain. She tried to tell how much daylight was left but knew her vision wasn't true. One eye was swollen entirely shut; a cut that kept reopening as she strained to pull herself up the ravine drained into the other one. Every part of her body was bruised and battered. She thought her left arm must be broken and both legs were badly sprained.

Sometimes she nearly succumbed to despair. If no one found her before nightfall, she would die of exposure. Perhaps it would be easier to just lie here and wait for death than to endure the intensified pain of trying to climb back up this wall of rocks to the trail.

Brenetta gritted her teeth. "I will not die," she gasped as she grasped a clump of wild grass and began pulling with her arm and pushing with what little strength was in her legs. "I . . . will . . . not . . . die . . ."

Bolts of pain shot up into her back from her legs. More skin was scraped from her useless arm as it dragged over the rocky ground. She felt herself losing consciousness again and fought against it. She had moved no more than two feet. She mustn't faint. She mustn't . . .

She found it more difficult to awaken this time. She felt as if she was floating in a black sea of nothingness. To reach the land of consciousness again would be to feel the pain. If she stayed here, she would feel nothing. Just nothing. No. No, she had to open her eyes. She had to try.

As she forced open her one good eye, she discovered she was on her back. She must have rolled over while she was out. Or worse, she might have slipped back down the little bit of ground she had gained. Then Rory's face appeared above her and she thought she was dreaming.

"Netta. Netta, can you hear me?" he said.

She moved her lips but nothing came out. Carefully he picked her up and carried her to the top of the ridge.

"I've got to find some shelter," he told her. "I'll be back."

As she gave in once more to the pain, she knew she would be all right. Rory was there to help her. Rory always came along to help her . . .

The sight of her, lying bruised and bleeding, had been almost more than he could stand. He was certain as he bent over her that she was dead, and he wanted only to die with her. He rolled her over onto her back. Then she opened an eye and he knew she was alive. Now his job was to keep her that way.

Nightfall was not long away. The temperature had already fallen drastically. October nights in the mountains of Southwestern Idaho could be bitter. It would be best if he could get her home but he knew she would never be able to make it tonight.

The small cave he found was hardly bigger than a wolves' den. It smelled of animals but was warm and free of the wind. Rory cushioned Brenetta's head with his jacket, then went out to his horse and got his bedroll. Before covering her with the blanket, he checked her injuries. Nothing appeared broken in her legs, but her left arm had to be set and secured as best he could. Before she could awaken, he went in search of a strong stick to support the arm.

After doing what he could for the broken limb, Rory washed her cuts with water from his canteen. Next he built a fire near the cave opening, and then he laid down beside her to share his body's warmth. He was relieved when she began to stir at last.

"Rory?" she croaked.

"Yes, I'm here."

"Am I going to die?"

"No, my little one. You will not die. I am here."

"I love you, Rory," she whispered as she slipped away again.

He tightened his arm around her, still trying not to hurt her by his touch. She had said she loved him. Could it mean . . . did he dare to think she meant she really *loved* him?

"Netta, don't leave me," he whispered in her ear. "I will always be yours even if we can't be together. I love you, little one. You must get well. Starr needs you. I need you."

Brenetta was alone again. The fire was dead, but she was still warm, wrapped tightly in Rory's blanket. Sunlight was streaming into the cave, warming her further. She tried to lift her head but gave up with a groan. She was too stiff to move an inch.

Rory appeared at the opening. "You're awake. I've rigged a stretcher for you. Do you think you can stand to be moved?"

"I can stand it," she replied stoically.

Bringing in his replenished canteen, Rory helped her drink from it. He brushed back her tangled hair and then laid her head back on his jacket, his eyes tenderly caressing each bruise on her face.

"I must be quite a sight."

"You are."

"Thank you for coming, Rory."

"Could I have been kept away?"

Despite her sore body, she wished he would take her into his arms and kiss her. She wished they could stay here and never go home. Just the two of them here in the wilderness.

"I'm going to take you out now," Rory warned her. "I'll be as gentle as possible. Are you ready?"

She nodded, bracing herself. "I'm ready."

Although she tried valiantly not to, she fainted again before they were outside, coming to on the stretcher, wrapped once more in the blanket and strapped on securely so she wouldn't fall out. The stretcher was made from another blanket attached to two long poles which in turn had been rigged to fit like traces of a buggy on Rory's buckskin.

"It's going to be rough," Rory warned her.

"It's all right, Rory. I'm sorry I've been such a coward, passing out all the time."

Running his finger down her cheek and under her jaw, he said, "You've been very brave, little one. Let's get you home."

Megan was furious. He hadn't come home last

night, and she had worked so hard to prepare a special dinner and to dress appealingly. She had been so careful lately, never raising her voice, always seeing to his needs, acting interested in his day's work. She really didn't mind that he still chose to sleep in Starr's old room. If there was some way to win him without sharing his bed, she would be just as pleased. She had discovered that sex didn't always bring the desired results and could, as had happened with Starr, only foul up a girl's plans. She was certain that he was almost convinced of her love for him. Men can be such fools, she thought.

But now he had failed to come home . . . and so had Brenetta. When Megan learned that Brenetta was missing, she knew they were together. So, he was cheating on her with Brenetta, and all the time saying he wanted to see if they couldn't make their marriage a better one. Brenetta, the girl who had everything Megan wanted—wealth and beauty and world travels and a beautiful house and fine clothes, now she was after the only link Megan had to ever gain those same objectives—her husband. Well, Megan wasn't about to let her win. Not ever!

She was waiting on the porch with her Aunt Taylor when Rory came into sight. Her fury was well concealed but still simmered in her breast. It made little difference to her when she saw that Brenetta was badly injured and heard Rory's tale of finding her. As long as she believed there was a threat to her hold on Rory, she would never let down her guard.

Brenetta was sitting in a rocking chair beside her bedroom window when Megan came to see her. The three weeks since her accident had erased the puffiness in her face and relieved most of her pain. Only her arm still caused her any real trouble, but Doc Marshall said Rory had done a good job of setting it and thought she would be fine in a few more weeks or so.

She wasn't exactly pleased to see Megan at her door, despite feeling better.

"May I come in?" Megan asked sweetly.

"Certainly."

Megan sat on the edge of Brenetta's large brass bed, her hands folded demurely in her lap, hidden in the folds of her bright yellow skirt. "Netta, I need to ask you a favor. I know you don't owe me anything but I must ask anyway."

Brenetta waited silently.

"You've taken such good care of Starr for me . . ."

For Rory, Brenetta corrected.

" . . . and I know I haven't deserved it. My only excuse is that I was young and felt unable to cope with a new husband I hardly knew and a baby too. It just all happened so fast." She sighed, sounding as helpless as her words. "Netta, I didn't even like Rory much at first, after what happened and all, but he's so wonderful, so sweet and kind, I . . . I've come to love him very much."

Brenetta pulled her shawl closer about her shoulders, feeling a sudden chill.

"I think he's grown more fond of me too and . . . I think it could be a good marriage if . . . if only . . .

Oh, how can I say it? If only it weren't for you!"

There were tears in Megan's eyes, and icy hands tightened around Brenetta's heart. "What about me, Megan?" she whispered.

"He . . . he thinks you love him and he thinks he should still love you too. I don't know. Maybe he does. But Netta, I'm his *wife!*"

"I know that." Brenetta felt as if she were choking.

"Then please, Netta. Oh please!" Megan cried, falling to her knees at Brenetta's feet. "Tell Rory to go away from you. Tell him you don't love him. Give me a chance. Once I know Rory's going to be my husband forever, I'll be able to bring Starr home and we can be a whole family. Please, Netta. Don't ruin my marriage."

Dear God, help me, Brenetta prayed. What do I say to her?

Deep in her heart, she knew Megan lied, that there was no love in this girl for Rory, for Starr, or for anyone else except herself. Yet she couldn't deny the truth of what Megan asked.

"Don't worry, Megan. Nothing improper has ever happened between us. Nor will it. Rory is your husband; I shan't forget it."

Megan rose swiftly. "Thank you, cousin," she said, kissing Brenetta's cheek.

Brenetta turned her gaze out the window as Megan left. The autumn world had turned an ugly grey.

Rory came with Starr, as had become his habit, directly after supper. He knew something was troubling her as soon as he saw her face.

"I'm a bit tired tonight, Rory. I don't think I'll have you stay long," she said when he sat down. "But I must talk to you for a moment."

"What is it?"

"Rory, I think we must put an end to these evenings. You should be taking Starr down to see her mother, not me. You should be relaxing with your *wife*." She was speaking quickly, as if the words had been rehearsed for hours. "I know you come because we're such good friends and you're worried about me, but your first duty is to your family. If you still feel Megan isn't ready to care for Starr, I'm glad to do that and so is Mother, but you don't have that same worry about yourself. You must go home to Megan."

Although he had told himself that he was doing his all to make some kind of life with Megan, always there had been his love for Brenetta getting in the way, always the unrelenting hope that somehow they could be together despite the mess he had made of everything. Now she was slamming closed that door of hope, sending him back to Megan and the coldness of his little room.

"You're right, of course, Netta," he said stiffly. "I didn't realize how much of your time I was taking up nor that Megan was alone so much. I'll see you around. Take care of your arm."

He didn't hear her muffled sobs as he hurried from the house.

She had won. It was almost more than she could manage to keep the smirk off her face as Rory told her they would be leaving for the East and Europe come spring.

"Thank you, Rory," Megan whispered tenderly, putting meaning into her kiss that wasn't in her heart. "Thank you so much, my darling."

She didn't care that he stood woodenly in her arms. She was going to Europe. She would be leaving this "no-woman's" land to see the world. She'd won!

CHAPTER THIRTY-THREE

APRIL 1882—HEART'S LANDING

Brent and Rory had ridden out at dawn. Late yesterday they had discovered another twenty head were missing. The rustlers were back. All winter the cattle had been undisturbed, but now as the spring drive drew closer, the thieves had returned. Brent was determined to catch them this time.

They had picked up their trail about an hour before. The going was slow. The trail followed along the side of a steep mountain, the earth falling sharply away to nothing on the left and rising breathlessly towards the sky on the right. They rode constantly skyward. Finally they were forced to stop their ascent to rest their horses.

"I'm going to hate to see you go, Rory," Brent said, resuming their conversation as he hunkered down, resting on his heels.

Rory did the same. "I'm going to hate it too, Brent. But this trip is important to Megan."

Important to Megan? It was more than important. It was all she thought about, morning, noon, and night. Sometimes he thought he would go crazy with her chatter. He had to admit she had managed to sheath, for the most part, her razor-sharp tongue, but there was nothing between them that could really be called a marriage. He knew everything she said and did was carefully calculated to get her what she wanted. Some time ago she had stopped telling him that she loved him, realizing at last that it made no difference to him as long as they lived in peace.

Rory was resigned to the life he had but sometimes he couldn't help imagining what it would be like if he was married to the woman he loved instead. He looked over at Brent, thinking how lucky he was. Take for instance this morning. As they were about the leave, Taylor had kissed him goodbye—kissed him passionately. She had told him to be careful, her eyes saying how much she needed him, how much he meant to her. Everything they did, they did with thoughts for the other.

Rory tried to avoid thinking of the same scene between himself and Brenetta. Since the day she had sent him back to Megan, the message clear there was no future for them, Rory had tried to block out such imaginings. They only brought renewed feelings of emptiness.

And really, he thought now, my life isn't completely empty. I work in the midst of the most beautiful country anywhere. I have an adorable daughter who loves me. I have good friends and never go in want of anything. That's more than most people can say. Actually it's not a bad life.

Then why did his heart still feel so empty?

"It was so nice of you to come calling again, Tom," Brenetta said as she set the tea tray on the table between them. "I'm sorry you missed Father."

"I think you know by now it's not your father I come to see, Brenetta."

Tom Parker's smile was friendly, showing slightly crooked teeth in his sun-darkened face. He was a tall man but rather ordinary in appearance with mousy brown hair and brown eyes. He had been calling on her since last November, and she was certain a proposal was in the works. She wondered what she would say when he asked.

Brenetta really knew very little about him. He had gone to work for Jake Hanson last year, he told her, but owned his own land just outside Boise. He hoped to be able to return there this year and begin working his own place. He had a fine sense of humor and joked with her often. She liked Tom, and he did help keep her mind off of Rory.

Looking at Tom from beneath lash-shielded eyes, she wondered if maybe she should accept when he asked, even though she didn't love him. She wasn't getting any younger, after all. She had just turned nineteen, and there wasn't exactly a line of men battering down her door. If she married Tom, they could go to his ranch, get away from here, away from Rory and Megan. If it was money he needed to work his place . . . well, she had money. I'm getting cynical, she thought.

"Brenetta, you're not listening," Tom said, snapping his fingers in front of her nose.

"What? Oh, I'm sorry. I was daydreaming. What were you saying?"

He laughed. "Nothing important. Just that I'm thinking of going back to Boise soon. I'm tired of doing Hanson's dirty work."

"Dirty work?"

"What I mean is, work he doesn't want to be caught doing himself. Ah . . . you know, work he doesn't *like* to do himself."

"Funny. Mr. Hanson never struck me as the type of man who really liked any kind of work."

Tom looked a bit uncomfortable. (Tom *never* looked uncomfortable.) "Guess what I really mean is I'm tired of working for him. I'm ready to go home."

"Now *that* I can understand."

Taylor came into the parlor. "Hello, Tom," she said absently as she walked over to the big window overlooking their valley.

"Mother, is something wrong? You look troubled."

"I don't know, Netta," Taylor replied without turning. "I just can't seem to stop thinking about your father today."

Jake focused on his target through the sight on his rifle. It was too great an opportunity to be

386

missed. There was no place they could take cover. And should he miss—by some wild stretch of the imagination—the terrain was too steep for him to chase him down. In fact, they would never even see him.

The moment between the crack of the rifle and Brent's tumble from his horse was fractional. Yet later it would play over and over again in Rory's mind in slow motion, everything agonizingly clear. Before Rory could react, another bullet split the air, this one meant for him. It missed him by less than an inch. He could feel its force as it whizzed by him and bored into the mountain at his right shoulder.

Brent's horse was already off and running before Rory could dismount. He vaulted to the ground, his eyes trying to spot the direction the shots had come from. Their assailant must have fled for no more shots were fired.

Kneeling at Brent's side, Rory knew at a glance that his friend was dying. He tried desperately to staunch the blood pouring from Brent's side. Brent coughed. The spittle that trickled from his mouth was red.

"Hold on, Brent. Hold on," Rory whispered.

Brent's eyes fluttered a moment. Finally they seemed to vaguely focus on Rory's face. "Rory," he said hoarsely, his voice weak.

"Yes. I'm here. Hold on, man. Hold on."

"Rory . . . tell Taylor . . . I . . . love her . . ."

Tears welled up in Rory's eyes, blinding him to Brent's struggling face. "Tell her yourself," he choked out.

"You're . . . best son . . . a man . . . could . . . have. Take . . . care of . . . them all." He was fading, his words hardly more than a whisper. "Tay . . . lor . . . Netta . . . Carl . . . all . . . need you . . . now." His final word came out with a sigh. There was no corresponding intake of breath.

"Brent! Oh, God," he cried as he crushed Brent's lifeless face against his chest, rocking mournfully back and forth. "Brent . . . Brent . . . Brent . . ."

She had always said she would know if something happened to him. Through those terrible war years, she had clung to that belief, hanging onto it like a lifeline, certain that he was alive and she would find him again. She had been right. She did know.

When she saw Rory walking towards the house leading his horse, Taylor didn't even have to look to know Brent's body was draped over the saddle. It was as if she'd been expecting it, waiting for them to arrive. She stood on the porch with one hand against the support beam, her eyes dry, her face seemingly unperturbed. Only the quivering arm that braced her gave away the numbing shock that was enveloping her.

Rory stopped at the bottom of the steps. His own face was ravaged by grief, a grief too great to be hidden behind his usual mask.

"Taylor, I . . ."

"Don't," she said gently. "Just bring him inside."

She didn't wait for him. She turned and entered the house, walking to the sofa—the long blue sofa they had picked out together in that quaint little store in Boise one summer—and placed a couple of pillows at one end, pillows where he could rest his head one last time.

Hearing footsteps, Taylor looked up to watch Rory and Sandman carrying Brent's body between them. Strange how normal he looked. His dusky hair was rumpled as usual, falling roguishly across his forehead.

Just like it did the day we met.

His eyelids were closed, hiding from her the golden twinkle that had always been lurking just behind the surface of his tawny eyes. His mouth seemed almost ready to smile.

Or to say he loved me. He always loved me.

Kneeling beside the sofa, she took his hand, a hand already grown cold, and pressed it against her cheek. A hand so strong. With its help he had fought a war. With it he had saved her life. He had brought her west and built this ranch. With it he had stroked her cheeks, her arms, her body.

"Brent," she whispered as one lone tear trickled down her cheek, "you said you'd never leave me again."

They buried him on a knoll overlooking his kingdom. The day was cool and the wind blew fiercely. A grey April day.

The Lattimer family—mother, daughter and son—stood beside the grave, all of them standing straight, their chins high and their eyes dry. The wind pulled at Taylor's and Brenetta's black gowns and veils until they appeared to be black wings about to carry them away. Carl held onto his mother's hand with a tight grip but tried hard to appear the man his father would have wanted him to be.

Behind the family stood the other mourners, friends and neighbors who had come to pay their respects to the memory of a man they all had liked and admired. Rory and Megan O'Hara. Tobias and Ingrid Levi and their five boys. There were the ranch hands and their families—old Sandman, Sam Wallace, Buck and Marie Franklin, Joe Simmons, Virgil Haskins and his wife, Emma, and all the others. Tom Parker was there and so was Abe Evans from Sage Hill Ranch and Rick O'Casey from the Lazy C and Mark and Matthew James from the Rocking Double J. There were men from Boise, dignitaries representing the capitol city, people Taylor had never seen before but who had known her husband.

As Taylor stared at the plain pine casket, she wondered at how suddenly her life was changed, what one instant in time had wrought. Never again would she hear his footsteps in the hall or brush his hair from his forehead. Never again would she find him laughing down at her in a sun-drenched meadow or race beside him on spirited horses, the mountain air kissing their cheeks.

Goodbye, my one and only love. Only the days with you were worth living. I shall never forget them . . . or you. Goodbye, Brent, my very life.

CHAPTER THIRTY-FOUR

MAY 1882—HEART'S LANDING

The study was oddly silent as Bob Michaels removed his glasses and laid them on top of the will. His eyes trailed from one person to another, awaiting some response, but everyone appeared to be lost in their own thoughts.

Bob had been witness to Brent's revised will last year when he had visited Heart's Landing for the first time. He was the only one who had known its contents besides Brent himself, and some of the recipients were obviously surprised.

His roving eyes stopped on Taylor. Still very beautiful, there were streaks of grey in her hair that hadn't been there before. Her lovely white complexion was nearly translucent. He hated to see the silent suffering hidden in her deep blue eyes. Brent had left her a large fortune, enough to keep a thousand widows in comfort, but his most important legacy had been a love that transcended death.

Then there was Brenetta. She was sitting beside Taylor, both of them dressed in black, their long hair caught back in snoods. They looked so very much alike except for the eyes. It wasn't just the difference in color and shape. It was that, instead of Taylor's sorrow, Brenetta's were filled with a fiery fury. Her only thought since her father's death was to find his killer. Bob almost believed she would. Brent had left his daughter half of Heart's Landing and a sizeable inheritance.

Young Carleton, not quite eight years old and already trying to shoulder his responsibility for his widowed mother and his sister. Bob had seen it the moment he arrived. He was definitely his father's son. Carleton was a handsome boy with Brent's dusky looks and his mother's blue eyes, and his good looks were not disguised behind the thick spectacles he was forced to wear. To him was left one of the surprises. In addition to his cash inheritance, his father had left this bequest:

Carleton, my son. How proud I have always been of you. From your infancy, you have been brave and so very quick. Should I not live to see you grown, it is my wish to assure you the dream you shared with me. I am leaving to you, in trust until your twenty-third birthday, the Lattimer Bank and Trust. However, as is my understanding, should you continue to desire to pursue another career, you

*may dispose of or maintain your interest in
the bank in the manner you see fit upon your
thirty-fifth birthday.*

*Carl, you have expressed a desire to become
a physician. It is a challenging career but a
more honored and noble profession does not
exist. Go after it, son. Seek to know all you
can. Stay humble, yet be strong. Remember, I
am proud to be your father.*

Despite himself, Carleton's face had beamed
brightly. He had his father's blessing to pursue
what he wanted to be. He wasn't going to be forced
to become a banker or a rancher.

Bob's gaze moved on, settling on Rory and his
wife, Megan. They were a striking pair, so very
opposite from the other, Rory so dark, the girl so
fair. Yet it was obvious to Bob it was an unhappy
union. He could also see that his young friend was
still in shock. To Rory Bear Claw O'Hara, Brent
had left the other half of Heart's Landing. He had
left the instructions that neither of them—Brenetta or Rory—could sell their share of the ranch
until such time as Brenetta was married and then
they could only sell it to the other part-owner, not
to any other third party. It was an unusual
bequest, one no one had been the least prepared
for.

Tobias Levi was a man Bob Michaels had taken
an instant liking to when they had first met. No
one could use the money Brent left to him as much
as Tobias could. He was still struggling to make
his own place a success, yet he had spent countless

hours helping Brent try to track down the rustlers. This in addition to the years he had spent at Heart's Landing, faithfully serving Brent. Tobias was a quiet, friendly, dependable and down-to-earth sort of fellow, the kind of man to give up everything to help out a friend. Brent's ten thousand dollars was going to make a big difference for Tobias and his family, and Bob believed it was well deserved.

To the other ranch hands who had been with him consistently through the years, Brent had left a thousand dollars each. None of these men were present for the reading of the will, but Bob had informed them of the gift Brent had left to them earlier in the day.

He cleared his throat as he stood up. "Assuming no one has anything to say regarding the will, I believe I'll step outside for a breath of mountain air."

Standing on the porch, his hands resting on the railing, Bob thought how peaceful it was here. No wonder Brent had forsaken New York for this. Yet, at the same time, Bob felt the urge to get back. The challenges he faced daily at the bank beckoned him home, and he knew it was time to go. His duty was finished here.

Taylor stood up slowly and turned to the others. "I don't imagine anyone has any questions as to what Brent wanted for each of us." She paused. "I have decided to take Carleton back east for a while. I don't know how soon we'll return. If Carl's to be a doctor, he needs more than my tutelage. I must find a suitable school for him. Brenetta will be in charge of the ranch, and Rory, of course, will help her. After all, they're partners now."

"I'm sorry, Megan. It's just out of the question right now."

She felt the heat rising in her cheeks. She clenched and unclenched her hands as she stared at Rory's serious features. She hated him. More than anything else in the world, she hated Rory O'Hara. To get the promised trip, she had pretended to feelings she didn't have. She had been submissive and obedient. She had even spent many hours with Starr, time when she would have rather been doing something else, just to please him. And now, just because Brent Lattimer got himself killed, she had to give up her trip abroad.

"Rory, you know perfectly well that Tobias or Sandman or any of the others will give her all the help she needs. You promised me this trip and no petty ranch problems are going to keep me from having it."

"Petty problems! Good gods, Megan, a man's been killed, the rustlers have taken hundreds of our cattle, and you call them *petty* problems."

"All right. Maybe they're not petty. Maybe they're important. But why should I have to change my plans because of something I can't control? Will my staying here change anything? Will it bring him back?"

Rory turned his back to her, and she could see the tensed muscles of his shoulders beneath his shirt. Megan bit at her lower lip to stop her torrent. She forced her breathing to slow before speaking again.

"Rory O'Hara, if I don't get my trip, I'm going back to Spring Haven and taking Starr with me," she said quietly.

"You may not take Starr," Rory answered, turning to face her again. "I forbid it."

Megan laughed sharply. "What right do you have to forbid it? She's not even your daughter."

Rory's skin turned from it's healthy tanned color to a shade of grey, his eyes hardening. Megan felt a satisfaction spread through her veins as she experienced the power she wielded because Starr was only hers.

When Rory spoke, it was a deathly tone. "Her name is O'Hara, Megan, and she's my child. You may not take her from Heart's Landing."

"Then we must take our trip."

Suddenly Rory turned on his heel and stormed out of their house. Megan looked after him, a small smile dressing her lips. Surely they would go soon.

Bob Michaels and Carleton were already waiting in the buggy. Taylor stood beside it, her arms around Brenetta in a tight embrace. Stepping away from her, Taylor studied her daughter's face.

"Mother, are you sure you're doing the right thing, leaving home?" Brenetta asked her.

Taylor gave her a shadow of a smile. Her face was still unwrinkled although her fortieth birthday was only a month away. Only the circles under her eyes suggested her suffering. The grey in her hair, instead of aging her, gave her an air of mystery.

"I'm certain. Please don't worry. I'm going to be fine."

"But you seem so . . ."

"So alone?" Taylor asked with a sigh. "We had almost twenty years together, Netta. That makes me alone now. But there's Carl to think about. Brent had a dream that he shared with his son. I mean to see that it comes true."

"Mother, I love you," Brenetta cried.

Taylor reached out with a gloved hand and stroked her cheek. 'I know, dear. And I love you." She took Brenetta's hand and pressed it against her own cheek. "Netta, listen to me. You have so very much here, and I know you can make all the right and necessary decisions in regard to the ranch. But be careful with your heart. Don't ever marry a man unless you love him with everything you've got. Don't cheat yourself or him. Remember, I've had it both ways so I know. Even with someone you like a lot, it's not the same."

Brenetta's eyes dropped to the ground.

"Netta," Taylor whispered, "don't ever give up hope. Not ever. Not if you love as I loved your father."

She hugged her daughter quickly, then got into the buggy, sitting beside Bob and holding Carl on her lap. Immediately they started off. Before they were far down the road, Taylor had to turn and look back.

"Oh, please don't let my advice be wrong," she whispered. "Let her be happy!"

Brenetta watched the buggy until it was out of sight. Her heart felt like lead within her breast. She was alone now too. Just like her mother. It was up to her to keep Heart's Landing going. Her . . . and Rory.

Why had her father done this, leaving half of the ranch to her and the other half to him? Of course, she wanted it. This was home; she loved it. But why shared with Rory? It was going to make everything so difficult.

Brenetta turned to look at the house. Tom was waiting for her on the porch, hat in hand. She sighed. She knew he was going to propose soon, as soon as a respectable period of time had passed, but she also knew she couldn't accept. Her mother was right. She wasn't going to settle for less than he who she loved, he who she wanted to spend every day of her life with.

Tom stepped off the porch and approached her. She thought there was something different about him, had been ever since her father's murder. But then, she was different now too.

"Brenetta," he said, stopping before her. "I'm sorry for barging in on you today. I didn't know your family was leaving."

"It's all right, Tom." She began walking towards the house, Tom falling in at her side.

"Brenetta, I know this isn't the time, but I must speak to you."

She glanced at him but kept walking.

"I'm leaving today. Going back to my own place. I can't stay another day."

"I had no idea you were going so soon. I'll miss your visits, Tom."

He put a hand on her arm, stopping her as he turned her towards him. "Will you, Brenetta? Then tell me you'll marry me."

"Oh, Tom," she sighed, wishing he hadn't asked, especially today when she was feeling so vulnerable. "Tom, I can't marry you."

"I know it's too soon after your father's death but . . ."

"It's not because it's too soon. I just can't marry you."

"Why?"

Brenetta tried to speak honestly, yet kindly. "Tom, I like you. Very much. But I'm not in love with you."

"It could grow."

"No. It would have to be there before we married."

A frown creased his forehead. "What if your father's killer is after you now?" he asked, looking over his shoulder and speaking softly. "Let me take you away from the danger."

"No, Tom," Brenetta repeated. "I'm not going anywhere except into the house."

"Then I'll say goodbye. I'll miss you, Miss Lattimer."

"I'll miss you too, Mr. Parker."

She watched him leave, feeling only vaguely sorry to see him go. Then with a brisk shake to clear her head, she entered the house. Rory, Tobias and Sandman were all waiting for her in her father's study.

"Don't get up," she told them as they started to rise when she came into the room.

She took her seat behind the desk and rested her

folded hands on the glossy top. Looking at their familiar faces, she wondered how she was going to be their boss. After all, they were all older than she was. They had watched her growing up. They were there when she fell from trees or skinned her knees or any of a dozen other childhood mishaps.

It was Rory who broke the ice. "Brenetta, I want you to know that Heart's Landing is really one hundred percent yours. I think Brent left it to me just to assure that you would have someone who he trusted always here to help you out. He didn't really mean for Heart's Landing to come to me."

"Why not, Rory?" Brenetta asked. "He considered you a son. He loved you dearly. Isn't it natural that he would leave part of the ranch to one of his own?" She shifted.

"Now to business," she said. "The ranch will pretty much run itself with the hands we've got here. Most of them have been with us for several years or more and know what needs to be done and who should be doing it. I wanted to speak to each of you about finding Father's killer. That's the single most important thing we have to do now. Tobias, will you help us?"

"You know I will. Your pa never stopped helping me when I needed it."

Sandman shoved his ratty hat back from his forehead and scratched the top of his balding head. "Miss Netta, what is it exactly you expect us to do? We've already scoured every inch of that mountain where your pa was shot. It's been more'n a month. The trail's long since dead."

"I know, Sandman," Brenetta answered. "No,

what I really mean is that I want each of us to be constantly on the alert for a clue that might help us to find that killer. Somewhere, somehow, it's going to happen. Maybe not this week or even this year, but find him we will."

The intensity of her gaze was so startling, it left no doubt in any of the men's minds that she would do just as she said she would. Brenetta Lattimer meant to find her father's murderer.

She stood up. "Thank you for waiting for me. I know that what I said may not have seemed like much but it was important to me to say it." As the three men started to leave, she added, "Rory, may I see you alone a moment?"

Rory stopped and waited as Sandman and Tobias left the room, Tobias closing the door behind them.

"Rory, we haven't had a chance to talk since the will was read. Father was right, you know. I *do* need you here. Up until this happened, I thought I knew a lot about running a ranch, but I really don't know anything at all." She held out her hand to him. As he took it, she said, "Welcome to your home, partner."

His returning gaze was unfathomable but his handshake was warm and firm.

CHAPTER THIRTY-FIVE

JULY 1882—HEART'S LANDING

Brenetta couldn't control the nausea. She leaned over a rock and threw up. Again and again her stomach spasmed. Tears stung her eyes. She didn't even look up when Tobias's hand touched her shoulder in understanding.

Wiping her mouth with her kerchief, she croaked, "Why?"

"I imagine things got too hot for them to steal anymore. Couldn't get 'em to market without getting caught."

"But to do this!" she exclaimed. "Why did they have to do this?"

Before them lay an unbelievable carnage. Cattle and horses alike had been slaughtered and the field was turned red with their blood. Tobias was wiped out.

The Levi family had come to visit Brenetta the day before and had stayed the night. She had enjoyed their company so much she decided to ride home with them just for a diversion. Brenetta and Tobias, on horseback, had arrived ahead of Ingrid and the children in the buckboard and had ridden on down to the pasture where his stock should have been grazing. Instead they found this.

Brenetta changed her question. *"Who* did this, Tobias?"

"The same rustlers as before would be my guess." (The same men who killed Brent Lattimer, they were both thinking.) "This was done outta spite, pure and simple."

Brenetta looked at Tobias, sympathy written in her almond eyes as she realized what this meant to him. "You can take as much stock as you need to replenish. You pick the very best that Heart's Landing has to offer."

Tobias shrugged. "We'll see." Turning his back on the grim scene, he added, "Let's get up to the house before Ingrid comes looking for us. I don't want her to see this."

"Tobias," Brenetta said as she swung her leg over the saddle, "we've got to do something to stop this. The rustling was one thing, but we've not dealing with just thieves any longer. Whoever's behind my father's death and this . . . this vengeance is crazy."

Tobias rode silently beside her, his eyes locked on his log home they were fast approaching. Despite his best efforts, Brenetta could read the sense of defeat written on his face. She turned away from him, unable to bear his sorrow too.

When he spoke, it was so softly she almost missed it. "When we find him, Netta, I'm going to kill him. With my bare hands, I'll kill him."

Brenetta's face was bathed in the golden lamp light. She was still dressed in the split riding skirt she had taken to wearing. The costume allowed her the freedom to ride astride, yet remain feminine, something it would have been hard for her not to be now that she was a woman. The light threw shadows across the planes and angles of her face, giving her an aura of intimacy. Rory drew closer.

He could smell the soft scent of soap and light cologne as he leaned over the desk. He was only half listening to her as she pointed out several different spots on her map. Instead he was thinking how much he would like to bury his face in her ebony hair, filling himself with her clean, fresh essence. It was almost more than he could resist to keep from reaching out and caressing her cheek.

These meetings with Brenetta were always difficult for Rory. He awaited them anxiously, then was tortured throughout by her nearness. She never indicated in any way that she felt other than friendship. Her brief expression of love for him seemed to have been forgotten, if indeed she had meant it that way at all.

Nonetheless, he treasured their moments together. Even tonight, as she outlined her plans for hiring more men to help in tracking down the rustlers, he felt the joy of just being near her.

"Well, what do you think, Rory?" she asked, lifting her eyes from the map.

I think you're beautiful, was the answer which popped into his head. Quickly he sat back in his chair, saying, "If they're still around, we've got a good chance of locating them. They've got to make a mistake soon." He paused, watching the determined set of her chin, the hard glint in her eyes when she spoke of their capture. "Brenetta, don't dwell on this too much."

"I can't help it. Blank faces obsess my every thought. I even dream of them." She got up from her chair and walked to the window. "Sometimes," she continued softly, "I almost know who they are. If I could just sleep a little longer, I'd get close enough to see him clearly. If I could just sleep a little longer . . ."

She seemed suddenly so frail and alone . . .

Pete Parker was a man after Jake's own heart. He was greedy. He thought like Jake, and they worked well together. Although his brother, Tom, had seemed promising, Jake hadn't been sorry to see him leave. Unfortunately, Tom not only still had some scruples and a sense of decency, but he had actually fallen for that Lattimer wench.

Jake frowned and spit at a bush, wondering what was keeping Pete. Again, he thought of Tom and how different the brothers really were—Tom, tall and brunette; Pete, shorter and blond. They were both hard workers, though. It hadn't been easy to smuggle all the cattle out of their hiding place, but they'd done it. Now Jake Hanson had more money than he had ever had in all the rest of his life combined. And he meant to have more. Grudgingly, he admitted to himself that his success was largely due to Tom Parker's expertise with the branding iron. As he sat on his horse overlooking the empty box canyon where they had hidden so many cattle for so long, Jake remembered the last time he'd seen Tom. Tom had been a very angry man.

"I agreed to help rustle a few cattle. I never agreed to be part of murder."

"Couldn't be helped, Tom," Jake replied. "They was on my tail."

Tom's eyes flashed. "Don't lie to me, Jake. You killed him in cold blood for your own damned reasons."

"And what if I did?" Jake asked, picking at his teeth with a dirty fingernail.

Tom could do nothing. He could tell no one unless he was willing to be hanged himself. Jake smiled as he watched the younger man struggle with his conscience.

"I'm going to see her today and ask her to marry me. Then I'm leavin' and goin' home. I don't want any of the money I've earned from you. It's got too much blood on it to suit me. Just forget we ever met."

Jake chuckled as he blinked away the memory. The fool. Not only had he given up the money he could have had, but the girl had turned him down too.

"Boss," Pete called. "Sorry I'm late. You ready?"

Jake spit again. "Yeah, I'm ready. Let's go."

The slaughter of his son-in-law's animals had happened almost accidentally. He'd seen the family riding towards Heart's Landing and had decided to have a look at their place. There were times he missed his girl, and he wanted to see just how she was living. Pete had been with him and had started chasing the animals in the fenced pasture just for the sport of it. One of the colts panicked and became tangled in the fence. Pete had shot it to stop its struggling. Somehow the next moment found them both shooting, cutting down one beast after another. As he fired his gun, Jake had begun to imagine Tobias Levi's despair, and he had laughed until tears streamed down his face.

Yes, it had begun accidentally, almost like the shooting of Brent Lattimer. The opportunity arose and he grabbed it. But Jake didn't intend to continue that way. From now on he operated by plans. He wasn't going to trust to chance to get what he wanted.

And he was doing it. Bit by bit, he was doing it. He was destroying the Lattimers and the Levis. He was destroying those who had scorned him and those who thought themselves better because they were wealthy or educated or whatever. One day this valley would all be his. In the meantime, he would hurt them anyway he could.

"Heard tell there's a big meetin' at the main house. Lotsa men comin' t' see 'bout workin' fer Miss Lattimer. Wouldn't mind takin' care of a thing or two fer her myself," Pete said as they rode south.

Jake eyed his partner. "You keep your mind on business, my friend," he said. "Play will come later."

Brenetta stood before the room full of men, her hands on her hips, her feet apart. Her hair was pulled tightly back and tied at the nape of her neck. Her hat lay against her back between her shoulder blades, held there by a thin string caught around her throat. Her dark brown riding skirt, white blouse, and brown vest were worn with an air of challenge, as if to say, "I may be a young woman, but I'm the boss."

"If you want to work and work hard, you'll have a job here. If you don't, don't bother to sign up."

Her eyes snapped from one face to another, daring someone to comment on her beauty or her sex. No one did.

"Rory O'Hara is my partner and my foreman. He'll assign you your duties. Mr. Levi is in charge when O'Hara or I am unavailable. It will be everyone's job to see that we don't lose any more livestock, and I expect the murdering vermin who've been doing the rustling to be caught soon. That's why I'm taking you men on. A reward of one thousand dollars each will be paid to the man or men who bring them in alive. Any questions?"

The room remained silent.

"Good," she said, relaxing a little, a slight smile gracing her mouth. "If you plan to stay, see O'Hara out on the porch. And welcome to Heart's Landing."

Brenetta left swiftly and climbed the stairs to

her room. Through her open window she could hear the low rumble of men's voices as they milled around the table where Rory was gathering their names and learning what he could about each one of them.

Sighing, she fell back on her bed, barely remembering her hat in time to keep it from being crushed. She felt weary clear to the bones. Ever since that morning in Tobias's pasture, she had been unable to rid her mind of that gruesome scene. That, and the sight of her father's body lying on the couch, his life snuffed out, played over and over again in her waking thoughts and haunted her fitful sleep. She must find them. She must.

"Bebe!"

Brenetta rolled onto her stomach, looking towards the doorway where Starr was standing with Mrs. Reichwein. The large German woman had been hired as a cook and housekeeper, but as Brenetta's responsibilities increased, taking her away more and more from the little girl, Mrs. Reichwein had become Starr's nanny, a position she thoroughly enjoyed.

"Come in, Starr," Brenetta said, holding out her arms.

The little girl ran towards Brenetta, her face aglow. They loved each other, these two, and no amount of trouble would ever change that. Megan's attempt at showing her maternal instincts had been short-lived. She had quickly dropped the pretense when she realized it was unnecessary for the fulfillment of her goals.

Brenetta was the only mother Starr knew, and Starr couldn't have been more Brenetta's child if she had been conceived in Brenetta's womb.

"Bebe," Starr said again as she pulled up onto the bed beside Brenetta.

Brenetta liked the name Starr had given her. She couldn't allow herself to be called "Mommy" and she hated the thought of being "Aunt Netta" to this child of her heart. Somehow, when Starr was first learning to talk, Brenetta's name had come out sounding like "Bebe" and the name stuck.

"How's my little starshine girl?" she asked, hugging the child.

"Fine."

"And what are you going to do today?"

"Help cook."

Brenetta looked at the woman in the doorway. "Is that right, Mrs. Reichwein? Is Starr going to make our dinner?"

"That she is. Come along, *liebling*. We must begin."

Starr threw her arms around Brenetta's neck and planted a wet kiss on her cheek.

"Bye-bye, Starr. Bebe will come see you later."

Starr slid off the bed, her chubby little legs scurrying to catch up with Mrs. Reichwein.

"You're the best part of my days," Brenetta whispered after her as the loneliness began closing in once more.

Rory was awake before dawn. He lay silently on his bed, allowing his mind to toy with the dream

411

he had been having before wakefulness disturbed him. It was still so clear, and he wanted to imagine what the ending would have been, could have been . . .

He is in the study with Brenetta. She is telling him once again that they must catch the rustlers. She will never be happy until they are found. Carefully he takes her by the shoulders and pulls her to her feet. They gaze into each others eyes, and he says, "Little one, I have found them. And your father is not dead. It was someone else."

She smiled brightly. "Oh, Rory. Thank you. I love you so much."

He is taking her in his arms, his lips leaning towards her to claim his kiss, his body straining to feel her against him . . .

It was always the same. Before he could experience the culmination of his desires, he would awaken. Suddenly he was back in his miserable little room, knowing that it would never happen. Instead he would be forced to listen once more to Megan's pleading about their leaving or her complaints about their staying. Instead he would be near Brenetta but never able to hold her, to touch her, or to really love her.

"Out damn spot," he mumbled as he began dressing, thinking Shakespeare's character had nothing on him when it came to being relentlessly haunted by memories and imaginings.

The July sun was just peeking over the edge of their valley as Rory closed the door of his house. He took a deep breath, filling his lungs with the crisp morning air. By the looks of the clear blue sky and the bright orange globe riding the rim of the mountains, the coolness that caressed him now would soon be forgotten, erased by an oppressive, breeze-free heat.

Dressed in a cotton shirt left open at the neck, a pair of worn Levis and brown leather boots, each step accompanied by the clink of his spurs, Rory sauntered towards the bunkhouse. Most of the men would already be up, and he would join them for breakfast before they began their morning's work. He enjoyed the camaraderie of the wranglers and often wished he could move into the bunkhouse with them. But he had promised Megan he wouldn't, so he stayed in his cabin, trapped by his word.

"Hey, Rory."

"Mornin', Sandman. How's it goin'? Mornin', Buck."

"Good. Goin' good, Rory."

The two cowpokes fell into step beside Rory. They had been at Heart's Landing nearly as long as Rory himself, and he felt relaxed in their company. He admired Sandman, recognizing in the wizened old man a quick grasp of any situation and a mind capable of deducing the most reasonable course of action. Perhaps the only man he felt closer to was Tobias.

Rory was glad to have Tobias back at Heart's Landing. He had never felt capable of running the place as Tobias had done for so many years. Ingrid and the children were staying at their own place, and Tobias rode home for a couple days each week. He had told Rory that before he could restock his place or even concentrate on what was left he meant to know that the man or men who had butchered his stock were caught and punished.

"Rory," Sandman said to him now. "I think we'd best check around Birch Creek again today. I got a feelin' that somethin's up there."

"What makes you think so?" Rory asked the crusty old cowboy.

Sandman shrugged. "Can't rightly say. Just a feelin' I got. Seen a man watchin' me and some of the boys in that area a couple days ago. Couldn't get a good look at him and I lost his tracks. Maybe it weren't nothin' but . . ."

"No. No, you're right. If you suspect something, anything, I'll go with your feeling. Have four or five of the men join us. We'll head out right after we eat."

The large kitchen and dining area behind the main house was already filling with men. The room had several long tables with sturdy benches for the men to sit on. Mrs. Reichwein was flipping flapjacks on the enormous grill, and the air was filled with the odors of frying pork and eggs and fresh baked biscuits. Rory slapped a few men on the back as he entered the room, pausing to say a word or two on his way to his place at the table. He was engrossed in conversation with Joe Simmons when Brenetta and Starr came in.

"Mornin', Miss Lattimer," someone said, and it was echoed many times over.

Rory looked up and stared at the two of them, his heart in his eyes for a moment.

"Daddy!" Starr squealed, struggling out of Brenetta's arms.

A smile brightened his dark face, his even white teeth showing as he began to laugh. Starr ran towards him, and he scooped her off the floor and swung her around. He loved the feel of her arms around his neck and the knowledge that she loved him. As he stopped turning he caught a glimpse of Brenetta's face. She seemed enraptured by the sight of the two of them together, but the look vanished when she caught him looking at her.

Walking towards them, she said, "Starr wanted to eat breakfast with her daddy this morning for a change. Is that all right?"

"All right? It's wonderful. Come, sit down with us, Netta. You must eat something yourself."

"Thank you. I'd like that."

Rory filled two plates and set one in front of Brenetta. Sitting down himself, he pulled Starr onto his lap and they began eating.

"Rory, I want to ride out with you this morning," Brenetta said after a few bites. "I'm going stir-crazy, waiting here. I know there's lots I could be doing, but I can't think of anything at the moment."

Rory nodded. He pretended not to look at her as he took another bite of sausage. He realized how drawn and thin she looked. Somehow she always seemed so perfectly beautiful in his eyes that he had missed the changes in her before this.

"It'd do you good to get out, probably. You can join us today. We're going to check out the Birch Creek area."

"Thanks for understanding, Rory."

Silently, he reached out and laid his hand over hers where it rested on the table between them. She lifted her eyes to meet his, and behind her pain at the loss of her father, beyond the worries of running this ranch and the obsession of capturing her father's killers, he caught a glimmer of something just for him. He tightened his hand around hers, then released it and helped Starr with her flapjack.

Megan had stopped in the doorway, her eyes finding her husband and child just in time to catch the tender exchange. Her blood raged in her veins. How dare he look at Brenetta like that when he couldn't spend five friendly minutes with her? Tossing her head angrily, she spun on her heels and returned to her cabin. This was the last time she would allow him to do this to her.

Those colts were the pride of Heart's Landing. If Pete and he could get them to the box canyon, it would be a severe blow to Miss Lattimer's morale. Besides that, they were unbranded and would bring a good price when he found a buyer for them.

Jake had posted himself on the side of the mountain. He was watching Pete carefully driving the small bank of brood mares and colts up the creek bed so they couldn't be followed. He was so engrossed in admiring how deftly Pete controlled the horses he almost forgot to keep a lookout for Lattimer's hired hands. When he did look, it was almost too late.

The riders, six or seven of them in number, couldn't see Pete or the horses as they rode towards Birch Creek, but it wouldn't be long until they could. And Jake was trapped. There wasn't time for him to make it to the draw and onto his own land before they would spot him. There was only one chance and Jake was not afraid to try it.

Spurring his horse, he shot down the hill, his big gelding's hooves scrambling for solid ground as they slid towards the creek. Pete looked up in surprise as Jake clattered towards him.

"Don't ask. Just shoot," Jake hollered at him as he drew is pistol and fired at the horse closest to him.

One thing you could say about Pete. He followed orders. Without the bat of an eye, Pete drew his own gun and felled three mares and two colts. He was smiling as he turned to look at Jake. As he stared into the barrel of Jake's gun, however, the smile was wiped away. He hit the ground with the same surprised look still in his death-glazed eyes. Jake dismounted and stood over him, waiting for the riders from Heart's Landing to arrive.

Rory pulled up at the first shot.

"Netta, stay here," he ordered her before galloping in the direction of the gunfire, the other men close behind him.

She waited a few moments. Everything was ominously quiet, the shots having stopped as quickly as they began. She clucked to her horse, unwilling to wait it out in hiding. She proceeded cautiously, not knowing what she might find. What she found was a dead man lying halfway out of the creek, his shirt turned red with his own blood. Around him lay the bodies of four mares and two colts. Standing over the human corpse was Rory, Sandman, and Jake Hanson.

"I couldn't do nothing else," Jake was saying as she approached the grisly scene. "I tried to stop him and he turned his gun on me." He shook his head. "I had no idea about Pete. To think he's been stealin' from me . . . and everyone else too. Must've been him that shot Mr. Lattimer."

"Rory?" Brenetta said softly.

His black eyes scolded her for being there but he didn't speak.

"Miss Lattimer? You've grown up a mite," Jake said as he looked her way. "Miss Lattimer, I don't pretend there ain't been trouble between our places, and your pa and me had our differences, but I wouldn't have hired no man who would do what this one's done. Not if I'd known." His voice deepened in outrage. "If I'd known Pete Parker was behind all the rustlin' and killin' that's been goin' on in these parts, I would've shot him sooner."

"Parker? Is this Tom Parker's brother?"

"Sure is."

Brenetta stepped closer to the body. She looked at the surprise frozen on his smooth-shaven face, the hazel eyes empty as they stared heavenward. Why would this stranger want to kill her father?

"You mean Mr. Parker worked for you all this time and you didn't suspect anything?" Rory asked Jake.

"He and his brother worked for me off and on, when they wanted to work. They never lived with me nor said what they did when they weren't workin' my place. And I never asked. Ain't my practice to pry into other folk's business."

"Why were you here, Mr. Hanson?" Brenetta asked, her eyes still transfixed on Pete's face.

"I was lookin' for some strays and seen him with these horses. Came to ask what he was doin' on your place with your horses and he drew his gun and started shootin'. Tried to get me but I got him first. Won't be no more rustlin' round here, I reckon." Jake turned away and mounted his husky gelding. "Well, I got strays to find," he said.

Brenetta watched him ride away, his enormous body seeming to dwarf the big horse he rode. He had changed little since the day her mother forced Brenetta and her father to accompany her on a neighborly call. Brenetta hadn't liked him then and she didn't like him now. But if the killing was over . . .

"Netta, you're shaking," Rory said as he took her elbow. "Let me get you home."

"Yes," she replied, her voice quivering.

"Sandman, take care of things here. I'll be back after I've taken Netta to the house."

"Sure thing, Rory."

As they trotted away, Brenetta looked back over her shoulder and whispered, "Is that the end of it, Rory?"

"I hope so, little one. I hope so."

CHAPTER THIRTY-SIX

AUGUST 1882—HEART'S LANDING/SAN FRANCISCO

Megan stared out the window at the seemingly endless desert. Dust, sand, chaparral, cactus, sagebrush. It was all she had seen for days on end, and she felt the urge to scream growing greater by the hour. The constant jerking and bouncing of the stagecoach didn't help matters any.

She had lost track of how many days she'd been traveling. Waiting until Rory and Brenetta and the others had ridden out that last morning home, she had entered the study and taken all the cash from the safe. Brenetta had never been very careful about locking it; she was too trusting. Megan had been ready to sneak off alone when she remembered the pleasant family scene of Rory and Brenetta with Starr that she had witnessed that very morning. No, she wasn't about to give them the pleasure of making that a permanent situation. She found Mrs. Reichwein and Starr still in the kitchen.

"Mrs. Reichwein, I've decided to take Starr to visit Mrs. Levi and the boys. We won't be back for several hours."

She'd left a note for Rory, telling him that she had taken Starr so that she and her daughter could become better acquainted, and she asked that he not disturb them for a few days. She was counting on Tobias not going home for at least three days, enough time to put some distance between them.

Megan had pushed the horses to their limit. Finally, at the station where she boarded the stagecoach, she was able to sell the outfit to a family going to Oregon. She hoped it would delay Rory a bit longer if he chose to follow her.

Many times, as passengers changed, she had been told what a lovely child she had. She liked hearing it but would have preferred hearing that she was the lovely one. Starr had been well-behaved, if a bit restless at times. Still Megan wondered what she was going to do with her in San Francisco. She certainly had no intention of being saddled with a child once she got there. Perhaps, in trying to spite Rory, she had only caused herself problems.

The color drained from his face. His knees felt weak. Rory stared at Ingrid, unable to believe what she had just told him. Megan wasn't here; she and Starr had never come for a visit.

"Rory, you'd better sit down," Brenetta told him.

Megan and Starr were missing. What could have happened to them? Were they lying somewhere, injured? If only he had checked on her sooner. If only he had known about Megan's visit before Tobias came home. If only . . .

As if she could read his thoughts, Brenetta said, "You couldn't have known. It's not your fault."

Tobias and the three men he had been riding range with had come in not too long after Rory brought Brenetta home the day Pete Parker was shot. After listening to Rory's description of that morning's events, Tobias had told him he was going home to be with his family for a few days and would come back the next week to look over some cattle to buy. Rory understood his wish to be alone with Ingrid; he would have liked more time with Brenetta himself. Later, when Rory learned that Megan and Starr had gone to visit Ingrid, he assumed she would be sent home soon. After all, Tobias would be wanting some privacy. But she didn't come home, and of course, Tobias didn't know she was supposed to be there.

A new thought struck Rory. "The money! Brenetta, it was Megan who took the money from the safe."

They had just discovered it was gone yesterday. With payday upon them, Brenetta had opened the safe for the first time in over a week only to find all the cash gone. Until this moment, it hadn't occurred to them that it might have been Megan who took it.

This morning, when Rory still hadn't seen or heard from either Megan or Tobias, he had decided enough was enough. If Tobias couldn't send her home, Rory would go get her. Brenetta had joined him for the ride.

"Where do you suppose she went, Rory?"

He looked at Ingrid and answered, "Not back to Georgia. I don't think she wants to live there again, even to get away from me."

"Rory," Brenetta said, "she only took Starr to hurt you. She doesn't care about that child."

"I know. I hoped, when I thought she'd come here . . . I've got to go after her, bring them back."

Ingrid reached out to touch his arm. "I'm sorry, Rory. I wish I'd known."

He nodded. "Tell Tobias I'd appreciate him keeping an eye on the place while I'm gone."

"I will."

They mounted quickly and galloped towards home.

"I'm going with you," Brenetta yelled above the thunder of hooves.

Rory slowed his horse. "No."

"Yes!"

He brought them both to a halt. "Why do you want to come? I'll be riding hard, moving fast. I don't know where I'm going or when I'll be back or what troubles I might run into."

"Listen, Rory O'Hara. I can ride as long and as hard as you or any other man. I won't slow you down. And I'm not going to wait here wondering about Starr. Or about you. I'm going along."

Megan liked San Francisco. It was a rough, bustling city with every type of person imaginable. There were the Spanish and the Chinese and the Negros. There were the miners and the cowpokes and the sailors. And they all thought Megan was pretty.

Shortly after arriving in San Francisco, Megan had located a woman who would keep Starr in her home for a reasonable amount. She had paid Mrs. Black three weeks in advance and then gave Starr no further thought. She came to San Francisco to have some fun, not to worry about a demanding child.

And she *was* having fun. She shopped for a new dress almost every day. She ate in the best restaurants, went to the theatre with her new friends, and spent hours flirting with handsome strangers. In the back of her mind, she was toying with the thought of finding her a man who would take care of her in exchange for her favors. It never occurred to her that she might be courting trouble

"Yup, I 'member 'em. Sold her buggy and team of horses t' some family on its way t' Oregon. She took the stage fer Californee."

"California?" Brenetta repeated.

"Yup. Bought her a ticket fer San Francisco, she did. She'll have been there a week or better now. She in some kind of trouble?"

"No," Rory answered, and to himself thought, at least I hope not.

It had taken them precious days to even learn

which direction Megan had headed. At least now they knew her destination. Wordlessly, Rory and Brenetta mounted their tired horses and turned westward into the afternoon sun. With luck, they could put another twenty-five miles or more behind them before sunset.

They made camp under a darkening sky. Few words passed between them as a weary Brenetta fixed them their meal over an open campfire. After Rory had watered the horses and turned them loose to graze, their legs hobbled, he joined Brenetta at the fire where she handed him a tin plate.

Since the terrible moment Rory realized Megan had taken Starr and run away, he'd barely given more than a passing thought to anyone or anything else. Therefore he didn't see the concerned frown on her face as she watched him set his plate on his knees, ignoring the food as he thought of Starr. He had to find her. He had to.

"Rory, you must eat."

The gentle appeal in her voice made him realize he'd been staring blankly into the fire for a long time. In the flames he had seen Starr's face—in laughter and in tears. He had heard her babbling voice and joyful squeals.

"Please, Rory. You haven't eaten right for days."

"I'm just not very hungry, I guess," he mumbled, stirring the beans on his plate with a fork.

Again his thoughts drifted away. He thought he could hear Starr crying. She was lost and frightened. She was calling for him. She was calling for her daddy and for Bebe. She needed him and he couldn't find her. Her voice was growing weaker and weaker.

Rory jumped to his feet, sending his plate clattering to the ground. With quick, jerky steps he left their camp, walking until he came to a sudden outcropping of rock. There, he leaned his forehead against the stone, still warm from the day's sun, and began to sob dryly. Months of hurt and frustraiton seemed to pour forth. Her hand on his back was so feather-like he didn't realize she had followed him until she spoke.

"It'll be all right, Rory. I promise."

For a moment he tried to swallow his pain, to resume the mask of self-control he had worn for so many years. Instead he found himself wrapped in her arms, still sobbing, his head on her breast and her lips pressed against his head as she whispered words of solace and understanding. She offered him comfort as a mother would her child, and slowly, it began to soothe him.

When did the moment change? He didn't know. One moment she was holding him in comfort; the next, he was holding her in passion. The touch of her mouth on his was like the sudden strike of a match in a dark room. It seemed to send a flash of light and heat throughout his body. She quivered in his arms as a low moan came from deep in her throat.

"I love you, little one," he whispered in her ear.

"And I love you. I love you."

Desire for her surged through the very marrow of his bones as he kissed her again. Another moan sounded, this one from his own lips. Following the sound, he swept her into his arms and headed

427

back towards the camp. Her face was hidden against his chest, her hands clasped around his neck. Her touch seemed to burn his flesh. He thought he could hear his own heart thundering in the desert night.

Rory laid her gently on his bedroll, then lay down beside her. He kissed her nose, her eyes, her lips, her cheeks, her ears, her throat. Her body melded with his and the world spun around him. He was drowning in his love and desire for her. His hand moved to the buttons on her shirt.

"Rory. Please. We mustn't."

Her whispered denial stabbed at his heart. He opened his eyes and stared into hers, pleading silently for her not to stop him.

"I love you, Rory. And I want you. I want you desperately. But not like this. Not when you have a wife, a wife who has disappeared with your child. I want you when it can be right . . . and forever."

He watched a tear trickle down her cheek, the moisture catching the light from the fire. She was right. He knew she was right and it broke his heart. Kissing her lips gently, he rolled onto his back beside her.

"Little one," he whispered, "when we've found Starr, I'm going to divorce her mother. No matter what I have to do, I'll be free of her. I'll never be happy until you are truly mine."

Brenetta moved closer to his side, touching his chest hesitantly. "I am truly yours, my love. I have been for a long time."

They slept beneath a star-studded sky, wrapped in the hope of their love.

CHAPTER THIRTY-SEVEN

OCTOBER 1882—SAN FRANCISCO

Megan could still taste the blood from her cut lip. She hesitated to open her eyes for fear he was still there. But she couldn't lie here forever; she needed to relieve herself badly. Slowly she opened her eye. She was surprised to find it was still dark. The room she was in was dark and reeked of salt water and fish. She could hear the slapping of the tide against the wharf and docked ships through the tiny window in the wall of her second story room.

Megan sat up, pulling her soiled and torn dress up to cover her bruised breasts. Her head throbbed painfully; her stomach complained over its emptiness. It was hard to believe that less than two weeks before she had been laughing and flirting with men in the bright lights of her motel lobby and at the opera house.

She had first seen him in the restaurant. He was an Adonis, a Greek god come to share his beauty with mere mortals. Megan had blushed when he caught her staring at him over her menu that first day. Then it seemed that wherever she went he was there, until one day he had introduced himself.

Richard Sunday. He had told her everything she loved to hear—how beautiful and witty and charming she was—and finally, he had offered his love, telling her he would take care of her in style, never allowing her to want for anything. By the cut of his clothes, his refined speech, and the manner in which he lived, she knew he was as wealthy as he was gorgeous. She was thrilled when he made his offer. She wanted nothing more than to be with him and be seen with him. Besides, her own money was nearly gone and she was growing desperate.

But her dream had become a nightmare. She had two days hidden away with him in their luxurious apartment before he brought her his first "friend." Too late she realized what price she was expected to pay for his care and protection. She had refused to do as he asked, angrily calling him every bad name she had ever heard. She could still see the cold, emotionless smile that was his only response.

Three days ago, he had brought her here. "To work out some of that feistiness," he had said. She'd been locked in this room, fed only a thin soup and bread. She had also been raped repeatedly by the stinking dirty men who lived and worked around the dock area.

When he left her here, Richard had said, "You'll be glad to see me when I return."

"Never!" she had spat back.

But he was right. She would welcome his return. At least the men he would bring her were clean, most of them wealthy and, hopefully, more refined in their approach, more gentle in their desires. She could wear pretty clothes and go to parties again. Yes, she would do whatever she had to to get out of this place.

At every turn, they seemed to run into a dead end. Megan had been swallowed up by the city of San Francisco like Jonah by the whale. There was not a trace of her anywhere. Everything she owned had been left in her hotel room. And what was worse, those who had seen her had never seen a child with her. Starr had vanished even before her mother.

Brenetta watched Rory out of the corner of her eye as they walked along the street. There was a desperate set to his mouth that grew more pronounced with each new day. Loving him as she did, his pain tore at her heart as nothing else could have.

Perhaps I'm wrong to make us wait, she thought. Maybe if he had the comfort of my body . . .

Rory pushed aside the doors and they entered another saloon. It was a plush establishment. The walls were covered with red and gold wallpaper. The gaming tables had bright green felt tops. The bar was of rich mahogany, polished to a mirror-like shine. A piano played gaily from a corner, and several finely dressed women, their eyes and lips painted brightly, stood and sat around the room, most of them on the arm of a man. The customers here were not the usual dust-covered cowboys or fish-smelling dock workers. These were the wealthy men of California. They were dressed in fine suits and polished boots. They wore the expression of the idle rich, though most had probably struggled hard at one time to make their fortunes.

A man rose from a nearby table and strolled towards them. He seemed to be about thirty-five years old, tall and slender, yet with shoulders broad enough to fill out his white linen suit coat admirably. His hair was dusky blond, worn long enough to brush his shirt collar, and a thick mustache, which had a sprinkling of red and white hairs in it, was perched above his smiling mouth.

"Welcome to the Sea Goddess," he said, extending his hand. "I'm Richard Sunday."

Rory shook hands with him. "O'Hara. Rory O'Hara."

"And is this lovely flower at your arm Mrs. O'Hara?" Richard asked, turning to Brenetta and bowing slightly.

"I'm Brenetta Lattimer, Mr. Sunday."

"Charmed." Looking once more at Rory, he said, "You're new to our fair city, am I right? What brings you to the Sea Goddess?"

"We're seeking someone," Rory replied.

"Well, come sit down. I know almost everyone. Maybe I can be of some help to you. Would you care for a drink?"

"No, thank you, Mr. Sunday . . ."

"Richard, please. I like things informal."

Rory complied. "Richard. I'm looking for my wife and daughter. They came to San Francisco over a month ago but have disappeared."

Richard frowned. "San Francisco can be a rough town. Do you expect foul play?"

"I . . . I don't know. She may just be hiding from me."

"Oh, I see," Richard said as his glance slid to Brenetta.

She bristled under the look. "I am Mrs. O'Hara's *cousin.*"

Richard smiled knowingly, making no reply.

"Mr. Sunday, I have been almost everywhere. I'm looking for even a small lead. Anything. That's why I'm even checking with the saloons. If there might be even a slight chance of someone knowing something . . ."

Richard motioned for the bartender to bring him a drink. "All right, my friend. I can see you're anxious to find your family. Describe them to me, though I doubt I would have met a mother and child in here."

"My wife's name is Megan. She may not be using my name as her own, though. She speaks with a distinct Southern accent. She's from Georgia. Megan has golden hair and blue eyes and is quite small, almost fragile looking."

"And the child?"

"Starr. She's not quite two. Blonde and pretty like her mother."

Brenetta watched as Richard shook his head. It

was as if she could see another chunk of Rory's strength being hacked out of him.

"I'm sorry, Rory. I've never seen them. But if I should, where can I reach you?"

"At the Chaparral," Brenetta answered. "Please, if you do see her, let us know."

Megan sat at the dressing table combing her hair. She was still feverish and sometimes she was doubled over by the harsh cough. But she knew she must look her best. Without him coming out and saying so, she knew that Richard would send her back to the wharf, or somewhere worse, if she wasn't appealing to the clients he brought to her.

She started at the click of the key in her door. She hadn't expected anyone so early. Megan met Richard's eyes in the reflection of the mirror and shuddered. Behind his gentlemanly smile lurked the sadistic evil she had come to know too well.

"Meg, my dove," he said in his wonderfully cultured voice. "Are you feeling better today?"

"Yes," she lied, her voice wavering as she held back another coughing spell. "I'm much better, thank you, Richard."

He sat in a chair by the door, his legs crossed and arms folded on his chest. "I want to ask you a few questions, Meg. And please don't lie to me. I know more than you might think I do, and if you lie, you'll regret it. Am I understood?"

Megan had twisted around on her stool. "What is it, Richard?"

"Tell me about your marriage and your husband, Mrs. *O'Hara.*"

She was shaken. She had given her name as Bellman since coming to San Francisco. No one here knew her married name . . . or so she had thought. Before she could answer she began to cough, deep, ragged coughs that tore at the lining of her lungs. When at last she was able to stop, her handkerchief was flecked with blood. She wadded it up in her hand, hiding it from his view.

"You're not well at all, are you?" Richard asked, sighing. "Now tell me before I lose patience."

"My husband is Rory O'Hara. He's a half-breed Cheyenne. I met him in Georgia where he'd come for business reasons. He's a partner in the Lattimer Bank and Trust and owns half of a large cattle ranch in Idaho."

"A very wealthy man then. Why did you leave him, knowing how much you love money?"

"Because we despised each other from the start," Megan answered with what vehemence she could muster, "and he's a very stingy man."

"And your daughter? Where is she?"

"Starr?" She hadn't given a thought to the girl in weeks. "I put her with a woman named Brown or Black or something like that. I paid her in advance. I suppose she's still there."

Richard stood up, his smile more obviously forced than she had ever seen it. "Meg, you are a totally heartless creature. Under other circumstances we might have made quite a pair, we two. So much alike." He opened the door, then said, "I have a friend who wants to meet you this evening, Meg. Make sure you please him. And get rid of that cough."

"Wait! Richard, why did you want to know about Rory?"

"Didn't I tell you? He's in town searching for you."

"Rory? Oh, Richard, when will he come for me?"

Richard laughed nastily, throwing back his head as if for a great joke. "Dear Meg, how naive you are. He won't be coming for you. He's still looking. He'll never find you."

Megan flew towards him but fell upon the closed door instead. "Richard! Richard, please!" she cried. Slowly she slipped to the floor, her cheek and hands still pressed against the door. "Oh, Rory. Help me," she whimpered.

Mr. O'Hara: I have information as to the whereabouts of your wife and daughter. Please meet me at the Sea Goddess at two o'clock tomorrow afternoon. Richard Sunday.

Rory reread the message for about the fortieth time. It had been delivered last night by a young boy of the streets, grubby and hungry-looking. Rory could still hardly believe what the note said. It had been ten days or more since he and Brenetta had gone into the Sea Goddess, asking questions about Megan. Now, at last, he had some hope of finding Starr.

"Netta, it's time to go," he called to her in the adjoining room.

She stepped into the doorway, dressed in a gown

of bronze-colored linen. A perky bonnet of the same shade was set on her head at a cocky angle and a parasol rested on her shoulder. It was quite a change from her riding skirt and boots.

"I felt like celebrating," she said by the way of explanation. "I just know we're going to find them."

He couldn't help but smile. What a strength she had been for him. He hated to admit it, for he'd always been dependent only upon himself, but he didn't think he could have stood these past few weeks without her with him.

"Come on, love. Let's go get our girl," he told her huskily.

They hired a buggy and drove to the Sea Goddess, not knowing if they should expect to find Megan and Starr there or not.

"My new friends!" Richard called in greeting as they came through the swinging doors. "Come in. Sit down. Juan, bring us some brandy. Our best."

Rory felt the hope surge again. As cheerful as Richard Sunday looked, he must have good news for them.

The saloon was nearly empty. A card game was in progress over in a corner, and a few of the saloon girls were standing around with bored expressions on their faces.

"What do you have to tell us, Richard?" Rory asked impatiently.

"I know a rather *unsavory* character, and I asked him to do some checking. He showed up yesterday saying he knew where your wife is but that the information would cost. Of course, I can't guarantee he's even telling the truth, but he did give me this."

He placed a gold ring on the table between them. Rory picked it up and read the inscription—"To M, for happier tomorrows together, R"

"It's hers. How much does he want?" Rory asked.

Brenetta was holding her breath. Five thousand dollars. Richard had told them the man wanted five thousand dollars to tell them where they could find Megan and Starr. As Rory prepared to answer, Brenetta caught a movement behind Richard. A young Mexican girl, perhaps about her own age, was walking slowly towards the stairs. With a glance that was almost indiscernible, she motioned for Brenetta to follow her. Something told Brenetta that whatever she wanted, it was important.

"Excuse me, Mr. Sunday," she interrupted, a convincing blush coloring her cheeks. "Is there . . . can you tell me where I . . ."

He smiled. "Certainly." Throwing a glance over his shoulder, he called to the girl who was now on the stairs, her back to them. "Calida! Show Miss Lattimer to the chamber room."

"Si, Ricardo. Come with me, Senorita."

Brenetta, her head dipped as if in embarrassment, followed her. At the top of the stairs, Calida looked sharply in all directions, then nodded towards the door in front of her and they entered together.

"Senorita," Calida whispered urgently, "I must

438

speak quickly. Ricardo, he lies. It is he who wants your *dinero*. The girl you seek. This Meg? She is *mucho* sick. He has sent her to the docks, to Hannah's. I think she dies."

"Dying?"

Calida nodded.

"And the baby?"

"The *nina* I have not seen, but I think Ricardo looks for her. She is worth more to you, no?" Calida put her hand on the door knob. "If he thinks I tell you this, he will kill me, *senorita*." She slipped out of the door and disappeared from view as she shut the door behind her.

Stunned, Brenetta stared at the closed door. Megan dying, the prisoner of this Richard Sunday? But these things didn't happen anymore. This was the nineteenth century, after all. But what if it was true? Then they certainly must hurry and find Hannah's.

Sometimes things worked out differently—even better—than a man thought they might. He had been lucky to run into Richard Sunday when he did, luckier still to be given this job to do for him. He hadn't expected things to be this easy for him. Mr. Sunday would never know just how much he appreciated this assignment.

He stared down at the girl on the bed. He remembered seeing her once before. She had been a pretty little thing then. She wasn't anymore. Cavernous black circles ringed her eyes and her lips were covered with cracks and blisters. She was too sick and too weak to do anything but lie still on the vermin-infested mattress.

"Miss, I don't care if I get what I want by hurtin' you or not, but it'd be better for you if I don't have to. Now tell me where I can find her. Mr. Sunday's losin' patience . . . and so am I."

"I've told you," Megan answered. "Her name was Black . . . or Brown. She had a boarding house and takes in children too."

"You won't like what I do to you, little lady," he growled unpleasantly. "I have a good imagination." ·

"Please. Please don't," Megan begged, and then succumbed to a coughing spasm.

"Where?" he demanded when she regained control at last.

"The house . . . the house had two stories. Brown. It was brown. It was on a street called Los something-or-other. Where the stagecoach comes into town. Please. That's all I remember."

The man laid his large, rough hand on her collar bone. "Okay, Miss. I'll try with that. But if I have to come back, you'll regret it."

The building seemed to lean precariously to one side, its clapboard siding bleached a greyish-white after years of salt water, wind, and sun. The stench of fish was nauseating. Brenetta pulled her shawl tight around her shoulders as protection against the lurid stares of the men on the docks. Hannah's was obviously a house of ill-repute, serving the sailors and fishermen of the area. Her spirit revolted at the idea of entering such a place, but Megan was thought to be inside and Calida had said she was very sick.

As soon as they had left the Sea Goddess, Rory promising Richard that they would return the next day with the money, Brenetta had told him what she had learned. They had inquired about Hannah's and been sent here.

The octoroon who opened the door was a gigantic man, very capable of keeping anyone from entering if he chose to.

"We've come for Meg," Rory said, using the name both Calida and Richard had used. "I'm her husband and Mr. Sunday told me she is ill. He wants me to take her home."

The man nodded mutely and pointed towards a door at the back of the building. Brenetta followed on Rory's heels, feeling the chill and dampness already creeping into her bones. If Megan was sick, this was the last place she should be.

The door wasn't locked and gave way to them at once. There was no reason to lock it. The girl on the soiled bed in the dark room was too weak to attempt to escape. Megan's arm came up to shield her eyes from the unaccustomed light and a bout of coughing gripped her at the same time.

"Dear Lord," Brenetta whispered. "Megan?"

The place hadn't been so hard to find, and Mrs. Black was an easily frightened old fool.

"You see these hands, ma'am?" he said, holding one up for inspection. "They could snap your neck before you knew you'd been touched. They've killed before and aren't afraid to do it again. You think about that before you tell anyone different than what I told ya. You understand?"

The woman nodded energetically.

"So what are you goin' to say?"

"The girl died. Got a terrible cough and died. Not knowin' where to reach her mother, I buried her myself."

"Right. You enjoy that money I gave ya, but if you take more from somebody else and change your story, I'll be back. Remember that."

Megan knew she was dying despite all Brenetta's efforts and protests to the contrary. The room they had brought her to was bright with sunshine, yet she always felt terribly chilled. She hadn't the strength to sit up or even to feed herself. When they brought her here, she had caught a glimpse of herself in the mirror. She never desired to do so again.

Brenetta was sitting beside her bed now, reading softly from a book of poetry. The verses spoke of rapturous love and of dreams fulfilled. Megan hated it. Nothing in her life had ever been as she had dreamed. Never. She was angry and she was frightened. With effort, she reached out and touched Brenetta's knee.

"What is it, Megan dear? Can I get you something?"

"No," Megan answered hoarsely. Weeks of coughing had left her throat raw and filled with sores. It hurt to talk. "Netta, I'm dying. The doctor's told you it's true, hasn't he? Well, never mind. You needn't answer. It doesn't matter."

A fit of coughing stopped her for a moment. When she stopped at last and Brenetta had wiped the blood from her mouth, she continued. "I'm only seventeen. I wanted so many things. I wanted to go places and to be somebody," she rasped. "I wasn't bad. Not really bad. Was I, Netta? I never meant to be. I wasn't really bad, was I? I was so pretty. I never went any place that the men didn't think I was pretty. Even here. Especially here. I could have had the pick of any man in San Francisco. I was so pretty . . . But look at me now, Netta. I'm going to die ugly. I don't want to die ugly!"

"Oh, Megan. Don't!" Brenetta pleaded.

Megan tried to smile. The blisters cracked and began to bleed. "Don't you ever get tired of being generous and loving? It makes *me* tired. Look at everything I've done to you. I took Stuart from you. While he was saying he loved you, he was sleeping with me. Rory really loved you, but I didn't let you have him either, did I? And I had Starr. You've never had a baby but I had the one that should have been yours. I've been selfish, so selfish I even deserted my own daughter. Why don't you hate me, Netta? I would hate you. I *have* hated you. Rory hates me. Why don't you?"

Brenetta dropped to her knees beside the bed, taking Megan's hand in her own. "Megan, Megan. He doesn't hate you. He doesn't!"

Again the coughing gripped her but her body was almost too weak to respond. Her breaths came in meager gasps, barely audible. Opening her pain-filled eyes, sunken behind circles of death, she croaked, "Then he's a bigger fool than I thought he was."

She closed her eyes and drifted into unconsciousness.

"How is she?" Rory asked as he removed his jacket.

"Not good, Rory. She knows she's dying. I think we should summon a minister." She paused and then asked, "Rory, did you find her?"

He shook his head as he stood watching the shallow rise and fall of Megan's breast.

As if sensing he had come, she opened her eyes. "Rory?"

"I'm here."

"Starr?"

"Yes, she's fine, Megan. You must get well for her soon. She needs her mother."

Megan's smile was grotesque. "Don't be silly. She won't miss me. She doesn't even know me. But I'm glad you've found her. I'm glad she's all right."

"She's fine," he repeated.

"Rory O'Hara," Megan whispered, her eyes fluttering closed for a moment. "Forgive me. It wasn't that I wanted to hurt you or Starr. I just wanted . . . I just wanted . . . what I wanted." Suddenly her eyes flew open, wide and filled with terror. "Don't let me die, Rory. I don't want to die!"

CHAPTER THIRTY-EIGHT

OCTOBER 1882—SAN FRANCISCO

Rory tenderly closed the blank eyes, then walked over to the window and stared out at the city he had grown to hate. San Francisco had claimed them both.

He had lied to Megan, offering his dying wife what little peace he could by telling her he had found Starr and that she needed her mother, when in fact Starr needed no one, would never need anyone again. Starr was dead. And now so was Megan.

"She's gone," he said quietly.

"Yes," Brenetta answered, "but at least her suffering is over."

Rory swung around to face her. "Not Megan. Starr! Starr is dead."

"What are you saying?"

"My little girl is dead, that's what I'm saying! She died over a week ago."

Brenetta came to him. He could read his own pain mirrored in her eyes where unshed tears glistened.

"She was the joy of my life, Netta. It didn't matter that she wasn't really mine. It never mattered. She was my daughter."

"I know that, Rory."

"I tried to love her mother. I tried to be a good husband and a good father."

"You were. You were."

"So why did I lose her?" he asked.

Brenetta kissed his cheek. "I don't know, my love. Why did my father have to die? Because death is just a part of life, and those of us who remain must go on. We must always go on."

Rory folded her in his arms, grateful for her presence. There they stayed, framed in the dusty sunlight pouring through the window, holding onto each other, locking themselves away from the world and life and death.

Brenetta stared at her reflection in the mirror. She looked tired and much, much older than her nineteen years. She felt more like a hundred. She had seen too much death in the last year. She was so very tired of death.

They had just returned from the graveyard. Megan had been laid to rest beneath a headstone that bore not only her name but Starr's as well. Though the child's body was not there, Rory had desired their names to be together at least. Upon return Brenetta had come straight to her room. Rory had gone for a walk.

She turned away from the mirror. She hoped they could leave here soon. She was ready to go back to Idaho, to be gone from this wretched place. There was no reason to stay any longer. It even looked like Richard Sunday would be properly punished, although a man of his influence could often get off more lightly than he deserved.

A soft rap on her door interrupted her thoughts. She was surprised upon opening it to see the pretty Mexican girl from the Sea Goddess.

"Calida!"

"Buenos tarde, senorita," Calida said hesitantly. "I am sorry if I disturb you."

"No. No, Calida. Please come in."

Brenetta ushered the girl to a chair and sat down across from her.

"Senorita, I am so sorry about Meg and the *nina.* If only I could have told someone sooner but . . ." Her voice trailed off as she dropped her guilty gaze.

"There was nothing you could do, Calida. You were as much a prisoner as Megan was, and you risked your own safety to help her."

Calida offered a tentative smile. "It is because of you that I am no longer a prisoner, as you say. That is why I have come. I am going home. Ricardo, he can no longer keep me here, and my parents, they have forgiven me all and have sent me the *dinero* I need to go home."

"Where is 'home'?" Brenetta asked.

"The *hacienda* of my family is two days south. It is a very pretty place. I have many brothers and

447

sisters and cousins there. I never should have left, but I am glad to go back." The smile vanished again. "But before I could go, I had to tell you how sorry . . . and that I thank you too. You have freed me, *senorita*. You and the *senor*."

"Please call me Netta. I'm glad you came and I'm glad you can go home and begin again. I'm sure you'll make a very good life for yourself with a fresh start."

"Gracias, Senorita, Netta."

Again there was a knock on the door.

"Excuse me, Calida."

This time Brenetta opened the door to another grubby little street urchin. Like the boy who had brought Richard's note about Megan, this one was holding a wrinkled envelope that had seen better days.

"Yes?"

"Your name Ladimar? Then this is yours," he said, shoving the letter towards her.

"Thank you," she mumbled, handing him a coin from her reticule.

The door closed, she tore open the envelope and scanned the brief missive.

"Senorita, what is it?" Calida cried as Brenetta slumped against the door.

It couldn't be true. It couldn't be.

Miz Latimer, I got the gal Star O'Hara. I payed Miz Black for her and to tell you she was dead. I'm taken her to Idaho. When you come back, I'll let you no what you gotta do to git her back. Signed, an old friend.

The floor was swallowed up by a murky blackness and she was engulfed by it . . .

Rory rapped on Brenetta's door and was surprised to hear a strange voice call, "Come in." He opened the door to find a vaguely familiar girl kneeling over an unconscious Brenetta, frantically waving an envelope in hopes of reviving her.

"What happened here?" he demanded.

The girl was obviously very frightened. "This came and she fainted."

Rory accepted the paper from the girl. The message, written in a rough, almost unintelligable hand, made him feel like fainting himself.

"What are you doing here?" he yelled at her, a defense against the weakness in his knees. "Did you bring this? Who are you?"

"Oh no, *senor!* I did not bring it. I am Calida. From the Sea Goddess. I came to thank the *senorita* and you for making it so I can go home. *Por favor, senor*, I did nothing."

Rory lifted Brenetta from the floor and carried her to her bed. "I can see that, Calida. I'm sorry for shouting."

"I will get some water for the *senorita*," Calida told him.

"Netta? Netta, wake up," Rory called softly. "Netta, it's Rory. Wake up."

She moaned; her eyelids flickered. "Starr," she whispered.

"I know. I saw it."

"But who?" she asked, opening her eyes.

"I don't know, Netta," Rory replied, "but we'll

find him, whoever it is."

Calida returned with a pitcher of water and a cloth. "Here, *Senorita*. Let me bathe your face. You will feel better."

"Thank you," Brenetta sighed as the damp cloth cooled her cheeks. "Rory, who could have done this? Is it true?"

"Don't ask me why, but I do think it's true. I'm going to pay a visit to Mrs. Black to make sure, but . . . yes, I think it's true. As for who, I don't know. Whoever it is, he must have followed us from Idaho and knew why we'd come. I'm afraid it's someone we must know."

Brenetta was sitting up now. "Surely none of our men!"

"I hope not, Netta," Rory said darkly. He knew this much, whoever had done it was going to pay dearly when Rory found him. There was no doubt about that.

"Rory, we must leave at once. We can't take any chances with Starr's life."

"Hold up. We'll leave before dawn tomorrow. In the meantime, I've got to arrange for supplies so we'll be able to make it back. Don't forget we're liable to run into snow before we get home. Besides, I've got to pay that visit to Mrs. Black first."

Rory picked up his hat and stalked to the door. Brenetta's voice stopped him as his hand rested on the doorknob.

"Be careful, Rory."

Mrs. Black's boarding house was a pleasant two-story house on the stage line coming into San Francisco from the northeast. Rory tied his horse to the post near the front door and climbed the steps two at a time. His knock was answered by Mrs. Black herself. Her eyes widened at the sight of him.

"Mr. O'Hara! Why have you come back?"

Rory could see she was considering closing the door and he reached forward to block her action. "Mrs. Black, I must ask you a few questions."

She was actually shaking as she answered, "But I don't know anything."

"I think you do, Mrs. Black," Rory said gently as he stepped inside. "Why don't we go inside and talk about it?"

Fifteen minutes later, Rory was standing on the walkway outside the boarding house. The description Mrs. Black had given him could only fit one man in a thousand, definitely only one who he or Brenetta would know. Jake Hanson was their kidnapper.

CHAPTER THIRTY-NINE

NOVEMBER 1882—HEART'S LANDING

"It can't be true. Surely it can't be true."

Three pairs of compassionate eyes were turned upon Ingrid as she shook her head and mumbled her denial.

Brenetta stood at the window. She turned to look out at the new snow dusting the earth. Her initial reaction had been the same as Ingrid's—total disbelief. Yet in the twelve days it had taken them to ride home, pushing their horses and themselves to the limit of endurance, Brenetta had begun to see that Rory had to be right. Pieces began to fall into place one at a time until the picture was complete. They were dealing with a man whose hatred for the Lattimers and all that was theirs had twisted his thinking until he would do anything to bring them down.

"Do you want me to go see him?" Tobias asked.

"No, I don't think that would be safe for you or Starr," Rory answered.

Ingrid spoke up again. "But why would he follow you to California? Why would he take an innocent baby who he'd never seen before?"

"Because he ruined his own rustling plans by killing Pete Parker," Brenetta said, not turning around.

Rory agreed. "I think he initially followed without having a plan. Other than maybe to kill Netta and me, that is. Somehow he found Megan ahead of us and learned of Starr's whereabouts. He's obvioiusly taken her for ransom. Our one advantage is knowing it's him while he thinks we're still in the dark about his identity."

Brenetta joined Rory on the couch as he finished. He took her hand and squeezed it in encouragement, causing a look of understanding to pass between Tobias and Ingrid.

"Could he really have changed so much, Tobias?" Ingrid asked.

Tobias's arm went around her shoulders. "I'm afraid I've suspected him for some time. I don't think he's even rational anymore when it comes to the Lattimers . . . or me."

"But then you might all be in danger!" Ingrid cried.

Rory shook his head. "No, not now at least. Not while he has Starr. He'll bargain with her first for whatever it is he wants."

Silence closed in around them as each thought of Starr, a captive of a strange man. Was she being fed and cared for? Was he mistreating her? Where was he keeping her? Was she cold, frightened, hurt?

They waited tensely for Jake to contact them. Their high mountain valley was blanketed several times by snow before the expected message came.

Miz Lattimer. Bring me the deed to Heart's Landing and you can have the girl. Meet me on Tuesday next week at the fork of Crooked Creek at noon. Come alone. No tricks or she's dead. If you bring the deed, I'll take you to her. If not, I'll deliver her body.

A lock of Starr's blonde hair was folded into the note. Brenetta held it to her cheek as she passed the letter to Rory. He read it quickly, then looked up at her.

"What will you do?" he asked, his eyes guarded.

"I'll take him the deed, of course."

"Just like that? You'll give away this ranch for her?"

"Rory O'Hara, what wouldn't I do?" Brenetta sputtered, anger and disbelief mixed in her voice. "She's my child, and don't tell me she's not. She's as much mine as she is yours. I've loved her, cared for her, nursed her and followed her to the coast and back. I can't believe . . ."

He silenced her with a kiss.

" . . . doubted me," she finished softly as his mouth released hers.

"I'm sorry, Netta. I knew better. Come into the study. We've got to make some plans."

Rory pulled a map of Heart's Landing from a desk drawer and unrolled it across the top, pinning down corners with books. Brenetta stood beside him, leaning forward to see what he was showing her.

"Here's the meeting place. It won't be hard for me to observe you unseen from this grove of trees but if he takes you back onto his place, which he's sure to do, I'll have to hang way back to keep from being seen. We're lucky there's snow. It'll make it easier to follow."

"But Rory, he said I must come alone. Wouldn't it be better to do as he says?"

Rory put both hands on her shoulders and looked deeply into her eyes. "Brenetta, I love you. I'm not about to let you go with that man alone. I don't trust him to follow through with his part of the bargain." He released her and turned back to the map. Pointing to its boundaries, he said, "Besides, I'm not going to let him have this place if I can help it. Your father built it and it's yours. I want it to stay that way."

"You forget," Brenetta whispered. "It's ours."

He kissed her again, this time letting his lips linger on hers as he tasted the promise of what life with her was to be like once they were married.

"Ours. And Starr's," she added when the kiss ended.

"Ours and Starr's," he echoed.

She was a cute little tyke. But he would kill her if he had to. He'd gone too far now not to follow through with his threats. They could only hang him once anyway.

Jake spat at the cuspidor beside the table. It had

been a birthday present from Ingrid years ago. Back when she cared about her pa and took care of him. Back before that damn Jew turned her head and stole her away. He spat again.

Jake pushed back his chair, the legs creaking under his weight as they scraped across the rough floorboards. He pulled a fur-lined cap over his head and slipped on his warm coat.

"You keep that kid quiet, you hear?" he said to the skinny girl on the bed with Starr.

"I hear," came her surly reply.

He had found her in San Francisco after taking Starr from Mrs. Black's. He'd paid thirty dollars to her old man, a drunk willing to do anything for money to buy whiskey with. He hadn't even cared what Jake planned to do with the girl; after all, he had plenty more kids at home without missing this one. She wasn't much to look at, but she was strong as an ox despite her slight build and she kept the little girl out of his way and the shack neat. He didn't even know what her name was and didn't care either as long as she did what he told her to do. Once Starr was gone, he supposed he would show her the door. She was too young and plain to be the type he would care to dally with.

A blast of cold air greeted him as he opened the door to their little hideaway. It looked as if it might snow again before the morning was gone. He pulled on a pair of gloves, knowing they wouldn't be enough against such low temperatures, and mounted his horse. It was a difficult climb out of the canyon with snow and ice on the ground but he hurried his horse forward. He wanted to be at the rendezvous point long before Brenetta Lattimer.

Upon arrival from California, Jake had brought the two girls to the box canyon and kept them in the tiny shack. If no one had found the rustled cattle all those months they were hidden there, no one was going to find one small child locked up in an old deserted shack. The entrance to the canyon was cleverly hidden by a natural maze of large boulders, intricately arranged, and further concealed by a dense stand of evergreens. Jake had stumbled on it by accident while chasing a calf during roundup one year. It had proved to be a very useful find.

Brenetta could see him clearly from some distance away, both he and his horse dark splashes against the white background. As she drew closer, it began to snow lightly again and she wondered if Rory was all right after so many hours in the cold. He had left the ranch early this morning to find his hiding place before Jake arrived. She had been worrying about him ever since.

She stopped her horse across the creek from Jake Hanson. For a moment they simply stared at each other. Then Jake kicked his mount sharply, and horse and rider splashed their way through the icy water.

"You bring the deed?" he asked.

"I did."

"Give it to me."

"Not until I see Starr. Not until I know she's all right."

Brenetta didn't flinch outwardly at his steely glare, but she was frightened, knowing that this was a man who had shot her father in cold blood.

"Okay then. Follow me. And no funny stuff."

Brenetta nodded as she nudged the Flame into the stream ahead of Jake. She wanted to turn around, to look for Rory, but she knew she mustn't. It might give him away.

Rory was so stiff from the cold he could hardly move. Quickly he slid to the ground and shook his arms and legs to speed up his circulation. He didn't have a lot of time to warm up. Rory was dressed all in white to help conceal him from view as he tracked after them on foot. Rifle in hand, he started after them at a trot, a pace he could continue for hours at a time.

The trail was easy to follow for the present but the falling snow worried Rory. If it increased he would soon lose them, something he couldn't afford to do. Not with Brenetta's and Starr's lives depending on him. He began to close the distance between them, counting on his white clothing to protect him from discovery.

He caught her doing it again. It was the third or fourth time she had tried to look back without him seeing her. Somone must be following them.

"Stop."

"Are we almost there?" she asked.

Jake drew his horse up beside Brenetta. "No, but your friend almost is."

His fist caught her under the chin, sending her tumbling backwards off her horse. He caught the

Flame's reins before she could race away, then dismounted. Brenetta was dazed, unable to resist as he dragged her towards the brush where he had tied their horses.

"You stupid fool," he muttered as he roughly gagged her and tied her hands behind her back. "Did you think I wouldn't expect such a trick? I'll probably have t'kill you, too."

Rory had an instant of warning, his instincts telling him that he wasn't alone, just before the rifle exploded, sending its deadly missile into his leg. He fell and rolled down an embankment. Pulling himself behind a rock, he waited, his rifle ready for a second attack. The pain in his leg was intense, and the cold made his hands and feet numb as his blood pounded in his ears like the seconds ticking away on a clock.

After what seemed an eternity, Rory dared to crawl out of his hiding spot. Jake must have either thought he was dead or injured too badly to follow. He might be right, Rory thought as he looked at the trail of red staining the snow.

With his scarf, Rory staunched the bleeding. Although it was painful and there was a lot of blood, he determined it wasn't too serious. He hoped he would be able to tend to the wound before there was any danger of infection, but for now, he had to resume pursuit. Brenetta's life depended on him.

He shoved her roughly towards the door. Brenetta stumbled and struck her shoulder against the wall of the shack. Tears sprang to her eyes but she stubbornly refused to let them fall. He may have killed Rory, he might be going to kill her, but she would never, *never* let him see her cry. She wouldn't crawl for this man. Not ever.

The interior was scarcely warmer than outside unless a person sat directly next to the stove. It was there that Starr was huddled in the arms of another girl, barely more than a child herself. Brenetta saw Starr shrink back from her and knew she must be a frightening sight, gagged and bound, her hair falling in disarray from beneath her warm cap. She wondered if Starr would even remember her at all after nearly four months.

"You, gal, untie her while I put up the horses," Jake ordered from behind Brenetta. To her he said, "Don't try to run for it. I'll gun ya both down."

Brenetta's mouth was dry and her wrists were bruised and rubbed raw from the rope, but she gave them little thought as she hurried towards Starr.

"Starr, it's Bebe. Do you remember me?"

There was a moment of fear, of drawing away, followed by a flicker of recognition and then a smile as Brenetta reached out and took her into her arms. Now the tears came. She cried silently as she sat down and began rocking Starr in her arms.

I won't think of Rory, she thought. I'll only think of Starr. She is alive and well. I'll get her out of here safely. We'll be fine. Just fine.

The young girl had crouched on the floor next to

461

the fire and Brenetta turned her eyes towards her.

"Who are you? Why are you here?" she asked kindly.

"My name's Jane. He," she said, cocking her head towards the door, "paid my pa for me. I'm to watch the kid."

"He *bought* you? But that's impossible."

"When you're really poor, you're for sale, one way or another."

"But . . ."

The door banged open and Jake entered, swearing loudly as he did so. "Damned animal. Should've shot it." He looked accusingly at Brenetta. "I should've killed that blasted horse of yours before it got away."

The Flame gone? How was she to get out of here now?

"Don't matter none. Won't be needin' it," Jake continued as he removed his coat and sat at the table. "Time we took care of business, Miz Lattimer. Where's the deed?"

Rory would never had found the passage if it weren't for the Flame. His wound was bleeding profusely and he didn't have enough strength left to maneuver his makeshift crutch through the snow. It was just as despair threatened to overwhelm him that the Flame, her reins dragging the ground, came trotting through the trees.

He whistled for her, unsure if she would bother to answer as she did in the confines of the corral. She stopped and listened. He whistled again, and this time she followed the sound, coming to a stop before him and nickering.

"Hello, Flame," Rory whispered. "How about a ride? Take me to Netta?"

He groaned as he pulled his injured leg over the saddle but managed to ward off the black cloud that was attempting to engulf him.

"Let's go, girl," he gasped, turning the Flame back in the direction she had come from.

He followed the Flame's tracks, hoping she hadn't been wandering around for long before he had seen her. Already the trail was disappearing in the fresh snow. Again hope was waning when the pathway opened into a box canyon. The shack was visible from where he stood, smoke curling from its chimney. He had found them.

Brenetta gagged as he kissed her again, the stubble of his day old beard scraping her cheek. He was twisting both her arms up behind her back, and as she struggled, he jerked them higher, making her think her arms were leaving their sockets. She screamed into his mouth. Jake chuckled as he pushed her away, sending her flying across the room, landing on the bed.

"Please, Mr. Hanson. Please. You've got the deed. Let us go." She hated herself for begging, yet she couldn't let him kill them.

He laughed again as he strolled foward. "You think I can let you go now? You or these two? I'd be hangin' from some tree in a week."

"But they'll know any—"

"No, they won't know. I got plans to fool 'em." His hands rested on either side of her on the bed as he leaned down close to her face. "But first I'm gonna show you that you ain't no different than any other woman just 'cause your name's Lattimer. You're put together just the same."

His body crushed down on top of her as he pinched her jaw with his fingers and kissed her again.

"No. Noooo," she moaned, trying helplessly to push him away.

His sudden jump off the bed knocked the wind out of her. He caught Jane by the scruff of the neck at the open door and swung her across the room where she slammed into the wall, her escape attempt foiled. Brenetta glanced frantically towards Starr where she cowered in a corner, wondering what their captor would do next.

Jake was still standing at the door, staring outside.

"I guess I didn't kill him the first time," he said as he turned around, the latch clicking shut. "I'll have to go do it right this time."

He tied them to the bed and then donned his coat again. Taking up his rifle, he said, "You keep thinkin' about what fun we're gonna have when I get back. You hear?"

CHAPTER FORTY

NOVEMBER 1882—HEART'S LANDING

Rory saw the door open, then close. He knew he'd been seen. He tied the Flame just outside the canyon and began the painful descent, trying to stay as much out of sight as possible. With his injury, he had to obtain the advantage by position, not by strength.

The snow was falling harder by the time he reached the base and started inching his way along the canyon wall. Along with his white clothing, Rory hoped the snow would provide him with adequate camouflage until he could reach the ledge overlooking the shack. Once there, he could better plot how to get inside and rescue his loved ones.

He wasn't sure what the sound was that alerted him to Jake's presence. He couldn't see him but he knew he was nearby. Rory pressed himself into the snow, praying his leg wasn't staining the white blanket that was his only protection. He waited, listening, resisting the urge to jump up and start firing blindly. Jake knew the area better than he did and was sure to win such a wild confrontation.

Jake moved on towards the canyon entrance, leaving Rory free to try to reach the shack. And he must get there soon. He could feel himself weakening fast.

Brenetta struggled with the rope around her wrists. She was sobbing quietly as she wrenched her arms first one way and then another.

"Rory. Oh, please. Rory," she whispered over and over again.

She had to get loose. She had to help him. He couldn't die. He mustn't die. She loved him. He *mustn't* die.

"It's no use. He knows how to tie a good knot," Jane told her.

Brenetta paid her no mind. She just kept sawing at the ropes and sobbing.

Jake found the copper mare and the bloody trail leading away from her. An evil smile spread across his face. Rory O'Hara was making it mighty easy to find him. Like a big bloodhound, Jake could smell an easy kill and quickened his steps. The sooner he found the stinkin' injun, the better.

The snowstorm was thickening, covering the bright red splashes, turning them to pink and then wiping them out entirely. But it appeared to Jake that Rory was headed directly for the shack. He must have seen Jake leaving and taken a chance that no one else was inside to stop him.

Well, Jake planned to stop him.

When the door burst open and Rory stumbled in, Brenetta couldn't suppress a scream. The white of his pants leg was turned to scarlet and he could hardly stand.

"Rory! Oh, dear God, you're hurt."

He motioned for silence as he shut the door. He laid down his rifle and moved to untie them.

Freed, Brenetta slid off the bed and threw her arms around him. "Oh, Rory. You've saved us. We're all alive."

"We're not saved yet," he answered, easing her arms from around his neck. "We'll have to get out of here. Who's this?" he asked, looking at Jane.

"Hanson got her to look after Starr. She's done a good job. We've got to take her too."

Rory nodded. "Get your coats on and be ready," he said as he limped back to the door. "Once we're outside, no one must make a sound. Understood?"

Brenetta hurried to bundle Starr in a blanket, then put on her own coat and gloves. Jane's jacket was hardly more than rag but Brenetta helped her wrap up in the blanket from the bed.

"Come on," Rory hissed. "The storm's letting up and we'll be easier to see. Once we're outside, we'll head that way," he said, pointing east, "until we reach the canyon wall. Then we'll climb as far up as we can go. Ready?"

Brenetta nodded as she clutched Starr to her breast. "Can you make it, Rory?" she asked.

"I'll make it."

He stepped out first, looked around, then motioned them out with the barrel of his rifle, mouthing the word "hurry" to them as they moved past him. Then he brought up the rear.

Brenetta ran as best she could through the drifts of snow, her heart thundering in her ears. She was afraid to look anywhere but straight ahead for fear she would see Jake waiting to kill them. Her lungs felt as if they might be freezing inside her as she gulped more cold air. The snowfall had nearly stopped when the first shot split the air.

"Keep going. Go!" Rory called after her as she hesitated, looking back at him. He had fallen to the ground and was swinging his rifle around, trying to find Jake. "Go!" he yelled a second time when he saw her still standing there.

She began running again, fear choking her. She reached the relative safety of the boulder-strewn east wall of the canyon where she thrust Starr into Jane's arms.

"Listen, Jane. I don't know you and you don't know me. But I've got to trust you with Starr. No matter what happens to us, you get her out of here. You tell anybody you meet who she is and what happened here and you'll both be taken care of until my mother returns from the East. Understand? Then go. Hurry . . . and be careful."

A rifle fired again and then again. Brenetta turned from Jane and Starr, silently praying for Rory's life. She didn't know what to do, but she couldn't just watch while he was shot down.

She saw the rifle spin away from him and knew another bullet had found its mark. Her worst fears had come true.

"Rory!" she cried, forgetting everything else except getting to him.

The bullet had sliced at his shoulder, sending his rifle flying away from him. His first reaction was surprise. It had only grazed him, yet now he was defenseless, his rifle out of reach. Surface wound or not, the shock to his body was the last straw, and he was left drained, too weak to try for his weapon.

When Brenetta reached him, falling to her knees in the snow beside him, he could only give her a vague smile. "I told you to go," he said.

She kissed his brow, cradling his head in her lap. "Rory, I need you. You must be all right."

"Get my rifle."

"You mustn't leave me. I need you!" She was nearly hysterical.

"Get me my rifle," he barked.

His tone somehow restoring reason, she shifted to do his bidding.

"Ain't gonna do you no good to try for the rifle."

Rory looked up into the barrel of Jake's weapon, the smell of powder strong in his nostrils.

"Cain't decide if I want you t'watch the lady die," Jake said, "or her t' watch you. Guess I'd best do you in first. I promised her a romp before she dies."

"Hanson, you lay one hand on her and I'll . . ."

The rifle jabbed his wounded shoulder.

"You ain't in a position to do nothin', half-breed.

You hear? Now say goodbye to the lady and breathe your last 'cause here it comes."

Brenetta threw herself across him, shielding his body with her own. "I don't want to live without you, Rory. I *won't* live without you," she whispered to him.

He tried to push her away with his good arm. "Little one, go. Starr still needs you. Go."

Brenetta stubbornly shook her head, and he knew that nothing he could say would change her mind. Slowly he turned his eyes to Jake . . . and to his own death.

He heard the rifle fire and waited to feel the bullet cut through his heart. At least he would die in her arms; they would die together. Instead of the pain, he watched in amazement as Jake's rifle slowly slipped from his hands.

Jake's face was a study in confusion. His right hand flew to his chest, and when he looked at it, it was covered with blood. His surprised eyes flashed to Rory just before he toppled forward into the snow, nearly landing on top of Rory and Brenetta.

The woman walked slowly into view, the big gun still gripped tightly in her quivering hands. She stopped beside the corpse, gazing blankly at the stranger who had once been her father.

"Ingrid?" she heard someone whisper.

She felt a million miles away from everything. Who were these people? Why were they staring at her like that? She wanted to run, she wanted to hide, to cry. But her feet wouldn't move. She could only stand there, the gun heavy in her hands, and shake.

Brenetta stared into the flames. She was home, in her own room, surrounded by warmth and those who loved her. Rory was in the next room. He was hurt, but the doctor had promised he would be up and around before long. Starr was once more in the nursery, her laughter slowly returning. The nightmare was over.

A light rap sounded at the door.

"Yes?"

Tobias leaned his head in. "Am I disturbing you? Mrs. Reichwein told me to come on up."

"No, come in, Tobias," Brenetta answered. "How's Ingrid?"

It had been over a week since the shooting. Brenetta had heard that Ingrid's baby, a girl this time, had been born the next day.

"She's fine. So's the baby."

"Has it been terribly hard for her, Tobias? She never said one word to us, you know. Not even one."

Tobias sat in the other chair by the fire. "It's been hard. Still is," he agreed, "but she's getting over the shock. Adina's birth has helped, I think."

"Did she . . . did she tell you why? How?"

"Yes. She told me . . . in bits and pieces," he replied, then stared silently at the flickering reds, yellows, and oranges in the fire before continuing. "She wanted so desperately to believe he hadn't really done everything we'd said he'd done. Maybe it was being pregnant that made her act so crazy.

She didn't know about the ransom note—the meeting place and the deed and all. She just decided to go see him. Without telling me, of course. I never would have let her on a horse in her condition, let alone . . ."

Brenetta touched his knee in friendly understanding. "I know."

"She heard the gun shot when she was at the house, so she took his revolver and went to find out what was happening. She followed Rory's trail of blood to the canyon. The rest . . . well, it's obvious." He paused briefly. "She . . . she asks that you forgive her for Brent's death."

Tears were trickling down Brenetta's cheeks. "Forgive her? Oh, Tobias, whatever for? She saved my life, Rory's life . . ."

"I know. I know," Tobias said as he clenched his fists, "but she still seems to feel . . . if she'd done something different, then . . ."

Brenetta squeezed his hand. "You tell your wife that I love her and that I'm sorry she lost her father, too, but that she's not to blame for anything. And you tell her that I'll be over to see her and Adina soon. You tell her that for me."

"Thanks, Netta."

She stood up as he did and hugged him tightly. "Tobias Levi, you've always been my friend and so has Ingrid. None of this will change that. Unless the change is to strengthen it. Now, come say hello to Rory. He's terribly bored and restless, stuck in that bed."

Brenetta remained at his bedside long after Tobias was gone. They were comfortably silent, simply enjoying the pleasure of holding hands and being together.

Rory loved how the firelight played with the strands of midnight blue running through her raven hair. Her lovely face was even more so in contented repose, a faint smile dressing her full mouth and sparkles of gold dancing in her tawny eyes. Her long, slender neck begged to be kissed and he pulled her towards him in response to the plea.

Brenetta laughed low in her throat as he released her. "I think you're nearly well," she said huskily.

He cupped her chin in his hand. Her smile departed when she noted how seriously he was gazing at her.

"Brenetta Lattimer, I love you. I love you more today then I did yesterday, and I'll love you more tomorrow than I do today. I wish I had the words to tell you all that I feel. But words somehow fall too short to express it all. Netta, you've been my little one nearly all your life . . . and most of mine too. Yet I almost lost you before I knew what you meant to me. I'm only beginning to know and I don't ever want to stop learning. I've wanted you and desired you for what seems an eternity, but I couldn't have you. Until now. Little one, will you marry me? Will you marry me tomorrow, if possible?"

For a man of few words, it had been a long speech.

She kissed him gently before answering, her eyes awash. "You are my everything, my all. I would die for you. But I would rather live for you. I will marry you anytime you say. I will share your life and your bed, your joys and your tears. I will raise your children and grow old with you, sharing all your tomorrows until forever. Rory Bear Claw O'Hara, I belong to you always.''

EPILOGUE

Brenetta took a deep breath and descended the stairs. She could hear all her guests talking gaily, the house filled with the warmth of family and friends, the cold January winds outside forgotten. A wedding of two young lovers was always a time of joyous celebration.

She paused in the doorway surveying the lively scene. Her mother was engrossed in conversation with Tobias, her deep blue eyes snapping in friendly argument. Age seemed to have no effect on Taylor Lattimer.

Rory stood near the large living room window. He was surrounded by his backslapping colleagues—Sam Wallace and Buck Franklin and Virgil Haskin. Even old Sandman had come, though it was getting more and more difficult for him to get around these days. Behind them, Brenetta could see the panoramic sweep of

Heart's Landing, the snow-covered ground unbroken by the herds of cattle that would be there in a few months when they returned from winter pasture.

Ingrid was sitting near the fireplace, several of her children around her as she visited with Father Duggan and Rabbi Jacobi. She was dressed all in yellow and hardly looked old enough to be the mother of such a large and handsome family.

There were others, too, so many others. So many loved ones and so many memories. Brenetta felt a sudden urge to cry at the years of joy and sorrow she had shared with these people.

"Feeling a bit wistful, big sister," Carleton asked as he slipped up beside her.

Brenetta nodded and sniffed quietly. "Yes, Carl. I am. It isn't every day that a daughter of mine gets married. Nor that a new century begins."

Carleton hugged her tightly and drew her with him into the living room. Rory looked up as they entered, his black eyes dancing with pride as they locked on to her.

"You're as pretty as a bride yourself," he whispered in her ear. "If I weren't already married, I would ask you to do me the honor this very moment."

Brenetta smiled softly and laid her head on his shoulder, feeling the peace of his closeness.

January 1, 1900. She still couldn't believe it. It didn't seem possible that more than seventeen years had slipped away from her since her own wedding day. It had been a very different day from this gala affair. Just her and Rory and the priest.

Yet there had been no shortage of love and happiness.

What had happened to the years in between then and now? Where had they gone? Together they had seen Heart's Landing through good years and bad, through drought and disease, and through growth and success. Together they had watched their children growing up—two daughters and two sons, Starr and Kathleen, young Brent and Travis. Her own brother, only seven when he left Idaho, had returned a tall, handsome man—a doctor of medicine. Dr. Carleton Lattimer had a successful practice and would soon be marrying as well.

The world was changing rapidly. Telephones. Electricity. Automobiles. Yet here, in the wilderness of Idaho, it was still the same as always. How could she possibly be nearly thirty-seven years old when she still felt seventeen?

"I love you, Brenetta O'Hara. More today than yesterday," Rory said as his arm tightened around her waist. He seemed to understand her thoughts and empathize with them. And why not? He knew her better than she knew herself.

She kissed his cheek, her smile returning. It was a glorious day. It was a glorious life. In a few minutes, her daughter, Bellamie Starr O'Hara, would float down the stairs in her great-grandmother Christina's wedding gown, made from yards and yards of old French lace and shiny satin, and studded with hundreds of tiny pearls. And in only a few minutes more, she would be the wife of Reuben Jacob Levi, eldest son of Tobias and

Ingrid, and embarking on the adventure of life on her own.

Yes, it had been a glorious life . . . and it would go on being so. The other children would grow up and marry, going their separate ways. They would face times of trial as well as joy. Friends would come and go, some would die. The world would go on changing, rushing by.

But nothing could change the O'Haras. Their love would go on as always. In each other they had found their own hearts' landing.